AVIDIAN

The Demon and the Savior
Book 1

Ashley R. O'Donovan

4 CHAMBER PUBLISHING

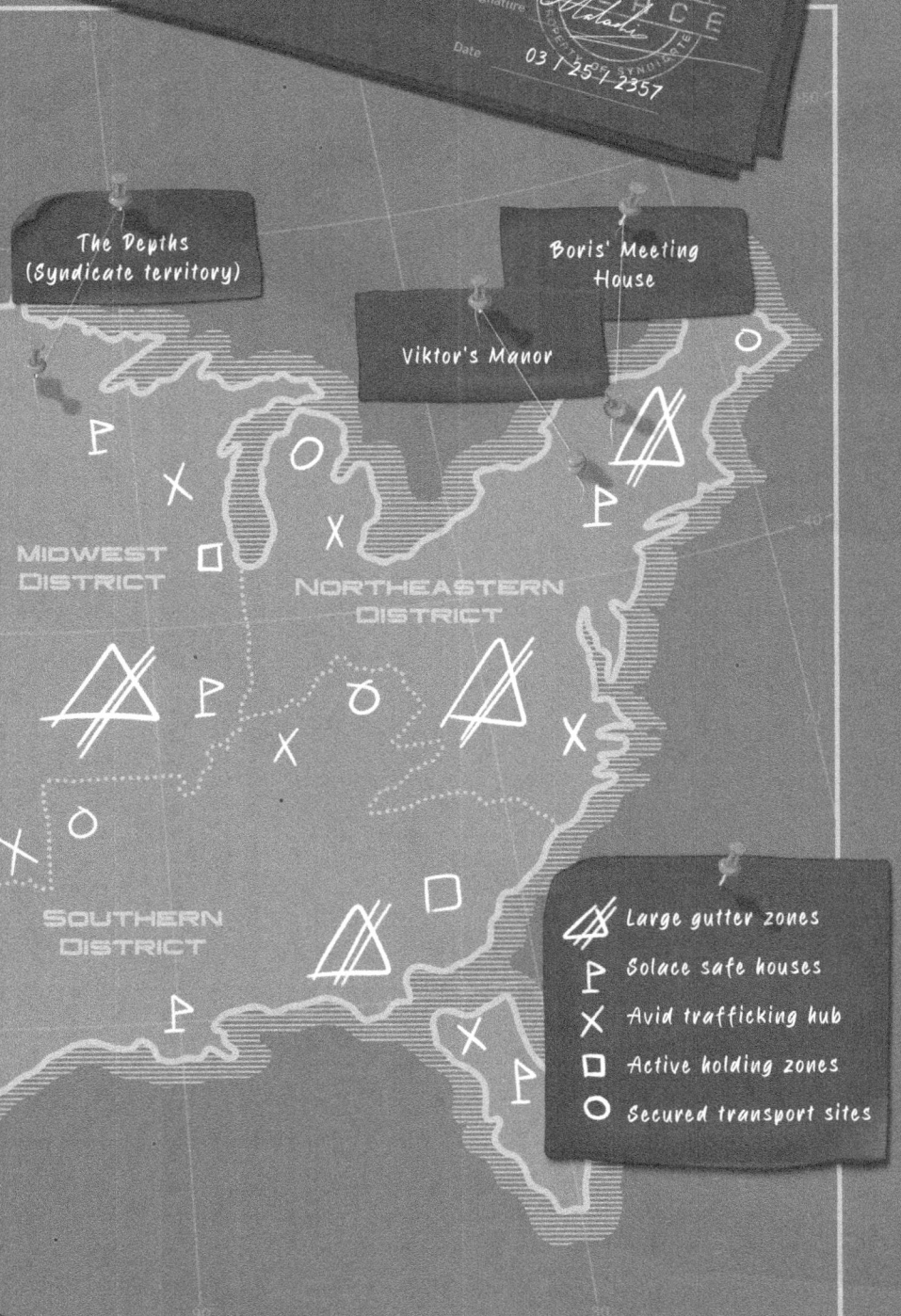

Avidian

By Ashley R. O'Donovan

Map and cover art by EKATHART Illustration

This is a work of fiction. All of the characters, organizations, and events portrayed in this novel are either products of the author's imagination or are used fictitiously.

For Mischka and Boris, who hold a piece of my heart in the stars.

CONTENT WARNING

Avidian is the thrilling first book in a new dystopian fantasy romance series. At approximately 100,000 words, it contains sexually explicit scenes, mature language, and themes intended for adult readers. Please note that the story includes depictions of violence, the trafficking and exploitation of a gifted race, and other intense situations that may be triggering for some readers.

Pronunciation Guide

Avidian (Uh-VID-ee-an)

Katja (KAH-tyah)

Avid (A-vid)

Malachi (MAL-uh-kai)

Mischka (MEESH-kuh)

Mish (MEESH)

Other Works By
Ashley R. O'Donovan

What Lies Beyond the Realms (Book 1)

What Beats Within the Tunnels (Book 2)

What Courses Through Her Blood (Book 3)

Destined for Darkness Omnibus

Chapter One

RULE 1 OF THE NEW ORDER: TRUST NO ONE—NOT
EVEN THE DEAD, FOR THEY HOLD MORE SECRETS
THAN THE LIVING.

I WANDER THROUGH THE GARDENS, admiring the night-blooming flowers, and find myself pondering the unthinkable—what it takes to kill another person.

Despite having never ended anyone's life myself, I imagine a long list of people I would like to kill. At the top of that list is Marco, the head of the family that claims ownership of me.

I sit against the trunk of my favorite weeping willow, gazing out as moonlight dances across the pond. This garden is one of the last sanctuaries here, surprisingly serene for the Western District. With the constant droughts on this side of the country, we're lucky if anything grows at all. My district hasn't seen rain in so long, and each year the days grow warmer, the air drier. It's hard to imagine that the other half of Sunderlands spends most of the year buried under snow and ice. Marco, along with a few other families, must be paying a pretty penny to keep this place looking so lush.

My heart nearly stops when a man appears, walking past me toward the water's edge. Considering I can see the dead, it's a significant reaction. The thought of Marco's men finding me here sends a chill down my spine. He would probably burn this entire garden to the ground to punish my insolence.

Frozen in fear, I watch silently as the man grabs a handful of rocks and begins skipping them across the pond, cursing under his breath with each throw.

His clothes reek of wealth: an all-black suit and pristine shoes.

"Fuck," he mutters, throwing the last rock into the water and running a hand through his reddish-brown hair.

He's probably pissed he was outbid today at the underground meeting where men like him go to bid on people like me —Avids—people with unique abilities who only the most wealthy families can afford to purchase.

Asshole.

He looks up, and our eyes lock. I debate standing and trying to outrun him, but in these heels and this fucking dress Marco made me wear, there's no way I'd make it.

"Rough night?" I ask, trying to keep my voice casual, like I belong here. Not like the prisoner I really am.

"Is it that obvious?" he says, taking a few steps toward me.

"The rocks didn't do anything to you, and neither did the water, so cursing at them is a bit of a giveaway," I say. He moves even closer, standing in front of me.

Play it cool, Kat. Don't give yourself away. You belong here.

"Do you mind if I sit?" he asks.

I glance at the grass next to me. "I don't own the park," I say, and he makes a slight chuckling sound, moving to sit next to me. Not too close though—he keeps a respectable distance, which I silently thank him for.

"Can I ask you a question?" he asks.

I look over at him, seeing him clearer now that he's on my level. He doesn't look much older than me, probably in his late twenties or early thirties if I had to guess. He has dark-brown eyes, but not the boring kind of brown; they have little flecks of amber and gold in them. His stubble-dusted face highlights a strong jaw, and his broad shoulders suggest strength. I wonder what he does for a living, but there's no way I'm going to ask him that.

"That depends—was that your question, or do you want to try again for something better?"

He laughs. "What's your name?" He leans back against the gigantic tree trunk we now share. I debate lying, but what do I care? I'm never going to see this man again, so I decide to tell him the truth.

"Katja, but my friends call me Kat."

He smiles, and I'm not sure why my name makes him happy. "Kat, I like that."

I smirk at him. "I didn't say we were friends." He has a nice smile, this mysterious man—perfect, straight white teeth and nice lips.

Why are you thinking about his lips, Kat?

"Katja then, pleasure to meet you. I'm Malachi."

"Malachi, why are you having a bad night?" I ask apathetically, not wanting him to know how curious I actually am.

"I'm missing home, I guess. I've been living in the Midwest District for the past seven years on business, and it's not the same," he says, clearly not one of Marcos's men then. Marco doesn't have any ties to the Midwest that I've ever heard of.

"I've never seen the Midwest before, but I imagine anywhere is better than here," I say, crossing my feet.

"All the districts seem to get worse every year. Nothing grows well anymore, here or there. This garden seems to be the only green place left in this entire district."

It's disappointing to hear, but he's not wrong about this place. It's why I love this garden, and any chance I get to sneak out, I come here. I love the flowers, the feel of the grass, the smell, and the sound of the pond. This is the only place I can ever find peace.

"I like to come here and imagine this is what the world used to look like—large bodies of water, hills covered in trees, and fields of wildflowers," I say, plucking a daisy from the grass and twirling it between my fingers.

"Maybe a few hundred years ago," he says, sitting up straighter and turning to face me. "So, Katja, what are you doing out here alone tonight?"

Do I tell him I'm a woman who's been trafficked for the last eight years and the family that owns me is the most prolific, murderous one in the entire country? And the reason I'm so valuable to them is because I can talk to the dead? No, I probably shouldn't tell him that, but it would be funny to see his face if I did.

"I was out with some friends and wanted some peace and quiet before I go home. There's usually no one here this late at night," I say, only lying about the first half.

"Aren't you a little young to be out here this late and alone?" he says, and I scoff at him.

"I'm twenty-three years old and can take care of myself."

"I mean no offense, but I'm surprised you don't have a husband already, given how beautiful you are," he says. I bite my bottom lip, a nervous habit I really need to stop.

"And what makes you think I don't have a husband waiting for me at home?" I ask, bending my knees and turning slightly toward him, leaning my shoulder against the base of the tree.

"If I were your husband, you'd never have to be alone. Not because you need protecting—but because I'd make damn sure you never wanted to be anywhere else."

I bust out laughing, throwing a hand over my mouth to stifle the embarrassing snorting sound. "Is this your go-to routine? Brooding in parks, skipping rocks, and sweeping women off their feet with possessive husband fantasies?"

With a furtive smile, he shakes his head and glances up at the night's sky.

"I'd say this is a first—trying to pick up a woman late at night in a park. And clearly it's not going well. Apparently these lines don't work. I can't say I've ever been called out quite like this before," he says, scratching his head.

"If you really want to have any chance at picking up women, be honest—be yourself. Skip the creepy pickup lines about husbands," I tell him, brushing a few strands of hair from my face. His gaze catches mine, holding it for a moment before I look away.

"And what about you?" he probes.

"What about me?"

"How do I get to see you again?" he asks, and inexplicably my heart skips a beat. I can't fathom why this stranger has such an effect on me. Perhaps it's his good looks and awkward sort of charm, or it's been too long since a man has seen me as more than an object to use for his gain.

"Oh, I'm not available," I clarify, crossing my arms.

"No husband, so you have a boyfriend?" he presses.

"It's complicated," I exhale.

"So he isn't your husband or your boyfriend, and it's complicated." He pauses, amused. "I don't even know the guy, and he sounds like a dick."

I can't help but laugh. If only he knew how right he was.

"Alright, Katja, if honesty is the way to win you over—I'm not only missing home tonight. I'm in town because my father wants me to start learning how to run the family business, and truthfully I can't stand him and want nothing to do with it," he admits, and I find myself both surprised and even more intrigued.

13

"What's so bad about the family business? And why don't you like your father?" I ask.

"Trade has never interested me, and my father... He's never been the same since my mother died. She passed when I was young, and my two older brothers and I were easy targets for him to vent his frustrations on." His gaze drops to the grass as he plucks at the blades, lost in thought.

I say, "When I was fifteen, I was learning to drive. I had been practicing all the time and loved it and couldn't wait to have a car of my own. One day, I was driving my parents, my best friend, and my dog to the beach. We got into an accident." I pause, not knowing why I'm sharing this with him. I've blocked it out for so long, but his vulnerability with me felt like it deserved honesty in return. "I woke up in the hospital two weeks later to learn I was the only survivor."

It was also when I learned I could communicate with the dead. My dog was there when I woke up, only she was no longer alive. I keep that detail to myself.

"Damn, I'm so sorry. Loss has a crazy way of shaping our lives, doesn't it? I often wonder how different things would be if my mother had lived. I'm sure you've had similar thoughts," he says, his eyes lifting to meet mine. I nod, feeling the weight of the conversation and eagerness to change the subject.

"So why not leave? If your father is as difficult as you say, and you have no interest in the trade business, why come here at all?"

His eyebrows furrow in thought.

"Nobody's ever really asked me what I want, and I don't know myself. This path has been laid out for me for as long as I can remember. My two brothers are already deep in the business, and it's my turn to start carrying my weight in the family," he explains, shifting his hands and repositioning himself against the tree. If I didn't know better, I'd say he seems nervous.

We both sit there in silence, our eyes drifting over the garden and the stars overhead. It should feel awkward sitting in a park late at night with a complete stranger, but instead it's the most relaxed I've felt in ages. I almost feel normal, and I savor the feeling.

He clears his throat, and I turn to face him, not ready for this moment to end. "Your eyes—fucking hell, Katja. You could start wars with them."

I look down, suddenly self-conscious. My eyes are a very light shade of blue—like my mother's. They stand out in stark contrast against my dark-brown hair and pale skin.

When I don't respond, he reaches over and touches my hand, drawing my eyes back to his. "What would you say if I asked you to get out of here with me? Let's go do something crazy—seize the night," he says.

"I'd say it sounds like the start of a horror movie, and I'm not in the mood to get murdered tonight," I reply.

He pulls his hand away, a charming smile spreading across his face—too charming, like he could get away with murder, maybe get away with anything. He's obviously wealthy and attractive, but that only makes him more likely to be an under-cover creep. And yet a huge part of me still wants to take him up on the offer.

"If I wanted to murder you, I could do it now. Knock you out and toss you over my shoulder," he says, teasing.

"Hmm, so you've thought about it," I giggle.

He has no idea. He'd be a dead man the second Marco realized I was missing. And Marco wouldn't merely kill him—he'd torture him, along with everyone he knows, anyone who's ever mattered to him.

"Tell me what happened after," he asks, and I meet his stare, studying his face for a beat.

"What?" I narrow my eyes, pretending not to understand.

"After the accident. You were so young—where did you go? How did you end up here?"

I shake my head, brushing it off. "That's a long story, and it's getting late. I should probably head back." I rise to my feet, smoothing my dress.

"Can I see you again?" he asks, quickly standing beside me.

I hesitate. "Depends—are you asking because you're genuinely interested, or are you hoping for a shot at redeeming that terrible attempt at flirting?"

I know damn well I can never see this guy again, but maybe...

"Both," he says with a wink.

I smirk, playing along. "I come here on nights when I need to get away. Maybe fate will bring us together again one of these evenings." I wink back and start walking toward the trail.

He quickens his pace to follow. "When you need to get away from what?" he asks, coming up beside me.

"Maybe I'll tell you if I see you again." I glance sideways at him, keeping my tone light. "It was nice meeting you, Malachi, but I really have to go."

He sets his jaw, his disappointment slipping through. "Why do I feel like I'm never going to see you again?"

I don't have the heart to tell him the truth. My life won't allow it. Once I leave this park, he'll become nothing more than a fun fantasy I think about on sleepless nights.

I pause, looking into his eyes for a beat longer than necessary, the cool night air swirling between us. Malachi doesn't move, but I can feel the shift in the space around us—like the world has stopped spinning.

"Are you sure you have to go?" he murmurs, stepping a fraction closer.

My breath catches. It would be so easy to lean in, to close

the distance. But I shouldn't—there are too many reasons why I should walk away.

He reaches out, his fingers grazing my wrist, sending a ripple of heat up my arm. His touch is light, almost hesitant, like he's giving me a choice—go or stay.

I know I should go, but my feet won't move.

"If I don't leave now..." My mind goes blank, too entranced to think.

"If you don't leave now," he whispers, leaning in, his breath warm against my cheek, "you'll have to kiss me."

I freeze. His lips are close, so close, that I could tilt my head slightly and—

No, I can't.

But I don't pull away.

Malachi watches me, eyes flicking from my mouth to my eyes, waiting. His hand lingers on my wrist, thumb brushing softly against my skin, like he's memorizing the feel of it.

"If I kiss you..." I whisper, not sure what I'm even trying to say, "it changes nothing."

His breath hitches enough for me to notice, and the world around us narrows down to the weight of his stare, the warmth radiating off his body, and the tension hanging in the air. He's waiting for me to make the first move, giving me the choice.

I close the distance between us, slow enough to feel his breath mix with mine but fast enough that I don't give myself time to overthink it.

Before our mouths have a chance to meet, I let my tongue glide across his bottom lip. A low, guttural sound rumbles in his throat, but before he can make a move, I turn my head, biting his earlobe.

My breath brushes against his skin as I whisper, "If you want a taste, Malachi, you'll have to earn it."

When I pull back, I catch the surprise in his eyes, and the

desire simmering beneath the surface. For a heartbeat, the air between us crackles, heavy with anticipation. I take a deliberate step back, leaving him rooted in place before he can act on anything.

"Goodnight, Malachi," I manage to say, my voice breathier than I intended. I give him a weak smile, turning on my heels and picking up my pace, putting as much distance between us as possible.

I don't hear his footsteps following. Good. I don't look back, not even when he calls out, "Goodnight, Kat."

The sound of my name on his lips makes me falter for a second, but I keep walking. I have to. Once I leave this park, this moment—it will only be a memory. One I might cling to but can never repeat. I don't have the luxury of kissing cute men in parks.

Behind me, his voice cuts through the air. "Wait—"

But I don't turn back.

I never turn back.

Chapter Two

RULE 2 OF THE NEW ORDER: NEVER
UNDERESTIMATE THE VALUE OF AN ENEMY'S
LOYALTY–IT'S EARNED IN FEAR AND MAINTAINED
THROUGH LEVERAGE.

I'M careful not to be followed on my way back to Marco's compound. The roads are deserted this time of night, and anyone with half a brain knows to keep their distance from the Volkov estate.

Marco Volkov—head of the Volkov family and ruler of the Western District—holds all the power here, like a king in the ruins of what was once a kingdom. We live in what used to be called California, though that name holds little meaning now. That was long before viral outbreaks, climate disasters, and total political collapse carved the world into what it is today. What was once the United States is now a bunch of fractured districts known as Sunderlands.

The population is a shadow of what it was, the billions who once lived here. At least, that's what we're taught. The history books in our schools paint a grim picture of the past, but when the curriculum is dictated by a monarchy that seized control in a time of chaos—one that rules with an iron fist—it's hard to know what's true. They rose to power when everything fell apart, and now they tighten their grip on what's left of this broken nation.

Fear keeps people in line. Fear of the unknown, of what lies beyond the realms of our borders, and of the Volkov family's reach. They say the monarchy saved us, but when the truth is written by those who rule, trust becomes a luxury none of us can afford.

At least this compound is perched on the cliffside. Even though few plants manage to grow here, I can still enjoy the ocean breeze. I breathe in the salty air and turn up the paved driveway to the place I call both my home and my prison. Sometimes I wonder if Marco chose this island deliberately, as if the isolation wasn't punishment enough. It makes escape that much harder. Too bad California fractured into the ocean, forming a series of islands, history screwing me over long before I ever had a chance.

I've learned the hard way that there's no point trying to run. The Volkov family has eyes everywhere. After so many failed attempts, I've finally accepted this as my life. The large iron gates come into view, looming in the distance. I stay close to the edge of the road, hugging the cliffside. The darkness hides the ocean beyond, but the sound of waves crashing below always resonates deep within me.

Banks steps out of the small guard post as I approach. He's one of Marco's many security personnel, but one of the few who actually fears me. Most of the men working for Marco have heard rumors about what I can do, but Banks knows the truth.

"I was starting to worry about you, Miss Sinclair," he says, sighing in relief as I approach the gates.

He was on the team that escorted me to a job a few years ago. A wealthy family from the Southern District hired me to find out what happened to their murdered daughter. They paid

Marco for my services, and I was able to contact the girl, uncovering exactly how she died. One of her father's enemies kidnapped her and tortured her for information about his company, since she was a valued stakeholder. The whole experience rattled Banks, who started letting me take walks without question or sneak off to the park when I need to clear my head.

"You know I'll always come back," I reply, flashing him some teeth.

Banks gives me a half-smile, his usual stoic expression softening. "One of these days, you might not. Marco doesn't take kindly to people disappearing."

I shrug, even though I know he's right. "It's a good thing you're here to keep an eye on me."

The gates creak open, the iron scraping against the stone in a way that makes my skin crawl. It's always like this—the sound, the sensation—like the gates are welcoming me back to my cage. As I step through, the weight of it all settles in my chest, heavier than before. The clang of the gates slamming shut echoes behind me, a reminder of the prison I can never quite escape.

Banks nods, his dark eyes tracking my movements, but doesn't say anything else.

I move as quietly as possible along the gravel path, the crunch beneath my feet sounding louder in the thick silence of the night. The path wraps around the mansion—no, palace—an enormous structure boasting wings and endless rooms. It towers above me, an architectural masterpiece on the outside, a fortress of control within.

I hug the shadows, keeping to the edges of the property, heading toward the back entrance closest to my room. The grandness of it all doesn't matter. Whether beautiful or opulent, it's still a cage.

A curdling scream rips through the house as I turn down

the hallway, echoing off the marble floors, sharp and jagged. My body goes rigid, every muscle locking as I press my back against the wall, instinctively slipping into a defensive stance.

Someone's being tortured tonight, and the thought of being dragged into whatever's happening claws at my insides. Another scream follows, a cry of raw pain, and my hand flies to my mouth, smothering the instinct to scream in return. I want to help, I want to run to them and make it stop, but I know better. I know that stepping in would only seal my own fate, and I'd be the one screaming next.

The thought of him hurting another Avid makes my stomach churn. The sickness twists inside me, and I force it down, swallowing hard. I tell myself it's not an Avid. Maybe it's someone who deserves it, someone who's done something terrible. But pretending that doesn't make me feel any better.

Marcos's made it clear, time and time again, how bad things could be if I stray. I don't even let the thought of escape flicker in my mind anymore. I've learned what happens if I try. I've been on the other end of those screams before.

The hall goes quiet, and the silence feels worse than the screams. It wraps around me like a noose. I push off the wall and move again, my steps quickening as the temperature plummets.

I feel it in my bones—the passing of life, so close. Whoever that was died, crossing over. I can sense it, the weight of it. My door is in sight, and I need to make it there before... A flicker of movement down the hall has my heart lurching into my throat. Is Marco sending someone to get me, to punish me for sneaking out? Or is it the tortured soul of his victim, seeking retribution?

I pinch my eyes closed, forcing back the rising panic, as my hand finally grips the doorknob. I push inside, quickly shutting the door behind me. I don't hear anything as I listen with my ear against the wall and my shoulders slump as I finally let myself relax.

Nights like this are far too common around here. You'd think I'd be used to it by now. I let out a long breath I didn't realize I was holding.

Safe. For now, at least.

I move to the window, pulling back the curtains to peer out at the black ocean below. I can't shake the feeling that no matter how quiet I am, no matter how dark it is, someone is always watching—dead or alive.

"MISCHKA, WHERE ARE YOU?" I call out as I slip into bed. Mischka was my childhood dog, a seal and white Boston Terrier who died in the car accident that claimed the rest of my family. She was the first spirit I ever saw, which nearly scared the life out of me.

When you wake up in a hospital and see ghosts, it's not exactly something you can tell your doctor, unless you want a one-way ticket to a padded room. Over the years, I've honed my gift, learned to control it. But Mish... She's always the easiest to summon. All I have to do is say her name, picture her in my mind, and there she is.

She doesn't look the same as she used to. There's a bluish glow to her now, like an aura surrounding her slightly translucent form, but she's still my sweet Mischka. Even in death, she's never left my side.

I've never told anyone about her—not that they could hurt her, since she's already dead. Maybe it's my way of protecting her, keeping something of my own safe. She curls up beside me, her ghostly form warm in its own strange way, and I feel the tension slip from my body. I stare up at the vaulted white ceiling, my mind still buzzing from earlier.

Tonight turned into one of the best nights I've had in a long time, all because of one mysterious man who appeared out of nowhere and left me reeling. I wonder where he would've taken me if I'd agreed to his offer to do something crazy. What was it he said? "Seize the night."

Maybe I will see him again—another late-night rendezvous in the park. Too bad I don't get to go there very often, only when Banks is on the night shift, and that's maybe once or twice a month if I'm lucky. I shake my head. Getting involved with Malachi would only put him in danger.

I already crossed a line tonight, but it felt damn good. I bring my hands to my lips, letting myself imagine what it would have been like to kiss him as I drift off to sleep.

CADE CHASES AFTER ME, grabbing me around the waist and lifting me effortlessly, carrying me toward the water. I scream and laugh, flailing my arms and battering his shoulders, but Cade is tall and built, even for someone our age. He finally sets me down, and the cold shock of the waves makes me cry out.

"Cade, no! It could ruin everything!" I push his chest, but the giggle bubbling up in my throat betrays me.

"Or it could make everything better! Come on, Kitty Kat." He grabs my wrist, pulling me into him, and our eyes lock—his soft green eyes filled with mischief. His disheveled black hair falls across his forehead in pieces, and suddenly it begins to rain. We both look up, completely dumbfounded. It never rains. In the Western District, rain is so rare it's practically a miracle if we get even one day of it each year.

The rain falls harder, sheets of it pouring down. I laugh, holding my hands out to feel it as it drenches my face and hair. When I look back at Cade, he's not watching the sky—he's watching me. Without another thought, we move together. He scoops me into his arms, and I wrap my legs around his waist. We kiss. His lips are soft, his tongue gentle as it explores my mouth for the first time.

A loud knock at the door jars me awake, and I sit up in bed, breathless. Mish is gone, and sunlight streams through the window. It's late.

"What is it?" I call out.

"Marco says to be ready by 5 p.m." It sounds like Zane, another one of Marco's men. He's not as fond of me as Banks.

"Will do," I say, listening for Zane's heavy footsteps to fade away from my doorway. God, I haven't dreamed about Cade in a long time. I guess it's only natural to dream about my first kiss after almost sharing one with Malachi. Maybe it's because I told Malachi about the car accident. Cade was my best friend for most of my life, and then one day things changed between us. It turned into something more.

But we never really got to explore it. Not long after our first kiss was the day of the accident.

I've never tried to contact Cade's spirit, or my parents' for that matter. For a long time, I was in denial and didn't think it was even possible. By the time I realized I could do it, I was too afraid of the pain that seeing them would bring. Or, if I'm being honest, too terrified of what they might say.

They must hate me for the accident. And that's a weight my heart can't bear. Obliviousness is easier to swallow.

"And Katja..." Zane's voice sends a jolt through me, I hadn't heard him approach the door again—God, I'm on edge today.

"Yes?"

"Dress warm and pack enough for a couple of weeks."

Weeks. My heart skips. That can only mean one thing—a case. And not just any case. A murder.

Chapter Three

RULE 3 OF THE NEW ORDER: THE DEAD LINGER
WHERE REGRET FESTERS–KNOW THEIR HAUNTS
AND USE THEIR GRUDGES.

"DON'T LOOK SO WORRIED, my little demon. You know I would never let anything happen to you," Marco says, lounging across from me in the plane.

His little demon.

He's called me that since the day we met. According to him, seeing the dead is the devil's work, so I must be one of his creatures.

I have no idea where we're headed. I went from packing to being hauled into the aircraft. Marco owns several planes and helicopters, but this one is reserved for his closest comrades—a dubious honor, if you ask me.

To my right sits Orin, one of Marco's sons. His cologne assaults my senses almost as much as his attitude. He lives for the work—or more specifically for the parts that get messy. If there's torturing to be done, Orin's the first choice.

To my left is Zane, quiet but no less dangerous, and across from me on either side of Marco sits Banks and Gary, who's the more level-headed of Marco's sons.

"I'm not worried," I reply, my face an effortless mask of calm. "I don't like to fly."

"I think you'll enjoy this trip. I don't believe you've ever been to the Eastern District," Marco says. I start to gnaw on the inside of my cheek.

The Eastern District—run by Marco's twin brother. Rumor has it the twins despise each other, which is one of the reasons they rule on opposite sides of the country.

This should be interesting.

"No, I haven't," I murmur as my gaze drifts past him to the window. The sun is beginning to set, its warm hues casting shadows over the horizon.

"Why don't you get some rest? I'm going to need you fresh when we get there in a few hours," Marco says, nodding to a small bedroom at the back of the plane.

It isn't a request, so I rise from my seat and ignore the way Orin leers at me—his light-blue eyes always teetering between lust and something far more disturbing. I can never quite tell if he wants my body for his pleasure or my pain. Either way, I'm used to it.

I step into the bedroom and close the door behind me. Lying down on the bed, I close my eyes, but my focus sharpens on the conversation happening through the thin wall.

"I don't know why you always insist on keeping her so close," Gary mutters, sounding irritated. "She gives me the creeps."

I roll my eyes. Creeps, huh? Guess I'll take that as a compliment.

"Yeah, Dad, what else does she do for you behind closed doors?" Orin sneers, his laughter grating.

"Enough," Marco snaps, cutting off the sound with one simple word. I silently thank him for it. Marco has never laid a hand on me—Orin is sick in the head, always looking for ways to twist the world into something uglier.

I already know why Marco keeps me close, and it's something he keeps from the others. Marco once had a wife and daughter. They both died before I came along, but I've always believed that loss is why he sought me out in the first place—why he purchased me. He missed them. Needed to know they were okay on the other side.

Sometimes, he still has me contact them. The conversations are brief, full of raw, quiet grief that I don't think he shares with anyone else. It's the only way he keeps himself moving forward in the hollow life he's built.

I may hate Marco and wish him dead for the simple fact that he owns me, controls my life, and dictates my every move, but there's a twisted sick part of me that loves him too—because, in many ways, he saved me.

Once I was out of the hospital all those years ago, I floated through a few foster homes and eventually made a friend—a girl named Aurora with red hair that matched her fiery spirit. She was the first person I ever trusted enough to share my gift with. To my surprise, she didn't run away screaming when I told her I could see the dead. Instead, she showed me a gift of her own.

Aurora could heat anything with a touch of her hand. God, we were kids then, still figuring out who we were. I can only imagine what her power must have grown into over the years—she's probably throwing fireballs these days.

She was the first Avid I'd ever met. Before her, I thought Avids were a fairytale, a myth whispered about in history books. Supposedly, Avids began appearing across the world as some kind of mutation—whether born from the Earth's wrathful elements or a disease no one fully understood. Personally, I blame the genetically engineered garbage they call food that we're forced to eat most of the time. No one knows for sure. Some call it evolution. Others whisper that we're demons walking among the living.

The term Avid comes from Avidus, meaning hungry, eager. They call us that because it represents our innate hunger for survival and freedom. Kind of sad when you think about it. Not just trafficked but condemned to slavery. History has a cruel way of repeating itself—those in power always seek to control what they fear. And they will always fear those who are different.

Aurora and I were taken in the middle of the night from our foster home. I'll never know how or why, but I'm pretty sure one of the other foster kids exposed us, figured out what we could do. Gladys, our bitch of a foster mom, probably got a nice payday for turning us in. The thought still makes my body tense up.

The days that followed our capture were dark—so dark I try not to think about them. Even now, eight years later, the memories make me want to vomit. The things that went on in those underground houses, the way they treated us like animals—or worse, like playthings—was the stuff of nightmares. The men who kept us, waiting for the next auction, were the most despicable humans I've ever encountered.

I met many other Avids while being shuffled from one house to another. Some shared their abilities with me, others stayed silent, too scared or wary to trust anyone. The range of powers I witnessed... I wouldn't have believed it was possible if I hadn't seen it myself.

There was a boy named Ramus who could channel electricity into a bottle. I watched him do it once, his hands trembling as sparks leapt from his fingertips into the glass—it was both mesmerizing and terrifying.

The night I was auctioned, they put me in a tall, round cage that descended into a room like an elevator. The walls were lined with two-way mirrors, giving the bidders on the other side a perfect view of me while my abilities were exploited, while I could only see myself.

But my ability is unique. You can't shove me into a cage and make me conjure lightning in a jar or something flashy like that. No, Marco made me prove my worth in his own way before he agreed to pay for me. That's when I met his daughter, Anya, in the afterlife.

I never saw Aurora or any of the others again after that night. I don't know if they were sold off to someone crueler or if they're even still alive. Over the years, Marco has collected a few Avids, but I'm the only one he keeps close to home.

He gave me my own room, a private bathroom, all the clothes and books I could ever want. It's comfortable, even luxurious. But it doesn't change what this is. I'm his prisoner, and his pretty palace is my jail.

Still, I don't doubt things could've been far worse if someone else had purchased me that night. And for that, as twisted as it is, I'm grateful Marco found me.

"Get up, terror. We're almost there," Orin says, pounding on the door.

I might have dozed off for a bit, but it wasn't nearly enough to prepare me for whatever kind of night lies ahead. With a sigh, I slip on my long coat and tug a light-blue beanie over my head to keep warm. The Eastern District is covered in snow almost year-round these days.

I've never seen snow in person before, and the thought sends a small thrill through me. I bury it quickly, forcing my face into a neutral mask as I head back to the main cabin and settle into my seat across from Marco.

It's too dark to see much of anything when we land. We quickly pile into the back of a black SUV, and as we pull away,

I catch a glimpse of the Volkov family's other plane unloading into three more cars behind us. Marco rarely travels with such an entourage, and the sight only solidifies the rumors about his twin. Whatever's waiting for us must be serious.

We drive for what feels like an hour, the darkness outside pressing in like a thick curtain. Finally, we come to a set of gates and turn onto a well-lit driveway. I glance out the window, and despite myself, a smile spreads across my face at what I see.

Trees. More trees than I've ever seen in my life. Here, on the other side of the country, I had no idea so many could grow, let alone in such harsh conditions. They're tall, thin, skeletal things, spindly branches drooping under the weight of heaping piles of white snow.

It's the most magnificent thing I've ever seen.

We pile out of the car, the crunch of snow beneath our boots filling the icy air. The sharp cold bites at my cheeks, and I pull my jacket tighter around me, though it's useless against the chill. Marco notices, shrugs off his thick black coat, and drapes it over my shoulders. The warmth of it is instant, and the scent —something rich and woodsy—lingers as I burrow into the heavy fabric. He might be a killer and my jailer, but moments like this almost make me forget. Almost.

Marco never loses his temper. I've watched him in situations where most people would snap—in the midst of interrogations, even while inflicting pain—and he remains utterly composed. I've tried to mirror that same calm, adopting it like armor. Letting people see what you're feeling or thinking is a weakness. That's one of my rules. After Aurora and I were taken, I learned quickly that the life I knew was gone and a new order had replaced it. I adapted. I made rules. And I carved them into my mind, one by one.

"Marco." A voice calls out from ahead, deep and commanding.

A man stands outside two massive double doors made of wrought iron, their surfaces etched with intricate patterns that glint in the dim light.

The house—or more accurately, the mansion—is a looming structure that makes Marco's estate seem modest. Its stark white walls rise against the bleak gray sky, framed by black trim that emphasizes its severity. Twisting branches creep along the exterior like veins, their tips coated in frost and snow. Once upon a time when we had warmer seasons, I imagine the vines might have been lush with greenery, but now they're skeletal, frozen in place.

Marco steps forward, his stride deliberate, and the rest of us —Gary, Orin, Banks, Zane, and I—fall into line behind him.

"Brother, it's been too long," Marco says as he opens his arms, and the two men embrace, a gesture of familiarity that feels forced.

As we draw nearer, I can finally make out the man's features. They're startlingly similar to Marco's—down to the sharp angles of their faces and the way their dark-brown, almost-black hair gleams under the faint light. Both men have intense eyes the color of rich chocolate, and they tower at least six feet tall. Their tailored suits fit them perfectly, the clean lines and dark fabric exuding wealth and power.

The differences, though subtle, are enough to set them apart. Marco's face is clean-shaven, his skin smooth and unmarred, while Viktor's beard adds an edge of ruggedness, even though it's meticulously groomed, trimmed to about an inch thick. I can't help but think it suits him, probably serving a practical purpose too, given the unforgiving cold here.

The two of them stand there side by side, like mirrored reflections, and I wonder how alike they are beneath the surface.

"Yes, I wish you were here under better circumstances.

Come, let's get you to your rooms," Viktor says and turns to the massive double doors. Two men, dressed in black and built like statues, pull them open with a synchronized motion.

As we step inside, I glance back over my shoulder. The headlights of the other cars glimmer faintly at the end of the long driveway. A pang of curiosity strikes me—I wonder who else Marco brought with us.

"All of you will stay here," Marco instructs as he looks at his men. "When the rest arrive, have them shown to their rooms." He looks from me to Viktor. "Now, I want you to take us to where it happened."

I glance sideways at him. Where it happened. Finally, I'm going to uncover the real reason for this visit.

"I take it this is her, the demon you mentioned?" Viktor's eyes flick to me, his gaze sweeping over me like I'm little more than an inconvenient curiosity. He doesn't look impressed—more wary than anything.

"Yes, this is Katja." Marco places a hand lightly on my back. I keep my expression neutral, unreadable, meeting Viktor's stare without flinching. Let him underestimate me. Let him be wary. I want him to fear me.

"Very well." Viktor gestures to one of the men near the doors. "Alex, get Bianca and Violet to show the others where they'll be staying."

Alex nods, a single sharp motion, though his presence dominates the room. He's massive, towering over everyone, even Marco, with arms that look like they could crush stone. Definitely more than a doorman.

"You two can follow me," Viktor says, pivoting and starting down the dim hallway. Marco taps my back lightly, urging me to follow, and I fall in step beside him.

The mansion's interior is as foreboding as its exterior. Hallway after hallway stretches before us, dark and cold, illuminated only by small, intricately carved wall sconces that cast faint, flickering glows. The walls are lined with enormous portraits—grizzled older men with piercing eyes that seem to follow us as we pass. The floors are hardwood with thick red rugs. The air feels heavy, oppressive, like the house itself is alive and watching.

After two flights of creaking stairs, we stop outside a dark wooden door. This part of the mansion feels different, older, and less meticulously maintained. The air smells faintly of damp wood and something metallic. Wherever we're going, it isn't Viktor's personal quarters.

"This is the place," Viktor says somberly. His expression is grim, his features set in a mask of discomfort. "I'll meet you back in the living room. Take all the time you need."

"You're not coming in with us?" Marco asks as Viktor starts to turn away.

"I can't stand another second in that room," Viktor mutters before he walks off. His figure disappears around the corner, leaving us in silence.

Marco and I exchange a glance then look back to the door.

He says, "Better see what you can find out."

I hesitate only briefly, my hand hovering over the cold brass knob. With a steadying breath, I turn it and push the door open, stepping into the room before doubt can take hold.

Chapter Four

RULE 4 OF THE NEW ORDER: EXPECT BETRAYAL AT
EVERY TURN—EVEN THE PUREST SMILE MASKS
KNIVES.

THE SMELL HITS ME FIRST, sharp and distinct, before my eyes adjust to the darkness. Sweet and coppery, it clings to the air, unmistakable. Fresh blood. Only fresh blood has that metallic sweetness. The scent of decay hasn't settled in yet, which means death is still new to this room.

I don't move an inch, my stomach tightening at the thought of stepping into a puddle of blood in my only pair of snow boots. Marco, far less hesitant, flicks on the light. The yellow glow floods the small space. I thought I knew what to expect from the smell, but I couldn't have imagined this.

Blood.

Everywhere.

My brain takes a second too long to process it all. The walls, the floor, the bed—it's all streaked, smeared, and splattered with red. When I glance up, my stomach churns. The ceiling too. I have to fight the absurd thought that a pack of rabid wolves broke in here and shredded someone to ribbons. There's no body, but the remains are gruesome—clumps of flesh, tufts of hair, and barely peeking out from beneath the dresser is a severed finger.

The room itself is modest—clearly a servants quarters. The tidy furnishings are jarringly at odds with the carnage. A simple dresser with a large mirror, a nightstand, and a narrow bed that might squeeze in two people if they didn't mind the closeness. It would all look neat and unassuming if not for the nightmarish coating of blood on every surface.

This room is chaos, a brutal explosion of rage.

"Whose room is this?" I ask Marco.

"Carmen's," Marco replies. "She was one of the cooks."

Cooks? I frown, my mind spinning. What could a cook possibly have done to deserve this?

"She's not why we're here," he says.

I whip my gaze toward him in disbelief. "Not why we're here?" I ask, incredulous. "A dead cook isn't enough?"

"My nephew," Marco says, his nose pinching like he can't stand the smell. "Damien. Viktor's son. He was found here. With her."

I swallow hard, keeping my expression locked in that carefully controlled mask I wear so well, but inside I'm blown away.

"Both deceased, both mutilated," Marco finishes, his pitch flat, like he's forcing himself to speak.

I bite my lips to keep myself from saying "fuck." Whatever happened here is worse than a murder. It's a tragedy, and one that reeks of secrets. If Viktor is anything like Marco, I almost feel sorry for the soul who did this when they find him.

"I'll be outside. Let me know when you're finished," Marco says, handing me an envelope before stepping out of the room. He always gives me space when I need to use my gift—or curse, depending on the day.

I glance at the envelope in my hand, its weight suddenly

heavier with the realization of what's inside. This must be what Viktor passed to Marco when we first arrived. That hug between them had seemed longer than necessary, even for brothers. Now I understand the secrecy. If Viktor truly believes someone close to him killed his son—someone possibly staying here under the same roof as all of us—this situation is far more precarious than I thought.

I shake my head to clear it. This isn't like summoning Mischka, my sweet dog and the closest thing to a constant in my life. With her, it's effortless. I simply think of her, and she's there. But reaching someone I've never met requires more effort. A photograph helps me focus, gives me a tether to their essence. Without one, it's like trying to navigate a maze in the dark.

Seeing the dead without seeking them out isn't common for me, but it's happened. And it's never pleasant.

I take a deep breath and open the envelope. The first photo I pull out is of Carmen. It's grainy, clearly cropped from a larger image, and not exactly ideal. The picture is of a crowded table full of people, but she's easy to spot. She's the only one wearing a cooking apron, a tray of food balanced in her hands. She's young, maybe my age or a little younger, with long blonde hair braided neatly back. Her face is freckled, light-colored eyes bright, and there's an unspoken kindness in her expression. *What happened to you, Carmen? What were you mixed up in?*

I slide her photo back into the envelope and pull out the next one.

Damien.

He's exactly what I'd expect the son of Viktor to look like— sharp features, short brown hair, and a chiseled jawline. He's clean-shaven and impeccably dressed in a tan suit, his posture rigid and composed. But it's his eyes that catch me. They're cold, calculating. Something about his expression doesn't suggest kindness. Not in the slightest.

I tuck his photo back into the envelope and slip it into my back pocket. I might need to look at them again later, but for now I need to focus. With one last glance at the bloodied room, I let out a steadying breath and prepare to do what I came here for.

There are two main ways I communicate with the dead—at least for me. The first is simple enough. I picture them in my mind, focusing on their essence, and silently call to their spirit until they answer. When it works, they appear to me as if they were standing right in front of me, tangible but not quite. Most of the time, they have a faint blue aura, but not always. And they don't necessarily look like they did when they died. Some spirits prefer to present themselves how they want to be remembered—maybe ten years younger or in a moment they cherished.

But it's never straightforward. Conversations are fragmented, like trying to piece together a puzzle in a dim room. Sometimes they give me images instead of words or a few cryptic phrases that don't make sense until later. I have to decipher it all, pulling meaning from the pieces they leave behind.

The second method is far more complicated—and infinitely harder on me. I call it projecting, and it's as draining as it is dangerous. It's something I've only been able to do in the last couple of years, as my gift continues to grow stronger, evolving in ways I never expected—or wanted.

Projecting requires me to send a part of myself—my soul, I guess—into the veil, the liminal space between life and death. It's not something I do lightly. Every time I go, it feels like a part of me is slipping away. Maybe the devil is taking a piece of my soul. I don't know enough about my gift or Avids in general to say for certain, but if demons exist—and Marco's cryptic warnings have me half-believing they do—then maybe he's right. Every projection could bring me one step closer to a place I can't come back from.

One day, I might project and my soul might not return. That thought terrifies me more than I'll ever admit.

It's as if my spirit leaves my body entirely, slipping through the veil and wandering the realm of the dead. From the outside, I probably look comatose, like I've drifted off into some deep, unreachable thought. But the reality is far stranger and riskier. On the other side, I can connect with spirits in their element, see the world through their eyes. It's disorienting and eerie, but it's invaluable. Otherwise, I wouldn't do it.

The details I pick up when I project—the whispers of what lingers where life and death collide—are often the only things that make solving certain cases possible. But it's always a trade. The longer I project, the more drained I feel when I return. Every trip leaves me feeling like I've left a piece of myself behind, scattered somewhere in that cold, endless in-between.

Sometimes, it's too much. There have been times when I've projected for too long and woken up days later, disoriented and barely able to move. I've passed out in the middle of the process, only to come to in Marco's bed, weak and barely able to sit up. He always takes care of me afterward. He could easily assign one of the servants to tend to me but never does. It's always him.

I don't know why. Maybe he actually cares about me in his own twisted, manipulative way. Or maybe he wants to ensure his prized asset, the obedient little demon he always boasts about, is safe. Either way, I let him.

As much as I hate what my life has become, it's the only one I have. And if projecting is what it takes to survive—to solve cases, to keep myself useful, and to maybe help others—then so be it.

I don't want to try option two now when I'm already too

tired, my energy frayed from how late it is. Instead, I close my eyes and picture Carmen and Damien as they appeared in their photos, focusing on the details. Carmen's braided hair, Damien's sharp eyes. I silently call to their spirits, pushing the image of them forward in my mind like a beacon.

One of you, answer me. Please.

A faint, floral scent fills the air, soft and out of place in the gore-filled room. My eyes snap open, and I feel the shift immediately. The temperature plummets, the air thick with an unnatural chill. Then she appears.

Carmen.

She sits on the edge of the bed, her figure faint and slightly translucent but undeniably present. Her form glows faintly, otherworldly, casting a pale light over the room. Her hands rest in her lap, her head slightly bowed.

"I'm here to help," I say softly, taking a cautious step closer, careful to avoid the blood and debris scattered across the floor.

She doesn't react or even look at me. Her presence is quiet, but the room grows cold enough for me to see each breath puffing white in the frigid air. I take another step, now a foot away from her.

"Who did this to you?" I ask.

Nothing. No flicker of acknowledgment, no movement. Her silence prickles at my nerves, but she doesn't feel hostile. Not yet. I press on.

"Carmen, I'm Kat, and I want to help you. Can you tell me what happened here?"

Suddenly, she lunges at me, her translucent form solidifying for a split second, enough to feel the cold weight of her presence as she collides with me.

I hit the floor hard, my ass slamming against the wooden boards with a painful thud. The shock of the fall rattles through me, but I barely have time to brace myself before her icy hands clamp down on my face.

Before I can even make a sound—a scream, a gasp, anything—the room shifts.

Suddenly, the cold vanishes, replaced by a stifling warmth. The metallic scent of blood is gone, replaced by something softer, more intimate—the faint aroma of wax and faintly sweet perfume. The lights are off, and the flickering glow of candles dances on the walls.

I'm not on the floor anymore. I'm in a bed. The sheets are soft against my skin, and someone's weight presses me down. His weight. Damien.

He's on top of me—no, not me. Carmen. I feel her body react beneath him, her pulse quickening, her breaths coming in short gasps. His hands grip her thighs, his movements possessive, demanding. His dark eyes are fixed on her, intense and unwavering.

"You're so fucking sweet," he growls against her skin, his voice low and rough. I feel the wet heat of his tongue as he licks the side of her neck. Carmen shivers beneath him, her body arching as a breathless giggle escapes her lips.

I can feel it all. See it all. Not as a witness but as her. Her emotions wash over me—fear, excitement, submissiveness, desire, nervousness. It's disorienting, a collision of sensations that aren't mine but feel as though they are.

I want to pull away, to break free from the vision, but I'm trapped in her memories, a prisoner to what she experienced in this room.

The door swings open, the sound cracking through the air as it collides with the wall. The force of it makes me jump, my body jerking back instinctively. Damien freezes, pulling away from Carmen—from me—as a figure cloaked in shadows steps into the room.

"Fuck, it's early," Damien mutters, annoyed.

But there's no time to question what he means, because in the next instant, the candles snuff out, plunging the room into darkness.

The warmth vanishes, replaced by an icy chill that seeps into my bones. I can't see anything, the pitch-black void pressing in around me. And then, pain.

Someone grabs the back of my head, yanking my hair so hard I swear a chunk of it rips free. A scream tears from my throat—no, her throat—a sound so raw and primal it echoes in my ears. Chaos erupts all around me, a cacophony of sounds that are impossible to make sense of. Crying. Heavy footsteps. Ragged breathing.

Hands clamp around my neck, strong and unyielding, cutting off my air. I claw at them desperately, wrapping my fingers around their wrists, trying to pry them off. But they're too strong. My lungs burn, my legs kick out wildly, my body thrashes in panic. The darkness makes everything worse—disorienting, suffocating, endless.

Then, as suddenly as it started, the warmth returns.

The room floods with light, too bright, and I'm no longer Carmen. I'm lying on the floor, gasping for air, drenched in a cold sweat. Blood pools around me, soaking into the floorboards, though it's not mine. The smell is sharp, metallic, and all too real.

I force myself to sit up, panting as my head spins. My hands tremble as I press them against the floor to steady myself. I replay the vision, trying to piece it together, but the details are fractured, incomplete. My heart pounds as the reality of what I saw starts to sink in.

Never in my life has anything like this happened to me. It's like his breath is still on my cheek, his hands still around my throat. I've seen snippets of the dead's memories before—fragments of their last moments—but I've never been pulled so deeply into their perspective, never relived what happened through their eyes like that especially without projecting. My entire body feels shaken, unsteady, like my mind and soul aren't quite aligned anymore.

I get to my feet, my legs wobbling beneath me and wipe the blood off my hands. Crossing to the mirror, I tug my shirt down, revealing faint bruises blooming around my neck. My fingers brush over the marks, and a cold shiver runs through me. How is this possible?

I don't wait to collect myself or come up with an explanation for Marco. I need to get out of this room—now.

I yank the door open, and Marco's eyes meet mine instantly. He's farther down the hallway, speaking with two men who have their backs to me, but the moment he sees my face, he strides over. His gaze rakes over me, sharp and assessing, and I can tell by the way his brow tightens that I look as shaken as I feel.

"What can you tell me?" he asks.

"I need more time," I gush. "Can I come back tomorrow? After I've slept?"

His eyes narrow slightly, studying my face like he's trying to peel back the mask I'm forcing into place. I steady my breathing, resuming the calm facade I've practiced for years, even though my heart is still pounding like a war drum.

"Very well," he says after a pause. "Bianca is waiting to show you to your room."

He waves, summoning her, and I exhale quietly as an older woman steps forward. Her white hair is pulled into a tight bun, and she carries a stack of fresh towels. The sight of them almost makes me sag with relief. The thought of a hot shower or bath feels like salvation right now. I nod silently, grateful, and step toward her, ready to leave this nightmare behind—at least for tonight.

"Before you go," Marco interrupts, stopping me in my tracks, "I want you to meet someone."

I stiffen, already knowing I don't have a choice. "My other son has finally decided to grace me with his presence," Marco continues, taking on that smug delivery I hate. "I've told him all about my talented little demon."

My stomach twists. His other son? Of course, he can't resist showing me off like some circus act. I shoot Bianca an apologetic look before following Marco reluctantly. My body screams for rest, but I press on, biting the inside of my cheek and reminding myself that I'm only moments away from being alone.

Marco stops where the two men are talking at the end of the dim hallway. "This is her—Katja, my special little demon."

One of the men steps into the flickering light.

"Katja," he says, his tone familiar in a way that punches the air from my lungs.

I look up, and there he is, towering over me with a slight, infuriating smile. His eyes—gold-flecked and chocolate brown —lock onto mine, and my chest tightens.

"Pleasure to meet you," he says, extending a hand. "Little demon, is it? I'm Malachi."

The name hits me like a slap.

It's him.

My mind races, the puzzle pieces falling into place too quickly to keep up. What a liar. His whole demeanor, his entire act—was it all a ruse? A game? His father works in trade—and not the kind you can talk about without blood on your hands.

I force myself to stay composed, though my pulse hammers in my ears.

"I'd be careful where you put that hand," I say, my voice cutting like a blade. "Demons tend to bite."

Marco laughs, clapping a hand lightly against my back. "She can be feisty when she's tired. Go with Bianca. I'll find you in the morning."

I narrow my eyes at Malachi one last time, but his smile doesn't falter. It's the kind of smile that hides more than it reveals, and it infuriates me further.

I turn on my heel and follow Bianca, my steps quick and determined. I don't look back, but I can still feel his eyes on me, watching.

Chapter Five

RULE 5 OF THE NEW ORDER: EVEN A DOG HAS
TEETH—NEVER FORGET YOURS.

I FINISH SCRUBBING my body clean and sink back into the warm water, letting it soothe my muscles. The tub—more like a small pool—is gigantic, easily big enough for three people. This entire bathroom is a testament to excess, from the sleek marble floors to the gold fixtures gleaming under the soft glow of an extravagant chandelier. It hangs in the center of the ceiling, its crystal pendants scattering tiny rainbows across the room like a private galaxy.

I let out a sigh and tilt my head back against the rim of the tub, staring at the flickering reflections. Before I got in, I checked the time, 2 a.m. This night has been relentless. I can only hope Marco doesn't have any early-morning plans for me. Knowing him, he probably does.

The events of the night replay in my mind, refusing to settle. The haunting scene with Carmen. The bruises still faintly visible on my neck. And then Malachi, Marco's son. My stomach twists at the thought. Good thing I didn't fucking kiss him that night. But that only raises more questions.

Why didn't he say he knew me? Why didn't he rat me out

for being in the park? Was it all part of a plan—had he been sent to follow me from the start? Did he already know who I was back then, or was I a random piece in some game I don't fully understand?

The questions swirl like storm clouds, heavy and unrelenting. Rest feels impossible, but I know I need it. I close my eyes, letting the heat from the water wrap around me, and try to convince myself to relax. If nothing else, I can stay here until the sun comes up.

But the peace shatters like glass.

"This is a strange turn of events," a voice says.

My eyes snap open, and I sit up with a start, water sloshing over the edges of the tub as I jerk forward. My heart leaps into my throat as my gaze locks on the doorway.

Malachi leans casually against the frame, arms crossed over his chest, his infuriatingly calm expression betraying no sense of decency—or respect for boundaries.

"What the fuck are you doing here?" I demand, heat rising to my face, though whether it's from anger, embarrassment, or both, I'm not sure. I instinctively reach for the towel draped over the edge of the tub, ready to use it as a shield if necessary.

He smirks, and the gold flecks in his dark eyes seem to glint in the dim light. "Relax, I just came to talk but you look tense. That bath's not working? Maybe you need me to help you unwind, little demon."

"Don't call me that," I hiss, grabbing the towel and holding it strategically so I can stand without giving him a show. I wrap it around me and tuck it tightly into place.

"I can't call you Kat, and now I can't call you demon," Malachi muses. "Everyone else seems to get free rein when it comes to what they call you though."

"You may call me Miss Sinclair, if you must," I reply, stepping out of the tub. My foot skids slightly on the marble floor, slick with puddles of water I sloshed over the edge. Before I can regain my balance, Malachi lunges forward, gripping my arms to steady me.

For the briefest moment, I catch his scent—fresh pine and crisp air, I imagine it's what a forest after a storm smells like. My breath hitches, but I quickly shake it off.

"I'm fine," I snap, swatting his hands away as heat rises to my cheeks.

"For a demon who bites, you sure are clumsy," he says, his smirk widening.

I roll my eyes and head toward the bedroom, leaving him standing by the tub. The audacity of this man is infuriating, but what bothers me more is that he's here at all. How did he even get in? Marco's security is tight, especially after tonight's murders. I'd assumed every room in this house was guarded, but I guess being Marco's son comes with its privileges.

"What do you want to talk about?" I ask over my shoulder, not bothering to look at him as I rummage through one of my suitcases at the foot of the bed. I pull out a pair of pajamas and plan to crawl into bed the second he leaves.

"I thought you should know," Malachi says, leaning casually against the doorframe now facing the bedroom, "I didn't know who you were in the park, but it doesn't change anything."

I glare at him, motioning with a sharp flick of my finger. "Can you turn around?"

He raises an eyebrow, his devious smile infuriatingly still intact, but obliges with a slow spin to face the bathroom again. I keep my eyes on him, making sure he doesn't peek, then quickly slip out of the towel. I pull on a pair of pink pajama pants and a matching tank top, the soft fabric soothing against my skin. Grabbing the clip from my hair, I toss it onto the dresser, running a hand through the loose waves that fall around my shoulders.

"Okay," I say, crossing my arms.

Malachi turns back around, his eyes immediately locking onto mine. He steps inside the room, leaning slightly forward like he's testing the waters.

"What's that supposed to mean anyway?" I ask, raising an eyebrow.

"It doesn't change," he says smoothly, his voice dipping into something softer, "that I still think you have the most marvelous eyes. That you're incredibly beautiful and clearly charming, even when you're trying not to be."

I snort, though the compliment strikes a chord I refuse to acknowledge. "Oh, please. I can see the creepy pick-up lines weren't an act."

"Let me get to know you," he presses, taking another step closer.

I force myself to stay rooted in place, even as my instinct screams to take a step back. His presence is overwhelming, like he takes up more space than his body should. I square my shoulders and tighten my crossed arms.

"What makes you think I'd let you?"

His gaze dips to my lips for a fraction of a second before meeting my eyes again. "Because you're curious."

"Curiosity means nothing," I say sharply, holding his gaze. "I don't have such luxuries. I'm not the son of a rich and powerful leader, like you. Look at me—you know what I am now. I'm nothing but property here, and not yours."

I shift my weight, tapping my foot against the cold floor, the sound a steady reminder of how much I dislike where this conversation is heading. His expression hardens, but his eyes remain locked on me, unyielding.

"Is there something more going on between you and my father?" he asks, suspicious.

I scoff, "Is that what you think, that I'm not just a prisoner but a common whore too? Are you here to collect, like the rest of your family?" I'm jabbering faster than I can think, and heat floods my cheeks. I take a step back and try to get control of myself.

His expression darkens. "So someone has touched you. My father? One of my brothers? Who?"

I tilt my head, narrowing my eyes at him.

"No one has touched me," I say firmly. "I have a job here—a purpose—when I'm needed. That's all. Your father may be my keeper, but it's completely platonic. I assure you."

The fire in his gaze doesn't dim, but his jaw tightens slightly, like he's fighting to keep his emotions in check. I stand my ground, refusing to let his presence intimidate me any further.

He reaches out to touch me, but I react without thinking, grabbing his wrist and shoving him away—hard.

"My God," he laughs, light but laced with something darker. "You really are a marvelously violent little demon, aren't you?" He takes a step closer. "Please, keep touching me by all means. I might even let you bite my ear again, if you're good."

I scowl, shoving his chest this time, trying to force him closer to the door. "Get. Out." My voice rises, not quite a yell but sharp enough to cut through his playful demeanor.

He freezes, his expression shifting. His eyes darken, and he tilts his head, studying me with unsettling intensity. When he reaches out to brush a strand of hair back from my face, I don't move. The look in his eyes leaves me frozen for a moment.

"Who did this to you?" he asks quietly, his warm fingers grazing the bruises on my neck.

I flinch, stepping back as the memory of that room and those hands on me resurfaces. "No one living," I say simply.

He doesn't look away, his gaze lingering on my neck like he's trying to piece together the truth. The tension between us stretches thin, and I shove him again, weaker this time, more to regain control than to actually move him. "Now go. I need to sleep."

Malachi's eyes finally lift to mine, and something flickers in them—a momentary softness—before he steps back toward the door.

"Fine," he says, pulling it open, but he pauses in the doorway, his hand on the edge of the frame. "This isn't over."

I move to close the door behind him, but at the last second he stops it with his hand, leaning in with that infuriating smirk. "Don't forget, Kat—you still owe me that kiss." He winks, and before I can retort, he's gone, disappearing into the dimly lit hall.

I glare after him, my chest tightening in annoyance. My eyes flick down the hall, but it's not because of him—I'm checking for the guard. Sure enough, Gary is a couple of doors down, leaning against the wall. His presence reassures me, though I'd never admit it aloud. But the fact that Marco is making his son keep watch instead of one of the guards does put me a little on edge. He must be worried—or suspicious of something.

Quickly, I retreat into my room and shut the door firmly behind me. The last thing I want is for Malachi to think I'm lingering out here for his sake. Let him think whatever he wants —I don't care.

I trudge over to the bed, exhausted. Climbing under the covers, I let out a long breath, the tension of the night slowly starting to unravel.

Sleep isn't going to come easy tonight. My thoughts are too

tangled, too heavy. I close my eyes and think of Mischka. Within a minute, she's there, curling up at my side, her ghostly warmth giving me a sliver of comfort after the day I've had. Her presence grounds me, but it doesn't quiet my mind completely.

What did Malachi even come here to talk about? He said this changed nothing, but that's not true. This changes everything. Not only is he a liar, but his family owns me. I shake my head, biting back the bitterness creeping into my throat. It had been a nice fantasy, daydreaming about some mysterious man in the park, thinking he was genuine, thinking he had good intentions. But that illusion is gone now—shattered.

It's not like I could ever have a relationship with anyone. Not ever. My life is this...coasting through each day, waiting for Marco to summon me for a job. That's all I am here for, all I'll ever be.

Most of my time is spent reading. Books are my only escape, since vacations and friendships are luxuries I'll never have. Sure, I talk to the other Avids, the servants, and even the guards from time to time, but to call any of them friends would be a lie. Getting too close to anyone is dangerous. Trusting anyone is impossible. That's the reality I've accepted, the life I've resigned myself to.

I didn't always feel this way. Early on, I tried to escape—a few times actually. But severe punishment, paired with failure after failure, taught me quickly that freedom wasn't an option. The scars of those lessons run deep, though they've faded with time. Now, I don't fight it and don't dream of something better.

This is my life. Marco's tool. His property. His little demon.

And I have to keep doing the job he brought me here to do, or else.

Chapter Six

RULE 6 OF THE NEW ORDER: EVERY GHOST HAS
UNFINISHED BUSINESS—SOME ARE BETTER LEFT
UNRESOLVED.

"GOOD MORNING, SUNSHINE," Malachi's voice drawls from beside my bed. I jolt upright, brushing hair out of my face as I blink at him in disbelief.

"What are you doing in here?" I ask, groggy and rubbing at my eyes.

He crosses his arms, looking far too comfortable for someone invading my space.

"Turns out Dad has a lot of catching up to do with my uncle, and I've been tasked with supervising you while you solve this case for him."

Fantastic. I didn't think this situation could get worse, but apparently it can.

"Usually, a knock on the door will suffice for a wake-up call," I mutter, pushing the blankets off and trudging toward the bathroom. My annoyance radiates off me, but I tamp it down. I've dealt with being supervised before—I can handle Malachi. He's no different from the others Marco's assigned to babysit me.

"So what's the plan for today?" he asks, following me as I grab my toothbrush and squeeze a dollop of toothpaste onto it.

I glance at him briefly in the mirror. "Isn't it your job to tell me what the plan is?" I say before shoving the toothbrush into my mouth.

He sighs dramatically, moving to sit on the edge of my bed like he owns the place. "Look, I think we got off on the wrong foot last night," he says gently. "Maybe we can be friends. I'm not here to make your life miserable. I don't want to force you to do anything you don't want to do. And for the record, not everything I told you at the park that night was a lie."

I spit into the sink, rinse my mouth, and pop my head out of the bathroom to glare at him. "Friends? That is something we will never be." I pause, leveling him with a pointed look. "And I hate to be the bearer of bad news, but it's literally your job now to make me do the things I don't want to do."

I roll my eyes for emphasis, disappearing back into the bathroom to wash my face. The cool water feels refreshing, though it does little to quell my irritation. Malachi supervising me? That's not going to make this trip any better.

"Fine. If that's how you want to play this, we won't be friends," Malachi says, the lightness from earlier completely gone. "Get dressed. I'll be waiting outside. We're going back to the crime scene upstairs so you can have another go at...whatever it is you do."

He closes the door with more force than necessary. The sound echoes in the silence, and I blink, surprised at his sudden shift. Hmm. I hadn't expected that reaction. Still, his moodiness might make things easier—less chatter, less pretending.

With a small shrug, I push the thought aside and focus on getting ready. I pull on a pair of warm pants and a thick sweater, tucking the hem into the waistband for extra warmth. Then I pull on my boots from last night, ignoring the blood specs on them. Finally, I grab my beanie and stuff it into my back pocket, in case we end up outside. Pulling my hair into a quick ponytail, I take a steadying breath and glance at the door. Time to get this over with.

I pull my bedroom door open, expecting to see Malachi, but instead there's another man standing beside him. Short and stocky with a completely bald head and a face that seems carved from stone, the man immediately gives me the creeps. His eyes are dark and cold, scanning me like I'm a piece of furniture to be assessed and dismissed. Jeez, this place is teeming with nice faces.

"This is Anton," Malachi says, his posture a touch more rigid than usual. "One of Viktor's men. He's going to, uh, oversee the investigation as well."

I nod with the least amount of effort. Great. Another babysitter.

Anton doesn't bother with pleasantries. He turns sharply and starts walking, his heavy boots echoing against the wooden floors as he heads back toward the stairs. Malachi falls into step beside me, close enough that his shoulder brushes mine.

"Anton's...thorough," Malachi mutters under his breath, sounding apologetic.

"Thorough?" I reply quietly, glancing at the man in front of us. "He looks like he'd enjoy breaking kneecaps."

Malachi's lips twitch, but he doesn't respond.

Anton stops in front of the door to the bloodied room and turns to face us.

"Time to see what you can do, Miss Sinclair," he says darkly.

I don't want to go back in here—not after last night—but I push the door open anyway, bracing myself for the metallic tang of blood. Instead, I'm hit with a sharp, stinging scent.

Bleach.

The room is spotless.

In the last several hours, someone sanitized the entire space. The floors gleam, the bed linens are crisp, and not a single trace of what happened remains. The violent scene I witnessed, both with my own eyes and through Carmen's memory, is gone, replaced by clinical cleanliness.

"Is there a problem?" Anton asks, startling me from behind.

I shake my head, uneasy. "No," I say, stepping inside. I don't need the blood and gore to reach the dead—it's their lingering presence I rely on. But this? Viktor scrubbing the place clean before collecting every shred of evidence? It feels wrong. He either has unshakable faith in what I can do or is hiding something. Both possibilities make my skin crawl.

"Usually, Marco waits outside," I say, glancing over my shoulder at Anton and Malachi, who have followed me in.

Malachi raises his hands in mock surrender, a shit-eating grin on his face. Anton doesn't move right away, his dark eyes fixed on me like he's assessing whether I'm worth his time. Finally, with a grunt, he steps out, Malachi following after him. The door closes with a soft click, leaving me alone.

I walk over to the bed, its stark white sheets a cruel contrast to what I know happened here. Sitting on the edge, I close my eyes and let out a slow breath, trying to push away the exhaustion weighing down my limbs. The memory of last night—the bruises, the chaos, the overwhelming presence of Carmen— lingers like a shadow.

But I push past it.

I focus on the cook, her image sharp in my mind. The long blonde braids, the freckled face, the soft smile from her photo. Almost instantly, I feel her presence, stronger than before. She's here.

But Damien isn't. Again.

I open my eyes, turning toward the faint figure of Carmen

now sitting beside me on the bed. Her translucent form glows faintly, her expression solemn but clearer than before.

"Tell me who did this to you," I say.

She turns her head slowly, her pale eyes meeting mine. For a moment, she says nothing, but her mouth opens slightly, and the air around me drops a few degrees.

Her lips move, forming words I can barely hear. "He... was...waiting."

"Who? Who did this?" I ask again.

Carmen's form flickers, her translucent glow dimming slightly. Her hands tremble as they rest on her lap, and when she looks at me, her expression is a mix of fear and heartbreak.

She whispers, but I can't catch it, like it costs her something to say it.

I lean in closer, my pulse quickening. "He? Who, Carmen? Who did this to you?"

Her lips part again, but this time they tremble, as though the words are too painful to release. Her form begins to blur at the edges, and I think she's about to vanish completely.

But then she says, "He promised. He lied." Her hands move, clutching at her throat. "I loved him. He said I wouldn't get hurt. He said I only had to lure him away, but then he..." Her voice cracks. "He...watched."

The air grows colder, the frost biting at my skin. My heart pounds. Watched? Who watched? Lure him away?

"Damien?" I ask before I can stop myself. But she doesn't answer—doesn't even flinch. Instead, her head snaps to the side, her attention drawn to the door as though someone is standing there, listening.

"No," she whispers, the word trembling as her entire form begins to waver.

Her presence flickers violently, and she twists to face me, her translucent hands reaching out but stopping short. Her eyes, wide and filled with terror, bore into mine. "Run," she says, "before he knows..."

And then she's gone, the glow fading entirely. The room is silent, the air heavy and cold, leaving her cryptic warnings burning in my mind.

I pull the door open, and Malachi and Anton are both standing right outside, tense and expectant.

"What did you see?" Malachi asks immediately, his gold-flecked eyes narrowing as they search my face.

"Nothing," I say automatically, my voice hollow, the words spilling out before I've even thought them through. My mind is too busy racing, trying to piece together Carmen's fragmented revelation. He promised. He lied. He watched.

"That didn't sound like nothing," Anton rumbles, stepping closer, his bulk making the narrow hallway feel suffocating.

I shake my head, avoiding his piercing gaze. "I need air," I mutter, trying to sidestep him.

"Air can wait," Anton grunts, moving to block my path with his broad frame. "We need answers. Viktor needs answers."

"I need air," I repeat, louder this time, straightening my shoulders as I meet his cold, unyielding stare head-on. "Unless you'd like me to pass out on your boots, I suggest you let me through."

Anton's jaw tightens, his lips pressing into a hard line. His eyes flick to Malachi, who shrugs. Finally, with a muttered curse, Anton steps aside.

I push past him, relief washing over me as I leave the room behind. Malachi, of course, falls into step behind me like a fucking shadow, his presence as persistent as ever. At least Anton doesn't follow. He's probably already back in that room, poking around.

I make my way to the double doors at the front of the mansion. Thankfully, I don't pass anyone on the way. The last thing I need right now is another confrontation or curious stares.

"Where are you going?" Malachi calls as I push the heavy doors open and step outside.

The cold air hits me instantly, sharp and biting, but it's a relief after the tension inside. I pull my beanie from my pocket and tug it over my head, ignoring him as I descend the side steps.

I stop a few feet into the clearing, the forest stretching out before me like a frozen canvas. The air is so still it feels like the world is holding its breath.

In the daylight, I can really see this place for what it is—it's stunning. A perfect winter wonderland. The snow covers the ground like a thick, untouched blanket, sparkling under the weak sunlight. The bony trees surrounding the estate are coated in frost, their dark branches glittering with small pillows of snow that cling stubbornly to the tips.

I close my eyes, taking a deep breath, letting the fresh air fill my lungs. The tension eases slightly as I stand there, the cold seeping through my sweater but somehow still comforting. This moment, however fleeting, feels like the first bit of calm I've had since I arrived.

Malachi's voice pulls me back. "Admiring the scenery?" His demeanor is lighter now, less pushy, though I can still feel the curiosity simmering beneath the surface.

I glance over my shoulder at him a few feet away, his hands shoved into the pockets of his coat. "Maybe I needed to breathe without someone watching me like a hawk," I snap.

"You did storm out dramatically," he says, his smirk reappearing. "What was I supposed to do, let you wander off alone in the snow?"

"Yes!" My lips twitch slightly despite myself.

He shakes his head, stepping closer but keeping a

respectful distance. "I'm here to admire the view too. No hovering, I promise."

I turn back toward the forest and stare out at the endless stretch of trees. Beautiful as this place is, it feels like the kind of beauty that hides something darker beneath the surface.

"Do you want to fill me in on what happened back there? Can you really talk to dead people like my father claims?" Malachi asks.

I step onto the path that runs along the edge of the forest, the snow crunching under my boots as I keep my eyes forward. I know he'll fall in line beside me.

I glance at him briefly. "Do you remember the accident I told you about?"

He nods, uncharacteristically serious. "The one where you lost your family."

I swallow hard, pushing the memory back down before it can surface. I don't let myself linger on that day—not for more than a second. "When I woke up in the hospital, that's when I saw my first ghost. My gift... It's changed over the years, but sometimes I can talk to the dead."

He doesn't interrupt, his footsteps keeping pace with mine as I continue, "If it's someone who passed a long time ago, it's usually easier to communicate with them. They've had time to settle into the spirit world. But cases like this?" I shake my head. "When they've died recently—and violently—it's different. Difficult. Sometimes they haven't fully crossed over or haven't accepted what happened to them. That makes everything...messy."

I look down, admiring the snow beneath my feet, its pristine blanket so surreal. It sparkles like the world's been dusted with starlight. I could look at it for hours if I weren't in the middle of this nightmare.

"So what do you do with cases like this?" Malachi asks. "If you can't talk to them, then what?"

I let out a long breath, watching it plume into the frosty air like smoke. "I have to try to decipher whatever images or words I'm able to get from them. And if that doesn't work..." I don't want to say it and admit where this might lead.

"If that doesn't work, then what?" he presses.

"Then I'll have to try other tactics," I say quietly. "More draining ones."

His footsteps halt behind me, and I pause too, turning enough to catch the look on his face. "Why do you let them treat you like this?" he asks. "Why do you let my father tell you what to do?"

I gape at him, the absurdity of his question hitting me like a slap. A bitter laugh escapes my throat. "I'm not sure how things are done wherever it is you came from," I say, shaking my head, "but clearly you've been gone too long if you think I have any choice in the matter.

"This isn't a life of options, Malachi. It's survival. And that means playing by your father's rules." I turn and keep walking, not waiting for his response.

Behind me, I hear the crunch of his boots as he catches up, his silence speaking louder than anything he could say.

I circle the mansion, the path winding in and out of the frost-covered forest. It's beautiful in a haunting way, but the cold seeps through my sweater, making my breath visible in the air. I pull my beanie lower over my ears and head back to the front steps. Then I hear the hum of an engine. A car pulls up the long driveway, and Orin steps out, his sharp gaze finding me immediately.

He closes the distance between us with purposeful strides.

"Who let you out?" he snaps, his hand grabbing my arm in a bruising grip. He yanks me hard toward the front steps, dragging me along like I'm nothing more than a troublesome pet.

I don't fight him. I've learned better. Orin thrives on resistance—he lives for the chase and the punishment that comes after. He's the most deranged of Marco's family, and I know firsthand how much he enjoys inflicting pain. He carried out my punishments when I tried to escape, and it wasn't duty—it was pleasure. Every bruise and scar came with his twisted laugh echoing in my ears.

"Hey! What are you doing?" Malachi's voice cuts through the icy air. He rounds the corner of the house, his eyes narrowing as he sees Orin's hand locked around my arm. He'd been keeping his distance like I'd asked, but now he looks furious, his eyes narrowing and his movements quick as he closes in.

Orin sneers, his grip tightening as he jerks me closer to him. "You were supposed to be watching the little bitch, not letting her wander around like this is a fucking vacation," he growls at Malachi. His nails dig into my skin, and I wince as he turns back to me. "Do you even have anything useful to report yet?"

"Not yet, but I will."

"Let go of her arm," Malachi says, glaring.

He's pissed—really pissed—and for some reason that makes the knot in my stomach twist tighter. I don't need a savior, and I sure as hell don't need him. He lied about who he was, showed up here thinking we could be friends, and now he's playing the protective act? It's infuriating.

"Oh shit, are you actually catching feelings for this little pest?" Orin laughs, his grin wicked and mocking. "Dad's going to love this." But he doesn't let go. If anything, his grip tightens.

"I'm looking after her," Malachi says, his voice razor-sharp now. "Now let go of her fucking arm."

Orin's smile falters, twisting into something darker. He

wants the fight. It's written all over his face, the way his stance shifts slightly, preparing for a physical clash.

"Stop," I yell, "I don't want you looking after me, and I don't need you sticking up for me either. Go back to wherever you came from."

Something soft flickers in Malachi's eyes—something I don't want to see. But it vanishes quickly.

Anton's gravelly voice booms from the front steps, catching all of us off guard. "I think you've had enough air."

We all turn to see him standing there. His dark eyes sweep over the scene, unreadable but heavy with authority.

"I will be taking Miss Sinclair into my care until this investigation is complete," he declares. "If you have a problem with it, speak with Viktor."

My stomach drops. Great. This whole thing is spiraling out of control, even by my standards.

"It's settled then," I say, ripping my arm out of Orin's grip and stepping away, the tension still crackling between the brothers. Orin is still locked in a silent stare-off with Malachi, but I don't stick around to watch it play out.

Without waiting for anyone to stop me, I follow Anton back into the house, the cold air finally replaced by the oppressive warmth of the mansion. I don't look back.

ANTON SHOVES me into Carmen's room with all the subtlety of a battering ram and barks out his decree, "Stay here until you have something to report." The door slams shut behind him, leaving me alone with the lingering smell of bleach and an overwhelming urge to punch something.

The asshole doesn't even understand how this works. I don't need to be in this room to contact her. I already saw her face and have her photo tucked away. That's all I need. But let him think he's cornered me. At least in here I'm free of Malachi's watchful gaze and Orin's insufferable presence.

Malachi.

My teeth grind together at the thought of him. What is his deal anyway? One moment, he's trying to flirt with me, acting like he's above all this family bullshit, and the next he's every bit the enigma his father likely trained him to be. Who is he really? Why does he even care?

He's probably no different than the rest of Marco's men, perhaps better at hiding it. My gut twists with suspicion every time I think about him, like there's a shadow behind his eyes I can't quite make out. Something about this place and this case feels wrong.

Off.

Like the air itself is too thick with secrets.

My thoughts are interrupted by a voice that sends a cold ripple down my spine.

"I'd like to get a piece of you."

I snap my head up, eyes wide. And there he is—leaning against the wall like he's been here the whole time. Damien.

His presence is sharper, darker, more tangible than Carmen's had been. His translucent form glows faintly in the dim room, and I can feel the weight of his spirit pressing against me like a cold hand on my neck. This is not a man whose company I'd have enjoyed in life.

"You finally decided to show yourself," I say, crossing my arms and peering hard. "Would you like to fill me in on what happened here? I'm not really in the mood to play games with the dead today. The ones I play with the living are exhausting enough."

He smiles, but it's not the warm, charming grin of a victim seeking help. No, it's twisted—dangerous. He pushes off the wall, taking a step closer, and the air around me chills further. My fingers twitch, ready to react if I need to, though I'm not entirely sure how to fight something that's already dead.

"Games?" he repeats, mocking me. "Sweetheart, the only game here is the one you're too blind to see. Do you know what happens to little girls who wander into the dark thinking they can survive among the monsters?"

"I'm guessing they survive fine when the monsters are as pathetic as you," I shoot back, leaning against the edge of the bed.

There's something deeply wrong about him. Carmen's spirit had been fractured, confused, but Damien's feels...whole. Like whatever bound him to this plane didn't bother tearing apart his soul. Instead, it made him stronger.

Crueler.

He takes another step closer, his figure flickering but never losing that predatory aura. "You think you're clever. But you don't even know whose game you're playing, do you? Whose rules you're following."

"Why don't you enlighten me?" I refuse to let him see how much he's rattling me. "Who pulled your strings before you ended up like this? Who's pulling them now?"

He chuckles, the sound low and humorless. "You think I'm a pawn? You're the one being played. The real monsters are right in front of you, and you're too busy playing detective to see them."

The temperature in the room drops another notch, and for the first time I wonder if I've underestimated him. But I don't flinch and instead step closer, my chin tilted defiantly.

"You're dead, Damien. You've already lost. Either give me the answers I need or get out of my way."

His wicked smile widens. "You're so sure this ends with me. But you'll see, Kitty Kat." He leans in close, his form almost solid now, his voice a whisper that feels like ice against my skin. "You'll see soon enough that the real danger isn't in the shadows."

He vanishes, leaving me alone in the freezing room, my heart pounding and my mind racing.

"Kitty Kat."

My skin crawls. There's only one person in the world who's ever called me by that name, and it sure as hell didn't sound the same on his tongue.

What the fuck is going on here?

My pulse thunders in my ears, and I glance around the room, half-expecting Damien to materialize again. But there's nothing—no flicker of his ghostly form, no mocking grin. Silence, heavy and suffocating, pressing against me like a weight.

It's a coincidence, I tell myself, though the thought doesn't comfort me. Spirits don't often share their secrets with one another—not in the afterlife, not in the in-between. But that fucking nickname...

My hands clench into fists at my sides, the chill in the room forgotten as something hot and sharp rises in my chest. If this is Damien's idea of a game, he's playing with the wrong person.

I pace the room, the soft creak of the floorboards the only sound breaking the suffocating quiet. Coincidence, I repeat, trying to convince myself. But the unease won't leave, gnawing at the edges of my mind.

I take a deep breath and think. But the name lingers, echoing in my head like a taunt. Whatever Damien is hiding is more twisted than I imagined. And if that name is more than a coincidence, then the stakes are now a hell of a lot higher.

The only person who's ever called me Kitty Kat is Cade. And Cade is dead.

What the hell did I get myself into?

Damien spoke to me like he knows me—like he knew I was coming. Could Damien reach my family in the afterlife? Could he reach Cade? But why? And how?

I yank my ponytail free, running a shaky hand through my hair. *Get a grip, Kat.* The fucking name rhymes—it's a shallow jab from some asshole spirit who doesn't want me solving this case. That has to be it. Spirits love their tricks, their cryptic bullshit. This isn't about Cade. It can't be.

But I can't stop thinking about him now, or about my parents. I haven't let my mind go there in years, and yet here it is. All because of a dumb nickname.

Kitty Kat.

The timing couldn't be worse. I had that dream about Cade the other night, told Malachi about the accident, dredged up things I'd buried deep for a reason. Now my brain is trying to connect dots where there aren't any. That's all it is, my head playing tricks on me.

But a darker thought creeps in, and it makes my stomach churn. What if all the spirits I've pissed off over the years have found a way to torment my family in the beyond?

My breath catches, and I stop pacing, gripping the edge of the dresser to steady myself. *Relax, Kat.* My fingers curl against the wood. *You're overthinking again. You're letting your mind get away from you.* The rational side of me tries to take control, grounding me. I've been through worse. I've faced spirits far more malevolent than Damien and lived to tell the tale. This is no different. It's noise—a distraction meant to throw me off.

Focus.

I need a plan. Damien's cryptic bullshit aside, I still don't have anything solid to tell Marco. Hopefully, he'll give me a few days before demanding answers. He usually gives me space when I'm working a case, and I'm counting on that now.

Do I contact Carmen again? The thought nags at me, but I

push it down. I can't keep pulling from the same shallow well and hoping for clarity. Carmen's answers won't fix this puzzle— not entirely. And I don't know if I can handle summoning Damien again.

One step at a time. I need to piece together what I have, block out the noise, and figure out what the hell Damien knows —and why he's focused more on me than his own death. Why not tell me who killed them?

Chapter Seven

RULE 7 OF THE NEW ORDER: KEEP YOUR ENEMIES CLOSE AND LEARN THEIR WAYS–SOMETIMES THE BEST VICTORY COMES FROM PRETENDING TO BE THEIR ALLY.

"I'VE BEEN MORE than patient, and my father has treated you well. But that can change if this isn't resolved soon." Orin's voice is cold, echoing in my ears as he pins me against the wall.

It's been two excruciating days since Damien showed up, and since then—nothing. Not a single sign of him, not a whisper from Carmen. But Marco wouldn't rush me this soon. No, this is Orin trying to push me.

"I wasn't aware Marco was in such a hurry," I reply, forcing myself to stay calm, even though every inch of me wants to shove him aside.

Orin's lips quirk up on one side, his eyes gleaming with mock sincerity. "I always have my father's best interests in mind," he says, stepping back with a wink. He opens his mouth to say something else, but then a soft knock interrupts him.

"Excuse me, miss, I brought you lunch. May I come in?"

I turn toward the door as a young redhead, wearing an apron and balancing a tray, pokes her head inside. She's barely in her teens, far too young to be working in the kitchen.

"Yes, thank you," I say, motioning for her to come in. She steps forward, carefully setting the tray on the side table by the window.

Orin sneers, "Soon, I'll be cutting back on your meals if you don't start pulling your weight—or maybe I'll have them switch you to the synthetic rations they hand out in the gutter zones." The girl flinches, looking even smaller as he pushes past her, slamming the door behind him.

The gutter zones are where people go to disappear—or where they're sent when they're no longer useful. Crumbling buildings, stagnant air, and the stench of desperation cling to every corner. It's not a place you survive; it's where you wait to be forgotten.

I throw my hands up, waving Orin off as if it's no big deal. "What's your name?" I ask before she can disappear.

She fidgets nervously, her eyes darting to the door.

"Kira," she says softly.

I offer her a small smile, trying to put her at ease. The last thing I need is to spook her before I can ask questions. "Did you know Carmen?"

Her head dips slightly. "Yes, very well."

I nod, studying her carefully. "I'm sorry for your loss." She shifts uncomfortably, her hands twisting behind her back. I need to keep this casual or she'll bolt.

"Did you know Damien too?" I reach for the sandwich on the tray and take a bite.

"Not well," she says quickly.

I suppress a sigh, annoyed at her short answers but not ready to push too hard. "Were they together romantically?"

Her nose wrinkles in visible disgust. "Oh no, Carmen had a boyfriend. I don't know who he was, but she was always sneaking off to see him. It wasn't Damien—she would never..." Kira appears to shiver.

I lower the sandwich and watch her carefully. That reaction says a lot more than her words. "Why do you say that? Did she dislike Damien?"

Kira hesitates, biting her lip before replying. "It's not that. She...knew what he was like. Everyone did. He wasn't..." She pauses, struggling with how to put it. "He wasn't a good man."

Her tone leaves no room for doubt, and my mind starts turning. If Carmen had a secret boyfriend, someone important enough to sneak away for, why hasn't he come up before? And why would Damien end up in her room—her bed—if she'd never associate with him? None of this is adding up.

"Kira," I say gently, "do you know anything else? I need help to understand what happened to Carmen and Damien."

Her eyes dart to the door again, and I know I'm losing her. "I don't know much, miss. She was scared sometimes and talked about leaving. But she never said why."

Carmen was scared and planning to leave? That doesn't sound like a cook who was content with her life—or someone who should have been anywhere near Damien.

"Thank you, Kira," I say, offering a smile. "If you think of anything else, will you let me know?"

She nods quickly, her relief palpable as she hurries to the door. Before she steps out, she pauses and glances back at me. "Miss...be careful."

And then she's gone, leaving me alone with more questions than ever. Carmen had a boyfriend. She was scared. And Damien was as one would expect, given he's a Volkov.

I need to remind myself of the priorities here—Viktor and Marco don't care about Carmen. They didn't bring me here to solve her murder. They want to know who killed Damien, and the fact that Carmen died alongside him? Collateral damage in their eyes. The help around here doesn't matter to them.

But are they one and the same? That's the question. The

vision I saw through Carmen makes me think they are. Whoever was watching in the doorway that night is the key. Could it have been Damien and Carmen's murderer? Or was it someone who decided to look the other way?

Still, something about Carmen doesn't sit right. Maybe she's not as innocent in all of this as she seemed. That look of disgust Kira gave when I mentioned Damien sticks with me. Did Carmen lie about her relationship with him? Maybe she was sneaking off to see him, not her supposed boyfriend. What if she was cheating? And what if someone found out? Maybe her boyfriend caught her that night and killed them both in a fit of rage.

It makes sense...doesn't it?

If that's true, then Carmen's mystery boyfriend is my number-one suspect right now. I need to figure out who he is—and where he is. But that won't be easy, not in this house where every whisper carries a secret and every look feels like a challenge.

I lean back in my chair, running a hand along Mischka while I eat my turkey sandwich. I replay the scraps of information I have. He's out there somewhere, the boyfriend—or whoever Carmen was sneaking off to see. And if he's involved, he either killed them or knows something that will unravel this whole mess.

Either way, I'll find him. The truth has a funny way of coming to light when you dig deep enough—and I'm not afraid to get my hands dirty.

"What the hell are you doing?" Malachi's voice startles me, breaking through the silence of the room. I whirl around from the window, dropping my hand to my side. Mish vanishes instantly.

How long has he been standing there? I was so distracted that I didn't hear him come in.

"I'm eating lunch," I say, waving my half-eaten sandwich in the air. "What does it look like?"

He doesn't look convinced, his sharp gaze flicking to my empty hand. "No, you were doing something weird with your other hand. Looked like you were trying to cast a spell or something." He steps further into the room, closing the door behind him as if I invited him in. "Do Avids cast spells? Is that another gift you have?"

I put down my sandwich and glare at him. "I wasn't casting a spell, and I have no idea what you're talking about." The last thing I need is Malachi sniffing around the edges of my abilities, especially when I don't even fully understand them. "Why are you here, Malachi?"

He leans casually against the edge of the desk, folding his arms like he plans to stay for a while. "Checking in on you. You've been locked away for days. Figured I'd see if you've cracked the case yet."

"Why? Are you suddenly Viktor's errand boy now?" I snap, grabbing the sandwich again and taking an angry bite.

"You're touchy today," he says, raising an eyebrow. "But, no, I'm not Viktor's errand boy. I don't trust Anton to actually keep you alive while you figure out who murdered my cousin."

I stiffen, the sandwich forgotten in my hand. His cousin. It's easy to forget sometimes how personal this all is for him too. "I'm fine," I say tersely. "Anton's annoying, but he's not exactly failing at his job."

"Glad to hear it," Malachi says, but his eyes are still locked on me, like he's trying to see into me. "Are you going to tell me what you were really doing just now, or do I need to start guessing?"

I clench my jaw, debating how much to give him. He's already suspicious, and denying everything will make him dig

74

deeper. But I don't owe him an explanation. Not about Mish. Not about anything.

"You really need to work on your boundaries, Malachi," I say, stepping away from the window and toward the tray of food Kira brought me. "Not everything I do is your business."

"You'd be surprised," he says, his voice low, teasing. But there's something beneath it, something sharp and curious. "Especially if it has anything to do with this case."

I set the sandwich down and glare at him. "Why do you even care? Don't you have better things to do than lurk outside my door, watching for spells that don't exist?"

He shrugs, a playful grin tugging at his lips. "You're interesting. And if you are casting spells, I'd like a heads-up. You know, in case you accidentally summon something worse than you."

"Get out," I say, throwing my hand toward the door. For a moment, I half-expect him to make another snide comment or otherwise annoy me. But to my surprise, he chuckles and pushes off the desk.

He moves to the door, and I think I've gotten off easy. But instead of leaving, he reaches out and turns the lock.

What the fuck?

I blink, caught between irritation and surprise as he casually kicks off his boots and sprawls out on my bed like he owns it. The sheer audacity of this man is unmatched.

"What exactly do you think you're doing?" I say, raising an eyebrow and crossing my arms.

He leans back, folding his hands behind his head like he's settling in for a nap. "I think I've gone about this all wrong. I have a proposition for you."

He pats the empty spot on the bed next to him, his smirk infuriatingly smug. "Come on. Hear me out."

If he thinks I'm going to sit—much less lie down—next to him, he's lost his damn mind.

I roll my eyes, shifting my weight impatiently. "Spit it out then," I bark, tapping my foot anxiously. I have better things to do than entertain whatever nonsense he's cooked up.

He doesn't budge, his gaze fixed on me with that infuriating mix of amusement and curiosity. "Relax. I'm not asking you to do anything you don't want to do. Yet."

I narrow my eyes at him, my patience fraying. "Malachi, if this is some ridiculous attempt to flirt—"

"It's not," he interrupts, sitting up slightly, his expression shifting to something more serious. "Sit down for a minute and hear me out."

"If it'll make you leave faster," I mumble under my breath, giving in and sitting at the very edge of the bed, my back to him.

"I get the feeling you don't like me much," he says, amused. "But that's not the vibe I got at the park that night."

I already regret sitting down. "Call it temporary insanity," I say, pulling my knees to my chest and wrapping my arms around them, waiting for him to say something interesting—if he's even capable of it.

"I've been watching you," he starts, and I suppress the urge to roll my eyes. "And I see that you don't have much to lose. You don't have much of a life at all."

I turn and blink at him, startled by his bluntness. "Uh, thank you for the compliment."

He leans forward, his expression uncharacteristically serious. "What I mean is that you're untethered. No family, no alliances, no loyalties—except to yourself."

"Again, a real ego boost here," I cut in, but he keeps going, undeterred.

"I'm going to risk telling you the real reason I'm here," he says, his voice lowering slightly. The way he's looking at me makes me pause. "I think we can help each other, but only if I can trust you."

My curiosity sparks despite myself. "The real reason you're here..." I tilt my head to study him. "You've been parading around like your father's perfect little soldier, so forgive me if I'm not entirely convinced."

His lips curl at the edges, but there's no humor in it. "That's the point, isn't it? Marco and Viktor think I'm here to fall in line, to play the good son and follow orders, learn the family business. But I'm not."

I narrow my eyes, my suspicion flaring. "So what are you really doing here, Malachi?"

"I want to learn the ins and outs of how they traffic people like you—Avids," Malachi says somberly. "I'm working with a group in the Western District where I came from. We've been rescuing Avids across our region."

He pauses, watching me as if waiting for a reaction. I stare back, arms crossed, not giving him anything yet. He exhales. "We want to put a stop to all of it—shut down as many houses as we can, save as many people as possible. Fuck, most Avids are kids when they're discovered. Then they're sold off to some wealthy family to be used for their gifts or exploited for wealth. My father and Viktor move more Avids than anyone else, and I want to destroy their operation from the inside out."

I let out the breath I hadn't realized I was holding. The way he huffs when he talks about the trafficking—it's not just hatred; there's something personal in it. But I don't let it show on my face.

I ask, "What's in it for me?"

His brows knit together. "Don't you want to help put a stop to the very system that ruined your life?"

I bite down on the inside of my cheek, willing myself to stay calm. "That doesn't exactly benefit me, now does it?"

I don't know why I say it. Of course I want to stop the exploitation, to save the kids who never stood a chance—kids like me, Aurora, Ramus, and the others I met before Marco bought me. But agreeing to Malachi means trusting him, and trust has never been something I've handed out easily.

I keep my glare steady, my stoic expression firmly in place, even as an unsettling feeling takes hold.

He doesn't back down. "If you help me, I won't just save others like you. I'll make sure you're free of my family forever. You'll be free to lead your own life."

My stomach twists.

Free.

The word lodges itself in my chest, dangerous and titillating. Hope like that can kill you. "Marco would hunt me to the ends of the Earth," I say darkly. "Don't make promises you can't keep."

He leans forward, his expression shifting. "What if my father was no longer in the picture?"

That gets my attention. I sit up straighter, narrowing my eyes at him. "You plan to kill your father?" My voice comes out louder than I intended, and I instantly clap a hand over my mouth, glancing toward the door.

He smirks, leaning back against the headboard. "Relax. These rooms are practically soundproof."

Convenient, I think bitterly, but the look in his eyes is deadly serious.

"I don't know what my plans are yet," he admits, running a hand through his hair. "That's why I need your help."

And there it is—the catch. "What do you need from me?"

His shoulders relax, like he's been waiting for this. "My father might trust me, but my brothers. Not a chance. They don't want me anywhere near their cut of the business. They see me as a threat, and they're not wrong." He pauses, grimacing. "I haven't seen the other Avids and don't even know where they're kept. But I know my father and Viktor own many. They have to."

"What does that have to do with me?" I ask, feeling skeptical. "I have no control here. No say over anything."

He shakes his head, a glint of something dangerous in his eyes. "You have more power than you think."

"How do you figure that?"

"For whatever reason, my father listens to you. He trusts what you say. It's like he has some weird infatuation with you or something." My skin crawls, but Malachi doesn't stop. "You can get me in, Katja. Tell him you need help with the case. Say you need to see what the other Avids can do, if any of them have abilities that might be useful."

The blood drains from my face. "You want me to use them as pawns? Like tools?"

"That's what they already are to him," he says, his voice hard. "You'd be playing along to get us closer to the truth. Once I know where they're kept, I can figure out a way to dismantle it all."

I shake my head, my chest tightening. "I don't like where this is going, Malachi."

"You don't have to like it," he says softly. "You have to decide if freedom—yours and theirs—is worth the risk."

I can't bring myself to answer. Because the truth? I'm not sure I know yet.

My pretty prison is safe, predictable, controlled, and survivable. But am I ready to risk it all for a chance at a real life? The thought gnaws at me, and I try to shove it down. Hope is dangerous. Letting myself believe there's a way out will only make it hurt worse when this all fails and falls apart.

I glance at Malachi, his brown eyes still on me, waiting for my answer. I think about Orin and the punishments I've endured. I don't know if I can bear another round of his sadistic shit. But can I let my fear, my cowardice, be the thing that keeps Malachi from saving so many others like me? What if he really can put a dent in the trade business and stop the trafficking of Avids altogether?

I sigh. "Okay, I'll do what I can to help. But that doesn't mean we're friends, and if this shit goes south, you can bet I'll throw your ass under the bus in a second."

A smile spreads across his face, and there it is—that stupid, dangerous smile.

Fuck.

It's too charming, far too dangerous. The kind of smile that could make someone forget all the red flags waving in the background.

"It's decided then," he says smoothly. "You keep working on the case and find a way to learn more about the Avids and how they manage things. Tomorrow night, Viktor's throwing some kind of party. I'll make sure my father thinks it's a good idea for you to attend. I could use a second set of eyes and ears."

I snort, the absurdity of it hitting me. "His son was brutally murdered in this very house, and he's throwing a dinner party? How deranged can your family get?"

Malachi laughs, the sound dark and full of irony. "I know, right? Let's say Damien wasn't exactly his favorite son. Haven't you learned yet that appearances are everything in the Volkov family? Viktor needs to put on a strong front and celebrate the arrival of his brother. Nothing screams 'strong leader' like a dinner party in a house still stained with blood."

I squirm but don't argue. The Volkovs thrive on appearances, power plays, and pretending everything is under control —even when it's clearly not.

"Was Gary or Anton out in the hall when you came in?" I

ask, steering the conversation away from the madness of the party.

"I saw Anton downstairs eating lunch, and Gary thinks I'm trying to get in your pants, so don't worry about him being suspicious of anything," Malachi says, adding a wink that makes my stomach churn.

"Nice. Real nice. Seems you've thought of everything, haven't you? Except how to do this all on your own," I say, narrowing my eyes at him.

His grin widens, and for the first time I notice the faint dimple on his left cheek. It's infuriatingly disarming. "You don't have to like me, Kat," he says. "At the end of the day, we want the same things. It only makes sense to work together."

He's right about that. I don't like him, and this changes nothing. But I learned from Marco to keep your enemies close. Malachi isn't my friend, but for now I'll play along. I'll help him, so long as I don't get the sense he's playing me.

"I still have a feeling you're not telling me everything," I say, watching him closely. "Was this your plan all along? Did you know who I was that night in the park?"

He opens his mouth to speak, but a knock at the door cuts him off. The handle shakes, and my stomach twists. Good thing he locked it, I guess.

"Viktor wants to speak with you," Anton says from the other side, his voice like gravel. There's no getting out of this.

I glance back briefly, but Malachi is already moving, slipping silently into the bathroom. Of course.

I crack the door open and nod. "Fine. Lead the way."

I step into the hall, the door clicking shut behind me. Whatever Malachi was going to say will have to wait. For now, I'm walking into whatever Viktor has planned.

Chapter Eight

RULE 8 OF THE NEW ORDER: NEVER
UNDERESTIMATE THE POWER OF PLAYING THE
FOOL. SOMETIMES THE EASIEST WAY TO GET WHAT
YOU WANT IS TO LET THEM THINK THEY'RE IN
CONTROL.

VIKTOR LEANS BACK in his chair and says, "Do you use your gift to speak to the family you killed?" It's like all the air is knocked out of me.

I don't flinch, but I feel it, hard and vivid. My hands twitch at my sides, desperate to hold something—anything—against the raw pain.

Grief has a funny way of sneaking up at the damndest times. You're fine for days, weeks, months even, and then it hits you— like a freight train, a sucker punch to the gut. One moment, you're coasting, even daring to smile at some memory of what you've lost. And then the next, it's like the world shifts, and your chest feels hollow, like your heart's been ripped out all over again.

I try not to think about my parents. About Cade. Memories of them creep in sometimes, and on good days I can handle it— a flash of their smiles, a laugh echoing in my mind. But the risk of those memories cutting deeper is always there. It's crazy how you can go from being fine to drowning in seconds.

I figure if I can speak to the dead, I should be the last person suffering from grief this way. But here's the thing. I can't speak to them.

I won't.

I'm a coward when it comes to my family. Too afraid to see their faces again. Too afraid to see Cade. What if they're angry? What if they're disappointed? What if they're at peace and I can't bear to let them go? I miss Cade so much that sometimes it feels like I'll never feel happiness again.

But I can't risk that kind of pain. The best way to survive is to bury it. To seal it off somewhere deep and dark and never let it surface.

I tell myself they're happy, that they've moved on to whatever peace the afterlife offers. That's it. End of story. I won't entertain anything more. Because if I did—if I let that grief sink its claws into me—I'm not sure I'd survive it.

"Are you deaf, or did I strike a nerve?" Viktor says, jolting me back to reality.

He's trying to get a rise out of me. I'll be damned if I give him the satisfaction.

"I do not use my gift for personal matters," I say flatly as I feel the weight of his words pressing down on me.

His expression doesn't change, but there's something in his eyes—a flicker of amusement or maybe triumph—that makes my blood boil. Why the fuck did he summon me here for this? Of all the things to ask me, this is what he chooses? To dig at a wound I've spent years trying to keep closed? Why does he even know about my family?

I swallow hard, shoving the grief back where it belongs. Deep, buried, untouchable. It will not seize me today. Goddamnit, it won't.

"I was told there was a boy in the car with you that day too.

You didn't only ruin your family's life in that accident—you ruined his as well," Viktor says.

I give him a cold look.

This man may be cruel, but I'll be damned if I let him see me break.

"With all due respect, sir, you're a very busy man," I say patronizingly. "I'd hate to waste your time with a decade-old story about a car accident. Is there something I can help you with today?"

I force a smile but know it's a poor imitation of one. I barely know this man, and yet I already despise him.

Across the room, Anton shifts by the door, his presence a quiet reminder that I'm not the one in control here.

"You can leave us, Anton," Viktor says, his focus entirely on me. The sound of the door clicking shut confirms Anton's departure, but it doesn't ease the tension in the room.

Viktor leans forward slightly, his broad, looming presence making the polished desk between us seem to disappear. "My brother has been treating you far too kindly, allowing you to walk around with a mouth like that," he says, his fingers drumming a slow rhythm on the desk.

I say nothing, keeping my expression impassive.

He purses his lips. "Anton tells me you're no closer to solving my son's murder. But he's also told me you've been speaking behind closed doors. When you're alone. In the room where it happened."

Apparently not all the rooms are soundproof.

"It seems your son doesn't want me to find his killer. He'd rather make a game out of it," I say matter-of-factly.

Viktor cackles, the sound sharp and hollow as he leans back in his chair. "I'd think you were lying, but that does sound like Damien. The boy always did have a flair for theatrics." His amusement fades quickly, replaced by his usual icy demeanor. "Still, no matter what trouble he gives you, I expect results. Marco assured me you would procure the killer in due time."

I nod once. "I will."

He studies me for a moment then sits up straighter, rigid and commanding. "Very well. I asked you here for another reason. Tomorrow evening, I am hosting a party to celebrate my brother's visit, and I want to make sure you are in attendance—and dressed appropriately."

His gaze flicks over me, a flicker of distaste crossing his face, as if my current outfit is an affront to his sensibilities. I resist the urge to roll my eyes. What does he expect me to do, solve his son's murder in ballgowns?

"I do not normally interact so openly with an Avid," he continues, "but my brother has an attachment to you, and I would like you present. However, let me make one thing very clear. No matter what my brother says, I do not want my guests knowing what you are or what you can do. Keep it to yourself. Do you understand?"

His eyes narrow slightly, and I nod, already regretting every part of this conversation. "Yes, sir. I understand."

"Good. The killer may very well be in attendance. If anyone asks, you're a friend of Orin's. He has enough of them to make it believable. I'll tell my nephew to say the same."

The thought makes my skin crawl. A friend of Orin's? Really? I want to argue but bite my tongue. Pushing back will get me nowhere, and I know Viktor well enough by now to recognize a command when I hear one.

"Understood," I say again despite my frustration.

He leans back, satisfied, and waves dismissively. "That's all. You may go."

I turn toward the door, my mind already racing with what

this party might entail and why Viktor seems so intent on keeping me hidden in plain sight. At least I know Malachi was being honest about one thing, and now he won't have to convince Marco to let me go, as I'm already invited—and by invited, I mean my attendance is mandatory.

As I reach for the handle, his voice stops me once more.

"Katja," he says, "do not embarrass me."

I nod without looking back, biting the inside of my cheek to keep from responding. Embarrass him? If anyone here is an embarrassment, it's this entire godforsaken family. But I swallow the thought and step out into the hall, closing the door quietly behind me. How would I embarrass him?

Asshole.

"TELL me what's on your mind," Marco says as he glances at me from the driver's seat.

He'd claimed he needed to run into town and wanted me to accompany him. It's not exactly unusual for him to make such a request, but something about it feels different today. Normally, we'd have a driver and at least one security detail. Today, it's the two of us. Marco rarely does anything without a reason, and I'd bet my life this is about the case. He wants to probe me without prying ears around.

I fiddle with my hands in my lap, glancing out the window at the forest lining the snow-covered road. The sun is beginning to set, casting soft pink hues through the trees.

"I'm admiring the snow," I say absently.

Marco doesn't give a shit what's on my mind. Whatever this ride is about, it isn't small talk.

He reaches over and tugs the beanie off my head, brushing

my hair back from my face with practiced ease. "I can't see your face with that thing on," he says gently.

I glance at him, my expression blank. Marco is an attractive man for his age. He's a young fifty, with only faint creases at the corners of his eyes betraying his years. But I know better than to let appearances cloud my judgment. Despite what anyone might think, Marco has never made a move to cross certain lines. This gesture, brushing my hair out of my face, might seem intimate, but it's not. To Marco, I'm a prized possession, a pet he keeps on a short leash. Something to admire, something to use to further his goals, and nothing more.

He's is a master manipulator, and while he can come close to fooling me sometimes, I know better. His charm is a mask, his kindness a means to an end. Greed drives him, not compassion.

"Tell me what you know so far about the case," he says, focusing on me.

I swallow, feeling the weight of his gaze even as I keep mine trained on the road ahead. Normally, I'd share my thoughts with him, brainstorm out loud, give him enough to keep him satisfied. But with Malachi's proposition hanging over me, I hesitate. If I'm going to play this game, I can't afford to be the obedient little pet Marco has always expected me to be.

Maybe it's time to start engaging my more cunning side.

"This case is proving more difficult than I anticipated," I say evenly.

Marco hums, his fingers drumming lightly on the steering wheel. "I gathered that much from Viktor. He's not pleased with your progress, but I told him you'd deliver. You always do."

"I hope I don't disappoint," I say apathetically.

He tilts his head slightly, studying me out of the corner of his eye. "You seem...distracted."

I stiffen but recover quickly, shrugging. "The details are messy. Nothing about this case is straightforward."

"Details always are," he says, thoughtful. "Do you trust Viktor?"

The question catches me off guard, but I don't let it show. "Does anyone?" I ask, deflecting.

Marco chuckles, "Fair point. But I'm not asking about everyone else. I'm asking about you."

I keep my gaze forward, carefully considering my next words. "Trust isn't something I afford easily."

"Good," he says. "That's how you've survived this long. I've taught you well."

I'm so confused by his question. Why is he asking if I trust Viktor? It's his fucking brother. His twin. If Marco is asking for my opinion of him, he's clearly questioning things about this place and their relationship in ways I don't fully understand yet. I want to tell him Viktor is vile, but I hold my tongue. Family loyalty runs deep, and the last thing I need is to cross a line I can't step back from.

"Does Viktor have any Avids?" I ask, testing the waters.

Marco doesn't reply immediately, and the silence feels heavier than it should. My heartbeat picks up, each second dragging longer than the last. I wonder if I made a mistake already.

"Afraid I might find another favorite while we're here?" Marco finally says, teasing, though there's something guarded beneath it.

I let out a light laugh, brushing off the tension. "Impossible," I say smoothly.

He snickers, clearly pleased with my answer, and some of the weight in the air lifts.

"I don't want to disappoint you," I continue, "and I may

AVIDIAN

need help with this case. Maybe he has someone who could be useful to me."

Marco hums, drumming his fingers lightly against the steering wheel. It's a noncommittal sound, enough to let me know he's considering it. Will he actually tell me anything? That's a different story.

But I planted the seed, and that's all I want to do right now. Pushing further would be too obvious, too risky. Let him mull it over.

"Viktor is very private," Marco says after a pause. "His view on people like you is different from mine. If it were up to him, he'd keep you in a cage. This is all very difficult for him. He's told me he arranged for you to come to dinner tomorrow night."

I'm not surprised. Of course the bastard would want to put me in a cage. Little does he know, I'm already in one—it has plush sheets and pretty walls. I think about the conditions the Avids he gets his hands on must be in...wherever they are.

Malachi is right. I have to do whatever I can to help, because this may be my only chance to make a difference. I'm tired of being complicit in this gilded prison of mine.

"Yes, he made it clear I'm to be Orin's, er, date. And that I'm a regular human—my only gifts shall be my looks," I say.

"Very good." Marco reaches over, patting my leg briefly, the gesture as dismissive as it is practiced. "Let's play by his rules since it's his home and these are his friends. Do you understand?"

I nod, hiding my irritation. Of course Marco wants to play nice. Everything is always nice on the surface with him. Polished, presentable, and dripping with charm, no matter what darkness lurks underneath.

He'll be your best friend right up until the moment he stabs you in the back—literally.

"Tell me everything you know about the case thus far,"

Marco says as we leave the forest and pass by businesses. I knew being vague wouldn't be enough.

I take a slow breath. "Damien's spirit is taunting me. He's difficult to communicate with because he thinks it's a game. It's as if he doesn't want his killer found. On top of that, he's keeping Carmen from communicating with me somehow. Her spirit is weak, and I'm struggling to get anything from her."

Marco listens intently, his expression unreadable, so I press on, testing the waters for my next move. "I suspect an Avid could have been behind this. I can't explain it, but when I went into Carmen's vision, I felt...power. I could probably sense it again if I were closer to it."

I hope I don't regret this lie.

Marco tilts his head but doesn't take his eyes off the road, "I thought you wanted to know if Viktor had any Avids so you could get help. You think one may be behind it as well?"

I force myself not to react, refraining from biting my lip or giving away any tells. "Yes," I say. "I could use the extra help, but I also thought that by working with them, I might be able to dig deeper into this case without coming off as a threat. I'm like them. If I seek their help, I could gain their trust and in turn find out who the killer is."

God, I hope I'm not making this a million times worse.

If Malachi doesn't come through on his promise to help free them, I might be setting these Avids up for some serious punishment. Viktor already despises our kind, and if he starts believing one of us killed his son... Fuck, please let this not be a mistake.

Marco's fingers drum lightly on the steering wheel. Finally, he nods. "I'll speak to Viktor about getting you more access, but let's keep this between you and me for now."

My heart slows. This is good. A step in the right direction.

Malachi may not think so, but I don't care what he thinks.

I'll do what I have to do, and if he has a problem with it, he can deal with it later. For now, I've opened a door. Whether it leads to salvation or disaster, only time will tell.

We pass through a dilapidated town, the kind of place that feels forgotten by time. Marco slows the car, the tires crunching over ice-covered asphalt, cracked and riddled with fissures that spiderweb across the surface like scars. The buildings lining the street buckle under the weight of snow and years of neglect. Roofs sag precariously, icicles dangling from their edges like jagged teeth, while shattered windows gape open, exposing rotting interiors to the bitter wind.

Streetlights, long dead and encased in frost, lean at unnatural angles, their warped poles twisted from years of brutal weather. A scattered few people shuffle along broken sidewalks covered in snow, hunched against the cold in mismatched layers that barely shield them from the biting air. Their faces are gaunt, hollowed by hunger, their eyes fixed downward as if even a glance in our direction could invite trouble.

Small clusters of them gather around barrels filled with burning scraps, the flames lighting up their weathered features. As we drive past, I can't help but wonder if the people here even remember what if feels like to be warm—to be full.

I feel bad for them—for anyone forced to live like this—but I know better than to dwell on it. This is how it is in so many places, and there's nothing I can do to change that. Marco could help. The political families in charge could change everything for these gutter zones. But they don't. They don't care, and it's a fucking travesty.

We turn up a narrow road that winds deeper into the forest, leaving the remnants of the forgotten town behind us. I know better than to ask where we're going, but my unease is growing with every mile. It's fully night now, and beyond the trees and the snow, there's nothing but darkness pressing against the SUV's windows.

"We're here," Marco says finally.

I squint into the blackness but don't see anything at first. Then he slows the SUV and turns down a barely visible snow-covered path. If it weren't for the four-wheel drive, I doubt we'd make it. My heart starts to pound as the headlights cut through the trees, illuminating a clearing up ahead.

There's a warehouse standing there, large and looming, its metal sides rusted and worn. It looks abandoned at first glance, but faint lights flicker inside. A few trucks are parked outside, along with one fancy SUV that looks out of place but similar to ours.

I don't like the look of this.

"Let's go," Marco says, putting the vehicle in park and stepping out.

I fall into step at his side as we approach the building. Two men step out to meet us, their appearances fueling my growing unease. They're scummy-looking with torn jeans and that "haven't showered in days" air about them.

"He's in the back room," one of them says, curt and dismissive. As we walk past, both of their eyes rake over me in a way that makes me want to run and hide. I stare straight ahead, refusing to give them the satisfaction of a reaction.

Once inside, it's not much better than the outside. The air is cold and damp, and the walls are missing panels, exposing beams and insulation in some spots. The concrete floors are uneven and coated in a fine layer of dust that clings to my boots as we move. The faint buzz of flickering lights echoes down the long, empty hallway. I hear someone cry out in the distance and the hair on the back of my neck stands up, but I don't stop. *Oh God, what am I walking into?*

Marco leads the way into what looks like a makeshift office, sparsely furnished and barely functional. A man in a suit sits at a small desk with a laptop in front of him. His clothes speak of wealth, but his features are rough—a long scar runs down his cheek, and his nose is large and crooked. Black and gray-peppered hair is cropped close to his head, but nothing about him feels polished, despite his attempt at refinement.

"I thought you weren't going to make it," the man says, standing and extending a hand toward Marco.

"Yes, I'm not used to driving in the snow," Marco replies with a charming smile, shaking the man's hand. "Didn't take into consideration I'd need to drive slower." His manner is easy, almost conversational, but I know better.

His attention shifts to me. His eyes sweep over me with open appraisal, and I force myself not to flinch. Marco steps closer, his hand moving to my back and gently pushing me forward a couple of steps.

"This is her," Marco says smoothly, as if presenting some prized possession. "My obedient little demon I spoke to you about. You see, she's not a fantasy after all."

Disgusted but impassive, I've had years of practice hiding how much I loathe moments like this.

The man's eyes linger in places that would make me uncomfortable if I wasn't already so desensitized to this kind of behavior. "I can see why you like keeping her close. She is quite something to look at, isn't she?"

I say nothing, standing still under his scrutinizing gaze. My pulse races beneath the calm facade I wear so well. *This is a game,* I remind myself. Play it smart. Watch. Listen. Don't give them anything to use against you.

"Boris, there is another way," Marco says. "Viktor's tactics may work, but it's not fun to have a caged beast when you can have an obedient dog."

I guess I'm the dog in this analogy now.

Lovely.

I swallow my pride, forcing myself to focus. It's all about survival. What are Viktor's tactics? Marco's words plant the question in my mind, unbidden. As much as I detest him, it almost sounds like he's positioning himself as the lesser of two evils. Not good, but not as monstrous as Viktor. Still, I can't bring myself to believe that Marco's motives are anything but selfish.

Boris steps closer, his boots scraping against the dusty floor. Before I can react, his hand clamps around my chin, tilting my head to one side then the other, like I'm some piece of merchandise he's inspecting. I'm repulsed by his touch, and every muscle in my body screams at me to jerk away. But I don't. Marco expects me to behave, and I know better than to challenge him here.

"Yes," Boris murmurs, scanning my face. "But is she the only one you've trained?" He releases my chin, turning to glance back at Marco, completely dismissing me now.

Marco leans casually against the edge of the desk, his demeanor relaxed as if this entire interaction is business as usual. "All of my Avids are like this," he says, a faint smile curling his lips. "I give them a nice place to stay, and they understand the work. In turn, I get the respect I deserve."

Respect? I almost laugh. Respect isn't what he gets. What Marco gets is fear. I don't stay in line because I admire him or appreciate the fancy cage he keeps me in. I obey because the alternative is far worse.

Boris looks me over again, but this time his eyes hold something darker, something calculating. "Interesting," he says, simpering. "Perhaps I've underestimated your methods."

"You wouldn't be the first," Marco replies.

He has pride in controlling me, and now he wants this man to see it, admire it. Marco is probably showing me off to seal whatever deal he's brokering. Boris must be a buyer—or worse. The whole thing churns my stomach.

I don't know what I expected before. Maybe I didn't let myself think about it at all, but deep down I wanted to believe those of us with abilities who were discovered and sold off were treated somewhat like human beings. Maybe not well, but at least given a home. A bed. Something. Not kept in conditions too horrifying to imagine.

"I don't suppose you'd like to sweeten the deal by lending her to me?" Boris asks.

I almost take a step back but catch myself, forcing my feet to stay planted and my face to remain unreadable.

"She's not a common whore," Marco says coolly. "You can find one of those, and it would cost you a lot less."

I silently thank him for that, even if his defense has nothing to do with my dignity and everything to do with preserving his property.

"I want you to think about this deal with Viktor," Marco continues, "and think about what I can offer you instead. You see her now in the flesh. Wouldn't you rather this than what's downstairs?"

Downstairs.

The word lands like a punch to the gut.

Fuck.

Is that where Viktor keeps the other Avids? I keep my face perfectly neutral, but inside my thoughts are racing. I need to pay attention when we leave—every turn, every landmark, every detail.

I need to come back here with Malachi and get everyone out.

"You've piqued my interest enough to make me think I'll pay your district a visit when you return home."

I can already tell Marco is silently basking in this victory.

He doesn't show it outwardly, but the way he carries himself now—the slight lift of his shoulders, the glint in his eye—makes it obvious. He's pulled it off. He's managed to sway one of Viktor's clients, turning him against his own brother.

"I look forward to it. I'll be in touch in a couple of weeks," Marco replies.

Thank God, I think, relieved. We're leaving. Finally.

Marco and Boris shake hands again, and I make a point not to look at Boris at all as Marco leads me out of the room.

This time, Marco turns us right, leading me down a different hallway. I think I hear the faint hum of whispers brushing against my ears. At the end of the hallway, a side door waits, but before we reach it, Marco stops abruptly.

He turns to face a stairwell that descends into pitch darkness, and the sound hits me. Clanging metal, the echo of bars being rattled. Faint, ghostly whispers of voices too distant to make out, but unmistakably human.

"I would take you down there," Marco whispers. "to remind you of your place and how bad things could be. But I know you would never try to escape again, would you?"

It's the closest he's come to being openly cruel in a long time. It feels like a slap, even though I hold myself in check. I haven't tried to escape in years. But that doesn't mean I've stopped thinking about it.

I shake my head, forcing myself to stay composed. Try to escape? No. Kill you? Absolutely.

I glance toward the stairwell, my heart sinking. There are people down there. Avids. I can feel it in my gut, and the sounds only confirm it. Who knows what kind of conditions they're being kept in or where they're going to end up?

This only solidifies my decision to help Malachi. Even if I can't stand him, he's my only chance at ever making a real difference. I can't keep burying this, pretending it doesn't matter. Staying complacent in my pretty prison isn't survival anymore—it's surrender. And it's turning me into someone I don't recognize.

"Let's go," Marco says, pulling open the side door. The rush of cold air hits me like a slap, sharp and bracing, but it's a welcome change. As I follow him back to the SUV, I make a silent vow to myself.

I won't bury this anymore.

I can't.

Chapter Nine

RULE 9 OF THE NEW ORDER: IN DESPERATE TIMES, EVERY MOVE IS SURVIVAL. NEVER JUDGE ANOTHER'S ACTIONS–YOU DON'T KNOW THE BATTLES THEY'RE TRULY FIGHTING.

"I THOUGHT you said the relationship with my father was completely platonic," Malachi says as he waltzes into my room without so much as a knock.

I really need to start locking my door. I'm not used to people barging in. At least Marco's men have the decency to knock when they're sent to retrieve me.

"It is. Why would you say that?" I sit up in bed and flick on the lamp beside me, squinting against the sudden light. I'd just gotten under the covers and turned everything off, ready to sleep. Now, I'm regretting not securing the door.

"You were gone all evening," he says, picking up a trinket from the bookshelf and examining it like he's studying some ancient artifact. "And I watched my father walk you back to your room. In that ridiculous outfit. Late at night."

I was wearing a dress and sweater, after Marco said I had to put on something nice. Hardly what I'd call ridiculous.

"I'm really not in the mood for any fuss tonight, Malachi. As fun as it is to go back and forth with you, it's been a long fucking day." I pull the covers up to my chin and flop my head back onto the pillow.

"What happened after you left? What did Viktor want? And where did you disappear to with my dad?" he asks as he sprawls out on the bed next to me, acting like he owns the place.

I turn my head toward him, raising an eyebrow. "Are you serious?"

He grins, unbothered. "Very."

I sigh, pinching the bridge of my nose. "Viktor wanted to remind me that I'm nothing more than a tool to him and to make sure I'll behave at his little party tomorrow. As for your dad? I had a front-row seat to why your family is so fucked up. Happy now?"

His grin falters slightly, and he tilts his head. "What do you mean? What happened?"

I glare at him, my exhaustion tipping over into irritation. "You really want to have this conversation now? Because I promise it's not going to make me any fonder of your charming family."

"Try me," he says, letting his guard down. "You have my attention."

I roll my eyes but quickly tell him about everything that happened with his father and Boris.

"You think that's bad?" Malachi says, leaning back with his arms behind his head, crossing his legs as if we're discussing the weather. "This is happening all across the country, and you're in a position to make a real difference—with my help, of course."

His casual demeanor grates on me, so nonchalant about people's lives. "How can you act like it's not a big deal?"

He turns his head to face me, his smirk unfaltering. "Hours

ago, you didn't want any part in this. You were happy to keep living the dream as a pet."

The word "pet" ignites something in me. I punch him in the arm, the motion quick and instinctive, driven by frustration.

"Fuck you," I mutter.

He rubs his shoulder, wincing slightly but still smirking. "For someone so tiny, with zero training, that actually hurt."

I roll my eyes, fighting the urge to hit him again. Little does he know, I've actually had some training. When you spend most of your days stuck at Marco's compound, you learn to occupy your time somehow. For me, that meant taking advantage of his extensive gym—and I mean extensive. Most of the security team uses it, and every now and then they show me a few moves—especially the ones who didn't see me as a threat. Banks even taught me a thing or two over the years. I might look scrawny, but I can hold my own in a fight.

"Maybe you should take me more seriously."

His grin widens. "Oh, I do. Believe me."

"Get out." I shove him, and he raises his hands in mock surrender, sliding off the bed with exaggerated care like I might lunge at him again.

"I'll see you tomorrow night at the dinner party," he says, heading toward the door. "And no one will know who you really are, so try to eavesdrop. The men will think nothing of a pretty girl hanging around."

If he were any closer, I'd hit him again. Harder.

"Are you trying to tell me how to act around men? I know what I'm doing. Stay out of my way," I say, flipping over and reaching up to turn off the lamp.

"Sweet dreams, Katja," he laughs as the door clicks shut behind him.

I HALF EXPECTED Malachi to show up today and deliver another infuriating lecture about the party tonight. But to my surprise, I haven't caught a glimpse of him all day.

Maybe he's finally learned to give me some space.

Anton stopped by earlier, gruff as always, to remind me to be ready by 7 p.m. That's it. No explanation, no details about the party.

Fortunately, I've learned over the years to pack for any occasion. I pull out the perfect dress, the one I'd tucked away for emergencies like this—when blending in is as important as standing out.

Sitting at the small vanity in my room, I do my makeup with precision, sweeping dark, smoky shadows across my lids and painting my lips in a deep crimson that matches the dress perfectly. My hair falls naturally into soft, dark waves, brushing against my shoulders with the right amount of effortless elegance.

Once I'm satisfied with the look, I slip on the dress, carefully smoothing the fabric over my body. The moment I stand in front of the full-length mirror, I pause. The dress feels like a second skin, every inch designed to hug my curves and make me feel exposed yet powerful at the same time.

The deep, daring red is bold—a challenge wrapped in silk. It's the kind of color that dares someone to underestimate me while knowing they'll regret it if they do. The single shoulder strap leaves one arm bare, framing my collarbone and neckline in a way that draws attention without screaming for it.

Sleek. Simple. And yet there's nothing remotely modest about it.

I tilt my head, taking in the reflection staring back at me. I hardly recognize her—the woman in the mirror. Bold. Untouchable. Maybe even dangerous. She's not me, but she's the perfect mask for tonight.

The mask I'll need.

At 7:15, there's a knock at my door. Clearly, Anton is not one for punctuality. I slip on my heels, take a steadying breath, and pull the door open.

"Oh, my pretty little menace," Orin says, his voice dripping with mockery as he strides in, uninvited, wearing a midnight-blue suit that somehow makes him look more sinister than polished. "Looking all fiery for me tonight."

I want to hit back with something sharp and sarcastic, but I bite my tongue, forcing a tight-lipped smile instead. Orin is a walking hurricane of brute strength and sadistic tendencies, but intelligence? Not exactly his forte. He's been working for his father for years though, which means he probably knows everything about the business—the inner workings, the deals, and, more importantly, the secrets.

Maybe tonight is my chance, an opportunity to use him. Orin has always made it clear he wants me, but I know he'd never cross that line without an invitation. He's too afraid of the repercussions Marco would rain down on him.

The thought of touching him makes me sick to my stomach, and I'm not very experienced in the art of seduction. But I can be fucking charming when I want to be. And with Orin, it doesn't matter what comes out of my mouth—he'll be more focused on my cleavage than anything else.

Seeing how far I can play him tonight might be worth it.

I lean against the doorframe enough to give him something to look at without being obvious. "I hear you're my date for this evening."

His grin widens, his gaze predictably dipping to my neckline. "I'm here to make sure you don't step out of line at the party. Lucky you, right?"

I flash him a small, calculated smile, already deciding how

far I'm willing to push this. "Lucky me," I echo sweetly enough to keep him hooked.

He extends an elbow to me, and I take his arm, letting him escort me through the sprawling mansion to the other side. The party is an event unto itself, occupying an entire wing. Guests move fluidly between a grand formal dining room, a library that takes my breath away, a polished bar, and a sitting room filled with men smoking cigars and swirling brandy in oversized glasses.

Orin leads me straight to the bar, but not before I catch several sets of eyes lingering on me as we pass. The dress is doing what I need it to—distracting.

Perfect.

I don't know what I expected when I imagined Viktor's party, but this wasn't it. It's much larger than I anticipated, at least fifty people milling about—maybe closer to one hundred. And the men outnumber the women significantly. I spot a few couples and small groups of women chatting quietly in corners, but the party feels overwhelmingly male, dominated by heavy laughter, low murmurs, and the clinking of glasses.

And in typical Volkov style, food and alcohol overflow in abundance. Most people can only dream of a proper meal—real meat, fresh vegetables—luxuries replaced by the genetically engineered trash they toil endlessly to afford. But here, among these people, it's nothing more than careless excess, squandered without a second thought.

No surprises there, I guess.

The bar is stunning—crafted from dark mahogany with an antique finish that gleams under the low light. But it's the library that catches my eye, its floor-to-ceiling shelves crammed with gorgeously bound books. I'd kill to have a collection like that back at Marco's. If I had a different life, I'd spend hours there, pulling volumes from the shelves and burying myself in the stories of worlds far away from this one.

But before I can linger, Orin keeps us moving, his attention already fixed on the drinks. He's nothing if not predictable.

"What can I get you?" the bartender asks Orin, his voice polite but neutral. He's a young man, slender, with dark hair neatly combed back.

"Whiskey neat," Orin says then glances at me. "And make something fruity for the lady."

I shake my head quickly, offering a polite but firm smile. "No, thank you."

The bartender hesitates, glancing between us. I've never been a drinker. I've tried it a handful of times, but it always tasted terrible, burning my throat in a way that made me wonder why anyone found it enjoyable. But that's not the real reason I avoid it. Alcohol dulls the senses, makes you vulnerable—and I can't afford that. Not tonight. Not ever.

"Make her the drink," Orin barks, startling the bartender. Then, without warning, Orin wraps an arm around my back and pulls me closer to him, the move possessive and overbearing.

"You're drinking tonight, demon," he whispers hotly against my ear, his breath brushing my cheek like an unwanted brand.

I stiffen under his grip, every muscle tensing as I fight the urge to shove him away. His voice is low, almost teasing, but there's an edge to it, a quiet demand that makes my blood boil. *God, if only you knew what kind of demon you were actually dealing with, Orin.*

The bartender sets two drinks in front of us, mine a pink frothy concoction that looks harmless enough. I pick it up, intending to fake a sip, but Orin has other plans. His hand clamps over the bottom of the glass, tipping it up and forcing me to swallow the entire thing in one go. It burns all the way down, like I remember from the last time I tried alcohol. At least this one doesn't taste entirely horrible—bubble gum with a kick.

"Nice of you to join us, brother," Orin says.

I glance over and freeze when I see Malachi stepping up to the bar, a few chairs down. The bar's L-shape gives me a perfect view of him—and his date.

His date.

He has his arm draped around a blonde woman who's curvy in all the right places. She's sophisticated, polished, and undeniably gorgeous. Looking at her makes my stomach twist uncomfortably. I don't know why, but I already hate her.

I narrow my eyes at Malachi, but he doesn't seem to notice —or pretends not to. Turning back to the bartender, I watch as he lines up more drinks, trying to distract myself.

"Lana, you're looking good this evening," Orin says, rubbing at his beard, his expression unusually pleasant.

She flashes a bright smile, her perfect white teeth gleaming. Of course. "Nice to see you, Orin," she replies smoothly, her voice as elegant as her appearance.

Lana. So that's her name. Who is this woman who knows Orin and is glued to Malachi's side?

Before I can think too hard about it, Orin tugs me closer, his hands firm on my hips. Now I'm practically wedged between his legs, and the discomfort is overwhelming.

"Another round," Orin says, twirling his finger in the air for the bartender's attention. "Make hers a double."

Great.

"Who is your date? I don't believe we've met before," Lana asks, gesturing to me with a polite smile.

I force myself to play nice. "My name's Katja. Pleasure." I

offer her a tight smile, adding with a touch of sarcasm, "And that's probably because I don't like to share."

Orin laughs loudly, his grip tightening on my hips. "You know I like my women feisty," he says and then slaps my ass. Oh, hell no.

It takes every ounce of self-control I have not to break my glass over his head right then and there. Instead, I bite down hard on my bottom lip, the sting keeping me focused. *Patience, Kat. You need him drunk enough to start talking—or give up and find someone less vile to get information out of.*

"How long have you two been together?" I ask Lana, redirecting my attention and trying to mask the venom behind my curiosity.

Lana lights up at the question, looking between me and Malachi with a beaming smile. "Oh, we've known each other since we were kids, but Malachi reached out to me when he arrived here a few days ago. I was delighted he called—it's been far too long."

She looks up at him with stars in her eyes, and my stomach twists again. There's an unsettling intimacy in her gaze, one that makes me wonder how much she knows about him now.

"Malachi wouldn't know how to have a casual fuck if a whore sat on his cock," Orin interrupts, his vulgarity making us all cringe. "He's always pining over one woman, more worried about soul mates and all that feminine shit that turns women off. A woman wants a tough guy who'll rough her up in the sack. Isn't that right, Katja?"

I swallow back bile, trying to ignore the heat rising to my face. He couldn't be more disgusting if he tried.

"He's always been the sweet one in the family, hasn't he?" Lana says, resting her hand on his arm.

Malachi clears his throat, taking a slow sip of his bourbon. "I think my brothers are tough enough for all of us."

The tension is palpable, and I can feel my pulse quickening. Malachi doesn't meet my eyes, but there's something guarded in his expression, like he's playing a role he doesn't quite believe in. *What are you up to, Malachi? And who the hell is this woman clinging to you like she's been waiting her entire life for this moment?*

"Down the hatch, sweetie," Orin says, his grip firm as he tips my glass again, forcing me to chug the alcohol. The liquid burns its way down my throat, and I cough slightly as I set the empty glass on the bar. This is clearly his twisted idea of fun—torturing me in front of a crowd, taking his role as my "date" to heart in the worst possible way. I need to start planning my escape, and fast.

"My girl loves to drink," he announces loudly, his hand sliding over my back in what he probably thinks is an affectionate gesture. "It gets her horny."

Heat rushes to my face, but not from embarrassment—pure fury. We're surrounded by people, so I swallow my pride and let his vile words roll off me like water on stone. He's nothing I can't handle, but that doesn't stop me from noticing Malachi's gaze trailing after the movement of Orin's hand, his jaw tightening ever so slightly.

"She'll have another," Orin demands, pointing at the bartender, who hesitates for a moment before setting about making the drink.

I dread the fresh glass appearing in front of me, the buzz of alcohol already starting to creep into my veins. If this keeps up, tonight will be a night I regret for many nights to come. I need a bread roll, a toilet, or divine intervention.

"Take it easy," Malachi says, glancing at me. "The night is young."

I turn and shoot him a glare that could kill. *Does it look like I have a fucking choice in the matter?* I want to scream at him, but instead I grind my teeth and look away before I lose control.

"Worry about your own date tonight," Orin snaps, puffing up like a peacock. "Trust me, I know how to show mine a good time. I can teach you a lesson or two if you'd like, brother."

Malachi leans back in his seat, entirely too composed, while Lana sips her martini like this kind of vile brotherly bickering is as offensive as talking about the weather.

"Maybe later," Malachi says, lifting his glass to his lips.

The bartender gives me an apologetic look as he refills my glass before moving down the bar to tend to other guests. *Great*, I think bitterly, staring down at the drink. If I keep playing along, I'll be drunk within the hour. If I resist, Orin will only make a scene, and that's the last thing I need.

Lana leans over, whispering something in Malachi's ear, and he smiles, that damn dimple on his left cheek making its unwelcome appearance. When his eyes flick toward me, I grab the glass in front of me and down it willingly this time.

"There she is," Orin sings, all too pleased with himself as I slam the empty glass onto the bar with more force than necessary.

"I need to find the ladies' room. If you'll all excuse me," I say, pushing away from Orin's possessive grip.

"Don't get lost on your way back, baby," Orin calls snidely.

There is no fucking way I'm going back to that bar.

I weave through the crowd, crossing into the study and heading down one of the quieter, darker hallways. I'm searching for the bathroom I spotted a couple days ago when I was on my way to meet with Viktor. The further I move from the party, the quieter it gets, the dull hum of conversation fading behind me.

I reach the door, push it open, and flip on the light, relieved to find the bathroom empty. Closing the door behind me, I glance at my reflection in the mirror. Despite feeling a little wobbly from the alcohol, I still look flawless on the outside. Perfect hair. Perfect makeup. The dress still daring and distracting. At least I have that going for me.

I reach to lock the door, but the handle turns suddenly, the door flying open and nearly hitting me in the face. I stumble back, startled, but a hand grabs my arm to steady me before the door slams shut and the lock clicks into place.

Malachi.

"What the fuck are you doing?" he says, his voice sharp, and the nerve of this man has me seeing red.

"What do you mean?" I glare at him, crossing my arms.

"You think getting drunk will make you of any use to me tonight? You're supposed to be working the room, finding someone useful to talk to, eavesdropping on something we can actually use."

He's scolding me, and I shove him in the chest.

"Did it look like I had a fucking choice when your brother was literally pouring the shit down my throat?" I spit back, my cheeks flushing hot with anger.

"That last drink didn't need any help," he says.

I roll my eyes so hard I almost give myself a headache. "Go back to your date, Malachi," I say, dragging out his name.

"If I weren't mistaken," he starts, a slow, infuriating smirk spreading across his face, "I'd say you sound jealous."

His arrogance ignites something primal in me, a fire burning hot and unchecked. "Get the fuck out," I snap, shoving him again. But he's unmovable, solid as a damn brick wall, and the action does more to hurt my hands than to faze him.

"I wanted to make sure you're okay," he says, which only annoys me further. "I know how Orin can be. You need to be careful."

I take a slow, steady inhale to keep from exploding. "You

think I don't know how Orin can be? Who do you think has lived with him for the last eight years while you were off doing god knows what on the other side of the country? I know precisely what kind of evil Orin is, and I don't need you to tell me how to handle him."

His features darken, and there's a flicker of something in his eyes that looks almost like guilt. "Has he hurt you before?"

The question sends a fresh wave of anger crashing over me. His concern feels misplaced, patronizing. "I'm sorry, where's your shiny armor, Malachi? You're not a fucking knight, and you sure as hell aren't my savior. So get out and let me do my job. I've survived fine thus far."

I can feel the alcohol coursing through me now, heating my blood, mixing with my temper in a dangerous cocktail. I need cold water. I need air. I need him gone.

"This isn't over," he grumbles and steps back, unlocking the door and slipping out.

The second he's gone, I lock the door again and turn to the sink, flipping the cold water on full blast. I lean down, cupping my hands to take a few sips, the icy chill grounding me. I want to splash it all over my face but stop myself. I can't afford to ruin my makeup.

I take a few long, deep breaths, forcing myself to steady the chaos inside me. Once I've gathered enough composure to face the room again, I straighten up and head back toward the party.

Avoid Orin like the plague. Find someone worth talking to. This place is practically swimming with powerful men, and every single one of them has secrets. Let's see which one I can get to spill them.

Chapter Ten

RULE 10 OF THE NEW ORDER: CONTROL IS AN ILLUSION—NEVER UNDERESTIMATE HOW QUICKLY ONE SPARK CAN IGNITE CHAOS AND UNRAVEL EVERYTHING.

I END up back in the sitting room, scanning the space for Orin and feeling relieved when I don't see him anywhere. Thank God. I haven't caught a glimpse of Marco or Viktor yet either. They're likely doing what men like them do—arriving fashionably late or holding court in some other room teeming with their guests.

I chose this room for its exclusivity, and because there isn't a single woman here. It's filled with tall tables where men stand chatting, a lower table with a group engrossed in a card game, and several oversized leather chairs occupied by gentlemen lounging with cigars.

It's the perfect place to eavesdrop. I stick out, of course, but I'm counting on that. A woman in a room like this will be seen as ornamental, not threatening. A pretty thing in a dress, I think bitterly. Far too delicate to possess a brain.

I keep my ears open, scanning the room while pretending to admire the card game, though I take no real interest. I'm about ready to move on when a conversation pulls me back.

"I was told there will be a silent auction at the end of the night," a middle-aged man says, lounging in one of the leather chairs to my right. He swirls a glass of brandy lazily in one hand. "Viktor himself gave me a preview earlier today."

"He's keeping the Avids here? In his house?" the younger man across from him asks, aghast, as if keeping us here were the equivalent of housing livestock.

"Only two of them," the older man replies, running a hand over his neatly combed black hair. "One male and one female, but he wouldn't tell me their abilities. Said it's a surprise for later."

The younger man sits forward, glasses perched on the bridge of his nose. "I need to get in on this. I better find Viktor and reserve a spot." He stands abruptly, leaving his drink on the side table before hurrying out of the room like a man on a mission.

Gross.

No wonder Viktor doesn't want anyone knowing what I am. It would cause a frenzy. To men like this, I'm not a person. I'm a prize. A status symbol to parade around.

Fucking pigs.

At least Marco—however manipulative—has always treated us with a sliver of respect, enough to acknowledge we're human beings. But these people? They'd line up like vultures for a chance to own me.

I grit my teeth, trying to control the sudden wave of rage. I need to know where Viktor's keeping them—the two Avids they spoke of. If they're here, tonight, maybe I could free them. No, I can't think like that. Not yet. I'd need Malachi, and this house is too massive to find them quickly. It's too risky to search blindly.

Instead, I turn my focus to the older man with graying hair at his temples and the slightest lines marking his face. He's my best chance at getting more information. But I can't simply approach him—I need him to think it's his idea to talk to me.

As I pass him, I make my move, letting one of my earrings fall to the floor with a soft clink. I stop, bending over slowly to retrieve it. "Oh my," I murmur, watching from the corner of my eye as he perks up and moves toward me.

"Allow me, miss—" He stoops to grab the earring before I do.

"Miss Sinclair," I say with a polite smile. "But please call me Kat." I give him my sweetest, most innocent look, and it works like a charm. His deep-blue eyes light up and then drop lower to the neckline of my dress.

"Kat," he says warmly. "I'm Eduard. Please, let me get you a drink."

"That's very kind of you," I say. "I'll have a vodka soda, please."

He looks delighted, taking my hand like a gentleman and guiding me to one of the leather chairs. He snaps his fingers at a passing busboy, not even glancing his way. "Vodka soda for the lady, and another for me," he orders, lifting his glass of amber liquid.

I settle into the chair gracefully, my mind racing behind the poised mask of politeness. *Let's see what secrets you'll spill, Eduard.*

I KEEP Eduard talking far long enough to get him through two more drinks. I'm hoping the alcohol loosens his lips, makes him sloppy enough to spill his secrets, but it also means I've had to force my way through a couple more drinks as well. And to say I'm feeling it would be an understatement.

Eduard, it turns out, loves to talk about himself. He's

divorced—hates his ex-wife with a passion, and complains endlessly about the "obscene" amount of money he had to pay to be rid of her. He loves golf but hasn't played in months because of the snow.

It's mind-numbing but perfect. The more he talks, the less I have to lie, and all it takes to keep him going is a lot of smiling, nodding, and fake laughing.

"Do you want to go talk somewhere more private?" he asks, leaning closer, his hand brushing over my leg. "I'm friends with the owner. I know a few spots that would be more comfortable."

I give him my most charming smile. "Please, lead the way," I say, taking the hand he offers to help me up.

When I stand, I'm glad for the support of his elbow because I'm not entirely sure I could walk straight without it. For the first time tonight, I'm worried I might be losing control.

You need to work on your alcohol tolerance, Kat, I think bitterly. Or better yet, make a deal with the bartender next time for soda water all night.

Eduard leads me out of the study, and we weave through a maze of rooms. I think we pass the bar, but the crowd is a mess of swirling color and blurry faces. I can't believe Orin hasn't come looking for me. Or maybe he did and didn't spot me in the chaos. Either way, it feels strange to be without a shadow tonight, and the unease nags at the edges of my drunken thoughts.

Eduard pats my arm reassuringly. "We're almost there."

Before I know it, we're in a guest bedroom I don't recognize. The fireplace clicks on with a flick of a switch, warm flames licking at the edges of the room. The heat makes my already flushed cheeks burn hotter.

"Fuck, you're gorgeous," Eduard says, his gaze hungry as it

sweeps over me. "There's a drink cart in here. Want me to get you something?"

"No, thank you." I reach out to fiddle with the lapel of his suit coat.

Stay focused. Keep him comfortable. I need answers, not another drink.

The firelight moves across his face, highlighting the greedy glint in his eyes. He's completely oblivious to the real game at play, and that's the only advantage I have right now. *You can do this, Kat. Let him feel like he's in control. A little longer.*

I lean in close, letting my tongue trace a slow, deliberate line up the side of his neck, twirling around his earlobe until he lets out a soft, guttural moan.

"You know what really turns me on?" I whisper, my breath warm against his ear.

"Oh, fuck, tell me, baby," he groans, his hands greedily caressing my hips and pulling me tighter against him.

"With my ex," I begin, low and sultry, "we used to make our Avid watch us. Being in control of something so powerful, forcing it to witness me...getting off... There's something about it that was so exhilarating."

It was easier to say than I thought, leaving me disgusted with myself.

"I knew you were going to be kinky the moment I saw you bending over in this red dress," he growls, his hand sliding up to my strap. He toys with it, running his fingers along the fabric a few times before pulling it down my arm, agonizingly slow.

The moment my upper body is exposed, he takes a step back, licking his bottom lip as his eyes roam over me like I'm a meal set out for him.

I swallow hard, forcing myself to hold my ground. I wouldn't be able to do this if it weren't for the alcohol numbing the humiliation. I need him to take me to the Avids before he pushes things too far.

"If you're good," he says, nearly giddy, "I might tell you a secret."

Bingo. That's exactly what I want to hear.

I trail my hands up my neck, letting them glide over my collarbone before moving down to my breasts, all the while keeping my eyes locked on his.

"I love secrets," I say, pulling my bottom lip between my teeth and biting down to add to the performance.

Eduard's breathing deepens, his eyes glued to the movement of my hands as I continue to touch myself, hoping to keep his attention fixed on watching me instead of touching me himself.

"Care to share one?" I ask.

His lips curl into a crooked grin, and I see it—his guard lowering. I'm reeling him in, and it's working. For now.

"How about this, baby? Let me have a little taste, and then I'll take you to where we can have an audience that won't disappoint for the finale," Eduard says, sounding like the sleaze he is.

I've got him.

He's going to show me what I want, and I didn't even have to be sober to pull it off. In your face, Malachi.

But wait.

Now I might actually have to kiss this guy. My chest tightens, but I try to focus. At least he smells good and has nice teeth.

"That sounds perfect," I murmur, and he grips my hips, lifting me onto the bed and positioning himself between my legs.

I tip my head back, looking up at him briefly before closing my eyes, preparing for what I have to do. But instead of feeling his lips on mine, I hear his voice again.

"I want to taste more than your mouth, baby."

He pushes my chest back and starts hiking up my dress. Panicking, I jerk back, and my eyes lock on the ceiling as I try to rationalize my actions.

I can do this. It's for the Avids. It's for the mission. Oh God, can I do this? What would Cade think if he could see me now, or Malachi? I'm not the first woman to dangle sex to get what she wants, but that isn't who I thought I was. Maybe it's not as bad as it seems. Am I in control or not?

His hands trace over my calves, and I squeeze my eyes shut, bracing myself. But then something changes—warmth spreads over me. No, not warmth—wetness.

My eyes snap open as Eduard's eyes go wide, his neck gaping open in a crimson slash. Blood spills down the front of him, splattering across me.

I freeze, my breath caught in my throat as his body collapses forward, sagging heavily against me. For a horrifying moment, I can feel the warmth of his blood soaking through my dress before his weight shifts and he crumples to the floor with a sickening thud.

I've seen my fair share of murders over the years—I live with the fucking Volkov family, after all—but this? This is something else.

I sit up, my heart racing, and my eyes meet Malachi's as he shoves a bloody blade back into the waistband of his pants.

For a moment, neither of us says a word. His eyes burn with fury, the intensity making me feel more exposed than I already am. When his gaze drops lower, I throw my hands over my chest, yanking the strap of my dress back into place.

"What the fuck is going on?" I wail, standing unsteadily as I look down at the blood smeared across my dress and pooling on the floor.

Malachi doesn't answer, doesn't even blink. Instead, he

strides forward, scooping me up like I weigh nothing and slinging me over his shoulder in one swift motion.

"Put me down!" I yell, pounding a fist against his back, but he ignores me entirely.

He moves around the room, rummaging through drawers and shelves. I can't see what he's doing from this angle, but his movements are quick and deliberate.

I think he's about to carry me out of the room but then he sets me down on the bed, not gently but not harshly either. His glare is sharp enough to cut through steel, the look of a disappointed parent—or maybe a frustrated executioner.

"Start talking," he says finally.

I cross my arms over my chest, staring back at him, defiance bubbling up despite my shaken state. "You just murdered someone!"

"And saved your ass in the process," he snaps.

"I had it under control," I hiss.

His laugh is cold, humorless. "Control? Is that what you call being drunk sitting half-naked on a bed with a predator between your legs?"

My cheeks burn with anger and humiliation. "I was working him!"

"Yeah?" Malachi steps closer, his towering frame casting a shadow over me. "From where I stood, it looked like he was about to work his way inside you."

"You told me to get information from these guys. How did you think I was supposed to do that?"

"You're reckless, Kat," he says, softer now but no less intense. "And tonight could've ended very differently if I hadn't been there."

I swallow hard, my throat tight with emotion. I want to argue, to yell, to push him away, but deep down I know he's right.

For once, I don't have a clever comeback. I sit there, glaring at him, before I spit, "And what if that's what I wanted?"

"I'm sure you could find someone better to fuck than that," Malachi says, hitting a nerve. My head throbs as the alcohol and frustration mix into a volatile cocktail.

I cross my arms. "He said there are two Avids being kept in this house tonight, and there's supposed to be a silent auction for them after the party."

Malachi's expression darkens, but I continue, sitting up straighter and taking a deep breath. "He said he'd take me to them. He..." I swallow, unwilling to say the rest out loud.

Malachi doesn't look away. His silence is heavy, expectant, as if he's waiting for me to finish the thought.

"He wanted something in return," I say finally, the words tasting bitter on my tongue. I don't elaborate. I don't need to.

"Get up. Are you sober, or do I need to leave you here to sleep it off?" Malachi's says condescendingly, like I'm some unruly child.

"Murder has a way of sobering someone up, if you know what I mean," I say, crossing my arms. I wouldn't call myself fully sober, but I'm definitely functional.

"Good, because we need to figure out where they are before it's too late," he says.

I glance at the bloody body in the room with us.

"Why don't I ask him?"

Chapter Eleven

RULE 11 OF THE NEW ORDER: A DEVIL IN DISGUISE IS
STILL A DEVIL. WHAT THEY DO SPEAKS LOUDER
THAN WHAT THEY SAY.

"GREAT IDEA. How do you plan to ask him now?" Malachi
asks, his gaze fixed on the man's lifeless body.

"I can talk to the dead, remember?" I roll my eyes, exasperated.

"I know that, but with the case dragging on... No offense,
we need answers—immediately." He crosses his arms, his impatience clear.

"Thanks. Glad to know you have so much faith in my abilities," I shoot back.

Malachi doesn't respond. I can feel his frustration, but he
knows as well as I do that there's no other way.

"Damien's different," I add, pressing my fingers to my
temples, as if it might ease the tension building there. "He
eludes me somehow, but that's not important right now. The
point is, I'll get the answers we need. Give me a minute." I step
away from Eduard's body, not wanting to look at the blood-
stains that mar my clothes.

I close my eyes and focus. I picture Eduard's face, fresh in
my mind, and the cold rush of air fills the room instantly. He's

freshly dead—this could get complicated if he's struggling to cross over. But tonight, I hope luck is on our side.

When Eduard appears before me, I know my chances have improved.

"What? Why?" His voice shakes with confusion, and the look in his eyes tightens my throat. For a moment, I almost feel sympathy for him. But I shake it off—now isn't the time for feelings.

"Listen, I'm sorry for what happened to you, but it's done now. I need you to tell me where Viktor is keeping the Avids tonight." I glance over at Malachi, who's staring at me, bewildered. He can't hear or see Eduard's ghost, and I know seeing this takes some getting used to.

"Why would I tell you anything, you conniving little bitch?" Eduard snarls, his form fading in and out with his rage.

I click my tongue, taking a step closer, my eyes narrowing. "Now, now, Eduard. You may think you can talk to me like that because you're already dead, but if you don't give me the answers I need, that man over there..." I flick my wrist toward Malachi. "He won't stop with what he did to you. And trust me, we'll find your entire family. Your death? It'll be merciful compared to what we'll do to them."

His eyes widen in outrage, but he bitterly spills everything I need to know before his spirit storms off.

"Now you can leave them alone. At least there can't be anything worse than you on this side," he howls and vanishes behind the veil.

Damn, that was easier than I expected—assuming he's not leading us into a trap.

I turn to Malachi. "He thinks they're under the stables."

His eyebrows rise in surprise. "Nice work. Let's go." He motions for me to follow him.

"Wait. If we're leaving, I need to change. I can't go out

there with blood-stained all over the front of my dress. What if someone sees me?" I gesture to the mess across the front of my outfit, emphasizing the obvious.

"I'm counting on it. If we do this right, we may get away with it. Put this on for now."

He takes off his suit jacket and drapes it over my shoulders. It's huge but warm, and I quickly button it up, the fabric drowning me but at least hiding the blood.

"Come on," he says, taking my hand.

I let him lead me into the hallway. It's eerily quiet—no guards, no servants. Everyone must still be at the party. Malachi moves quickly, and I struggle to keep up in my heels, the pace almost sending me stumbling a few times.

He catches me, his muscles firm beneath the fabric of his shirt. Without hesitation, he offers his elbow for me to hold onto better, and I reluctantly take it.

"Come in on the south side and stay within the tree line until my signal," he murmurs, and I stare up at him in confusion.

"Uh, what?"

"It's my comms," he explains. "I have a safe house near here where some of my people have been waiting. I told one of my men to stay close tonight in case anything went down."

We reach the back door, and the freezing air bites at my exposed skin as we step outside. The snow crunches underfoot, icy and slippery, and I instantly regret my choice of shoes.

"I take it wearing boots would've been a giveaway if we're seen," I mutter, clinging tighter to his forearm for balance.

"You're quick," he says with a self-indulgent look on his face.

"Quick enough to know I'm going to break my neck if you keep this pace," I retort, glaring at him.

He slows slightly, guiding me more steadily as we navigate the slick path.

"Fuck," Malachi mutters, fiddling with his ear again.

"What?" I ask, glancing up at him.

"He's not answering. He must not be in range," he says, frustrated.

"Maybe you'll reach him better from the stables, especially if he's on the outskirts of the property," I suggest, trying to sound optimistic.

In the distance, I can make out the stables, their shadowy outline faintly illuminated by the snow. I glance back at the mansion behind us. Thankfully, the party is on the opposite side of the house, and I don't see any movement or light from back here.

God, I hope no one sees us. If someone does, we'll have to play it off. We could always pretend we're sneaking off to hook up. Malachi already has Gary convinced that's his goal, so it would probably work. But Marco? He'd... I don't even want to think about it.

"Stay quiet and stay behind me. If we get caught, run back to your room and make sure no one sees you," Malachi whispers, not giving me time to object before sliding the large stable door open.

The heavy door creaks slightly as it moves, and we slip inside. The scent of hay and horses fills the space, mingling with the faint tang of manure and wood polish. The overhead lights are on, casting long shadows across the stalls. At least twenty horses peek out from their enclosures, some snorting softly at our presence.

"What now?" I ask as I scan the space.

I half-expect to see some obvious clue—a trapdoor or hidden staircase—but there's nothing immediately out of place. Rows of pristine stalls and the lingering quiet of the stable.

"He said under the stables, right?" he asks.

I nod, and he starts moving further in, his boots muffled against the hay-strewn floor. "Let's find out how to get down there."

I follow closely, scanning the walls and floors for any sign of an entry point. The horses shift in their stalls, their ears twitching as if sensing the tension in the air. My pulse quickens.

"Look over here," I say, pointing to the floor near the feed bin. The faint scratches across the wood look too deliberate, like the bin's been moved over and over again.

Malachi steps closer, narrowing his eyes as he examines the marks.

"Stand back," he says with unnecessary authority.

I roll my eyes, crossing my arms. Men.

He braces himself and pushes the bin aside with a grunt, revealing a small hatch door flush with the floor. No lock, no chain, only a plain metal handle. I guess Viktor trusts that no one would dare be out here doing what we're doing right now.

Malachi pulls the hatch open, the faint creak of the hinges making my nerves jump. He peers into the dark space below, the faint glow of a single, dim light visible through the opening.

"I'm not waiting here, so don't even say it," I snap before he has a chance to speak.

He gives me a disgruntled look, one brow raised like he's about to argue, but then he shakes his head and grabs the sides of the ladder bolted to the edge of the hatch.

He descends quickly, his movements quiet and deliberate. The moment his boots hit the ground, he glances back up at me, waiting.

I lower myself onto the ladder, but after a few steps down, I jump the rest of the way, landing with a soft thud beside him.

We've made it.

The air is damp and cold, with the faint scent of earth and rust lingering in the space. A narrow corridor stretches out ahead leading to a single door, lit by a flickering bulb hanging from the low ceiling.

"Not creepy at all down here," I mutter as we approach the door.

Malachi pulls it open instantly, as if he has no reason to believe anyone other than the Avids would be down here. I guess he figures the hatch wouldn't have been covered if someone else were lurking.

The smell hits me like a physical blow—an unbearable mix of feces and ammonia. I gag, pressing my hand to my nose to block out the stench.

Malachi stops inside the doorway, his broad frame blocking my view. I peer around him and immediately wish I hadn't.

The room stretches out far beyond the size of the stables above, dimly lit by wavering, uneven bulbs. Rows of rusty, decrepit cages line the walls, old jail cells with thick, corroded bars. Each one contains a bucket and a filthy, tattered mattress —if there's a mattress at all. Some have nothing but a pile of hay.

These conditions aren't fit for animals, let alone people.

"It's worse than I thought," Malachi says with unmistakable anger.

I glance up at him. For once, his usual smug expression is gone, replaced by something raw and unguarded. It's unsettling to see him shaken, though I can't blame him—this place feels like a physical embodiment of despair.

The quiet sound of shuffling pulls my attention to one of the cages. In the dim light, I can make out a figure huddled in the distance, too still. The sight makes my stomach drop, and I grip Malachi's arm without thinking.

"Are they even alive?" I whisper, unsure if I want to know the answer.

His jaw tightens. "We're about to find out."

He steps forward, the soft clink of his shoes on the concrete floor echoing through the room.

In the far corner, there are two stalls, each caging one person. The figures are huddled together on the floor, pressed against the bars, their hands gripping each other tightly like it's the only thing keeping them alive.

I stop dead in my tracks. The world slows, my knees buckle beneath me, and I think I'm falling, but Malachi grabs my arm, steadying me before I hit the ground.

"What's wrong? What's happening?" he asks, his gaze flicking between the cages and my face.

"Kat."

The sound of my name—soft but familiar—cuts through the haze. It doesn't come from Malachi.

He freezes, his head turning slowly toward the cage then back to me, his expression shifting as realization dawns.

"Aurora," I whisper, the name barely escaping my lips as tears blur my vision and stain my cheeks.

Her red hair is matted, tangled, and lifeless, but it's her. Even thinner than I remember, her face hollowed and her body frail. Yet it's undeniably her.

She's clutching the boy in the neighboring cage, her arms wrapped around him protectively. Her hands are pressed to his skin, her gift shimmering faintly as she channels warmth into him, keeping him from freezing to death in this hellhole.

Her tired, pained eyes meet mine, and for a moment I'm fifteen years old again, back on the night we were torn apart.

I stumble forward, but Malachi holds me back. "Kat, wait—"

"I have to get to her!" I pull free of his grip.

Aurora shifts closer to the bars, her face softening despite the evident exhaustion. "Katja, is it really you?" Her voice cracks, as if she hasn't spoken in days.

Luckily, there's no lock on the bars, only a handle that can only be opened from the outside. Malachi pulls the cell door open, and I drop to the floor, wrapping Aurora in the tightest hug I've ever given anyone. She squeezes me back as hard, her tears streaming freely now, and I feel my own matching hers.

I want to ask her everything—where she's been, how she ended up here, what happened after Marco took me. What comes out is altogether different.

"Are you hurt?"

She shakes her head. "No, I'm alright."

"I hate to break this up," Malachi says, "but two of my people are outside in the tree line, ready to get them somewhere safe."

I glance at the other Avid as Malachi opens his cell. He steps out cautiously, looking younger than us, maybe by a year or two. Thank God there are no kids here in these conditions. But they may be somewhere else.

Aurora and I pull apart, and I stand, helping her to her feet. I check her over for injuries, but she looks me up and down, her expression shifting as she takes in how different I must look. Not to mention how out of place I am in this ridiculous dress, in the snow, in a fucking underground prison.

The room feels like it drops a few degrees, the air suddenly freezing, and then my chest goes cold.

"Tick tock, Kitty Kat," a familiar voice echoes, smug and mocking. "He's closer than you think."

Damien's faint form appears beside Aurora, his presence like a shadowy stain against the dim light. He winks at me, his smile twisted, and then he's gone.

"What did you see?" Aurora asks, gripping my shoulders

tightly, her eyes wide with concern. She knows that look on my face all too well.

"We need to leave. Now."

I wrap an arm around her, pulling her close as Malachi leads the way. We rush out of the hatch, carefully putting everything back the way we found it. At the stable door, Malachi pauses, peeking out into the night before speaking into his comms.

"Is it clear for us to come out?"

There's a pause, my pulse hammering in my ears, before he nods to us, his movements brisk. "Let's go."

He slides the large door open enough for us to slip through, and we step out into the frigid night air. The cold bites at my skin, but all I can think about is Damien's warning. "He's closer than you think."

Who's closer? The killer? Or someone else? The answer feels like it's hiding in the shadows around us, and it's all I can do to keep moving forward.

We reach the edge of the forest where two figures are waiting—fully geared up like soldiers with masks covering their faces, weapons strapped to their backs, and heavy coats keeping them warm and hidden. One of them steps forward, and I can tell by the build it's a woman. She moves straight to Aurora, draping a thick jacket around her shoulders.

"You're safe now. I'll see you soon," I say softly, though I have no idea when or if I'll actually see her again. My voice trembles, not from the cold but from the uncertainty. I don't know these people, but she's safer now than she was in that godforsaken stable—or if one of those sick bastards from the party had bought her tonight.

Aurora pauses, glancing back at me, and then shrugs the coat off, handing it to the boy beside her. Of course—she won't be cold. She never is. The boy, on the other hand, looks like he's been through hell, his shoulders hunched and his movements stiff. He takes the coat with a grateful nod, his eyes meeting mine for a fleeting moment before darting away.

Malachi steps forward, exchanging low words with his people. I can't make out what he's saying. The woman gestures toward the deeper forest, and Aurora and the boy begin to follow her.

The second figure, the one in full military gear, lingers behind, his gaze fixed on me. There's something about the way he tilts his head, like he's trying to place me, or maybe he's curious. Either way, I've had enough people staring at me tonight. I turn away, pulling Malachi's jacket tighter around me as if that could shield me from the weight of his attention.

I feel Malachi's arm drape over my shoulder, pulling me close as he steers us back toward the mansion. His touch is warm, steadying, and for once I don't shove him off. As we hurry across the snow, I glance back over my shoulder, but there's no sign of them anymore. They've disappeared into the shadows of the forest, swallowed by the night.

Still, I can't shake the feeling that someone is watching. Not them, not Malachi—it's something deeper, like a presence I can't name, prickling at the back of my neck and settling heavy in my chest. Damien's voice echoes faintly in my mind, and I wonder if his warning meant more than I realized. "He's closer than you think."

Who?

I swallow hard, forcing my eyes back to the mansion. Whatever it is, I can't deal with it now. I have to focus on surviving the rest of this night.

Malachi and I don't speak on the walk back. I'm still reeling from seeing Aurora, still piecing together everything that happened. By the time Malachi opens a door and ushers me inside, I realize we're in a part of the mansion I've never been to before.

The room is grand—far larger than mine. A four-poster bed dominates the space, draped with rich, dark fabrics that match the wooden walls. A cobblestone fireplace is built into one side, the flames within lighting up the dim room with a amber glow. It's warm and inviting, but that only makes the tension in my stomach churn harder.

"What is this?" I ask, turning to face him.

"Stay here," he says firmly. "Don't do anything. Sit by the fire and follow my lead when I get back."

I open my mouth to object, to demand answers, but he's already out the door, shutting it behind him before I can utter a word. He's moving fast, like time is running out, and for all I know, it is.

The room feels suffocatingly quiet, and I let out a shaky breath, trying to steady myself. Why leave me here? What's the plan?

I walk over to the fireplace and lower myself onto the large stone ledge that juts out in front of it. The flames crackle softly, and I hold my hands out toward the heat, letting it thaw the lingering cold in my bones. My cheeks begin to flush as the warmth seeps into my skin, chasing away the frigidness from outside. Slowly, I start to feel human again, my fingers no longer stiff, my nose no longer icy to the touch.

Only a handful of minutes pass before the door opens again. I jump to my feet instantly, my body tensing. But it's not Malachi who enters first.

It's Marco.

He stands in the doorway, his expression unreadable, his presence filling the room like a storm about to break. My pulse quickens, and I try to steady my breathing as his sharp eyes rake over me.

"Katja," he says with an undercurrent of something I can't quite place. I have no idea what he knows or what's about to happen, and all I can do is stand my ground.

Marco closes the distance between us, his movements deliberate, reaching out to undo the buttons of the coat— Malachi's coat. My body tenses, frozen in place as his hands part the fabric, revealing the front of my gown. Blood stains the once-pristine dress, dark and glaring against the crimson fabric. Marco's eyes harden at the sight, his sharp features tightening like a vice.

"Is it true what my son tells me? This man was forcing himself on you," Marco says.

I nod, struggling to speak as Malachi steps into the room, shutting the door behind him. The sound feels deafening in the silence. I know how I must look—a mess, my hair disheveled, my face streaked with tears. It makes the story all the more believable.

Marco's jaw flexes, the muscle ticking—a rare tell for a man who prides himself on control. He takes my chin in his hand, surprisingly gentle as he tilts my face up, studying me intently for a long moment. His dark eyes burn with something fierce, but I can't quite decipher whether it's anger, concern, or both. He lets go without a word and turns to Malachi.

"Stay in this room with her until I come back tomorrow. No one else enters," Marco says. It's an order, plain and simple.

"What are you going to do?" Malachi asks. It's strange hearing someone question Marco. No one does that—not even me. But Malachi is his son, and the dynamic between them is clearly different.

"I'm going to take care of it," Marco says, straightening his suit jacket with precise movements.

He strides toward the door but pauses before leaving. I think he might look back at me, but he doesn't. The door clicks shut behind him, leaving the room suffocatingly quiet once again.

I glance at Malachi, who watches the door for a long moment before turning to me.

"This...isn't exactly what I had planned," he says quietly, running a hand through his hair.

I sit back down by the fire. "What is he going to do?" I ask, my voice trembling despite myself.

Malachi doesn't answer right away, his eyes darkening as he sits in the chair across from me.

"It doesn't matter what he does," Malachi says, stretching his legs out with a casual ease. A small smile begins to play on his lips.

"What?" I ask, unable to decipher the shift in his mood.

"It's... Damn." He chuckles softly, shaking his head. "If you think about it, this night turned out perfect."

"Perfect?" I repeat, staring at him as if he's lost his mind. "Are you serious? Perfect is not even in the same universe as how I would describe this night."

"Think about it, Kat," he says, sitting forward, the smile still lingering. "We saved two people tonight—one of them someone you clearly care about. And not only that, but we've got the perfect alibi. My father thinks that man was attacking you, and I stepped in to stop it. Then I brought you straight here to keep you safe. No one will suspect us of anything."

I stare at him, wide-eyed, trying to process how he's finding a silver lining in this mess.

"Don't you see?" he continues, leaning back in his chair. "It's a small victory. My father's trust in me will only grow after tonight, while Orin's credibility is going to take a hit for not keeping an eye on you. And when they realize the victims of their precious silent auction have vanished, everyone else will be too busy pointing fingers to look at us. Marco's word will protect us. We're in the clear."

I stare at him in disbelief. As messed up as it is, it is a win. A small, tenuous victory in the middle of this fucked-up night.

I shrug, letting out a long breath. "I can't disagree with you."

"See?" he says, the smug smile returning. "Enjoy the win, Kat. They don't come around often enough in this kind of life."

I roll my eyes but feel some of the tension in my shoulders ease as the reality of what he's saying sinks in. This night might have been a disaster, but we've come out of it unscathed. For now.

He drops to his knees in front of me, and I instinctively lean back. "What are you doing?" I ask, eyeing him suspiciously.

He laughs softly, a sound that somehow makes me feel more on edge. "Relax, I'm going to run you a bath." His hands are already undoing the straps of my heels, his touch surprisingly gentle as he slowly slides them off my feet.

"Why would you do that?" I study him, hesitant, my arms crossing over my chest.

"Just because you don't like me doesn't mean I can't do something nice," he says, amused and exasperated. "You've had a rough night, Kat, and contrary to what you might think, I'm not a complete monster."

He sets my heels neatly on the mantle, their delicate straps hanging over the edge, and then strides into the bathroom. A moment later, I hear the rush of water filling the tub, the sound oddly soothing despite my still-jumbled nerves.

I remain rooted to the spot, staring after him, unsure whether to be grateful, suspicious, or both. "You didn't strike me as the 'bubble bath and pampering' type," I call out.

"You'd be surprised," he responds, his voice echoing faintly over the sound of the faucet. And for some reason, that annoyingly smug tone of his almost makes me smile.

Chapter Twelve

RULE 12 OF THE NEW ORDER: FIRST IMPRESSIONS ARE RARELY THE WHOLE TRUTH. SOMETIMES, THE PERSON YOU LEAST EXPECT BECOMES THE ONE YOU CAN'T IGNORE.

"THIS IS GOING TO BE FUN," I mutter under my breath as I step out of the bathroom, feeling better after scrubbing every last trace of blood off me.

The bath helped, though Malachi's lack of a proper brush made dealing with my wet hair a nightmare. At least his oversized white t-shirt serves as a makeshift nightgown, falling to my knees and sparing me from the burden of wearing his equally ill-fitting pajama pants.

He's stretched out on top of the bed wearing gray sweats and a white shirt, a book in his hands, looking far too comfortable for my liking. I clear my throat to announce my presence, feeling uncharacteristically awkward. His gaze doesn't even flick to me. He doesn't say anything and keeps reading, like I'm a ghost he's choosing to ignore.

I hesitate for a moment, debating whether to demand he sleep on the floor, but I shove the thought away. I'm an adult. Sharing a bed shouldn't be a big deal. Right?

"What are you reading?" I ask, craning my neck to catch the title.

He startles, quickly sitting up and shoving the book into the drawer of the nightstand like a kid caught sneaking candy. "Must be good if I caught you off guard," I tease, crossing my arms and giving him a sly grin.

"It's okay," he mutters.

"Oh, really?" I step closer to his side of the bed, and his eyes narrow like he's trying to figure out what I'm up to. Before he can stop me, I reach over, yank the drawer open, and grab the book.

"Hey!" he protests, making a half-hearted swipe to snatch it back, but I sidestep, flipping the cover up so I can see the title.

"A romance novel?" I blurt out, blinking at the embossed letters and the couple locked in a passionate embrace on the cover.

His ears turn the faintest shade of pink as he crosses his arms, glaring at me. "It's not a romance novel. It's...literature."

"Uh-huh." I tap the book against my palm, biting back a laugh. "You know, I pegged you as the brooding action thriller type. But this? This is adorable."

"Are you done?" he grumbles, clearly annoyed but not making a move to take the book back.

"Not even close," I say, dropping onto the bed next to him and flipping through the pages. "Let's see what kind of literature you're into, Malachi."

"Don't you have anything better to do?" he asks, exasperated.

"Not really." I glance over at him, a half-smile starting to form. "Honestly, this is the most fun I've had in days."

"I'm glad making fun of my choice in literature is fun for you. By all means, keep making jokes," Malachi says, his lips twitch like he's trying not to smile.

I stop flipping pages when a particularly spicy line catches my eye. Grinning wickedly, I start reading aloud, "'Calliope grasps his hard length—'"

Before I can finish, he snatches the book from my hands and shoves it back in the drawer, slamming it shut. "Okay, that's enough," he says, clearing his throat.

I burst out laughing, clutching my sides as I flop back onto the bed. "That's great. Who knew we'd have the same taste in books?" I tease, still giggling.

He gives me a look—a mixture of amusement and irritation —but I catch the faintest hint of a smirk tugging at the corner of his mouth. "I'm glad you think you're funny," he mutters, leaning back against the headboard and crossing his arms.

"Oh, I know I'm funny," I say, sitting up and wiping a stray tear from my eye. "Seriously, you could've told me you like romance novels. I wouldn't have judged. Much."

He shakes his head, finally letting out a soft chuckle. "You're impossible."

"And you're full of surprises," I quip, still grinning as I settle back against the pillows. "Maybe I'll borrow it when you're done. Seems like a real page-turner."

"Not a chance," he says, glancing at me out of the corner of his eye, that half-smirk making a brief reappearance.

For once, the tension between us feels a little lighter, and I can't help but think that maybe this night isn't a total disaster after all.

"Are you tired? What time is it? Do you think they discovered that Aurora and the boy are missing yet? Do you think Marco confronted Viktor about Eduard?" I ask, my thoughts spilling out in no particular order.

"I can see that bath really gave you a second wind," Malachi says, amused. I reach over and swat his chest lightly.

"I'm not tired, and it's only 11 p.m.," he answers, leaning

up to check the clock on the bookshelf. "I don't know if they've discovered the Avids are missing yet. The party will probably go on until the early hours of the morning, so it's very possible they won't realize until then."

He pauses, his expression hardening slightly. "As for my father... I don't know what he's going to do. But either way, Eduard deserved to fucking die." His jaw ticks as he speaks, and I peek over at him, unsure how to respond. "What were you thinking tonight, getting in a situation like that?"

I avoid his gaze, staring up instead. I didn't mean to steer the conversation back to this.

My eyes stay fixed on the ceiling, as if the wooden beams above could offer me an excuse or a way to justify my actions. "I saw an opportunity, and I took it. That's what I have to do."

"You don't have to do anything like that," he counters, frustrated. "You think throwing yourself into the lion's den is the only way to get results?"

I finally look at him, and the way his dark eyes search mine makes my chest tighten. "What do you want me to say, Malachi? That I planned to let it go that far? That I wanted to let him touch me to get information?" My voice shakes, and I hate that it does. "Do you know what it's like to be me? To constantly weigh every action against what's expected of me? To know that no matter what I do, it's never enough and I'll never be free?"

He stares at me for a long moment, his jaw still tight. Then he sighs and scrubs a hand over his face. "No, I don't know what it's like to be you," he admits. "But I do know you don't have to put yourself through hell to prove anything to anyone. Fuck my father and brother and the entire Volkov family."

I let out a bitter laugh. "You make it sound so simple."

His hand moves to mine, brushing against it lightly before

pulling back as if he's not sure if he's allowed to touch me. "You don't have to prove anything to me, Kat," he says quietly.

I shake my head and sit up, pulling my knees to my chest. "I wasn't trying to prove anything to you," I say. "I was trying to survive, Malachi, like always."

"I promise I'm going to get you out of here, free of my family. You'll have a life of your own one day. But until then, promise me you won't be reckless."

Malachi sits up and reaches out, his hand brushing my back briefly until I finally turn to face him. "Don't ever do what you did tonight again. I don't care if you're trying to get information to save someone's life. It's not worth it. What if I hadn't gotten there in time and—"

I stare at him, confused.

I've seen so many different sides of Malachi tonight, and this one throws me off the most. Why does he care what I do or what happens to me?

"If you didn't get there in time," I say, keeping my expression steady and cold, "then I would have fucked him and gotten the location of the Avids, and he'd probably still be alive right now." I bury the sensitive side of me that's trying to claw its way to the surface.

Malachi leans back, his head hitting the headboard with a soft thud as he exhales sharply. "I take it you're experienced in using your body to get what you want," he mutters, staring across the room, his expression unreadable.

"You have no idea." I stand, pulling back the covers before climbing into bed, deliberately keeping my movements calm and indifferent.

Little does he know, I'm a twenty-three-year-old virgin, and the closest I've come to kissing a guy in years was that night in the park—with him.

I turn on my side, facing away from Malachi, and focus on Mischka. It takes only a moment before she appears at the end of the bed, her tiny tail wagging as she does a few excited circles. I call them scuttle-butts because of the way she tucks her butt in like something's about to chase her. It's a Boston Terrier thing.

I can't help but smile, holding back a laugh as Mischka finally settles, climbing up to lie on her side right against my chest. Her comforting presence lifts the weight of the evening a little.

I start to relax, assuming Malachi has fallen asleep.

But sleep is impossible for me. My mind races with questions after everything that's happened tonight. I want to see Aurora again, to find out where she's been all these years, if her powers have changed, and if she'll be okay. I reach out, running my fingers along Mischka's ghostly fur in slow, soothing strokes.

"What are you doing?"

I freeze, my hand stopping mid-motion. "What do you mean?" I ask, trying to sound casual, but my heart skips a beat.

"You're doing that weird spell shit again," he says, his voice closer than I expected.

I press my hand to my mouth to stifle a laugh. "As far as I know, Avids don't cast spells, and wizards don't exist," I say, peeking over my shoulder at him.

Malachi's eyes narrow, though his expression softens when he sees the smile on my face.

I roll over to face him, and Mischka hops over my body, settling herself perfectly in the space between us. I watch her, and Malachi follows my gaze, his brow furrowing slightly.

"You're going to have to fill me in on what's going on here," he says.

"If I tell you, do you promise never to share it with anyone?" I ask.

His lips curl into a faint, teasing smile as he shifts, propping himself up to face me more comfortably. "I promise, Kat," he says, and somehow I believe him. After tonight, I feel like I can trust him—something I never thought possible.

"My childhood dog, Mischka, died in the same car accident as my family." I pause, reaching out to pet her, and his eyes follow the motion, though he says nothing. "She was the first spirit I ever saw. When I woke up in the hospital, there she was, sitting by my bed like she hadn't left my side. Before her, I had no idea I was an Avid. No clue I could see the dead."

His brows lift slightly, but he doesn't interrupt.

"All I have to do is think about her, and she materializes. A piece of her is always with me, but I can only see her when I will it. She's here now, cuddled between us." My hand strokes her oddly warm fur, and his gaze drops to follow the motion.

"Why don't you want anyone to know?" he asks, his hand moving tentatively toward where mine rests. His fingers graze the empty air, searching as if he might feel what I see. "It's not like they could hurt her. She's already dead, right?"

I smile faintly, shaking my head. "No one could hurt her, but I like knowing it's something special only I have. She's comforted me through some really dark times, and keeping her a secret is my way of keeping her safe, even though she doesn't need protecting."

He tilts his head. "Makes sense," he murmurs. His fingers hesitate in the space between us, and I realize he's not mocking or dismissing me. He's trying to understand.

"What will happen to Aurora and the boy?" I ask.

Malachi glances at me. "We have a safe house not far from here. My team will keep them there, protect them until I give the all-clear for them to move on. After that, we'll help them find a real place to call home—a life where they can live without fear of being hunted or exploited."

"I want to see her again. When can we make that happen?"

"I'll figure something out soon," he says, and I beam at him, the prospect of reuniting with my only real friend filling me with a small, fleeting joy.

"One of these days, you'll have to tell me how you know her," he adds, his fingers grazing mine, but I don't move away.

"That's a long story," I admit. "A story about a really dark time in my life—one I don't want to relive tonight. But one day, I'll tell you...I promise."

He studies me for a moment. "Alright. I look forward to it," he says. In a gesture so simple yet oddly intimate, he reaches out and brushes a stray strand of hair from my face, tucking it behind my ear.

The touch makes my chest tighten in a way I can't explain.

"One of these days, you're going to have to tell me more about this team of yours," I say, shifting the conversation. "How it works, how you got into the business of saving people who are trafficked."

His lips curl faintly at the corners, but his eyes hold something heavier. "Yes," he says, "one day soon, I'll tell you everything you want to know."

I don't push for answers now. The exhaustion in my bones outweighs my curiosity. "Good," I murmur, leaning back against the pillows, Mischka curling against me.

Malachi shifts, sliding under the covers beside me, the mattress dipping slightly with his weight as he repositions. I glance over at him as he settles in, his arm brushing mine for a fleeting moment before he folds his hands behind his head and stares up at the ceiling.

I try to focus on the firelight dancing across the walls, but the warmth radiating from his side of the bed is distracting.

It's ridiculous—the odd urge to inch closer, to let my head rest against his chest like this is something normal, something safe. I grip the edge of the blanket tighter instead, willing the feeling to go away.

"Goodnight, demon," Malachi mutters.

"Goodnight, savior," I reply sarcastically. It's a fitting nick name after his actions tonight. He chuckles lightly before silence falls over us, and I shut my eyes.

Chapter Thirteen

RULE 13 OF THE NEW ORDER: A KIND TOUCH CAN
HIDE A CRUEL HAND. ALWAYS QUESTION WHY THEY
REACH FOR YOU.

I WAKE up with my head pressed against Malachi's chest, my arm and leg both draped over his warm, solid body. Oh God, I'm practically bear-hugging him. I freeze, trying to keep my breathing steady as I feel his chest rise and fall in the slow rhythm of sleep. I need to get out of this without waking him.

Carefully, I lift my head, only to notice something worse—there's a tiny drool spot on his shirt.

Oh my God.

I must have been in a deep sleep to drool on him. This is beyond embarrassing.

I pull my arm back and start to lift my leg, glancing up at his face to make sure his eyes are still closed.

"Restful night?"

His voice catches me mid-sneak, and I snap my gaze up to find him already watching me, his eyes bright with amusement. He's clearly been awake for a while.

I shove him away, sitting up and running a hand down my face in an attempt to gather some dignity. "Shut up."

He chuckles, still lounging like he owns the world. "I was

enjoying all the cute little sounds you were making in your sleep."

I turn to glare at him, my side-eye sharp enough to cut. "I hope you're joking."

"Not at all. Adorable, really." He grins, and it's infuriating how good he looks first thing in the morning.

I throw the covers back and get to my feet, ignoring the warmth creeping up my neck. Stretching my arms above my head, I let out a long exhale and mutter, "You're impossible."

"And yet here I am, your favorite bedmate," he teases, swinging his legs over the side of the bed and smirking like he's won something.

"Yeah, don't get used to it," I say, crossing my arms and glancing toward the window. "Did you hear anything last night after I fell asleep? When do you think Marco will come for me?" All I want is to brush my teeth, shower, and get back to my room.

"I haven't heard a damn thing," he says, stretching like he has all the time in the world. "But that's not surprising— I told you, most of these rooms are practically soundproof. It's already 7 a.m., so I imagine my father will be coming to retrieve his precious demon pet soon. Don't look too excited to get away from me." His sarcasm is as sharp as ever, and I roll my eyes in response.

"I'm not excited to get away from you, and I'm definitely not excited to see Marco," I shoot back, turning toward the bathroom. "I want to know we're in the clear after last night and that know no one saw us or suspects anything."

I step into the bathroom and splash cold water on my face, hoping it will wake me up—or at least wash away the unease gnawing at the edges of my mind.

"I know Marco said we were both to stay in here, but I want to shower and change into my clothes. Can't I go to my room, and you can keep watch or whatever?" I step out of the bathroom, catching sight of Malachi mid-dressing. He's already pulled on a pair of jeans, and my eyes betray me, catching on the dip of his waist and the muscles along his bare chest and arms. Damn it. I clear my throat and quickly turn toward the window, focusing on the snow-covered trees outside. Neutral. Innocent.

"Why don't you get in the shower, and I'll go grab whatever you need from your room?" he says, buttoning up his shirt, his tone annoyingly practical. "No one's going to come looking for you in here, and the last thing I want to do is piss off my father this morning by not following orders."

I hesitate, glancing back briefly before looking away again. "Fine. I have a small bag on the bathroom sink with all my toiletries in it—grab that. And I still haven't unpacked one of my suitcases. It's on the left side of the closet. Bring the whole thing so I can go through it myself."

He smirks faintly as he adjusts his cuffs. "You don't trust me to pick out your clothes? I'm hurt."

"I don't trust you to pick out anything without some kind of ulterior motive," I shoot back, crossing my arms and keeping my gaze out the window. "Bring the suitcase and the bag. That's it."

"Got it," he says, and I hear the faint sound of him slipping on his shoes.

I stay fixed on the snowy expanse outside as the door clicks shut behind him, letting out a slow breath.

MALACHI STILL HASN'T RETURNED, which feels odd. And now here I am, alone with Marco, who was already waiting when I stepped out of the shower. He says the last thing I expected to hear.

"What do you mean you're sending me away?" I ask in surprise.

I bite down on the inside of my cheek immediately, trying to temper the edge in my tone. The last thing I want right now is to push his mood further into the red. He's already tense, and I've seen what happens when he's not in control.

I can't help feeling frustrated. I was starting to—maybe, barely, reluctantly—enjoy Malachi's company. Now Marco wants to send me away? This will ruin everything. Our plans, the mission to save more Avids, my slim chance at freedom...all of it. I knew better than to let hope creep in, but it still stings.

"I mean," I try again, softening my voice, "I haven't finished the case yet. I want to help you."

Marco's furrowed brows relax slightly, and he takes the chair across from the fireplace in Malachi's room. His usual calculating gaze is heavier today, more serious, and it puts me on edge. I grip the towel wrapped around me, tucking it tighter for security before hesitantly sitting in the chair next to him.

"Something happened last night, Katja," Marco says, crossing an ankle over his knee. "And there's more going on here than the case with Damien."

I keep my expression neutral, but my mind is racing. Damn right a lot of things happened last night.

"What happened?" I venture cautiously, my demeanor careful, respectful. Normally, I don't ask Marco questions—I respond, act, obey. This feels like a dangerous line to cross, but I have to know.

Marco studies me, the firelight illuminating his face in the dimly lit room. "Avids went missing from Viktor's property last night. He's furious, as you can imagine. And I suspect there's more going on here. They didn't just escape—it would have been impossible."

He rubs his chin, his eyes narrowing like he's sifting through possibilities. I stay quiet, trying not to betray the rapid pounding of my heart.

"I don't feel comfortable keeping you here when one of our rivals—or Viktor's enemies—could be murdering or stealing Avids."

Internally, I sigh with relief. He doesn't suspect us.

"I don't fully trust my brother," Marco continues. "And I especially don't like this situation. But I'm not ready to go home yet. I have unfinished business here. You, however..."

His piercing gaze lands on me, and I sit perfectly still. I don't want him to send me home, but I can't risk protesting any more than I already have.

"You have to understand," Marco says, leaning closer, "I care for you, Katja."

His hand lands on my knee, and I instinctively stiffen. This is an unusual side of Marco—softer, almost sincere. It has me holding my breath.

"You are my most prized possession," he says tenderly. His hand moves from my knee to cup my chin, tilting my face toward him.

I force a wan smile, swallowing down the urge to roll my eyes. Yep. You only want to send away your precious pet to keep her from being stolen.

"Do you trust me to keep you safe?" Marco asks, his eyes boring into mine like he's daring me to say otherwise.

I nod and lie through my teeth. "Of course, Marco."

"Very good." Marco drops my chin, his hand retreating as if the moment of closeness never happened. I glance down at my lap, avoiding his gaze.

"I want you to continue the case," he says, his tone shifting back to its usual authority. "You and I both know you have enough of a connection now to work on this from a distance. I still expect you to solve this, and Viktor will want results."

He's right. I don't need to stay here to contact Damien or Carmen. The connection is already forged.

"Will I be returning home today then? Should I pack?" I ask, trying to keep my voice even.

"You won't be returning home," Marco says, and my head snaps up before I catch myself, quickly glancing toward the fire to cover the slip.

If not home, then where? The question buzzes in my mind like a warning. But I keep my expression neutral, my curiosity masked.

"Your things are being packed for you as we speak. I'll see you in a few weeks," Marco says, rising from his seat with a finality that leaves no room for argument. My mouth almost drops open—a few weeks. This is so out of character for him. Something else is going on, something I'm not privy to, and I want to know what it is.

"And Katja," he adds, pausing at the door, his sharp gaze slicing into me, "don't disappoint me. I expect you to deliver the next time we meet."

The weight of the threat presses on me. Solve the case by then or face the consequences—Marco's way of ensuring obedience without saying too much.

"I understand," I manage to say, though my insides twist at the thought of dealing with Damien and whatever games he has in store.

He nods once and strides out, the door clicking shut behind him. No further explanation, no reassurance—only expectations. And now I'm left to wonder where I'll be sent and how

I'll manage to untangle this mess before time runs out. I'm going to have to project. It's the only way to get to the bottom of this. Contacting the spirits on their playing field is the only move I have left.

"HOW ARE YOU NOT READY YET?" Malachi asks as he hauls my luggage into the room, his eyes scanning me where I still sit in front of the fire, wrapped in a towel with my wet hair dripping down my back.

"Hello, you have all my stuff," I retort, throwing up my arms. "I'm not using that ridiculous excuse for a comb again." I hurry over, opening one of my bags on the bed.

"I see you packed everything. That must mean you spoke with Marco," I say, digging through the bag for clothes and a toothbrush.

"He came to you already?" Malachi asks, crossing the room to grab a duffle bag from the closet. He starts tossing his things into it with no real care or organization.

"What are you doing?" I ask, stepping into the bathroom to brush my teeth.

"I'm getting ready to go," he replies simply.

I peek my head out of the bathroom, toothbrush in hand. "He's sending you away too?"

A devious smile spreads across his face. "Oh no, little demon. He's sending me to take care of you," he says.

I spit out my toothpaste, glancing at him in the mirror. "Creep," I say, laughing as I wipe my mouth and start working a brush through my hair.

"So where are you taking me? What security is coming with us? And what does this mean for your mission? How are you going to figure out what's going on here—Viktor's operation and all—if Marco's shipping you off to babysit me?" I ask.

Malachi leans against the closet doorframe, arms crossed, clearly amused by my rapid-fire questioning. "Aren't you full of curiosity this morning?" he says, grinning. "Don't worry. I've got a plan. But I'll let you sweat it out a little longer before I tell you."

"Malachi," I warn, giving him my best glare.

"Relax," he says, grabbing his duffle and tossing it onto the bed next to my open suitcase. "All you need to know is you're stuck with me for the foreseeable future. Now hurry up. We leave in fifteen. Meet me at the front door when you're ready."

I dry my hair as fast as I can. There's no way I'm stepping out into the snow with wet hair. I'm already poorly acclimated to the cold as it is. Once it's mostly dry, I pull on the black pants and blue sweater I'd set aside. It's not my best outfit, but it's warm, and that's all I care about right now.

Malachi must have taken all the luggage while I was getting ready—probably loading up one of the cars. At least he's making himself useful. I glance in the mirror, swipe on some chapstick, and toss my hair behind my shoulders before heading out into the hallway.

I take one last look around the mansion. I'm not going to miss this place, with all its dark secrets and suffocating rules. But the snow, the trees, and the quiet beauty of the grounds? Those, I might actually miss.

I round the corner and suddenly find myself shoved hard against the wall. Orin's hand is pressed to my shoulder, pinning me in place. His face is so close I can feel his thick beard scratching on my cheek.

"Don't think I'm not on to you, pet," he growls.

I turn my head away, pressing my cheek against the cool

surface of the wall to avoid his glare. "What are you talking about?" I say evenly, though my heart pounds in my chest. I try to shove him off, but he doesn't budge.

"You may have my father fooled, but not me. I know you're up to no good. Mysteriously disappearing last night? I'll get to the bottom of it," he sneers, his grip tightening momentarily before he lets go and steps back. "And when I do? It's right back into that not-so-pretty cage for you."

He storms off down the hall, and I let out a shaky exhale.

Fucking asshole.

He's bluffing. He doesn't know anything but hates me enough to want to keep me looking over my shoulder. Still, I can't shake the uneasy feeling that lingers in his wake.

By the time I reach the entry hall, Malachi and Banks are waiting for me. I plaster on a smile for Banks, who as always remains stoic and unreadable. Malachi catches the smile and looks between us with a curious expression.

Banks, ever the professional, opens the door for us and then heads to the driver's seat of the car. No security detail. Malachi climbs into the front seat, and I slide into the back. As we drive away, I watch through the window as the mansion disappears behind the trees. The farther we go, the lighter I feel.

At the airstrip, Banks and Malachi load up one of Marco's small planes. Banks is careful to avoid looking directly at me as usual. "If that will be all, then safe flight," Banks says curtly before stepping back from the plane.

Malachi waves him off. "Take care, Banks."

We board the plane, and after a few quick words exchanged between Malachi and the pilot, we're in the air.

Malachi reclines in his seat next to me, arms crossed as he glances over with an amused expression. "So what was that back there with Banks?"

I shake my head, laughing lightly. "Banks isn't so bad. I think he finds me creepy."

Malachi lets out a loud laugh. "Who doesn't?"

I punch him in the arm, but a small smile tugs at my lips despite myself.

I'm ready for some answers about where the hell we're going.

Chapter Fourteen

RULE 14 OF THE NEW ORDER: CERTAINTY IS THE
GREATEST LIE–WHEN YOU THINK YOU KNOW
EVERYTHING, THE TRUTH WILL UNRAVEL YOU.

"IS Mischka coming along on this little trip with us?" Malachi asks, taking a sip from his water bottle.

"Duh, she goes everywhere I go," I laugh, and Mischka appears instantly, doing her signature little run up and down the aisle before hopping onto my lap.

Malachi shakes his head with an amused smile. "I wish I could see the world the way you do. Must be a trip."

"Yeah, it's always changing too," I say, taking the water bottle he offers me.

"What do you mean by that?" he asks, tilting his head curiously as I take a sip.

"I don't really know much about Avids or even my own abilities. I've never really had anyone to talk to about it. All I know is that over the years I've gotten stronger, and the more I use my gift, the more it evolves," I tell him, stroking Mischka's fur absentmindedly.

"Then why aren't you using it all the time? If I were you, I'd be trying to become as powerful as possible," he says, and I glance out the window, my thoughts drifting to the veil.

"Seeing the dead is still creepy, even for me, you know. Every time I project, it takes a toll," I admit, watching the clouds blur past.

"When you project? I overheard my father and Orin talking about it before. Orin wanted to force you to do it. My father said it wasn't a good time because it knocks you out for days—what the hell is that all about?" Malachi places his hand over mine, and I let it fall to my lap, Mischka disappearing in an instant.

I glance down at his hand then up to meet his eyes. When did he become comfortable enough to touch me? And why does it feel like something's shifted between us? I don't want to acknowledge it, so I quickly turn my gaze back to the window. After a moment, he pulls his hand away, as if he feels the tension too.

"Projecting is when seeing the spirits in our world isn't enough," I begin, my voice softer now. "I push a piece of myself—my soul—out into the veil, where I communicate with them on their terms. I see things from their perspective. That's the best way I can describe it." I pause, my fingers tightening slightly on my lap. "But when I do it, it's...draining. And things feel different over there. It's darker on that side of the veil."

He leans back slightly, his brows furrowed, but he doesn't speak right away, giving me the space to finish my thought. It's oddly comforting. For someone I swore I didn't like not too long ago, he sure has a way of making me feel heard.

But I don't want to talk about projecting right now. I want answers. Real answers.

"Will you tell me where we're going now?" I ask, my gaze flicking nervously to the window. All I see are endless clouds, but that doesn't stop me from looking every few minutes, hoping for some clue.

"I'm taking you home. To my home, where I've been for the last ten years," he says casually, like he's discussing the weather.

I snap my head back toward him, eyes wide in shock. "Your home? You mean the Midwest District? I can't believe Marco is letting you take me there. And without any security."

"Yes, Midwest is right. And why is that so hard to believe?" He leans back, folding his arms like he's challenging me.

I let out a soft, bitter laugh. "Because I've never gone anywhere without Marco. Ever. Not once since I met him." It's the unspoken truth of my life.

Malachi's lips press into a firm line, his jaw tightening slightly. He doesn't say anything, but his expression shifts, like he's deep in thought. I can't tell if my answer bothers him or if it's another piece of information he's filing away. Either way, the silence stretches between us until I find myself resting my eyes.

"RISE AND SHINE." Malachi's voice jolts me awake. How long was I asleep? How long was the flight? I sit up, brushing my hair out of my face, blinking at him as he's already halfway out the plane door. By the time I get to my feet, the pilot is shaking his hand, and then I watch as the plane takes off again. Malachi begins loading our luggage into a truck parked inside the hangar.

I step out, surprised by the biting cold and the blanket of snow surrounding us. I'm not sure what I expected, but I guess it makes sense—it is the middle of winter.

"Ready?" he asks, sliding into the driver's seat. I follow, climbing into the passenger side and glancing around the hangar. It's eerily quiet, nothing like the chaos I'm used to. No one else is in sight. I like it. I feel like I can breathe better here.

I buckle my seatbelt, idly looking out the window at the shelves inside the hangar—random items scattered across them: a gas can, some old folders. But then I notice we're not moving. Turning my attention back to Malachi, I find him leaned back against the window, watching me.

What the fuck?

"Why aren't we driving?" I ask slowly, raising an eyebrow. My mind flashes through a series of worst-case scenarios, and I shake my head, trying to rid myself of the intrusive thoughts.

"We need to have a little talk before I take you to my home," he says.

"A little talk?" I repeat, crossing my arms as suspicion settles into irritation.

He nods, his expression unreadable. "You have to understand, Katja. I need to know I can trust you."

I glare at him, my annoyance flaring. "How can you not trust me after last night? I helped you. We saved those people together. If anything, I should be the one questioning if I can trust you."

His gaze sharpens, but he stays calm, leaning forward slightly. "Last night was a start," he says, running a hand over his hair, "but trust isn't about one night or one action."

I let out a heavy sigh, pinching the bridge of my nose before meeting his eyes again. "What else do you want from me, Malachi? How can I prove myself? And why the hell is this something we need to hash out right now in this creepy old hangar?" I narrow my eyes at him.

"If I take you to my home, if I let you see things there—if I let you into my life—there's no turning back. No one can know the things you will be privy to."

I sit back. There's already no going back, not for me.

"I have nothing to go back to," I say aloud, studying his face. "That's the truth. Do you think I can go back to Marco after this? To that prison? After everything? I've already crossed the line, Malachi. You don't see it yet."

"You say that, and maybe you believe it," he says finally. "You seem like you're willing to help me, to do what it takes to take down my father—but you have to see why I hesitate to believe you."

I feel the heat rising to my cheeks, frustration burning in my chest. "No," I say even though I want to scream, "I don't see why you hesitate to believe me. I've been nothing but honest with you."

His jaw tightens, his eyes locked on mine. "My father treats you like you're more than some prisoner to him," he says, the words biting. "He treats you like you matter to him. Like there's something more to your relationship than you're letting on. He worries about your life more than any of his sons'. He gives you everything—nice clothes, a nice room. The first time we met, for fuck's sake, you were alone in a park, not even trying to escape." His voice sharpens, and I can see the questions burning behind his eyes. "How am I supposed to believe you don't enjoy whatever it is you have with him?"

Something cold and sharp coils in my chest at his words, anger mingling with the raw sting of his accusations. "You don't know what you're talking about," I say, trying to keep my emotions in check.

"Then you're going to have to give me something, Kat. A reason to believe you, to trust you," Malachi says, like he's issuing an ultimatum. "If you can't, that's fine. I won't be upset. We'll go stay in a hotel, you'll solve the case for Viktor, and in a few weeks I'll take you back home to Marco."

He says it so easily, like last night meant nothing. Like none of this matters. The thought makes my chest ache.

Last night meant everything to me, I think bitterly. I was willing to let that creep touch me, willing to do something I'd never done before—something that made me sick to my stomach—to help his mission, to help free the Avids. And now he sits here questioning my loyalty, questioning me as if my relationship with Marco could ever mean more than the chance to truly help people...or the chance at my own freedom.

What kind of deranged shit is he believing right now?

I know what I have to do. What I have to say. What I have to show him. But it's not something I'm ready for—not this soon. I wasn't prepared to have this conversation in this drafty old hangar with his eyes boring into me like he's dissecting my every thought.

My throat starts to burn, and tears threaten to sting my eyes. I can't let them fall. Not in front of him. I bite down hard on the inside of my cheek, forcing myself to focus on the physical pain until I feel more grounded. Until I regain some composure.

"I did try to escape, you know," I finally say, exhaling slowly. "A few times."

He watches me with that same thoughtful expression, his jaw tightening like he's bracing himself for whatever comes next.

"The first couple of times, I was caught right away," I say, my voice steady even though the memories threaten to overwhelm me. "They were poor excuses for attempts. I took a beating for it both times, but it only made me more hardheaded. I was so stubborn, so determined to get away back then."

I let my gaze drop to my hands, twisting my fingers together in my lap as I continue. "I will admit I did have a sick appreciation for Marco—maybe I still do—because he saved me when he purchased me. He saved me from a place that was far worse than the pretty prison his home became for me."

I tug my bottom lip into my mouth.

"Being knocked around by Marco's security the second time fueled a fire inside me. I started plotting. Watching. Learning everything I could about the staff, about Marco's security detail, the routines, the weak spots. When Marco took me out on my first real job, I thought it might be my chance." I take a deep breath, the memory of that night still sharp even now.

"I was left alone to contact the spirit, to 'get comfortable in the scene.' At least that's what Marco told his men. And I had spent months plotting, waiting, so when the opportunity came, I couldn't refuse it. I barricaded the door, snuck out the window, and ran as far as I could. I stumbled across a woman working in her yard, and I begged her for help. She took me in, fed me, gave me water." The fury I felt back then resurfaces. "But it only took Marco's men a day to find me."

Malachi shifts in his seat, sitting up straighter, his attention locked on me. He doesn't interrupt, but some uneasiness in his eyes suggests he has an idea where this is going.

"You have to understand," I say, my voice softening, "I was only sixteen at the time. I should have been smarter about it, but I was so desperate to get away that I acted irrationally. I was naive enough to believe I had a chance."

He exhales, the sound heavy in the confined space of the truck. "What happened when they found you?" he asks. It's like he doesn't want to know but feels he has to hear it.

I look away, my stomach churning. "They killed the woman without a second thought then dragged me back to the compound. And Marco... He made sure I'd never try to run again."

I let out a heavy sigh. "How do you create an obedient pet? How do you make a girl determined to escape stay willingly and obey with a smile on her face?"

Malachi's expression hardens, his eyes never leaving mine.

"You break her," I continue, my gaze distant. "You tear her

down until she's ashamed and powerless. But Marco would never dirty his own hands—that would make me hate him even more. No, that's when I met Orin."

"Dammit," Malachi mutters under his breath.

"Orin took me to a place not much different than those cages under the stables," I say. "He stripped me of my clothes, my food, my water—my dignity. He shoved me into a cage in the dark. I lost track of time. He didn't touch me, not then. He taunted me, broke me down piece by piece. He reminded me how I 'killed' my family and my best friend, made me believe it was all my fault. He convinced me I was nothing, that I should be honored to serve someone like his father. He actually made me feel guilty for embarrassing Marco by escaping."

I let out a hollow laugh. "I don't know how long he kept me down there. Without daylight or meals to keep track, everything blurred together." I turn slightly, gazing out the passenger window, not wanting to meet Malachi's eyes for this next part. "On the last day, Orin finally pulled me out of that cell. He forced me to shower in front of him then took me to his bedroom where Marco was waiting. I thought maybe it was over, that Marco would forgive me. But he didn't say a word. He watched, emotionless, as Orin shoved me onto my knees before him."

I take a slow, steadying breath, tracing a foggy trail on the window with my finger. "I can still hear Orin's voice. 'Hold still now. Don't want this to get messy.' He pulled a rod from the fireplace—only it wasn't a rod; it was a brand. A shield with a wolf on it."

"The Volkov family crest," Malachi whispers.

"'Now everyone will know you belong to us. Try running again, and I'll make sure the next mark is somewhere a lot more visible,' Orin said. He left me there, crying on the floor. But Marco held me while I cried, told me it hurt him as much as it hurt me. He said I brought it upon myself but that no one would ever touch me again as long as I obeyed him. He kept me in his bed, healed my wound, fed me until I started to look like myself again. And I buried that day deep inside."

A single tear escapes down my cheek, but I quickly wipe it away before Malachi can see. I grab my sweater and pull it off over my head.

"What are you doing? You don't have to—" Malachi hesitates mid sentence as I grip the hem of my shirt and lift it, exposing my back to him.

"I buried that night, but he gave me this so I could never forget," I say quietly.

His fingers brush over the scar at the top of my back right in the center, tracing its jagged outline with a gentleness that contradicts the rage I see building in him. My skin prickles under his touch, the memory of how I got that mark still so vivid now when I let myself remember.

"He fucking branded me," I say, struggling to hold my composure. "How could you not trust me?" I glance over my shoulder at him, and his face is an open book. Anger, guilt, regret—and something else, deeper, darker, that he's holding back.

A tear slips down my cheek before I can stop it, hot and unwelcome. I lift my hand to swipe it away, but Malachi beats me to it. He pulls me into him, his arms strong and unyielding as they wrap around me, holding me against his chest like he's trying to shield me from the weight of my own pain.

And I break.

The tears come, unchecked and relentless. I sob quietly into his chest, his warmth and steady presence holding me in a way I hadn't known I needed. He doesn't speak, doesn't try to offer platitudes or empty words. Instead, his hand moves slowly through my hair, smoothing it in soft strokes, while his other hand tugs my sweater back down, covering the scar like he wants to hide the evidence of what's been done to me.

Minutes pass—maybe more. The truck is quiet except for my uneven breaths and the occasional sniffle. His embrace doesn't falter, his strength a silent reassurance that he's here, that I'm safe. And for a fleeting moment, I let myself believe it. I let myself exist in this fragile, fleeting bubble of comfort.

But then the weight of reality creeps back in. I can't stay like this. I can't let myself fall apart in front of him. I push gently against his chest, forcing some distance between us, and he lets me go without protest.

I swipe at my damp cheeks, trying to erase the evidence of my breakdown, and straighten my sweater. "I'm fine," I murmur, my throat tight and voice raspy.

Malachi watches me carefully, his eyes still stormy.

"At least he put it somewhere I can't see it every day, and my hair usually covers it when my clothes can't," I whisper. "So you see, I have plenty of reason to hate Marco. I, more than anyone, have reason to want him dead." I press my lips into a thin line, holding his gaze.

Malachi remains silent, his eyes searching mine. "Kat... I didn't know," he finally says, strained.

"Now you do," I reply softly, the weight of my confession settling between us.

Malachi sits frozen, his hands gripping the steering wheel so hard his knuckles turn white. He doesn't say anything for what feels like an eternity, his eyes locked on some distant point outside the windshield.

"You didn't have to show me, Kat. I believed you."

I cross my arms over my chest, leaning back into the seat, and stare out the windshield. "Maybe I needed you to see it," I say. "Now I don't want to talk about this anymore. The point is, you can trust me. I'm not hiding some twisted affection for your father. I did what I had to do to survive. That's it."

I glance at him briefly. My fingers dig into my arms as the weight of everything I've said presses down on me. "Now take me to your home or to a hotel—whatever you want—but don't bring this up again."

The only sound is the low hum of the engine idling. I keep my eyes fixed on the hanger shelves, wishing I could get out and pace. I feel too exposed, too vulnerable. I need to move, to be anywhere but stuck in this moment.

"I'm taking you home," Malachi finally says, shifting the truck into gear.

Chapter Fifteen

RULE 15 OF THE NEW ORDER: TO REVEAL YOUR PAIN
IS TO SHOW YOUR POWER–BUT ONLY DO SO TO
THOSE WHO HAVE EARNED THE RIGHT TO SEE IT.

THE LANDSCAPE here is starkly different, as it is in every district, I assume. The terrain stretches out in endless, desolate plains—a sea of white broken only by the occasional jagged tree. Snow blankets everything in a thick, unbroken layer, concealing what I imagine were once sprawling farmlands. The horizon blurs where the Earth meets the sky, both the same cold, unyielding shade of gray. Low-hanging clouds hover ominously, so dense and dark it feels like I could reach up and brush my fingers against them.

"This is home," Malachi says as we turn through an open wooden gate.

I blink, taking in the scene. It looks like an old ranch sprawling across an enormous piece of land, so isolated I can't see a neighbor in any direction.

There's a large, weathered main house, several smaller cabins scattered about, a barn, and a stable. The entire place feels rooted in a time long gone, but it's charming in its way.

"You live here all alone?" I ask, surprised at the sheer size of the property. It's no mansion like Viktor's and not a fortress compound like Marco's, but there's a warmth to it, even in the freezing cold.

Malachi shakes his head. "No, I don't own the ranch, but I do call one of those cabins home." He gestures toward a modest log house tucked further back.

We pull up in front of the largest building, which I assume is the main house. Malachi gets out and opens my door for me. I hesitate briefly then follow him up the steps. He doesn't bother knocking and pushes the front door open like he owns the place.

The moment we step inside, I'm hit with the unmistakable smell of something baking—apple pie? It's comforting, and I take in the cozy interior. The living room is filled with inviting couches and well-worn armchairs, and the warmth from a potbelly stove radiates through the house.

"Malachi, are you really home?" A woman's voice catches me off guard. I turn to see a tall, athletic woman with dirty-blonde hair stride into the room. She walks right past me and wraps Malachi in a tight embrace.

"Aunt Irina," Malachi says warmly, returning her hug. My eyes widen in shock.

"Aunt?" I whisper, but he catches it. He steps back and smirks, clearly amused.

"Katja, this is my Aunt Irina—my father and Viktor's younger sister," he says casually, as if this isn't a bombshell.

I blink at him, and the full weight of the revelation settles in. The Volkov brothers have a sister? I never once heard her mentioned—not by Marco or anyone. How does she fit into all of this?

I extend my hand, forcing a polite smile. "Nice to meet you. You can call me Kat."

Irina shakes my hand firmly, her expression warm. "It's a pleasure, Kat. Welcome to the ranch."

"Oh, she can call you Kat right away, but I still get shit for it?" Malachi teases, clearly enjoying himself.

I shoot him a sharp look, making it very clear I am not in the mood for jokes—not until someone explains what the hell is going on.

"Why don't you take Kat to get settled and come fill me in on everything as soon as you can. I'll make some coffee. You both look exhausted," Irina says, and I'm surprised by how kind she sounds. Not fooled by what I'm sure is an act, I offer her a polite smile and let Malachi lead me back out to the truck.

He drives us to his cottage, which isn't far. We could've walked, but with all the luggage and the snow, I can see why he chose to drive. The cottage is charming from the outside—a log cabin with a round stained-glass window centered above the front door.

"Come on, make yourself comfortable," Malachi says as he hauls the bags inside.

I take a look around, and it's perfect—cozy and simple. There's a cobblestone fireplace with a large fur rug spread out in front of it, and a loveseat that makes me want to sink in with a good book. There's also a couch, a small dining table with chairs, a breakfast nook, and a clean kitchen.

"Let me give you a quick tour," he says, motioning for me to follow. He takes me down the hall and shows me the bathroom —nice enough.

Further down the hall, he opens the door to a bedroom. "This is my room. I can take the couch, or if you'd rather, I can find you a guest room in the main house," he offers politely, almost too polite.

I cross my arms, raising an eyebrow. "You're saying you'd rather be uncomfortable than share a bed with me? Wow, Malachi. That's a real blow to my ego."

He lets out a low chuckle, leaning against the doorframe.

"Oh, don't worry, demon. It's not you. I assumed you'd want your own space. You know, considering how much you dislike me most of the time."

I glance past him into the room raising an eyebrow. "What about Lana? She seemed pretty cozy with you at the party. Won't she be upset when she hears you're bunking with another woman for weeks?"

His jaw tightens slightly, but the flash of annoyance is quickly replaced by amusement. "There's nothing going on with Lana. Or here for that matter. So no one has anything to worry about."

I step into the room, spinning to face him with a sly grin. "Nothing going on here, huh? You sure about that? I mean, what if I sleepwalk and accidentally end up on your side of the bed? Or worse, snore so loudly it drives you crazy?"

He smirks, leaning into the doorway. "I'll risk it. But if you drool on me like last time, all bets are off."

Heat rushes to my face, and I point a finger at him. "I do not drool!"

Oh God, I did drool.

"You definitely do. But it's not the worst thing. You're cute when you sleep," he says, and I can't tell if he's teasing or serious.

I huff and turn to the window, looking out to see the view. I can see the stables in the distance, and the large icicles hanging off the edge of the roof sparkling in the sunlight that's trying hard to peek through the clouds.

"I guess this'll work," I finally say, glancing back at him over my shoulder.

"Good," he says, the earlier tension gone. "Because it looks like you're stuck with me, Kat. At least for a fortnight."

I sit on the edge of the bed, sinking into the fluffy covers that practically swallow me. "Are you going to fill me in on what's going on here?" I ask, watching him as he fiddles with the straps on one of the bags.

He looks up, brow furrowed. "What do you mean?"

I roll my eyes, gesturing around us. "You live with Marco's sister. How does that work? Is she..." I pause, unsure how to put it.

"Is she like him?" he finishes for me, a faint smile tugging at the corner of his mouth. "No, she's not like the rest of our family. She's great—you're going to love her."

Something about his easy answer doesn't sit right with me, and a quiet unease starts to creep into my chest. "Great," I say slowly, though I'm not convinced. "I guess I'll take your word for it."

Malachi shifts his weight, his expression turning thoughtful. "Look, there's a lot I could tell you, but it'll all make way more sense if I show you."

"Show me what?" I press, my patience already thinning.

He grins, like he knows how much this is driving me insane. "Let's start with a cup of coffee. We'll catch up with my aunt, and then I'll take you to see the real operation."

He's being coy, and it's irritating as hell. "You could tell me now," I mutter, crossing my arms.

"And ruin the surprise?" He tilts his head, a knowing smirk tugging at his lips. "Trust me, it's worth the wait."

I huff but stand anyway. "Fine, but this coffee better be life-changing if you're making me wait for answers."

He chuckles, heading for the door. "Oh, you're in for way more than coffee."

THE HOUSE IS warm and inviting when we return, the scent

of freshly brewed coffee filling the air as we settle down by one of the fireplaces, warm mugs in hand.

"My brothers...we've never agreed on what it means to lead, let alone how to treat people. Malachi found his way here because he understands something my father and brothers never could—power doesn't have to mean cruelty," Irina says, her voice even but weighted with history.

She takes a slow sip from her mug, glancing between me and Malachi like she's trying to measure how much to share.

"I used to come here every summer as a kid," Malachi adds, leaning back in his chair, his expression softening with the memory. "Gary and Orin came too, at first. Back then, this place felt like freedom. But once they started buying into my father's way of thinking, they stopped coming. That's when things changed. We were close once."

He pauses, a shadow crossing his face. "Eventually, I begged my father to let me stay here. He figured I was too much of a disappointment at home and hoped my aunt could knock some sense into me." His lips quirk in a faint smile, but it doesn't reach his eyes.

"Little does he know..." Irina murmurs with a soft, wry laugh.

I try to piece together this family dynamic that feels both alien and too close to home. "So you help Malachi save people like me?" I ask, leaning forward. "And there's an entire organization behind this?"

Irina places her mug down, folding her hands over her lap, her gaze steady. "The Syndicate," she says. "That's who we are. Yes, we help Avids who have been trafficked. We find them, free them, and give them a safe place to rebuild their lives. But that's only part of what we do. The families—the ones like my brothers'—they're trying to keep the world in chains, ruling through fear, control, and violence. We're fighting to break that system."

"You're fighting the families? To what end?" I ask, still trying to untangle the enormity of what she's saying.

"We want to restore democracy," Irina says. "A government of the people, by the people—like what existed before humanity burned the world to the ground. We want to dismantle the districts and strip the ruling families of their power. The world needs more than tyrants hoarding what's left of it. It needs hope."

I lean back, the idea sparking something deep in my chest. "Democracy. I remember learning about that in school, but it always felt, I don't know, like a fairy tale or propaganda. Something unattainable."

"It's not unattainable. The Syndicate has scientists and strategists working tirelessly. We're on the cusp of breakthroughs that could level the playing field. What my brothers—and others like them—fear most is losing control. That's exactly what we're planning to take from them."

What she says swirls in my mind, part of me wanting to believe it possible, part of me hesitating. "And, Malachi, where do you fit into this grand plan?"

He straightens in his seat, raising his eyebrows and exhaling. "What I do is...more specialized. My team and I handle the dirtier side of things. We infiltrate operations, gather intel, extract Avids, and remove threats when necessary. Call it deep-cover work, if you like. The Syndicate handles the big picture. We're the scalpel they use to cut out the rot."

"So you're like a special task force," I say, starting to see the picture more clearly.

"Yes," he says, his gaze steady. "We call ourselves Solace."

"Solace," I repeat. It feels almost too peaceful, too clean for what he's describing, but then again I did call him the savior. The thought makes me want to laugh, but I refrain.

"You're wondering why we'd choose something so...gentle sounding," he says, catching my expression. "It's not about being intimidating. Solace is what we offer the people we save. A way out. A second chance."

"And how many members does the Syndicate have? And Solace?" I ask, trying to strike a balance between curiosity and caution, testing how much they're willing to reveal.

Irina sets her mug down and leans back slightly, considering her answer. "That's where things get a little complicated," she says with some discomfort. "We have numbers in the hundreds but not thousands. It's a tightrope to balance. We want as many people as possible working toward the cause, but every new member is a risk. If the wrong person joins us, it could mean the end of everything we've built."

I nod, digesting that. It makes sense, but it also makes me wonder how they've kept this network hidden for so long.

Irina stands, smoothing down her sweater. "I still have a lot of work to do today, but something tells me you'll have more questions for me later." She smiles warmly, but something about it leaves me unsettled.

"Why do you say that?" I ask, setting my empty mug on the table and rising to my feet.

"You'll see," she says, a knowing glint in her eye before she collects our mugs and disappears into the kitchen.

I glance at Malachi, crossing my arms. "Well, that was...cryptic. I don't think I've ever been told so much information so openly and yet still felt like I'm missing something huge. What's with all the mystery?"

Malachi shrugs, an amused smile tugging at his lips. "It's better if I show you. You'll understand why it's not something we can explain once you see it for yourself."

"What are you going to show me?"

He tilts his head toward the door. "Get your coat. You'll see soon enough."

Chapter Sixteen

RULE 16 OF THE NEW ORDER: LIFE IS
UNPREDICTABLE. IT CAN SHIFT IN THE BLINK OF AN
EYE, NOT ONCE BUT OVER AND OVER AGAIN.

"TRACT HOUSES? You brought me to a neighborhood in the middle of nowhere where every house looks the same?" I ask skeptically as we stand outside one of the beige-painted homes.

"You don't miss a thing, do you? I always imagined demons were supposed to be clever, but I guess all the brains are reserved for the devil." Malachi smirks, and I punch him in the arm.

"Very funny," I mutter, following him up the path to the front door. He doesn't bother knocking and lets himself in, and my suspicion flares.

"Do you always break into houses, or is this a special occasion?" I ask, stepping into a space that looks almost too perfect. The house is clean and orderly—simple furniture, neutral tones, not a personal touch in sight.

"Relax. This is one of ours." He's already moving, leading me down the hall to a large living room. As I look around, I can't shake the sterile feeling of the place. It's livable but devoid of life.

Malachi approaches a built-in bookshelf on the far wall and tugs on one of the books. The entire shelf swings open, revealing a hidden passageway.

"Okay, really? That's not predictable or anything. You know how many books I've read with secret bookshelves?" I say, crossing my arms even as my inner nerd fights not to fangirl over the sheer coolness of it.

"Yeah, we're all clichés here," he says, rolling his eyes. "Not everyone can be an endlessly clever demon." He steps into the dimly lit corridor beyond the bookshelf, his footsteps echoing faintly as he approaches a set of double doors.

He presses a button, and the doors slide open, revealing an elevator. Without hesitation, he steps inside and waves for me to follow. I glance back at the slowly closing bookshelf, and those intrusive, self-preservation instincts kick in.

This is how nightmares begin...

"Well?" Malachi raises an eyebrow. With a deep breath, I step into the elevator.

"Okay, let's recap," I say as the doors slide shut. "Secret bookshelf, creepy hallway, hidden elevator in the middle of a too-quiet neighborhood. So tell me—are you a serial killer, or is this a cult?"

He grins.

The elevator doors slide open with a soft hiss, and I step out into another world—one that leaves me momentarily breathless.

The first thing I notice is the light. It isn't harsh or fluorescent like I'd expect in an underground bunker. Instead, it's a warm, ethereal glow emanating from crystalline fixtures embedded into the walls, ceilings, and even the floors. They cast a soft shimmer that dances across the vast expanse before me. The space is massive, and as I take another step forward, the enormity of it hits me.

The floor stretches out in a sprawling circular pattern, tiered like a grand amphitheater. Each level is lined with laboratories, rooms, and what I can only describe as workshops, their windows glowing faintly with different colors depending on what's inside. Some pulse with blue, others with gold, and a few with vibrant greens and reds, making the entire place feel alive.

The center of the space is open, plunging deep into what seems like an endless abyss below. Far above, I catch a glimpse of other levels spiraling upward, their occupants mere specks bustling about. A massive chandelier-like structure hangs in the open space, its tendrils dripping down like frozen waterfalls made of light. It's mesmerizing and overwhelming all at once.

To my left, there's a railing looking out over an atrium, allowing us to see many levels above and below ours.

To my right, long glass panels reveal people in lab coats working. Inside one room, a man has his hands pressed to a sphere of glowing liquid, the energy arcing around him like lightning. In another, someone examines a floating object—a dagger suspended midair that seems to hum with power. The halls themselves are like arteries, stretching outward in every direction, connecting this vast labyrinth.

Above and below, balconies wrap around the open center, where I can see people walking, talking, and working. I assume some must be Avids and others part of The Syndicate, some wearing lab coats, others carrying books. There's a hum of activity, a low buzz of machinery, and the sound of faint laughter and conversation echoing across the cavernous space.

The air is warmer than I expected, and it carries the faint scent of ozone, like the moments before a storm. There's something vibrant and alive about this place, a stark contrast to the stillness above.

I turn to Malachi, who watches me with a small smile, clearly enjoying my reaction. "This is the Depths," he says.

I take a slow, deep breath, marveling at everything in front of me. The possibilities. The secrets. The sheer magnitude of it all. What the hell have I gotten myself into?

"I thought you were going to be away a lot longer this time."

A voice rings out from behind us, smooth and warm, and I turn to see a man with tan skin, a mop of curly black hair, and the most extraordinary blue eyes. He looks like he stepped out of a painting, all charm and confidence.

"You know I can't stay away from this place for long," Malachi replies as he steps forward to embrace the man. It's a quick, familiar hug, and I take a moment to size up the newcomer. He's no boy, despite the youthful energy radiating from him. Late twenties, maybe pushing thirty.

"This is Kat," Malachi says, motioning toward me. "I'm showing her the Depths for the first time."

The man turns his attention to me, his smile easy and disarming. "Sebastian," he says, extending a hand. "But everyone around here calls me Bash."

I shake his hand, offering a small smile of my own. "Nice to meet you, Bash."

He pats Malachi on the back, and there's an unmistakable camaraderie between them. Bash glances at me, his grin widening. "I'll tag along for the tour. I'm better at explaining all the scientific stuff anyway. Malachi here struggles with anything outside of combat."

"Combat, huh?" I glance over at Malachi, raising an eyebrow.

Malachi turns a shade pinker. "Ignore him," he mutters, waving Bash off.

"Oh, it's true," Bash says, chuckling. "Anyone joining

Solace has to pass Malachi's training before he'll let them on the team. It's basically a rite of passage."

I can't help but smirk. "Good to know. I'll keep that in mind."

"Alright," Malachi cuts in, clearly eager to change the subject. "Why don't you lead the way?"

Bash moves to the other side of me, grinning like he's won some unspoken game, and I find myself flanked by the two of them as we start walking.

"The level we're on right now," Bash begins, "is all about discovery. We've got some of the best scientists—including yours truly—working on ways to make Avids stronger, harness the power we have, and improve conditions up above. Take Atlas, for example. He's a genius botanist a couple of levels down, working on altering plants to thrive in the harsh climates topside."

I pause in front of one of the windows, peering inside. The equipment is impressive, intricate, and completely incomprehensible to me. My reflection stares back, a mix of curiosity and wariness.

"Make Avids stronger? Power we have?" I glance at Bash, realization dawning. "You're an Avid?"

Bash stops, turning to face me fully, that ever-present grin softening into something almost proud. "Sure am. And don't let this charming demeanor fool you. I'm more useful than I look." He winks.

"Wait—how did you know about me?" I ask, narrowing my eyes slightly.

Bash grins, the picture of casual charm. "Ran into Irina before meeting you. She told me Malachi was bringing someone back. She mentioned you had the gift but didn't get into specifics. Word travels fast down here, especially when Malachi brings home a guest."

Malachi groans, "I'll have to thank Irina later."

I follow them down the hallway as we pass an array of rooms bustling with activity—labs humming with energy, a dining hall full of chatter, and various stations filled with people absorbed in their work. It's organized chaos, fascinating and overwhelming all at once. Eventually, we reach another elevator at the far end of the corridor.

As we step inside, Malachi hits a button, and the elevator begins its descent. The hum of motion combined with the faint sounds from the floors above has my mind wandering. How did they build all this down here? It's insane.

"This is the training level. Physical training, that is," Bash announces as the elevator doors slide open, revealing a noisy, chaotic scene.

The sounds of boxing gloves meeting punching bags and loud, encouraging yells echo through the cavernous space. We step out, and I take in the sight of a giant gymnasium. Bleacher-style seating lines the walls, and four makeshift rings dominate the center, each one occupied by people sparring or practicing. The air buzzes with adrenaline.

"These are the rings where people can practice," Malachi explains, leading us inside. The energy in the room is palpable, and I find myself drawn to the crowd gathered around each ring. Most of the faces are young, some teenagers, while others look closer to my age. Everyone's animated, eyes alight with either excitement or focus.

"Mal, I'm so glad you're back! You have to see Alex and Nasha. I think they might be ready for Solace," someone calls out, and I turn to see a petite woman with striking purple hair pulled into a long ponytail weaving toward us.

"This is Rain. She and I run the only two Solace teams," Malachi says.

"Nice to meet you. I'm Kat." I extend a hand, and she

shakes it with a grip so firm it nearly makes me wince. She may be small, but there's nothing weak about her.

"Kat," she repeats, sizing me up with a critical eye, "you could use some training. No offense, but it doesn't look like you've got a strong right hook, especially not after that handshake."

I force a smile. "It's cute how your mouth does all the fighting for you."

Bitch.

"Don't listen to Rain," Bash interjects before Rain has a chance to say anything else. "All she cares about is being fit. Rain, leave the poor girl alone—she's seeing the Depths for the first time. This is all new to her."

Rain smirks, unbothered. "New or not, we can't have weak links, Bash. That's all I'm saying."

Malachi clears his throat. "We'll see about training later. For now, we're here to give Kat the lay of the land, and I happen to know first hand her right hook isn't that bad."

Rain shrugs, her ponytail swinging as she steps aside. "Fine. But when you're ready, come find me. Everyone starts some-where." She points at the closest ring, where two fighters are trading rapid blows. "Including them."

I glance at the fighters, noting their intensity. I'd love to take her into the ring right now and show everyone here some-thing they don't expect. She thinks she's hot shit, but I'm pretty sure I could take her. For now, I follow Malachi and Bash as we move deeper into the gym and out the door on the other side.

"Okay, I want her to see Atlas's garden first. Then she needs to see your lab," Malachi says, and Bash nods, already leading the way down a spiral staircase.

"Who built all this?" I ask, trailing after them. "I mean, it's incredible, but how did you guys manage something like this?"

Bash glances back. "The government built plenty of these silos back in the day—safe from the elements, even radiation. But this one? It's a whole other level. Fancy as hell, right? Some eccentric billionaire with too much money and a wild imagination."

Malachi rolls his eyes, nudging me lightly. "Don't listen to him. This place was a wreck when we found it. It's taken years for Irina to turn it into what it is now. Every new member who joins the cause brings something to the table, whether that's engineering, design, or sheer determination. It's a constant work in progress, but it gets better every year."

We reach the bottom of the staircase, and Bash pushes a heavy door open. Instantly, a burst of cold white smoke billows around us, hissing like steam. I instinctively jump back, grabbing Malachi's arm.

"It's alright," Malachi says, steadying me. His hand lingers long enough to make me feel even more self-conscious. "This is the cleaning room. Atlas is...particular about keeping contaminants out of his garden."

I let go of him quickly, trying to ignore the rising embarrassment. *Get a grip, Kat.*

"Alright, time for the enchanted forest," Bash announces with dramatic flair, shoving open a mirrored glass door.

"Enchanted forest?" I mumble, stepping forward hesitantly.

"Bash likes to name everything," Malachi says, shaking his head.

When I step inside, my breath catches in my throat.

The ground isn't a sterile floor but a carpet of vibrant green moss and soft grass that cushions every step. Massive, ancient-looking trees stretch skyward—or at least as far as the high ceiling allows—draped in vines that shimmer faintly as if laced with starlight. Exotic flowers in every color imaginable bloom along the edges of a crystal-clear pond, their petals in blues, purples, and golds.

Butterflies—no, not butterflies, something more magical with wings that sparkle like shards of glass—flutter lazily through the air. Small streams meander through the garden, their water so clear it's almost invisible, except for the soft light refracted in rippling patterns. The air smells of earth, sweet blossoms, and something indescribable, like magic itself.

"How is this possible?" I gasp, mesmerized.

"Atlas," Bash says, gesturing grandly. "The guy's a genius. He's blended botany and Avid abilities in ways no one else has even dreamed of."

Malachi watches me with a faint smile. "It's why we call him Gardener. He can make things grow anywhere, no matter the conditions. Everything here thrives because of his magic—and his science."

"This is far beyond anything I imagined," I murmur, slowly stepping forward, my fingers brushing over a glowing vine. "It's like stepping into a dream."

"And this is the beginning," Malachi says, motioning for me to follow them. "Wait until you see what comes next."

"You mean there's more?" I say, throwing my arms up dramatically to encompass the magical garden surrounding us. The sheer scale of it all already feels impossible, like something out of a storybook.

Malachi's lips twitch, a small smile breaking through.

We pass through another sterilizing chamber, the cool mist enveloping us before we step out into the main hall again. Malachi stops abruptly, turning to me. "Go with Bash to his lab. Pick his brain—he loves questions and showing off. I have a few things I need to take care of, but I'll find you afterward."

I nod, glancing at Bash, who immediately slings an arm around my shoulders. The casual gesture catches me off guard, and I go stiff for a second before reluctantly starting to walk with him.

Out of the corner of my eye, I catch Malachi's smirk as he turns and heads off in the opposite direction.

"Relax. I don't bite—hard," Bash quips, his grin teasing as he steers me toward a set of sleek, silver double doors. "You're in for a treat. My lab is where the real magic happens."

Chapter Seventeen

RULE 17 OF THE NEW ORDER: POWER IN EXCESS, EVEN WITH GOOD INTENTIONS, BREEDS UNINTENDED CONSEQUENCES.

"WHAT IS YOUR ABILITY?" I ask Bash, leaning back into one of the wheeled chairs scattered around his lab. The room itself feels like a futuristic hospital—a pristine maze of white walls, glowing screens, and complex machines performing functions that are completely beyond me. The air smells faintly sterilized, like alcohol wipes.

"Bioelectric tuning," he says casually, and I blink at him, doing a double take.

"Uh...you're gonna have to break that down for me. What does that mean?"

Bash grins and swivels his chair closer, his elbows resting on his knees. "You know how all living beings have electrical signals running through them?" he starts, and I nod slowly, not entirely sure where this is going. "Well, those signals? They're like music to me. Avids—especially Avids—have their own frequency, a unique bioelectric signature. I can hear it, feel it, manipulate it. It's like tuning into a specific radio station."

I tilt my head, intrigued despite myself. "So what can you actually do with it?"

His grin widens, and he raises his hand. Faint blue static crackles between his fingers, like a miniature storm dancing across his skin. "A lot. I can stabilize someone's vitals, keep them alive until a healer steps in. I can track an Avid by their unique frequency. I can mess with power grids or short-circuit machines. And I can amplify an Avid's power for a short time. Make them stronger, faster, more... potent."

I straighten in my chair, alarmed but also intrigued. "Wait, how do you even do that?"

"Every Avid has a bioelectric signature," Bash explains. "Think of it like a fingerprint, but for their powers. My gift lets me tap into that frequency and amplify it. But that's not the most interesting part." He stands and strides toward a long cylindrical machine in the corner of the lab, gesturing for me to follow.

Curiosity gets the better of me, and I trail after him. "What does this do?" I ask, watching as he presses a few glowing buttons on its sleek surface.

"This," he says, patting the machine fondly, "is something I built to work in tandem with my gift. It's like an amplifier for the signals I sense, but it does more than that. It turns those signals into something tangible."

I watch him walk over to a wall of white cabinets and refrigerators opening one, pulling out a small orb that glimmers faintly in his palm. He tosses it toward me, and I scramble to catch it, nearly dropping it in my lap.

On closer inspection, the orb is mesmerizing. It looks alive —an ever-shifting swirl of stars, galaxies, and structures unfathomable, like the night sky captured only brighter and condensed into a bottle. I hold it up to the light, and the swirling contents shimmer, almost like they're responding to my movements.

"Do you like it?" Bash asks, proud.

I can't tear my eyes away. "What... What is it?"

He takes a moment, letting the suspense hang before finally saying, "I call it Avidian."

"Avidian," I repeat. "Clever. What does it do?"

Bash steps closer, taking the orb from my hands. "With my gift and this machine, I've learned how to extract the essence from Avids—the very core of their powers—and make it tangible. It's pure, concentrated essence."

I stare at him, a chill creeping up my spine. "You're telling me that's what our power looks like after you...extract it?" My eyes widen slightly, caught between fascination and horror.

"Precisely," Bash says, unflinching. "It's not just power in its raw form—it's potential. Bottled and ready to be used by anyone."

"Used?" My stomach twists. "You mean someone can take this and...borrow our abilities?"

Bash nods, his expression turning serious. "That's the idea. A single inhale, and someone could temporarily wield the power of the Avid it came from."

I take a step back, the implications hitting me all at once. "And who decided that was a good idea?"

Bash shrugs, his easy charm momentarily dimmed. "The world isn't kind to Avids, Kat. We've been exploited for generations. This could make a huge difference. For a little while, at least."

I look at the orb again, its swirling contents almost hypnotic. Beautiful and dangerous all at once.

"What happens to the Avid after you take their power from them?" I ask, even though I'm not sure I want to know the answer. My fingers fidget against my leg, bracing for something awful.

Bash shakes his head quickly, his expression softening. "No, Kat, it's not like that. I can't take their power. An Avid's gift is part of who they are—it's constantly evolving, replenishing itself. It's not something you can completely remove, even if you wanted to."

I narrow my eyes, studying his face for any sign of deception. "So you take a piece of it? And the Avid feels nothing?"

He exhales, leaning back against the counter. "The process is painless. They don't lose anything, and their power isn't weakened in any way. It's like drawing a drop of blood for a test—what I extract is so small that they'd never notice it was gone. And because their essence is tied to their bioelectric field, it regenerates naturally. The only symptom I've seen is fatigue for a few hours, as if you used too much power."

I bite the inside of my cheek, my gaze dropping to the orb in his hand. "And what about me? If you put me in that machine, what would it pull from me?"

Bash tilts his head, his sharp blue eyes studying me with an intensity that makes me feel exposed. "Irina mentioned you can see the dead. Is that true?"

I gulp, hesitating for a moment before nodding. "Yes, but it's not like I see dead people walking around all day. I have to will it—and sometimes I have to cross the veil," I explain, giving him the short version.

"It'd pull the essence of your gift," Bash says, his tone thoughtful, almost reverent. "Your connection to the dead, the way you see and interact with spirits. It'd be pure and raw, like capturing a piece of the veil itself. And if someone used it, they'd see the dead too, for a little while."

The idea is unnerving, cold and unwelcome. "That sounds horrifying."

"Or incredible," Bash counters, his lips quirking into a faint grin. "Depends on how you look at it."

I scoff, shaking my head. "You really are a scientist through and through, aren't you? Always looking for the potential, not the consequences."

Bash chuckles, spinning the orb between his fingers like it's a toy instead of the bottled essence of someone's power. "Can't blame me for being curious. Curiosity's what got us this far, after all."

"I guess so." I cross my arms as the weight of the situation settles on me. "So how effective is this stuff? How long does it last? Can an Avid use another Avid's power, or is this something for regular people?"

Bash's grin widens. He clearly loves questions—or being the one with all the answers. "This orb is the largest quantity we keep. If you inhaled it all, it'd last a good twelve to twenty-four hours. But in the field, something like this would be way too bulky to carry. We collect smaller vials instead. A vial typically lasts about thirty minutes—enough to get the job done."

My mind races, piecing together the implications. "So you're already using these when you go undercover? Solace is using them? Malachi has these vials?" The thought of Malachi keeping this from me rankles, even though I know he doesn't owe me every secret. Still, this is a lot to drop on someone all at once.

"No, not yet," Bash says, shaking his head. "It's still being tested. Atlas has used it in his garden, and we've been trialing it in controlled environments, but we haven't taken it out into the real world. It's risky, because in the wrong hands..." He grimaces.

"Oh, so you do think about the consequences," I say, a little too smug. "But they don't stop you from playing god."

His grin fades, replaced by a more serious expression. "We're careful," he says firmly. "But this could give us an edge. We want to take down the Volkov family—yes—but they're only one family. There are dozens more leading this country into the ground. The districts are suffocating, Kat. People are suffering. And I don't see another way forward."

I fall silent.

My world under Marco's thumb suddenly feels so much smaller, more isolated. I'd ignored the chaos outside, pretending it wasn't my problem. But now it's impossible to ignore.

How will I ever go back after seeing all of this?

"HOW ARE YOU FEELING? You look like you've got a lot on your mind," Malachi says from across the table, his eyes studying me like he's trying to gauge the weight of the day on my shoulders.

After leaving the Depths, we picked up takeout for dinner, and now I'm cozied up in the booth side of the breakfast nook, savoring chicken tacos. I glance at him between bites, considering my answer.

"I'd say that's an understatement," I reply with a smirk. "But I'm okay. Hopeful. Maybe. I dunno—anxious?" I say.

"Yeah, that's understandable," he says, nodding as he digs into one of his steak tacos. Silence falls between us, the comfortable kind that settles when you're both too focused on food to fill the air with small talk.

Then my thoughts overflow. "What do you see happening? I mean, what's going to happen when Marco's ready for me? Is he going to try to come here? Will he want you to bring me back? And...how am I supposed to go back to living like that after seeing all of this?"

I drop my taco onto the plate, suddenly not as hungry.

Malachi leans back, his expression thoughtful. "I don't think he'll come here, but it's possible. Either way, it doesn't matter. Everything here is hidden. He doesn't know about the

Depths, and he thinks Irina is running a ranch and living in peace like she's always wanted. He has no idea what's actually going on right under his nose."

His gaze softens as it locks with mine, "I told you I'd free you, and I'm going to. My father's days are numbered, Kat. When he comes—or when he summons you—we'll be ready to handle him."

My heart twists at the certainty in his voice. It feels like hope, like someone's taken the impossible and cracked it open enough to see light shining through. But his assurance only stirs more questions.

"I still need to finish the case," I say, almost expecting him to argue against it, to tell me it's too dangerous or unnecessary now.

"Agreed," he says, surprising me. "We'll want Viktor to stay ignorant of everything, so we have to play along for now. And Marco may still expect updates from you."

I nod, taking another bite of my taco, even though the food tastes dull compared to the storm of thoughts whirling in my head. There's so much to process, so much I want to ask, but I focus on one truth: for the first time in years, I'm not entirely alone in this fight.

"So, Mal," I say, popping a chip into my mouth and swirling another in salsa, "what did you do today when you disappeared for so long?"

He looks up from his plate, his mouth twitching like he's holding back a grin. "You caught that, huh?"

"Of course," I say, smirking. "I notice everything. By the way, I've decided 'Savior' is a much better nickname. It's more fitting, especially now that I know your team is called fucking Solace." I lean forward. "Speaking of names, what's the deal with you and Rain? You say there's nothing going on with Lana, but what about Rain? She seemed awfully comfortable calling you 'Mal.' Is that her pet name for you?"

Malachi's eyes widen, but a chuckle escapes him anyway. "She's called me Mal forever. And there's nothing going on there either. We're friends. She's a hell of a fighter though. You should train with her sometime."

I mull that over for a second, dipping another chip. "I'll consider it, but that still doesn't answer my question. What were you actually up to?"

He shakes his head, leaning back in his seat with a look that says you're relentless. "I had to call my team back in the Eastern District to check in. I wanted to make sure everything's going smoothly with the two Avids we saved and see if they've picked up anything unusual while surveilling Viktor's place."

That grabs my full attention. "Is Aurora alright? Did they say anything's going on at Viktor's?"

"Your friend's fine," he assures me. "Better than fine, now that she's out of that hellhole. As for Viktor's place, they said there's been a lot of people coming and going but no one they recognize yet. They must be interrogating suspects or gearing up to retaliate against whoever they think broke in."

I sit back in my chair, exhaling a breath I didn't realize I'd been holding. "I'm glad we're not there anymore. It's nice to talk freely here...and breathe. No shadows hovering."

Malachi quirks a brow. "I'm not sure if I should take offense to that. Technically, I'm close by all the time now. Does that count as hovering?"

I glance at him, my lips curving into a small smile. "No, it doesn't feel suffocating like before. It's different. I can't explain it, but I'm starting to enjoy your company."

He doesn't say anything at first but watches me with those unreadable eyes. Finally, he smirks, reaching for another taco. "Careful, you're starting to sound like you actually like me."

I roll my eyes, shaking my head as I take another bite. "Don't push it, Savior."

"Now that nickname has to go," Malachi says, laughing harder, and I can't help but join him. It is ridiculous, but I like it.

Maybe a little too much.

I tuck the thought away, letting the laughter fade naturally. "I kind of like 'Mal' too," I tease. "Maybe I'll use them both."

He shakes his head, grinning. "You're incorrigible."

"What's your plan for after dinner?" I ask, noticing we're both nearly finished with our food. I have no idea what his evening routine looks like—or if he even has one.

"That all depends on what you're doing," he says, his eyes questioning.

I narrow my gaze playfully. "Remember when I told you about projecting and how I'll probably have to do it to get through to Carmen and Damien? I think I'm going to try it before bed."

His expression shifts immediately. "Then I'm staying to supervise this. Marco told me how it usually goes when you project—he said he has to carry you to bed afterward."

I tug my bottom lip into my mouth, suddenly feeling awkward for reasons I can't quite pin down. "Yeah, it can make me really tired—like dead-to-the-world tired—but I'm going to test the waters tonight. I won't be out long, so I'm hoping it won't be too bad."

He nods, getting up to clear the plates. "Alright, but don't push it."

I head to the bedroom to change into my pajamas, moving quickly so he doesn't think he'll need to help with that later. Not that I'd let him, but still. The thought makes my cheeks warm.

Once I'm dressed, I start pacing the room, my nerves building. It's been a while since I've done this, and no matter how many times I project, the anxiety always lingers. There's something about willingly stepping into the veil—a world that feels as if it's constantly shifting, always watching—that makes my stomach twist.

For a brief second, I wish Bash were here. Maybe he really could experiment on me, figure out a way to make me stronger, more resilient. Maybe even take away the exhaustion afterward.

Malachi knocks lightly on the door. "Are you going to do it in the bedroom? Or does it not matter where you are?" he asks, and I pull the door open and walk out. "You don't care if the ghosts see you in tiny pink pajamas?"

I roll my eyes. "It doesn't matter where I am or what I'm wearing. I figured I'd try in here since it's closer to the bed."

He moves to one of the leather chairs at the foot of the bed and takes a seat, stretching out like he plans to settle in for the show. His attention is fully on me, making the whole situation even more awkward. Great. Last thing I need is an audience.

"You look nervous," he says, his brows pulling together. "Is this dangerous? Maybe you shouldn't do it."

I force a smile, though my nerves are real. "I'll be fine. But whatever you do, don't interrupt me. I won't be able to respond until I'm done."

He rubs his chin thoughtfully, the faint shadow of stubble making him look more serious. "I won't interrupt, but I'm here if anything goes wrong."

Nothing's going to go wrong.

But his concern doesn't help the knot forming in my stomach. Taking a deep breath, I nod and step toward the bed. "Alright. Let's do this."

I cross my arms over my chest, close my eyes, and take a few steadying breaths. Malachi, thankfully, remains silent. I try to pretend he's not sitting there, probably staring at me like a hawk. The thought almost breaks my concentration, but I refocus, imagining the veil—the thin, intangible wall between space and time.

I force my mind through it.

When I open my eyes, the world has shifted. The room is dim and shadowy, like all the color and warmth have been sucked out of it. I glance back and see my body still seated on the bed, arms crossed, chest rising and falling slowly as if I were simply meditating. Malachi sits in the chair, his posture tense, eyes locked on me—or rather on my physical body. His intensity hasn't changed, and seeing him like that, unaware of my presence, is both unsettling and grounding.

The temperature plummets suddenly, the air turning icy and thin, and I shiver. A soundless vibration ripples through the space, a low hum I feel more than hear. Then the room begins to change around me, the walls stretching, melting, twisting like ink spreading across water. I know I've crossed over.

The veil has opened.

Chapter Eighteen

RULE 18 OF THE NEW ORDER: THE VEIL BETWEEN
WORLDS IS THINNER THAN YOU THINK. STEP
LIGHTLY, OR YOU MAY FALL THROUGH.

"ALRIGHT, Damien, you like to play games. I'm here now—come play with me." My voice echoes into the abyss, taunting him because I know he won't be able to resist.

The darkness around me feels alive, almost tangible, and when I glance back, I see Malachi's bedroom glowing faintly in the void, like a beacon of warmth in a cold, forsaken world. It's strange—like peering through a foggy window at another life. I can still see us there, Malachi watching over my lifeless body, his expression unreadable.

But out here, in the veil, everything is different.

I turn away, facing the expanse of what has melded from darkness into what looks like the forest outside Viktor's compound. The snow-covered ground and skeletal trees are familiar but twisted. The snow doesn't crunch beneath my feet. It's eerily silent, and when I reach out to touch a tree, my hand sinks into its bark—it feels warm, slimy, and wrong, as if the tree is breathing.

When I project, the world bends to the will of the spirit I'm calling. It's always unpredictable, always unsteady, and now I know either Damien or Carmen has brought me here. The question is who.

A breeze stirs, light but unnatural, carrying a faint whistle that snakes through the trees. It whispers, "Here, Kitty Kat." I roll my eyes. Of course.

"Don't you think it would be better if you showed yourself, Damien? We could talk face-to-face, save us both some time," I say, crossing my arms as I scan the shadows.

The air shifts. The sensation of being watched creeps down my spine, raising the hairs on the back of my neck. My breath hitches as I catch something in the distance—a figure, dark and jagged, peeking out from behind a tree. Or maybe it's the tree itself. No. It moves, slipping out of sight before I can focus.

"What's the matter?" I call out. "Are you afraid of me?"

Then, all at once, his voice is there. Too close. Right against my ear, soft but sharp enough to cut. "To what do I owe the pleasure of your visit?"

I whip around, stumbling back as my heart races. Damien stands there, grinning, his dark eyes gleaming with something too sinister to be amusement.

"Miss me?" His voice drips with mockery, and his form glitches, like static on a broken screen. One moment he's whole, the next he flickers, jagged edges melting into shadows before snapping back together. His body doesn't move like it should— too fluid, too unnatural.

"You brought me here, Damien. Let's not pretend you didn't want this." I steady my breathing, locking eyes with him.

His grin widens, showing too many teeth. "Oh, Kat, I didn't want this. I needed it. You're far too much fun to ignore, especially now that you've seen the intriguing depths beneath my father's house."

My stomach tightens. He knows. Of course, he knows.

"Is that why you're haunting me?" I ask, forcing a smirk.

"Daddy issues? Trying to screw over Viktor from beyond the grave?"

Damien's laugh echoes, the sound bouncing unnaturally through the trees. "Sweetheart, my issues go way beyond Daddy dearest. But this is...a little personal." He steps closer, and I fight the urge to retreat.

"Yeah, I can tell you're pretty fucked up. I can only imagine what you were like when you were alive," I say steadily despite the unease crawling over me. "Why were you with Carmen that night? I heard she had a boyfriend, and it wasn't you."

Damien's grin sharpens, and he tilts his head, a look of sick amusement plastered across his face. "That little whore was playing me. I was playing her too, but I'll admit—I didn't see her coming." He lets out a low chuckle, the sound echoing unnaturally around us. "She's smarter than I gave her credit for, but not smart enough to stay alive. Clearly."

He starts circling me slowly, his steps soundless on the snow that isn't really snow. His gaze pierces me, dark and predatory, like he's savoring the thought of whatever game he's about to play.

"Why don't you tell me who killed you?" I ask, refusing to let him see how much he's unsettling me. "I'll figure it out eventually. You know that, right?"

Damien stops in front of me, leaning in close enough for me to feel the icy energy radiating off him. "Oh, I know you'll figure it out. That's what you do, isn't it? Little Katja, solving puzzles and crossing veils. But where's the fun in making it easy for you?" He sighs, his form flickering in the dark fog around us. "No, no, no. You'll have to work for this one."

I clench my jaw, frustrated. "You're scared," I say, taking a step closer to him. "Scared to face the truth. Scared to admit who got the better of you."

His expression darkens, the grin fading into something

colder, more menacing. "Scared? Oh, Kitty Kat." He leans in. "I'm dead. There's nothing left to be scared of. But you? You're still breathing. Still vulnerable. Still playing in a world you barely understand."

He straightens, his grin returning as he takes a slow step back. "I'll give you a little hint, because I'm feeling generous." He lifts a hand, gesturing vaguely to the shadows around us. "The truth isn't hiding where you think it is. And Carmen? She's not the only one who played you. Better keep your eyes open, little kitty. The answers you seek may be closer than you think."

My irritation boils over. "Fuck you, Damien, and fuck your games. No wonder your father couldn't stand you. He didn't even care when you died and threw a fucking party days later while your blood was still on the walls upstairs. He drank with his friends, laughing like nothing happened."

I don't care about holding back anymore, not with him. "Carmen," I call sharply, hoping to shift the power balance. But before I can utter another word, Damien is on me, smothering me with his closeness.

"I think you're getting a little too comfortable with that mouth of yours," he hisses, his hand tightening around my throat. Cold spreads through me, biting and unrelenting. His other hand tangles in my hair, the motion almost tender if it weren't so laced with menace.

How is he touching me? It shouldn't feel like this.

I claw at his arm, but my hands pass through him like smoke, futile and maddening. I try to gasp for air, but his grip tightens.

"Oh, the things I'd do to you if I were still alive," he croons, stroking my cheek as his grip remains firm. His touch is unnervingly intimate, and bile rises in my throat as panic surges. I try to shove him away again, but my hands meet nothing solid, only the cold, swirling vapor of his form.

"Get off her." Carmen's voice cuts through the suffocating tension like a blade.

Damien freezes, his smirk fading into something darker. His form begins to dissolve. His grip vanishes, and I stagger back, gulping for air as his low, mocking laughter echoes in the void. He's gone, his presence whisked away on an unnatural gust of wind.

"Carmen?" I call out, but I don't stop to find her. I can't— I'm too shaken. Instead, I turn and run, my feet pounding against the eerie, soundless ground. The skeletal forest around me blurs into darkness as I chase the faint glow of Malachi's room, my only tether to reality.

The light grows closer, but so does the suffocating black void that devours everything else. My chest heaves as I push forward, the forest disintegrating around me until only that beacon remains.

As I reach out, the scene starts to unravel, the veil collapsing in on itself.

"He's not dead," Carmen's voice echoes around me, but it's too late.

I grasp onto my body and slam back into myself, gasping as I fall to my knees clutching my throat, Malachi's room around me once more. I can't be sure who she was talking about.

My breaths come too fast, shallow and erratic, as if the air itself refuses to settle in my lungs. Malachi is suddenly there, crouched in front of me, his hands hovering near my shoulders like he's unsure if touching me will help or break me.

"Kat! What happened?" His voice is urgent, and there's something raw in his eyes—concern, fear.

I try to speak, but my throat feels tight, and my thoughts are a storm I can't control. "Carmen...she set up Damien," I manage to choke out, trembling. "He's alive."

I see the disbelief flash across his face, quickly replaced by something harder. His hands move to steady me, his grip firm yet careful, but I'm already slipping.

The room feels like it's spinning, the walls pressing closer, and I can't focus on anything but the weight of what I saw, what I felt. The edges of my vision darken, and the exhaustion settles over me.

"Kat!" Malachi's voice is the last thing I hear as the world goes black.

I FEEL the soft graze of fingers along my cheek, the gentle touch of someone brushing strands of hair out of my face and tucking them behind my ear. I don't open my eyes. Instead, I breathe him in—fresh-cut wood and the faintest hint of something minty.

My leg is draped over Malachi's waist, my arm thrown across him, and my face rests on his chest. His arm cradles me firmly against him, the warmth of his hold grounding me. I know he's awake. The way his fingers move through my hair, slow and deliberate, makes that clear. Yet I don't stir. Something inside urges me to pause, to savor this moment—the safety of his embrace, the steady rhythm of his breathing, the quiet comfort of the dimly lit room. It feels too good, too natural.

I inhale slowly, blinking a few times before daring to peek up at him through my lashes. The hand tangled in my hair drops, and his expression falters for a second, like a guilty child caught doing something naughty. But it fades quickly, replaced by the more serious demeanor I've grown accustomed to.

"How are you feeling?" His voice is softer than usual, gentle in a way that catches me off guard.

"I feel good. Rested," I murmur, still groggy. "How long did I sleep for? Is it morning yet?" I glance around the dim room, noticing the candle on the end table and the dark curtains drawn tightly over the window.

"The opposite, actually," he says, shifting slightly as his gaze darts toward the clock. "You slept for an entire day. It's already night again." His thumb brushes lightly against the small patch of skin exposed where my shirt rides up my back, a motion so absentminded yet so tender it makes my breath hitch. "Twenty-six hours, to be exact. It's about midnight."

I blink, surprised. "An entire day?" I try to piece together how long I might've been in the veil. It hadn't felt like I was there for more than minutes, but sometimes the toll is unpredictable. "That's...longer than I expected, but not unheard of."

His brows knit together slightly as he studies my face. "I know you said this happens—that projecting takes a lot out of you—and Marco warned me you'd need rest. But I didn't expect it to hit so hard."

He looks past me, his jaw tightening slightly as if he's replaying the last twenty-six hours in his head. His hand, still tracing gentle lines on my lower back, seems to move without him realizing it.

"Are you sure you're okay?" he presses, his voice dropping into something more serious, more personal.

I nod, resting my chin lightly on his chest as I meet his gaze. "I'm fine, really. Sometimes it's worse, sometimes not as bad. This was...manageable."

He doesn't look convinced but doesn't push further, and I don't tell him how comforting it feels to wake up like this, in his arms, instead of in Marco's room, him or one of his guards watching me.

I slide out of bed, Malachi's gaze trailing me as I move, but he doesn't stop me. He watches, his eyes tracking every step like he's trying to unravel a puzzle he hasn't quite figured out yet. It makes my skin prickle under the weight of his attention.

"Why do you look at me like that?" I ask, hesitating near the bathroom door, my hand hovering over the frame.

"Like what?" Malachi replies casually despite his eyes being anything but.

"Like you're trying to figure me out," I say.

A smirk tugs at the corner of his lips as he leans back slightly, arms crossing over his chest. "Maybe I am," he says, his gaze locked on mine. "Or maybe I can't stop staring."

The way he says it has me giggling like an idiot. "You're ridiculous," I mutter, ducking into the bathroom, but the warmth in my cheeks is unmistakable.

The cold water on my face helps wake me up fully, washing away the haze of sleep and the strange heaviness left behind from projecting. I brush my teeth, run a comb through my hair, and push it back over my shoulders, wanting to feel human again after sleeping for so long.

When I crawl back into bed, Malachi lifts his arm without saying anything, inviting me to settle against him. I hesitate for the briefest moment then tuck into his side, letting his arm wrap securely around me. His hold is warm and firm, and the way my body fits against his catches me off guard. It feels good —too good—and I inhale a shaky breath, trying to steady myself.

I tilt my head slightly, my eyes finding his in the dim, shimmering light of the candle on the nightstand. The golden-brown of his gaze is more vivid up close, tiny flecks of amber scattered like shards of firelight against a backdrop of deep, endless mahogany. He's staring right back at me.

"You know," he says suddenly, "you still owe me a kiss." His lips curve into a slow, teasing smile, the kind that flashes the dimple on his left cheek and makes it impossible to look anywhere else.

I swallow hard, my pulse quickening. I don't have a quick, biting comeback. Because the truth is—I do want to kiss him. Worse than that, I want him to kiss me.

My gaze drops to his lips before I can stop myself, and I feel a rush of heat crawl up my neck. I bite the inside of my cheek, wrestling with the war raging inside me. One part of me screams to close the space, to feel the heat of his mouth against mine. The other part—the one that's built walls and thrived behind them—warns me to keep my distance.

But then he tilts his head, his smirk softening into something deeper, more intense. His hand slides from where it rests on my back, his thumb brushing lightly against my side as his fingers press into me slightly, holding me closer. "What's the matter, Kat? No snarky remark this time?" he asks.

I force myself to meet his eyes again, and I see the challenge there, the unspoken dare. I tilt my chin, feigning confidence I don't feel, and murmur, "Maybe I'm waiting for you to take it."

For a moment, I think he's going to move. That he's going to close the space between us, and—

But he doesn't. Instead, his thumb grazes my side again, sending another shiver through me. "Careful what you ask for, demon," he whispers, his voice like a velvet caress.

I hold his stare, my lips parting slightly, my breath caught somewhere between anticipation and defiance. His thumb pauses on my side, the heat of his touch penetrating through the thin fabric of my shirt. For a heartbeat, neither of us moves, as if the world itself has stopped to hold its breath.

Then he shifts slightly, his hand sliding up my back as he leans in, his face mere inches from mine. I can feel his breath on my lips, warm and teasing, and it sends a thrill racing through me. He hesitates, his eyes searching mine, like he's giving me one last chance to pull away.

I don't.

His lips brush against mine, tentative at first, like he's testing the waters. I sigh into the kiss, my hands sliding up to rest against his chest. He deepens it, his fingers tangling in my hair as he pulls me closer, erasing the space between us entirely.

The kiss is slow and deliberate, yet it steals the breath from my lungs. His lips move against mine with an intensity that leaves no room for doubt—no room for anything else but him. My heart races, my pulse roaring in my ears, and for the first time in what feels like forever, I don't care about anything but this moment.

He tilts his head, his nose brushing against mine as he explores, his other hand anchoring me against him. I lose myself in the warmth of him, in the way he tastes, the way he feels, like a force of nature I never saw coming.

When he finally pulls back, it's slow and reluctant, his forehead resting lightly against mine. My eyes flutter open, meeting his smoldering gaze, and I feel my chest tighten all over again. His voice is low and husky when he finally speaks.

"Was that what you were waiting for?"

I don't trust myself to speak, so I nod, running my tongue across my bottom lip. Then I feel something softer, something dangerously close to safe. I start to let my mind wander, worrying if letting my guard down around him might be reckless.

But then, with a breath, I push the intrusive thoughts aside, a spark of boldness flaring within me.

Fuck it.

Before I can second-guess myself, I close the distance between us, my mouth finding his. The contact sends a jolt through me, and when I press my tongue against his lips, he responds immediately, opening for me. He's half-sitting, his back resting against the headboard, and it's not enough. I want to be closer. I need better access.

I shift, crawling on top of him, straddling his waist as I deepen the kiss. His hands move instinctively, trailing down my sides, gripping my hips. The heat of his touch sends a delicious shiver through my body. My fingers thread into his hair, tugging gently as his tongue meets mine, exploring, teasing, and pulling soft, shaky breaths from me.

His grip tightens, pulling me flush against him, and I feel his chest rise and fall rapidly beneath me. I tilt my head, angling the kiss for more, giving into the moment entirely as his mouth devours mine.

When I finally pull back for air, I rest my forehead to his, both of us breathing heavily. His gaze locks onto mine, his pupils dark and dilated, his lips red and glistening. He exhales a single word, low and hoarse, his voice like a rumble of thunder in the quiet room.

"Fuck."

His hands remain on my hips, and I feel his fingers flex slightly, like he's trying to rein himself in. But the look in his eyes tells me he's anything but in control.

Suddenly, he flips me onto my back, his lips trailing a searing path along my jawline, his breath warm against my skin. His hand slips under my shirt, his fingers grazing my stomach before moving upward, cupping my breast with deliberate tenderness. A soft moan escapes me when his thumb and forefinger tease my nipple, rolling it until it peaks beneath his touch. His other hand grips my hip, grounding me, holding me steady as his body presses against mine.

I can feel his hardness through the thin layers of fabric between us, and the realization steals my breath. My pulse races, my heart thundering in my chest as a flood of emotions surges to the surface—excitement, desire, and something heavier, something uncertain. The weight of every assumption I've let him make about me presses down on me. He thinks he knows me—what I've done, what I'm capable of—but he doesn't. Not really.

I shift slightly beneath him, trying to steel myself against the storm of feelings building inside me. His lips skim the edge of my neck, his breath igniting my skin, and I can't help the way my voice trembles when I whisper his name. "Malachi..."

He stills instantly, pulling back enough to look at me. His dark eyes search mine, soft yet intense, his expression a mixture of concern and restraint.

"What is it?" he asks, his teasing tone gone, replaced by something infinitely more serious.

I bite my lip, suddenly unsure if I can say it aloud. But I have to—before this goes any further. "I need you to know something."

He shifts his weight, giving me enough space to breathe, his brows knitting together as he waits for me to continue. "You can tell me anything," he says, his voice steady, reassuring.

I take a shaky breath, forcing myself to speak before I lose my nerve. "I've never...done this before. Any of it."

His expression falters, confusion crossing his face before realization sets in. "Wait, you mean..."

"Yes." Heat rushes to my cheeks, and I look away, unable to meet his stare. "I've never been with anyone. Everything you've heard, everything I let you believe...it was all a lie."

The silence that follows is deafening, stretching so long that I almost regret saying anything. When I finally glance back at him, his expression is unreadable. His mouth opens slightly, as though he wants to say something but can't quite find the words.

"All this time…" he mutters more to himself than to me. He shakes his head, and I see something briefly in his eyes—regret, guilt, or maybe a mix of both. "Kat, why didn't you tell me? For fuck's sake, what were you thinking letting that fucking pig touch you for information?" His jaw tightens, his frustration palpable.

"I was thinking people like you always assume the worst about me," I say, releasing years of pent-up frustration. "It was easier to let you think I was someone else. Someone…stronger. Someone who wouldn't let themselves be used."

His hand cups my cheek, his thumb brushing against my skin with a tenderness that catches me off guard. "You're already the strongest person I know," he says quietly. "And I'm sorry for ever assuming otherwise."

I search his eyes, looking for any trace of mockery, any hint of disbelief, but all I see is sincerity. "You didn't have to lie to me," he adds, "but I get why you did. And for what it's worth, I don't care about what you have or haven't done. I care about you."

It relieves an ache I didn't realize I was carrying, but then his expression darkens slightly. "And I want to go back and kill that fuck Eduard all over again for touching you."

He rolls off me onto his side, still facing me, his gaze unwavering. "You don't have to prove anything to me," he says. "Not tonight. Not ever."

I let out a slow breath, "I don't need you to go easy on me, Malachi. I'm not fragile."

He smirks, the corner of his mouth quirking into that infuriatingly charming half-smile. "I know that," he replies, "but that doesn't mean I'm rushing you into something you're not ready for."

His patience disarms me, and I hesitate, unused to someone being so careful with me—with my feelings. It's always been the opposite—people trying to take, to use, to bend me to their will. But Malachi...waits. His hand moves to my side, tracing slow, soothing circles over my shirt, his warmth steadying the chaos inside me.

"What if I want this?" I whisper, my fingers toying with the edge of his shirt where it meets his skin.

His eyes darken, his breath hitching slightly, and for a moment I think he might give in. But then he leans forward, pressing a kiss to my forehead so tender it makes my chest ache.

"Then we'll take our time," he says softly, his lips brushing against my temple. "I'm not going anywhere."

Undone, I bury my face in his chest, letting his heartbeat steady me. His arms wrap around me, strong and secure, and for the first time I let myself fully relax into someone else's care.

We stay like that for a long time, the candlelight dancing across the walls. His hands trace gentle patterns along my back, as if he's content to hold me, and I realize I've never felt anything like this before.

"You're going to ruin me, Kat," he murmurs against the top of my hair, sounding like he's not sure if he's teasing or confessing a truth that terrifies him.

I let out a soft laugh. "Good," I say, my fingers curling against his chest, feeling the steady beat of his heart. "Someone should."

Chapter Nineteen

RULE 19 OF THE NEW ORDER: DAYLIGHT HAS A WAY OF SOFTENING TRUTHS SPOKEN IN THE DARK, BUT IT DOESN'T ERASE THEM. WHAT IS SAID AT NIGHT LINGERS, NO MATTER HOW MUCH THE MORNING LIGHT TRIES TO CHASE IT AWAY.

I SNEAK out of bed and into the shower before Malachi wakes up. God, even asleep he looks good—his hair all disheveled, his body relaxed. I don't know what's come over me. The kiss, the way his hands felt on me, the sound of his voice saying my name... It's too much. I need this cold shower to wake me up, to get my mind out of the gutter.

The cool water shocks me, grounding me as I run my fingers through my hair, rinsing away the heat clinging to my skin.

I crossed a line last night, and I'm not sure it's one I can come back from. Not that I want to take it back, but I don't want things to be weird. What even are we? I don't know how Malachi feels, not really, and I groan, tilting my head back under the spray.

None of it matters. I don't even know what my life is going to look like in the next couple of weeks. It's reckless to think I even have the luxury of entertaining these feelings.

Get it together, Kat.

I shake my head, forcing myself to focus on the mission. *Don't let a hot, charming, infuriatingly sweet guy distract you.* If —and it's a big if—Malachi really does find a way to free me from Marco, then maybe I can revisit whatever this is. But until then, I need to protect myself, because if I fall too hard, the crash will destroy me when reality sets in.

I turn off the water, towel off quickly, and dry my hair. A little makeup helps me look more put together, and I decide on something cute but practical: warm tights and a form-fitting long-sleeve blue dress. It's thick enough not to look completely ridiculous in the snow but flattering enough for me to feel confident in. Satisfied, I open the bathroom door, expecting Malachi to still be passed out in bed.

Instead, he strolls in from the hallway wearing nothing but a towel slung low on his hips, his dark hair damp and tousled.

Not today, God.

My eyes betray me, dragging over the hard lines of his chest, the strength in his arms, the sharp curve of muscle at his waist.

He clears his throat, a knowing smirk pulling at his lips. "See something you like, demon?"

I cough, snapping my gaze to his face, my cheeks heating. "You wish."

He chuckles, walking to the window and pulling the blinds open, flooding the room with blinding light. Then he turns and closes the distance between us in three slow strides, his gaze raking over me. "You look so good I could take a bite out of you," he teases, leaning down, his mischievous smile daring me to push him away.

"Hey, I do the biting around here, remember." I show him my teeth and chomp.

As his face nears mine, he freezes, his body going rigid. His eyes narrow, locking on my neck like a predator spotting prey.

"What's wrong?" I ask, my heart skipping as his hand brushes my hair back over my shoulder. I know immediately what he sees. Oh, Damien. The bruises. They must have surfaced by now.

His jaw tightens, and hisses through clenched teeth, "Who did this to you?"

"No one alive, remember?" I force a half-smile, trying to lighten the mood, but he doesn't take the bait.

"Kat." His voice is tight, his eyes dark with restrained fury. "I let it slide the first time, but this is the second time you've had bruises on your neck. What the fuck happened in the veil? I thought spirits couldn't touch humans."

I shift, moving to sit on the edge of the bed. "It's complicated," I say quietly, looking at my hands instead of him.

"Try me," he says, crossing his arms but staying close, his tension palpable.

I exhale slowly, bracing myself for the explanation I'm not sure how to give.

"Spirits can't touch humans—not usually," I begin. "I don't even know if it was Damien the first time. It was all confusing. I couldn't make out his face. But this case is different."

Malachi sits beside me on the edge of the bed, still only wearing the damn towel. His presence is steady, grounding, even as his dark eyes bore into me. "I've seen you pet Mischka," he says, his tone probing but not unkind. "You're spell casting."

I nod, tucking my legs under me. "Yes, I do pet her, but it's not the same as it was when she was alive. She doesn't feel solid, but there's...something. It's warm, faint. Like touching a memory." I glance back at Mischka, who chooses that exact moment to appear, doing her usual circles around the room before stretching out on the bed behind us. Her presence always makes me smile.

"It wasn't always like this," I continue. "I couldn't feel her for a long time. Our connection grew stronger because I keep her near me. She's here so much now that it's like she's closer to crossing back over, if that makes sense."

Malachi leans forward, resting his forearms on his knees, his focus unwavering. "So how is this case different? Why is Damien so strong? Why is the connection there so intense?"

I shrug, frustration bubbling under my skin. "I don't know," I admit. "But it scared the shit out of me. That's why I wasn't in the veil for long after he..." I falter, my throat tightening as the memory sweeps through my mind. "After he grabbed me, I panicked and ran back to you."

His lips twitch into the briefest smile, gone almost before I register it. There's a softness in his expression, like he's holding onto the fact that I said I ran back to him.

"I don't like this at all, Kat. I don't want you projecting again. The strength of that connection..." He pauses, running a hand over his damp hair. "And you know the first thing you said before you passed out after you crossed back over was that Carmen set up Damien and he's alive. Want to fill me in on what that means?"

After the heat of last night, I'd completely forgotten about my conversation with Damien—and Carmen's warning. I was too busy thinking about him.

"Can you get dressed? It's very distracting having you next to me like this," I say, throwing my hands out in mock exasperation.

He chuckles, entirely unbothered, strolling over to the closet. And then he drops the towel.

Fuck me.

My eyes betray me again, drinking in every inch of him before I can stop myself. His back, his shoulders, his...everything. And by the smug look on his face when he glances over his shoulder, he knows what he's doing.

"This," I say, turning abruptly to face Mish instead. My hand rests on her fur, petting her with more focus than necessary. "This right here is why I forgot to tell you about my conversation with Damien."

His low chuckle carries across the room as he pulls on his clothes. "I'm sorry you're so easily distracted, clever demon," he teases.

When he comes back to sit in front of me, now dressed in a perfectly tailored dark-brown suit that somehow makes him even more frustratingly attractive, I finally let out the breath I've been holding.

I narrow my eyes at him, catching the satisfied smirk playing on his lips. "You're insufferable, you know that?" I grumble, crossing my arms.

"And yet," he says, leaning forward with a cocky grin, "you can't seem to look away."

"I don't know who killed Damien, but I do know Carmen was playing him. She might have had something to do with his death too," I say, my voice steady despite the unease I feel.

Malachi's expression hardens, his jaw tightening. "But you said before—he and Carmen were having sex the night they were killed, right?"

"They were, but Carmen had a boyfriend, and it wasn't Damien. He made it sound like she set him up or something. I wish I knew who her boyfriend was, but no one at Viktor's would tell me when I asked. They all acted like they didn't know—or didn't want to get involved. And she's been too evasive to get an answer out of."

Malachi leans back slightly, his brow furrowed in thought. Mish stretches beside me, her movement so lifelike it almost pulls me out of the conversation. I stroke her fur absently as I continue.

"Why won't Damien tell you who killed him?" Malachi

asks, his voice edged with frustration. "Maybe he doesn't know. Maybe he never saw the killer's face either and he's messing with you, using this as an excuse to keep getting his hands on you."

His fists clench slightly in his lap, the muscles in his forearm taut with restrained anger. I reach over, resting my hand on top of his, grounding him.

"I think Damien knows exactly who killed him," I say. "But he's bored. And an asshole. It's a game to him, Malachi. He's doing it because he can."

Malachi's gaze flickers down to my hand then back to me. I pull my hand away, the contact lingering in the air like a silent promise.

"I don't like it," he growls. "The idea of him touching you—even in the veil—it pisses me off."

"Trust me, I'm not thrilled about it either," I say, managing a faint smile. "But I'll figure this out. I always do."

"I don't want you projecting again," Malachi says, almost commanding. "If he can leave bruises on your neck like this, what's next? How far can he take things over there? I'll call Marco and tell him you're done working on this. Viktor can find someone else."

He stands, pacing as if he's already made up his mind.

I shoot to my feet, spinning to face him. "Yeah, that would go over great. Marco would come get me or demand you take me home and—"

I don't want to say it. Don't want to admit to myself what that would mean for us...for me.

"And what?" Malachi presses, his eyes narrowing. "You're not going back to him, Kat. I told you I'm going to take care of him. Give me and my team time."

I want to believe him. I want to lean into the hope he's offering. But Marco isn't someone you "take care of." He's a storm, a hurricane of calculated power and paranoia. I glance at Malachi, his jaw tight with resolve, and my chest aches with the fear he doesn't fully understand what he's up against.

He has the Syndicate, sure, and they're good—hell, they're better than good. But Marco? He's a monster, and monsters don't fall easily.

"I know you believe that," I say, treading carefully, "but I know Marco. Killing him isn't one option of many; it's the only option. And when that time comes, it's not going to be as simple as you think. He's still your father."

Malachi's expression hardens, a flicker of something unreadable flashing in his eyes. Pain, maybe. Or guilt.

"Do you think I haven't thought about that? Every single day, Kat. I've made my peace with what I have to do. He's not my father anymore—not in any way that matters. He hasn't been for a long time."

I search his face, trying to gauge if he really means it. If he truly knows what he's walking into.

"In the meantime," he says, breaking the heavy silence, "I know what we're doing today."

The shift in his tone catches me off guard, and I blink at him, my thoughts scattered. "What do you mean?"

A sly smile tugs at the corner of his mouth. "You'll see. It's going to be therapeutic."

Therapeutic? Knowing Malachi, that could mean anything from target practice to a fight ring.

"DON'T WORRY about the why—tell me if you think it will work," Malachi says to Bash, standing in front of the cabinet filled with small vials and swirling orbs of Avidian. His tone is sharp, urgent, and it sets my nerves on edge.

Bash runs a hand through his dark curls, typing something furiously into the machine beside him. "I don't know," he admits, not looking up. "I've never tried it on a power like hers before. What she can do isn't tangible—like creating fire or manipulating elements. But in theory, it should work."

Malachi nods, like that vague answer is all he needed to hear, but I'm not convinced. "Wait," I say, holding up a hand. "Didn't you tell me you could amplify an Avid's power for a short time? How does that work?"

Bash glances at Malachi then back at me, his brow arching in curiosity. "I did," he says slowly, clearly wondering where I'm going with this.

"Then that's a much better idea," I press. "Amplify my power tonight. Let's see what happens. Putting me in this machine, pulling some piece of my gift to test it out on Malachi? That's risky. Even if it worked perfectly, I don't think you're ready to project with me," I say, glancing from Bash back to Mal.

Malachi turns, his jaw tight, his hands braced on the edge of the counter. "And what happens if I do nothing? You go into the veil alone, like always, and I'm left standing here with no way to protect you."

Before I can respond, Bash speaks up. "Wait a minute, did something happen between you two in the last couple of days?" There's a glint of suspicion in his eyes that makes me flush.

"No," I say quickly, shooting Malachi a look that dares him to contradict me. "And I think you need to tell him he's being irrational. Tonight, we test the amplification theory. End of discussion."

Bash leans back in his chair, his grin widening. "Mmm-hmm. Sure, Kat. No tension here at all."

Malachi lets out a long exhale, his hand dragging down his

face. "Fine. We'll try it your way, but not tonight. Let's do it tomorrow during the day. Is that okay?"

I nod, relieved to have won this round. I need to get a grip on this case fast.

"THIS FEELS awkward to do while I'm wearing a dress. People are looking at us," I mutter, glancing toward the gym floor, where groups are practicing sparring techniques or watching from the bleachers.

"It's even better that you're wearing a dress," Malachi counters with a smirk, stepping closer. "Real-world scenarios, Kat. You're not always going to be in gym clothes when something goes down. Besides, no one's looking because of your dress."

I shoot him a skeptical look as he moves behind me, slipping his arm around my waist in a mock grab. And I think I might go on a while letting him believe I'm weak. "Alright, here's the deal—if you can't escape like this," he begins, tightening his hold slightly, "you stomp on his foot, elbow him in the kidney, or—"

"Hit him in the dick?" I interrupt with a grin.

"That'll work. Whatever you do, don't grab his arms and try to wrestle free. You're not strong enough to flip someone like me over, and it won't hurt him," he says, releasing me.

"Good to know," I say sweetly before immediately elbowing him in the gut.

"Low blow," he chuckles, rubbing his stomach.

"How many Avids are here anyway? What can they all do? I want to know more about their gifts. Maybe someone can help me understand mine better."

"Curiosity suits you," he teases, dodging when I try to poke him in the ribs. "There's a lot to learn, but tonight," he starts, pausing to give me an unreadable look, "I was thinking we could do something you probably haven't done in years."

I cross my arms, tilting my head. "Oh yeah, what's that?"

Malachi grins, stepping toward me again. "Have fun."

"Fun?" I arch a brow, stepping out of reach. "Define fun."

"Let loose. Stop worrying about who's watching or what's happening next. The case can wait until tomorrow," he says.

I turn to face him fully, catching his sly grin.

"You mean do something crazy?" I ask, throwing his own words back at him, the memory of that night in the park surfacing between us.

"Exactly," he replies, and the intensity in his gaze sparks something reckless in me. Something that makes me want to seize the night, as he put it before.

"Come on, Mal, you're going too easy on her," Rain calls out as she approaches. She's dressed in fitted training gear, her purple hair braided back today, and I notice a faint scar above her left eye that only adds to her no-nonsense demeanor.

"We're letting off some steam," Malachi says, his voice calm but firm. "She's not starting a full training regimen yet."

Rain doesn't seem to care. She steps into the ring without waiting for an invitation and waves him off. "Get out. Let me show her how to really defend herself."

I glance at Malachi, who hesitates. His eyes linger on me, reluctant, like he's expecting something to go wrong. I almost want to roll my eyes—if he thinks I can't handle this, he's got another thing coming.

Rain cracks her neck and rolls her shoulders like she's about to take on a heavyweight champion. "Alright, new girl," she says, grinning, her eyes gleaming with mockery. "Come at me. Let's see if you're more than just talk."

I raise an eyebrow, sizing her up. "Is this really necessary?"

She doesn't answer, and I look over at Malachi again, but Rain is already on me. "Don't look at him. Focus on me."

Before I can respond, she's coming at me, faster than I expect. Her fist taps lightly against my arm, more a reminder than an attack. "Come on, that's it?" she sneers. "Fight back. You don't want to be a disappointment, do you?"

I clench my jaw, feeling the irritation simmer. She's underestimating me, and that's a mistake. I throw a punch, aiming for her shoulder. She blocks it easily, and I let my training kick in. I've never had to use it outside of Marco's gym before, but I can take this bitch and show her I'm not someone to be walked all over—not here—not when I don't have to obey anyone's rules.

"Is that all you've got?" Rain taunts, circling me like a predator. "Hit me like you mean it, or are you all talk?"

My blood boiling, I swing again, this time putting some real force behind it, but she catches my arm in midair and twists, sending me crashing to the mat with humiliating ease. The crowd murmurs, some laughing, some watching in silence.

I push myself up quickly, my face hot with embarrassment and fury. I glare up at her, she stands over me with that smug look still plastered on her face.

"That all you've got?" she says, circling me. "No wonder Mal's going easy on you. You'll never make Solace like this."

I bite back the retort rising in my throat, but something inside me snaps. Who the hell does she think she is? I don't need Solace, and I definitely don't need her approval. My fists clench, but I hold back—a little.

Rain smirks wider and takes a step back, giving me room. "Alright, precious, let's see if you've got more than a pretty face."

The insult hits a nerve, and I'm done. I stand up straighter, wiping my palms on my sides, determination setting in.

This time, I don't hesitate. I move fast, landing a clean

punch to her mouth before she can react. I step back, watching as shock flashes across her face. She spits blood, and for a moment I think I've won. But then that dark gleam returns to her eyes, and I know this isn't over. It's going to take a lot more than one hit to appease her appetite for fighting.

Her lips twitch into a twisted smile. "Nice try," she mutters, before lunging at me, pulling me off balance. Her grip on my wrist is tight, and before I can recover, she drives a punch into my side. I gasp as pain shoots through my body, but I won't let her control me. Not now, not ever. I slam my knee into her gut, forcing her back.

We both hit the ground, rolling and scrambling, limbs tangled in a chaotic mess. She's strong, but she's not faster than me. I fight through the pain, pushing myself to stay on top.

Rain drills an elbow into my chest, the impact sharp. I grit my teeth, shoving the pain aside, and force myself on top of her, pinning her down. I'm ready to finish it, but she's still thrashing, trying to break free.

I throw a punch at her jaw, solid and deliberate, like I've been taught. The first one lands, then a second. The third hits harder, a sickening crack echoing through the ring. I feel her resistance falter, and I know I've finally got her.

But as I pull back, trying to make my point without really hurting her, she seizes the opportunity. She yanks me down, and I hit the mat hard, my back slamming into the floor.

I look up at her, breathless. Really? This is how we're doing it? I'm in a damn dress for crying out loud.

I throw my arm up to block her next move, but before I can react, Malachi's voice cuts through the chaos like a blade. "Enough."

The word hits like a thunderclap. Everything stops. I freeze, feeling the tension evaporate instantly.

Malachi steps into the ring, his presence commanding.

Rain, panting and sweaty, freezes too, her expression turning from amusement to something else.

"Alright, new girl," she says between labored breaths, "turns out you might be hiding a few surprises after all."

She grabs my hand and yanks me to my feet, her strength surprising me. I sneer at her, but she laughs it off, unbothered.

"She's tougher than you think, Mal. Don't baby her. She just needs to learn how to throw a proper punch so she doesn't break her wrist."

"Yeah, work on that another day," Malachi says, his hand on the small of my back as he guides me out of the gym.

A proper punch, yeah right. She knows I landed more than one proper punch on her face.

"Sorry about Rain," he continues once we're inside the elevator. "She can be a handful. But I'll admit that was impressive back there. I don't think Rain saw that coming. The look on her face when you pinned her down..." He laughs

"Don't be sorry," I reply, straightening my dress and fiddling with my hair. "It was kind of exhilarating. If I end up staying here, maybe I could join Solace. Be on your team. Do what you all do...after I train more."

He pauses, and I feel his gaze on me, sharp and searching. The air between us shifts, and I glance up to find him giving me a look I can't quite place. "Do you want to stay?" he asks.

I blink, caught off guard by the question. My initial reaction is to deflect, but instead I find myself looking away, mulling it over. "I mean, if we take care of Marco...if I'm free. I haven't really let myself think about it much. I don't want to get my hopes up, you know?"

The elevator dings, and the doors slide open. We walk in silence through the tract house, the sound of our footsteps the only noise. Something feels different—charged—and I can't shake the sense that Malachi is upset with me, or maybe deep in thought.

When we reach his truck, he climbs into the driver's seat, the faint hum of the engine filling the silence as he starts it up. Finally, he breaks it.

"What do you want, Kat?" His voice is calm but weighted, like he's laying something bare. His eyes lock with mine. "Because you are going to be free. You should let yourself start thinking about it. You'll be able to go anywhere, do anything. No one will be controlling your life but you."

The idea of freedom—of having no strings, no one pulling me in any direction—should feel exhilarating, but all I can focus on is the hollow ache it leaves behind.

I want to tell him.

I want you.

I want to go where you go. I want to fight alongside you, be a part of your world. But it sounds ridiculous in my head, too raw and vulnerable to say out loud.

Instead, I look out the window as the truck rolls forward, watching the snow-covered landscape blur past.

"I'll think about it," I say softly, my voice almost lost in the hum of the engine.

Chapter Twenty

RULE 20 OF THE NEW ORDER: SOMETIMES, THE
ONLY WAY TO FEEL ALIVE IS TO DANCE ON THE
EDGE OF DISASTER.

"COME ON, tell me where we're going," I say, blindfolded in the passenger seat. My fingers fidget in my lap, anticipation getting the better of me.

"I want it to be a surprise," Malachi replies. "Trust me, it's better this way."

I huff but can't deny the thrill. No one's ever done anything like this for me before, and as much as I hate giving up control, the excitement outweighs my nerves. Or maybe it's the two drinks we had at dinner loosening me up. Either way, the suspense is killing me.

Thankfully, the drive isn't long. It feels like only a few minutes before he finally says, "Okay, don't move. I'm coming to get you."

I hear the engine cut off, and a second later his door slams shut. My senses heighten in the darkness as his footsteps crunch through the snow. When he opens my door, his hands are warm and steady as they grip my hips, lifting me effortlessly out of the truck. The motion sends a jolt of something through me, making my breath hitch.

"Alright," he murmurs, guiding me a few steps forward with his hands on my shoulders. His touch lingers for a beat longer than necessary before he steps back. "This is perfect. Ready?"

"I'm ready."

His fingers brush against my temple as he unties the blindfold, and I catch the warmth in his gaze before the cloth falls away. I blink, my eyes adjusting to the brilliance of lights.

"Oh my God," I breathe.

In front of me stretches a winter wonderland come to life—a carnival blanketed in snow, but the first thing I notice is the Ferris wheel, its gondolas glittering like jewels in the moonlight.

"Welcome to the Winter Carnival of Devil's Lake," Malachi says, stepping beside me, his hands slipping casually into his pockets as he watches me take it all in.

"Devil's Lake?" I repeat, the name snagging my attention.

"Yeah," he says with a mischievous grin. "Isn't it fitting I bring my very own little demon to a town called Devil's Lake?"

I blink at him, stunned for a second, before his laughter becomes contagious, and I burst out laughing too. "You're impossible," I say, shaking my head, but I can't stop the smile tugging at my lips.

He nods toward the bustling scene before us. Strings of glowing lights crisscross above the snowy lot, bathing everything in a soft, golden glow. A giant ice castle stands at the heart of the carnival, its jagged spires glittering like diamonds under the twinkling fairy lights. The air smells of roasted chestnuts, sweet pastries, and something warm—mulled cider maybe? Booths line the streets, selling everything from handmade crafts to steaming mugs of hot cocoa. Children dart past us, laughing and chasing each other with snowballs, while couples stroll hand-in-hand, bundled up against the cold.

"We have a winter carnival every year around this time," Malachi says, stretching his arms. "What do you think?"

I let out a slow breath, marveling at the scene. "It's magical." The kind of magical that feels too good to be real, like something out of a storybook.

He leans closer, his breath warming my ear in the chilly night air. "Good. Tonight's about fun. About us. No missions, no ghosts, no training. You deserve this, Kat."

That sends a flutter through my chest, and I look up at him, seeing something unguarded in his expression, something I haven't seen before. "Alright, Savior," I say with a smile, trying to shake off the sudden vulnerability I feel creeping in. "Show me how Devil's Lake does winter."

He holds out his hand. "Let's start with the ice maze. Try not to get lost, demon."

Malachi's smile is infectious as I take his hand, the warmth of his fingers a welcome contrast to the biting cold. "An ice maze?" I echo, raising an eyebrow. "You do realize that sounds like an excellent place to get frostbite and die."

"Come on, where's your sense of adventure?" he teases, tugging me toward the glowing entrance.

The maze is enormous, its walls made of thick, perfectly translucent ice that reflects the twinkling lights above like a kaleidoscope. The entrance arch glows with a soft blue light, and I can hear the muffled laughter and shouts of people trying to navigate its twists and turns.

"After you," he says with a playful bow, gesturing for me to enter first.

"Chivalrous," I remark, stepping in, the ice crunching softly beneath my boots.

The maze's narrow pathways wind in unexpected directions, and the further in we go, the quieter it becomes, the walls absorbing the noise of the carnival outside. At one point, I reach a fork and glance back at Malachi, who's still holding my hand.

"Left or right? I'm thinking left," I ask.

"Right," he says without hesitation.

"Why?"

He grins. "Because you asked, and I like being contrary."

I roll my eyes but follow his suggestion, only for us to hit a dead end a minute later. I stop and turn to face him, narrowing my eyes. "Contrary, huh? What's it like always being wrong?"

"I wouldn't know," he fires back, stepping closer, his grin widening.

I'm about to retort, but he catches me off guard, backing me gently into the icy wall behind me. The chill seeps through my coat, but the heat of his body so close to mine is enough to keep the cold at bay.

"Malachi," I warn, though I lack any real conviction.

"Yes, Kat?" he says, the mischief in his eyes softening into something deeper. His free hand comes up to tuck a stray strand of hair behind my ear, and I swear the world outside the maze fades away.

"Are you trying to distract me?" I ask, my breath visible in the cold air, mingling with his.

"Maybe," he murmurs, his lips curving. "Is it working?"

"Not even a little," I lie, my pulse racing.

"Good," he says, leaning closer. "Because you deserve to be distracted. From everything."

And then he kisses me, slow and deliberate, like he's savoring the moment. The cold of the ice at my back vanishes under the heat of his touch, and I lose myself in him, in the way his lips move against mine, in the way his hand slides to my waist, anchoring me like he never wants to let go.

When he finally pulls back, I can't help but laugh softly.

"What?"

"I'm pretty sure we're lost," I say, and he chuckles, pressing a quick kiss to my forehead before taking my hand again.

"Good thing I'm an expert at finding my way out of tricky situations," he says, tugging me back through the maze.

Malachi navigates us out of the maze so quickly it feels like he's been holding back and letting me stumble around a little longer. The thought makes me smile. By the time we emerge on the other side, cheeks flushed from the cold, he grabs two mugs of boozy hot chocolate from a nearby stand.

The first sip warms me from the inside out, the alcohol cutting through the chill in the air, and we spend the next hour playing carnival games. He wins me a small plush polar bear at the ring toss, which I absolutely do not gush over, even though it's kind of adorable.

"Let's ride the Ferris wheel," I say, pointing toward the glowing wheel lighting up the sky. Malachi doesn't hesitate, guiding me through the crowd to the line. He exchanges a few words and slips a bill to the teenage operator before ushering me into one of the creaky little carts.

As soon as we sit down, he drapes his arm over my shoulders, pulling me closer. I tuck into his side, grateful for the warmth radiating from him. "What did you say to that kid?" I ask, squinting up at him suspiciously.

"I paid him to stop the ride while we're at the top," he says with a teasing grin.

"You didn't," I laugh, but the ride slows sooner than I expect, and our cart jerks to a halt at the very top. "You did!"

I turn to him, my laughter spilling out into the quiet night air.

He grins, unapologetic, as the first snowflakes of the evening start to fall. I look out over the carnival, the snow glittering in the glow of the twinkling lights below. The flakes catch on the air, sparkling like tiny stars as they drift lazily around us. It's stunning, and I lose myself in the beauty of it all.

But when I glance back at Malachi, I realize he's not looking at the snow. He's looking at me. His expression is warm, steady, and unflinching, and when he leans in, brushing a few stray flakes from my beanie, my heart skips a beat.

His lips press against mine, desperate and wanting, I let him explore my mouth as I try to get closer to him. The snow falls around us, catching in his hair and melting against my cheeks. It's perfect, almost too perfect, like something out of a dream. His hand cradles the side of my face, his thumb brushing lightly against my skin as he deepens the kiss, and the world fades away.

When he pulls back, his forehead rests against mine. "Worth every penny," he murmurs.

"You bribed a kid so you could make out with me in the sky?" I ask, my own smile spreading wide despite the teasing lilt in my voice.

He shrugs, unrepentant. "You make it sound so calculated. I'd call it...spontaneous."

I laugh, nestling back into his side as the Ferris wheel begins to move again, our cart swaying gently as it descends. "I'm not sure what's worse—your smugness or the fact that it actually worked."

"I'll take that as a win," he says, his arm tightening around me as he looks out at the carnival lights below. "You seem like you needed a night to just...be."

I glance up at him. "To just...be?"

"Yeah," he says, his expression thoughtful now. "No missions, no projecting into creepy veils, no looking over your shoulder every five minutes. Be Kat. Laughing. Smiling. Forgetting the rest of the world exists, even if it's only for a little while."

As the ride slows and we near the bottom, I tug on his coat sleeve. "Thank you."

"For bribing a Ferris wheel operator?" he jokes, but his eyes soften when he sees my expression.

"For tonight," I say, looking away. "For making me feel like...me."

Malachi's smile turns softer, more genuine. "Anytime, demon. But don't thank me yet. We still have to go ice skating."

"Ice skating," I repeat, raising an eyebrow. "So you're saying you want me to break my neck tonight too?" I joke, though I've never actually tried any kind of skating before.

Malachi grins, that infuriatingly charming half-smile that somehow always gets me to go along with his plans. "I won't let you get hurt."

The way he says it, so confident and easy, makes it impossible to argue. I roll my eyes but follow him willingly, my nerves already tangling with a mix of excitement and apprehension.

It's not as hard as I thought it would be, but I have a death grip on Malachi's arm the entire time, clinging to him like my life depends on it. Every now and then, he glances down at me with a teasing look on his face, but he doesn't say anything. He steadies me, his hand warm and secure on mine.

The skating trail is breathtaking. It's not some big circular rink like I imagined. Instead, it weaves through a cluster of lonely trees and is lined with holiday decorations that glow against the dark night. There's a snowman made entirely of Christmas lights, its bulbous form cheerfully flickering, and a sleigh with fake, lit-up reindeer poised as if ready to take off into the starry sky.

It reminds me of being a kid, of those rare, magical winters when my parents would string lights around the house and hang stockings by the fireplace. A pang of nostalgia hits me hard, mingled with the ache of loss. I haven't celebrated Christmas—or any holiday, really—since they died.

Marco's family throws extravagant holiday parties, but they're nothing like what I remember. They're cold and impersonal, and thankfully I'm usually not invited.

"Are you okay?" Malachi's voice pulls me out of my thoughts. He slows his stride, steadying us both as I wobble slightly.

"Yeah," I say, forcing a smile. "This is really nice."

He squeezes my hand lightly and guides me along the glowing path.

The skates slip out from under me without warning, and before I even have time to yelp, Malachi's hands are on me. He reacts so fast it's like he was waiting for this to happen, catching me before I hit the ice. But instead of keeping us both upright, he lets himself fall, landing on his back with a soft grunt—me sprawled right on top of him.

I blink down at him, my heart racing from the near-disaster. His face is inches from mine, and he's laughing, his eyes crinkling at the corners.

"Hey!" I shove at his chest, which doesn't budge because he's basically made of stone. "You let me fall!"

He chuckles harder, his deep voice rumbling under me. "I never said I wouldn't let you fall," he says, one hand still steady on my waist. "I said I wouldn't let you get hurt."

I narrow my eyes at him, my mouth twitching with the threat of a smile I don't want to give him. "That's semantics."

"That's survival," he counters, his smile widening. "And clearly I'm very good at it. You're not hurt, are you?"

"No, but I might hurt you if you keep laughing," I mutter, but I can't keep the heat out of my cheeks or the laugh that escapes me despite myself.

He props himself up on his elbows slightly, forcing me to

shift so we're even closer. "You're cute when you're mad," he teases.

"You're impossible," I shoot back but don't move away. Instead, I find myself lingering there for a moment too long, caught in the warmth of him and the way he's looking at me like I'm the only thing that matters.

The cold ice beneath us is a stark contrast to the heat building between us, and as much as I want to make some sarcastic retort, I...don't. Instead, I bite my lip, the tiniest of smiles creeping onto my face as I finally push myself up, standing on wobbly legs.

"Come on," I say, holding out a hand to help him up. "Let's get more of that hot chocolate before we freeze to death."

WE MAKE IT BACK HOME, and Malachi heads straight for the fireplace, stacking logs and coaxing a fresh fire to life. The crackling warmth fills the room, and I can't help but plop down on the big, fluffy rug right in front of it, kicking off my boots and pulling my beanie from my hair.

"Tonight might have been one of the best nights I've ever had," I admit, stretching my legs out toward the fire's glow.

Malachi sits down beside me, the light casting shadows over his sharp features. "Me too."

I scoff, shaking my head with a laugh. "Malachi Volkov, rich and charming. I'm sure you've had countless nights far better than this one."

But he doesn't laugh. Instead, he leans in, brushing his fingers through my hair, tucking the loose strands behind my ear. His touch is so gentle it steals the air from my lungs.

"Yeah," he murmurs, his dark-brown eyes locking with mine, "but the company is what made tonight so great."

I smile, feeling strangely shy even though I don't know why. "Tell me what you were like as a child," I ask, changing the subject. I can only imagine how awful it must have been growing up with Orin as a brother.

Malachi tilts his head back, thinking for a moment before answering. "Hmm, I guess I was a bit of a dick," he admits, the corner of his mouth quirking up. "But Aunt Irina whipped me into shape. My father would say she made me soft, but I think that's because I don't have the stomach for the things my brothers do."

He stretches out beside me, and I can't help but smile at the idea of a young Malachi—mischievous but with a good heart, already resisting the darkness of his family. "If I stay here, would you want me to join Solace? Be on your team?" I ask, watching his face closely.

His expression shifts, and he looks away toward the fire, the flames flickering in his eyes. "It's dangerous," he says. "I wouldn't stop you if it's what you wanted, but I don't want to see you get hurt either."

I lean my head on his shoulder, letting the warmth of the fire and his presence soothe me. "It can't be any more dangerous than what my life has been until now," I point out.

He doesn't answer right away but moves his arm, draping it around me and pulling me closer to his side. The weight of it feels grounding, protective in a way I'm not used to.

"You're nothing like what I expected, you know," he says.

I glance up at him. "What do you mean?"

He looks down at me, his gaze steady but thoughtful. "I don't know. The way my father spoke about you, I thought you would be...different."

I turn to face him fully, raising a brow. "Different how?"

His lips twitch into a small smile. "Colder, maybe. Hardened by everything you've been through. But you're not. You're strong, but you're also warm. Kind."

I can see how serious he is. "You're not what I expected either," I finally say.

"Good unexpected or bad unexpected?" he asks, the teasing lilt back.

I laugh softly, shaking my head. "Good," I whisper, steeling a glance back at him.

"Have you ever been in love?" The question escapes before I can stop myself.

Malachi's brows knit together as he leans back, his fingers absently running along the seam of the couch. "I don't think so," he finally says, his gaze fixed on the fire. "I've been in relationships, cared for people, but love? I wouldn't go that far."

I tug my knees up, wrapping my arms around them as I try to shake the surprised feeling.

"What about you?" He shifts slightly, angling himself toward me. A faint smirk curves his lips, softening the weight of his question. "Has the clever demon ever been in love?"

I laugh quietly, running a hand through my hair to buy myself a second to answer. "Once," I admit.

He tilts his head, his interest sparking. "Really?"

"Really."

His gaze sharpens, studying me like he's trying to peel back my layers. "I'm surprised," he says. "Given—"

"Given that I've been in captivity for eight years," I cut him off, smirking slightly to hide the sting behind it. "You can say it. It's true."

Malachi exhales softly, his hand dragging over his jaw. "So who was he?" He hesitates then adds, "Where is he now?"

I toy with a loose thread on my sleeve, the action grounding me as I search for the right thing to say. "He's dead." I keep my tone light even though the truth weighs heavy. "So don't worry —you don't have any competition."

The joke doesn't land as easily as I'd hoped. Malachi's shoulders tense. "What happened?"

I lean forward, resting my arms on my knees. "He was in the car," I say, letting the words settle between us, "the day of the accident I told you about. We were kids, but he was my best friend growing up—until one day, he was more than that. I'll always love him in some way, but he's gone."

The room feels impossibly still. The fire crackles, its warmth contrasting the ache in my chest. Malachi doesn't look away, his eyes darker now, unreadable.

"I'm sorry," he says, and the way he says it feels different— like he's not sorry for my loss but sorry for everything I've endured.

I nod, pressing my lips together and looking away. "Me too."

We sit there in the glow of the fire, the unspoken weight of the conversation wrapping around us. His hand shifts closer to mine, resting on the rug between us, as if offering comfort without saying a word.

"Can I ask you an...uncomfortable question?" Malachi leans forward slightly, his hands fidgeting in his lap.

I cringe, uneasy about what he might ask. "You can ask me anything, but I don't guarantee an answer," I say, trying to keep the mood light.

He pauses, his jaw shifting like he's trying to figure out the right way to phrase it. "How have you never been with a man?" he says cautiously. "I mean, you were in love...you were young, but not too young. Teenagers have sex all the time. And then, after everything—" He takes a deep breath, his shoulders rising and falling. "I can't imagine what things were like for you once you were taken."

I take a deep breath, and he continues, "I know what men in those trafficking rings are like, Kat. I know what the men who work for my father are like. And you're—" He pauses, his voice dipping lower. "You're gorgeous. So, how?"

I'm not sure if I should feel insulted or validated. I straighten my back and hold his gaze. "I would have slept with Cade eventually," I say, my tone measured. "Cade—that was his name. But I wasn't in a rush to have sex at fifteen years old. You can love someone without sex being involved, Malachi."

He leans back slightly, his expression softening. "I know," he says quickly. "Don't take offense. I... I had to ask."

I shift my gaze to the fire, as if the flames could somehow burn away the sting of old memories. "As for the men who captured me and kept me until Marco bought me at that underground auction..." I pause, letting the weight of it settle between us. "Those men were disgusting. And, yeah, they tried. They tied me up, kept me filthy, unkempt. But nothing ever happened."

Malachi sits up straighter, his entire body going rigid. His fists clench in his lap, and I know he's picturing it all too clearly.

"Honestly," I continue, "I think most of them were too afraid of us. They knew we were different, gifted. And they didn't know what all of us could do. That fear kept them in check to an extent."

He exhales through his nose, his eyes locked on mine, sharp and unreadable.

"And Marco's men would never risk it. They're so terrified of him and wouldn't dare. I'm his most precious possession, his...pet. Marco would kill them himself without hesitation if they tried anything."

Malachi's lips thin, and a muscle jumps in his jaw as if he's barely holding himself back. His voice is low, rough around the edges. "Yeah, I believe that. After seeing how he reacted when I told him about Eduard the morning after the party."

"Yeah, and clearly you inherited the Volkov temper, because you slit his throat without even assessing the situation. For all you knew, maybe I liked that guy," I tease, though the memory of that night makes my stomach churn.

Malachi scoffs, "I knew you were drunk, and after watching Orin force you to keep drinking at the bar, I could barely fucking contain myself. Then, when I couldn't find you..." He pauses, running a hand through his hair like the memory still burns in him. "I started to worry. And then seeing you with him, that's when I knew you were trouble. I mean, I knew it in the park, but seeing you then, with him? I realized I had feelings for you. No matter how intolerable you were acting up until that point, I might add."

I half-smile, nudging his arm. "You have feelings for me," I say, teasing.

"I think that's obvious now," he replies. I like hearing him say it anyway.

I take a close look at his brown eyes and the contours of his cheekbones. "How many people have you killed?" The question comes out suddenly, but it's been weighing on me ever since I saw how easily he took Eduard's life.

His eyes darken, but he doesn't flinch. "Too many to count," he admits. "But all of them deserved it. I only kill bad men who do bad things."

There's no hesitation, no trace of guilt, and I don't push further. I believe him.

Maybe I'm desensitized to a lot after living with Marco all these years, but I'm more turned on by the fact that Malachi will kill to protect—kill those who have harmed women and children, those who deserve punishment—than I am afraid of it.

If this is a red flag, it's one I accept openly.

As if sensing the dark turn our conversation has taken, Mischka appears, circling the room in her usual graceful way before curling up at our feet in front of the fire.

"Why are you smiling like that?" Malachi asks, breaking me out of my thoughts.

"Mischka showed up," I tell him, nodding toward the empty space in front of the fire "She's right there."

His gaze flicks to where I pointed, and he exhales a soft chuckle. "I want to meet her. If you're unwilling to let Bash extract enough essence for me to project, maybe we could try a small amount, enough to fill a vial. That way, I could see what you see for a few minutes."

I nod, liking the idea more than I probably should. "I think I'd be willing to give it a shot, especially if Bash can help me tomorrow. I'm really hoping he can make a difference with my power when I project. I need to be stronger."

"Then stronger we shall make you," he says, rising to his feet and offering me a hand. The moment I take it, he catches me completely off guard, swooping me up into his arms. A surprised laugh escapes my lips as I grab onto his neck for balance.

"Are you feeling tired yet?" he asks, his demeanor playful, as his dark eyes glance down at me.

I lean in, brushing soft kisses along the curve of his neck, savoring the warmth of his skin against my lips. "Not even a little," I whisper, my breath teasing his ear before I gently nip at his earlobe.

His grip on me tightens, and he narrows his eyes, taking me in. "Good."

Chapter Twenty-One

RULE 21 OF THE NEW ORDER: LET THE WORLD BURN
FOR A NIGHT—TOMORROW ALWAYS BRINGS A NEW
FIRE TO LIGHT.

MALACHI CARRIES me into the bedroom, his movements deliberate, as though he's savoring every second. The firelight spills in through the open door, casting a golden glow across the walls. He lowers me onto the edge of the bed, his hands lingering on my hips, warm and steady.

"Stay right there," he murmurs, his lips brushing my forehead before he pulls back. His gaze locks on mine, intense yet soft, like he's searching for something unspoken in my expression.

I watch him as he steps back, the dim light highlighting the sharp angles of his face and the corded muscles of his arms. He peels off his shirt, revealing the lines of his chest, and I can't help the way my breath catches. He's beautiful—strong, sure, yet somehow vulnerable in the way he looks at me.

He steps toward me, and I lean back on my palms, suddenly hyperaware of the weight of this moment, of him, of us. His hands cup my face, thumbs brushing against my cheeks as his eyes search mine. "You're nervous," he says, his voice gentle, and I shake my head, though I know he can see right through me.

"Maybe a little," I admit.

His lips curve into a soft smile, and he leans down, pressing a kiss to my temple. "I've got you. We don't have to do anything you don't want to do," he says, and I record that in my memory.

I've got you.

He kisses me, slow and sweet, as though he's mapping out every inch of my mouth. My hands move on instinct, threading into his hair, pulling him closer. The kiss deepens, and I surrender to the feel of him—the warmth of his lips, the way his hands trail down my sides, leaving sparks of heat in their wake.

When he pulls back, his forehead rests against mine, our breaths mingling in the quiet. His hands slip under my sweater, and he pauses, giving me a chance to stop him. When I don't, he pulls it over my head, his eyes darkening as they sweep over me.

"You're so fucking beautiful, Kat," he says, his voice low, reverent. The way he looks at me makes my skin flush, my heart race.

His hands slide over my shoulders, down my back, unhooking my bra with an ease that feels practiced yet respectful. The straps slide off, and I let it fall to the floor, exposed yet strangely unafraid under his gaze.

His fingers trail across my skin, light and teasing, until his hands cup my breasts, his thumbs brushing over the sensitive peaks. I suck in a breath, my body arching toward him, and the sound pulls a low growl from his throat.

"You're going to be trouble," he whispers, and the rawness in it makes my heart stutter.

I pull him back to me, seeking his mouth again, needing the reassurance of his kiss. He moves us slowly, lowering me onto my back, his body hovering over mine, his warmth blanketing me. His lips never leave mine, but his hands begin their journey downward, exploring, worshiping, until they find the curve of my hips.

His fingers slip beneath the waistband of my pants, and he pauses, giving me a moment to object. Instead, I lift my hips, silently giving him permission. He slides them down, his eyes never leaving mine. When he removes my panties, I feel vulnerable, exposed, but the way he looks at me—like I'm the most beautiful thing he's ever seen—chases away my nerves.

He kisses me again, slow and tender, as his hands explore my body, leaving goosebumps in their wake. When his fingers find the heat between my thighs, I can't stop the gasp that escapes me, my body instinctively reacting to his touch.

"Is this okay?" he asks, his eyes searching mine for any hint of hesitation.

"Yes," I breathe, absorbing his devilish smile.

His fingers move slowly, gently, circling the sensitive bundle of nerves with a precision that sends waves of pleasure coursing through me. My hands grip his shoulders, holding onto him like he's the only thing keeping me grounded.

An embarrassing moan leaves my mouth, and I quickly meet his eyes, seeing them fixed on my every reaction. "You have no idea how long I've wanted this. To touch you. To taste you. To make you mine in every possible way," he says, and, my God, I'm going to come if he keeps talking to me like that.

Then, with maddening slowness, he presses a finger inside me, and the sharp gasp that escapes my lips has my hands tightening on his shoulders.

"You're so fucking tight," he groans, his voice thick with something primal, as his finger begins to move, stroking me with an almost torturous rhythm. His thumb finds its way back to my clit, pressing down with the right amount of pressure to make my back arch off the bed.

"Malachi," I whisper, his name falling from my lips like a plea, almost overwhelmed by how good it feels, by the way he's unraveling me piece by piece.

"Do you trust me?" Malachi asks, his finger stills inside me. My mind is a haze of sensations, overwhelmed by how good his touch feels.

"Yes, I trust you."

"Good," he says, commanding and soothing. "Then don't move."

I freeze, my body taut with anticipation, as his mouth lowers to my breast. His lips are warm, his tongue flicking softly against my nipple before his teeth graze the sensitive tip, sending a shiver cascading through me. The wet heat of his mouth is almost too much, and I fight the urge to squirm beneath him, every nerve ending sparking to life.

He releases my breast with a deliberate slowness, the cool air brushing against my damp skin where his mouth had been. He trails soft, teasing kisses down my stomach, each one igniting a fire beneath my skin. The intimacy of the moment, the way his hands hold me steady, has me both nervous and craving more, even as I try to process what's happening.

When his lips reach my hips, my breath hitches, and then his mouth is on me, closing over my clit with a warm, gentle pressure. The sensation is electric, his tongue pressing and circling in a rhythm that has my hips jerking involuntarily.

"Stay still," he murmurs, his voice vibrating through my core, but I can't stop the way my body reacts, instinctively chasing the pleasure he's giving me. His hand grips my hip, firm but not harsh, holding me steady as his mouth continues its exploration. "You taste like sin, and I plan to indulge in every damn bit of you."

"Fuck," I breathe.

Then he presses a second finger inside me, the stretch both

unfamiliar and intoxicating. My body tightens around him, a mix of sensations overwhelming me—heat, pressure, and something building deep inside, coiling tighter and tighter with every stroke of his fingers, every flick of his tongue.

I'm burning, too hot, my skin flushed and damp, and I can't stop the sounds escaping me—soft moans and breathless gasps that seem to spur him on. His movements quicken, his tongue and fingers working in tandem, and I'm squirming beneath him despite his earlier command, unable to stay still under the onslaught of pleasure.

"Malachi," I cry out, but he doesn't let up, his touch relentless and precise. My hands grip the sheets beneath me, anchoring myself as the pressure inside me builds to an unbearable height.

It's too much yet not enough, and I know I'm on the edge of something I've never felt before, something that sends shockwaves through me.

I squeeze my eyes shut as my body shudders with pure ecstasy, waves of pleasure rolling through me, leaving me trembling and breathless. Time seems to blur, the sensation lingering, until I finally open my eyes to find Malachi watching me. His expression is soft but undeniably proud, a satisfied smile playing on his lips.

He slowly pulls his fingers from me, and my body immediately misses the warmth and fullness of his touch. A shiver runs through me, and he moves without hesitation, grabbing the blanket and pulling it up over us.

"Are you cold?" he asks, tucking the edges snugly around me with a tenderness that makes my chest ache.

I shake my head, still catching my breath. "No, I'm okay. Better than okay. That was..." I struggle to put into words how utterly incredible I feel.

His chuckle is warm and low as he shifts to lie beside me,

wrapping his arms around me and pulling me close. I melt into him, feeling the steady rise and fall of his chest against my back, grounding me. The fire crackles softly in the distance, the room dim and intimate, but all I can focus on is the heat of his body and the quiet strength in the way he holds me.

His erection presses against me through his shorts, a reminder of what we haven't yet done. My hand drifts back, brushing against him, emboldened by how safe he makes me feel. I want to feel all of him, to know him in every way, to be closer to him.

But before I can go further, he catches my hand in his, his grip gentle yet firm. He lifts it to his lips, pressing a soft kiss to my knuckles before settling it back against my chest.

"Sleep, Kat," he says, a low rumble against my ear, warm and steady. "We have all the time in the world."

The last thing I feel before sleep takes me is the steady beat of his heart against my back, a rhythm I never want to lose.

THE SUN FILTERS through the garage window, casting golden patches of light on the ground. Cade's laughter echoes before I see him, that carefree sound pulling me toward him. We're back in my family's garage—the makeshift hangout we turned into our sanctuary, a place to hide from the world when everything else felt too heavy.

"You're so slow," he teases, sliding the door shut behind him, his grin lighting up the room. His black hair is tousled from the breeze, and he's already dropping into the oversized chair across from me, his energy infectious.

"I'm not slow. You're a cheat," I fire back, collapsing into the chair next to him. My pulse races, not from the sprint here but from the way he looks at me—like I'm the only person who exists. "I thought you wanted to run away."

He leans toward me, his gaze locking with mine, steady and sure.

"I do," he says softly, his voice carrying the weight of unspoken dreams, "but not without you."

I blink, and suddenly we're somewhere else—on the beach, our hands clasped together. His jacket is draped over my shoulders, shielding me from the cool evening air. The horizon glows in shades of orange and pink, the waves rolling in a steady rhythm that matches my heartbeat.

"You're the only person who makes me feel like this, Kat," he says, his voice low, intimate.

"Like what?" I whisper, my throat tightening with emotion.

"Like I could stay," he murmurs, his green eyes dropping to my lips. "Like home isn't a place but a person. And you'll always be my person."

He leans in, brushing his lips against mine. The touch is fleeting, but it sends a jolt through me, grounding me in the moment.

"Cade," I say, my voice trembling, "wait until we graduate. Then we can leave together, save the world, right?" I try to keep it light, but the heaviness in his gaze stops me.

"Come stay with my family for a while," I urge. "Get away from that house."

He cups my face, his fingers tangling in my windblown hair. "I love you, Kat Sinclair. I'll always go where you go."

My heart swells, and the words spill out of me like they've been waiting for this moment. "I love you more."

I climb into his lap, my lips finding his, the world falling away until there's nothing but us. His weight shifts, and I fall back onto the sand, his body pressing against mine. It feels endless, timeless—perfect.

In an instant, it's gone. I wake with a gasp, my chest heaving as I shoot up in bed. The room is dim, lit only by the dying glow of the fire through the doorway, and reality rushes back to me.

"What's wrong? Bad dream?" Malachi's voice cuts through the haze as he sits up beside me, his hand finding my back to steady me.

I shake my head, unable to speak, the remnants of Cade's voice still echoing in my mind. "No," I whisper. "A good dream."

He gently coaxes me back down, his hand guiding me with a soft yet firm touch. I turn into him, burying my face in his chest, letting his touch comfort me. His arms wrap around me, strong and protective, his fingers tracing slow, soothing circles on my back.

As the warmth of his embrace settles over me, I feel the weight of the dream linger—bittersweet and heavy. A single tear slips down my cheek, disappearing into his skin, but he doesn't say anything. He holds me closer, like he knows I need this moment.

The tension in my body ebbs away, piece by piece, until sleep finds me again.

"ALRIGHT, I think I'm ready. Is this going to hurt? Should I be doing anything specific? Like, what should I do with my hands?" My mouth runs faster than my nerves, and Malachi chuckles from where he's seated in one of the armchairs, his legs crossed and arms folded like he's trying not to intervene.

Bash grins, bemused. "Come sit here," he says, patting the couch beside him.

I plop down, trying to ignore the way my heart is racing. He scooches closer, his usual cocky energy tempered by focus. "Okay, first step, close your eyes and relax. Think about your gift—how it feels when you use it. I'll find your frequency and amplify it."

My brows furrow. "Frequency? That sounds...technical."

"It is. Sort of," Bash replies with a devious smile. "It'll make sense."

It all still sounds crazy, but my entire life is crazy, so who am I to judge? I close my eyes, trying to focus on the sensation of the veil—the strange pull I feel when I cross over, the faint whispers that brush against my mind like a forgotten melody.

Bash's hands settle on my shoulders, his touch warm and grounding. "This will only last for a couple of hours," he says, his expression softening. "So be careful. Don't overdo it."

That immediately yanks me out of my calm. My eyes snap open, and I catch Malachi's sharp glare cutting through the room. "What the fuck does that mean? How can she overdo seeing spirits?"

Bash shrugs, his fingers flexing lightly on my shoulders. "Look, I've never amplified a gift like hers before. If you try projecting and things feel...off, get out of there. Don't push it."

Malachi looks ready to call the whole thing off. "Maybe this isn't a good idea."

Bash sighs, exasperated. "Relax, Dad. Kat's a big girl."

I giggle despite myself, but Malachi's glare remains locked on Bash, his jaw clenched. "I'll be fine," I say, winking at Malachi before closing my eyes again.

"Yeah, famous last words," Malachi mutters, but he doesn't stop us.

I focus, willing my body to relax, and Bash's hands settle more firmly on my shoulders. The room falls silent except for the faint hum of electricity building in the air. At first, nothing happens, and I'm about to open my mouth to say it's not working when it hits me.

A vibration stirs beneath my skin, soft at first then stronger, until it feels like every nerve in my body is waking up all at once. It's like my entire being is resonating with something ancient and vast, something out of reach. A brilliant light flares behind my closed lids, so bright it forces my eyes open—and that's when I realize everything has changed.

Chapter Twenty-Two

RULE 22 OF THE NEW ORDER: MORE POWER
DOESN'T ALWAYS MEAN MORE CONTROL–
SOMETIMES, IT'S THE QUICKEST WAY TO LOSE
YOURSELF.

I'M STANDING in the living room, but Malachi isn't looking at me.

He's looking through me.

A chill races down my spine as I whirl around. My body is still seated on the couch, Bash's hands glowing faintly where they touch my arms, his head bowed in concentration. This is wrong. I never cross into the veil this way—without trying, without intention.

"Malachi?" I say, testing the air, but he doesn't react. It's like I don't exist.

I glance back at Bash, my voice trembling. "Bash, something's—"

Then I hear it.

A whisper. Soft at first then louder, like dozens of voices layered together. The air thickens, and shadows ripple along the edges of the room, stretching and twisting as if they're alive. My heart pounds as I turn in a slow circle, the temperature dropping with every second.

This isn't the veil. This is something else entirely.

"Katja." The whisper carries my name, disembodied but familiar. A woman's voice. Then a man's. Then another. The air vibrates with their chorus, each word tugging at me like invisible threads.

I stumble back, my foot catching on nothing, and suddenly I'm falling. The world tilts, and I tumble out of the living room, out of the light, into endless darkness. The room I left hangs above me like a distant window, glowing faintly in the void. I scramble to my feet, reaching for it, but something—someone— shoves me back.

"You don't belong here...but you will soon."

The voice brushes against my ear, cold and hollow, as though the speaker is right behind me. The icy breath freezes me in place, and I scream, spinning around to find...nothing. Only the darkness stretches on, endless and suffocating.

But then the void churns, swirling like ink in water, and shapes begin to emerge. The ground beneath me solidifies into a desolate, cracked landscape. Wisps of mist curl around my ankles, cold and clinging, and then they take form.

Spirits.

They materialize all around me, flickering in and out like broken projections. Men, women, even animals—some look almost normal, their faces solemn and pale. Others are horrors. Twisted bodies, gaping wounds, and empty eyes, frozen in the moments of their violent deaths.

I take a shaky step back, but they're everywhere. A crowd, restless and shifting, growing thicker with each second. My chest tightens, my breaths coming in shallow gasps. This isn't like the veil I've known. This is chaos. This is...wrong.

Amid the spirits, something else moves. Shadows. They dart between the dead, fast and deliberate, always narrowly out of sight. I whip my head around, trying to follow their movement, but they're too quick, slipping between the figures like predators stalking prey.

"Who said that?" My voice wavers as I turn, searching for the source of the voices.

A woman stands beside me, her face pale and lifeless, her eyes wide with something that might have been fear—or madness. Her lips curl into a wicked smile, too wide and too sharp, and she begins to laugh. It's a high-pitched, manic sound that claws at my nerves, and then she's gone, vanishing into the air like smoke.

The laughter lingers, echoing around me, picked up by others in the crowd. More spirits turn toward me, their hollow eyes fixed on mine. I stumble back again, my foot slipping on the uneven ground.

I've never seen so many at once.

The sheer weight of their presence presses down on me, until I think I may be sick. Their whispers grow louder, a thousand overlapping voices clawing at the edges of my mind. My head throbs, and I press my hands over my ears, but it doesn't help. They're inside me now, their voices wrapping around my thoughts, making it impossible to think, to focus.

I try to will it all away, to block them out like I've done before, but it's too much. The darkness is alive, crawling with restless energy, and I don't know how to control it. Panicking, I spin in place, searching for a way out.

The spirits close in.

"Help," I whisper, but there's no one here to hear me.

"Here, kitty, kitty." Damien's voice slithers through the crowd like smoke, wrapping itself around me and making my skin crawl. My heart jumps at the familiarity, a bizarre cocktail of relief and dread settling over me. At least it's someone I know—if you can even call Damien a "someone" anymore.

"The very person I wanted to talk to," I call out, forcing my voice to stay steady even as the weight of the veil presses in on me. My eyes dart through the sea of dead, searching for him, but he's nowhere to be seen. The air feels charged, the overwhelming energy of so many voices, faces, and emotions making it hard to focus. I clench my fists, trying to keep control. Bash said I'd be stronger. If I can see all of this—feel all of this—then I should be able to control it. Shouldn't I?

I close my eyes, forcing three slow, steady breaths as I try to quiet the madness around me.

I can do this.

I focus on the cold, electric hum of the dead—the constant, grating vibration that surrounds me—and attempt to shut it out completely. Normally, I'd lean into it, tuning in to each thread of energy to pull the answers I need. But this time, I push back, trying to create some semblance of peace in this cacophony.

When I open my eyes, it's barely better. The dead still swarm, flickering and murmuring like static-filled apparitions, their voices blurring together into an unbearable din.

"Want to take me somewhere quieter to talk?" I ask as I glance at Damien. He tilts his head and takes the bait. His hand grips my wrist, and the world around me shifts.

The suffocating darkness melts into the snowy forest I've come to associate with him—Damien's haunting reflection of home. The skeletal trees, their black branches heavy with snow, stretch endlessly, casting jagged shadows over the pale ground. The murmuring dead thin out, their flickering forms still visible but distant now. For the first time since I crossed into the veil, I exhale.

I don't pull my wrist away, even though the chill of his touch makes my flesh prickle. If he lets go, I might get dragged back into that overwhelming nightmare. For now, I'll tolerate it. "Thanks," I say carefully, keeping my tone light. No need to poke the bear when I need answers.

"You certainly know how to draw a crowd for someone who's supposed to be invisible," Damien says.

I narrow my eyes. "What's that supposed to mean?"

"You Avids," he says snidely, "you're supposed to be the untouchables. The pets no one wants to play with but that everyone wants to own."

That puts a sour taste in my mouth. He would see us that way. After all, I've seen how his father treats people like me. I want to snap at him, to tell him where he can shove his twisted perspective, but I hold back. Losing my temper won't get me the answers I need.

"Carmen said something before," I say. "She said, 'He's not dead. He's alive.' Who was she talking about?"

Damien's expression barely changes, but there's something behind his eyes—something smug. "Fuck if I know. Why don't you ask her yourself?" he says lazily, shrugging as if the thought of Carmen bores him.

"I've tried. She's not exactly easy to reach. Either someone's keeping her away, or she doesn't want to talk to me."

He lets out a sharp laugh, cold and humorless. "Maybe she's got her reasons. Ever think of that?" He licks his lips. "But I'm more fun to talk to anyway. You keep coming back, playing my games, hoping I'll throw you a breadcrumb. Maybe if you keep being entertaining, I will."

He's already getting under my skin, but I force a smile, knowing I need to keep him talking. "If you want me to keep showing up, you'll have to give me more than breadcrumbs."

He leans closer. "I have enough to keep you wanting more."

I steel myself, meeting his gaze head-on. "Your father, did he know? Did Viktor have anything to do with your murder? Did you do something to piss him off, something you couldn't come back from?"

Damien's smile falters, his expression darkening. "He's

innocent—if you think being uninvolved makes him innocent. Do you really believe something like that could go down under his roof and he wouldn't know?" His thumb brushes over my wrist, causing goosebumps to spread up my arm. "My father's no saint. He didn't pull the trigger, but he's never clean."

Damien's right—Viktor's reaction to his son's death was cold, calculated. A party mere days after Damien's murder, blood still staining the walls upstairs? That's not the grief of an innocent man. I already knew that. But Damien's certainty that Viktor didn't directly order the kill throws me off.

"Oh, Kitty Kat," Damien says, mocking affection. "You are going to be so surprised when you find your killer."

A chill creeps down my spine. "Why don't you tell me?" I ask, exasperated. "You know who did it. Why play these games?"

"Because it's fun," he says simply, his smile widening. "And because watching you figure it out is so much more satisfying. Careful who you trust out there. Us Volkov men can be very resourceful—all of us. Killing is in our blood."

I stiffen. It feels like a jab at Malachi, but I can't tell if it's meant to rattle me or if there's truth hidden in his taunt. Either way, I don't like it.

I narrow my eyes, forcing myself to keep my expression neutral despite the unease creeping into my chest. Damien thrives on reactions, I remind myself. Don't give him one.

"Good to know," I say. "Not that I'd expect anything less from you."

He grins, taking a step closer, "You really should be careful who you trust. Not everyone has your best interests at heart. If only you could see what I see."

I retort, my voice cold, "I don't take anything you say at face value, not anymore."

"Smart girl," he says, something dark lurking in his gaze. "But even the smartest fall for the wrong person sometimes."

I swallow hard, refusing to let his words shake me. "Is that what you think this is? Some cheap attempt to scare me off?"

Damien's laugh echoes through the trees, hollow and haunting. "No, Kitty Kat, it's a warning. Trust is a fragile thing, and you're in a world where even the closest bonds can shatter like glass."

He's not going to get under my skin, and I sure as hell won't let him turn me against Malachi. Damien loves screwing with me, twisting everything he says into a barbed threat or a cryptic taunt. His games may have been mildly interesting at first, but now? They're exhausting.

Damien releases my wrist with a sudden, icy shove. The snowy forest around us dissolves into darkness, its serenity melting away like smoke in the wind. The noise returns—voices, so many voices. It's a cacophony of whispers and cries, spirits clawing at my mind, each one desperate for attention.

It's like they want a piece of me, to give me a message, to take something from me. I can barely think, barely move, as the overwhelming sensation drags me down, my knees buckling beneath the weight.

As I'm about to lose myself completely, Mischka bursts into view, her glowing form leaping into my arms. Her warm, shadowy presence grounds me, and her familiar licks on my face help silence the relentless noise. I cling to her, drawing strength from her, until she wriggles free, barking sharply and darting ahead.

I follow her, my eyes snapping to where she's heading. That's when I see it—my window. My way back to Malachi's living room.

Except the sight before me freezes my blood.

The window is surrounded by the dead, their translucent hands clawing and grabbing at my physical body.

My body.

They're trying to drag it into the veil.

"What the fuck?" I gasp. This has never happened before. I don't even know what would happen if they succeeded. Would I be trapped here, my soul severed from my body forever? The thought sends a jolt of panic through me, and I take off running, my heart pounding as I chase after Mish. She weaves through the crowd of spirits, her calls guiding me.

I can see the living room beyond the window now. Malachi has his arms wrapped tightly around my waist, focused intently, while Bash flails wildly, his movements erratic as he tries to swat at something he can't even see. They have no idea what they're up against—no idea how to fight off the spirits threatening to drag me into oblivion.

"Mish, go!" I shout, my voice echoing through the void. She leaps through the window without hesitation, disappearing into the room. I charge forward, shoving past the spirits. Their cold, spectral hands claw at me, some passing through me with a bone-deep chill, others dragging me down with their weight. I can barely see, barely breathe, but I throw myself into the writhing mass, pushing and clawing until I reach my physical hand.

The moment my fingers connect with my own, everything snaps back into place. I gasp awake, my lungs burning as though I've surfaced from deep underwater.

I'm back. I'm in Malachi's living room.

Malachi's arms are still around me, his grip so tight it's almost painful, and Bash is breathing hard, his wild eyes scanning the room as if the spirits might have followed me through.

"What the fuck happened?" Bash demands, his voice loud

and sharp in the silence. But all I can do is sit there, trembling, as Malachi falls to the couch with me in his arms.

He grips my face, his hands firm but careful, his wide eyes scanning me like he's searching for something—any sign of injury.

"Kat, talk to me," he says, his expression tight with panic.

"I'm okay," I manage, slurring as exhaustion starts to pull me under. "That was intense, but I'm—"

A wave of heaviness crashes over me, my body sinking like lead into the couch. My head feels too heavy to hold up, my vision blurring at the edges.

"Kat!" Malachi sounds distant now, as though it's coming from somewhere far away. My last blurry glimpse is of him shooting Bash a look so sharp, so full of fury, it could cut glass.

"It's not his fault," I want to say, but the words don't come. I try to lift my hand, to do something, but the overwhelming pull of sleep takes over before I can process another thought.

Darkness swallows me whole.

Chapter Twenty-Three

RULE 23 OF THE NEW ORDER: ANSWERS OFTEN HIDE IN THE MOST UNEXPECTED PLACES—KEEP AN OPEN MIND AND LET GO OF ASSUMPTIONS, OR RISK MISSING THE TRUTH.

PRESSURE on my chest pulls me from sleep, and my eyes snap open. "Time to wake up, demon." Orin's voice invades my senses, and I find him standing over me, shaking me awake. Confusion and a spike of horror flood my system as I sit up abruptly.

I'm in Malachi's bed, but he's nowhere to be seen. The blinds are drawn, cloaking in a dim, disorienting light. What time is it? What day? Panic claws at my throat. Is Marco here? Did something happen?

My breathing comes too fast, and Orin, ever the opportunist, presses his hands against my shoulders and shoves me back down onto the mattress.

"What are you doing here?" I ask before I can think it through.

He sits down beside me—too close, the mattress dipping under his weight. "I think I'll be the one asking questions," he says smoothly.

I bite the inside of my cheek, my gaze darting toward the

doorway, my thoughts racing. Where's Malachi? What's going on? I force myself to inhale deeply, willing the panic to subside. I need to keep my composure. With practiced precision, I arrange my expression into a calm mask, the one I've spent years perfecting.

"My father sent me to deliver something he thought you'd find useful," Orin says, his eyes narrowing on me. "Why he trusts you, I'll never understand. But I think he'll find it very interesting how cozy you look in my brother's bed, barely dressed."

He tugs at the edge of the blanket, and I clutch it to my chest instinctively. Beneath it, I'm in pajamas—a tank top and shorts. How did I even get into these? The realization adds another layer of confusion, but I push it aside, refusing to give him the reaction he's fishing for.

I flatten my lips, meeting his stare with unwavering calm. "I think Marco would like you to deliver whatever it is you came here for," I say evenly, devoid of emotion.

Orin smiles, his eyes lingering a moment too long before he leans back, propping himself on one arm as though he owns the room. "Feisty as ever. You know, I don't think I've ever met anyone as skilled at manipulation as you."

I glare at him, gripping the blanket tighter around me. "I don't manipulate, Orin. So, whatever this is, whatever message or object Marco sent you with, deliver it and get out."

Orin chuckles, a low sound that echoes through the room. With deliberate nonchalance, he reaches into his inner coat pocket and tosses something small at me. Instinctively, I catch it. It's a plain blue book, unassuming and worn at the edges.

I flip it over in my hands before cracking it open. The pages are filled with handwriting, slanted and rushed in places, careful and neat in others. A jolt of recognition hits me as I glance back up at Orin.

"I did some interrogating of my own while you've been off playing house," he says, flicking some invisible lint off his coat. "It's Carmen's journal. One of the servants handed it over after a little...persuading."

He winks, and I feel a cold dread settle in my stomach. My grip tightens on the journal. "What kind of persuading?"

He waves me off dismissively, leaning back across my legs. "Relax. Nothing too serious." The implication makes my skin prickle.

"What's in it?" I ask, flipping through a few pages but finding no immediate answers.

Orin shrugs, already losing interest. "I didn't bother reading it. I'm not dying to dive into the inner ramblings of some dumb broad." His lips curl in disdain as he adjusts his coat. "My father thought you might find it useful to close this case. Don't think anyone's forgotten—your time is running out. Viktor's getting restless."

"Anything else?" I ask, my voice flat, leaving no room for further small talk, I don't want him to know how worried I am about figuring this case out.

He chuckles again, standing and stretching his arms over his head.

"You know, my father thinks I broke you all those years ago," Orin says with smug satisfaction. He grabs my shoulder and tugs me forward, forcing me into a hunched position. My stomach churns as he brushes my hair aside, his fingers pulling at the corner of my shirt to reveal the brand on my back. His touch is slow, deliberate, as he traces the scar with his fingers, and the revulsion rising in me is almost unbearable. I want to punch him in the face, to shove him away, to scream—but instead I stay still, biding my time, my teeth clenched so tight my jaw aches.

"He thinks you're still his loyal little pet," Orin continues, his voice sickly sweet. "But that's why he has me—so he doesn't have to worry about such things. I hope you don't need any reminding of who you serve."

His fingers linger on my skin, the weight of his threat coiling around my chest like a vice, making it harder to breathe.

I shake my head slowly, keeping my expression blank, though the urge to fight against him burns through me. My mind races, every nerve on edge. First, Marco drags me to see where the Avids are kept with that man—Boris, his twisted reminder of how much worse things could be for me under his rule. And now Orin, digging his claws in to assert control. Is it all because Malachi killed Eduard? Or because of what we did for Aurora and the boy? Or is there something bigger at play—something I haven't pieced together yet?

Orin pulls back, his fingers finally leaving my skin.

"Get up. We're going," he says abruptly. My stomach twists.

"I thought you were dropping off the journal," I say, forcing myself to sound calm, though my pulse races.

His mouth twitches, the expression cold and calculating. "I could smell my aunt's cooking when I snuck past to pay you a visit. I think we should go join her for dinner."

Dinner with Irina should feel safe, comforting even, but with Orin, nothing is ever as simple as it seems. What awful thing is waiting for me at the table? And where the fuck is Malachi?

I nod stiffly, slipping out of bed, and make my way to the bathroom, needing a moment to gather myself. "Hurry up," Orin calls as I close the door behind me.

I move quickly, splashing cold water on my face to wake myself up and shaking off the grogginess clinging to me after who knows how long I've been asleep. My reflection stares back at me, the faint shadows under my eyes and the tension etched across my brow revealing more than I'd like. I need to hold it together.

After a quick stop to pee, I pull my hair back into a pony-tail, but when I look around for something decent to wear, I realize all my clothes are by the closet—out there with Orin. Peeking through the crack of the door, I see him pacing the bedroom like a predator.

"I need to change," I say, motioning to my black shorts and tank top.

He stops, turning to me with a dismissive wave. "No, you don't. Put on your boots and grab a jacket," he growls, pushing me along without a second thought.

The cold air hits me like a slap to the face as we step outside, the chill biting through my thin layers. I hug my jacket tighter around me, trying to ignore the dread pooling in my stomach.

"About time. I was starting to—" Irina falters mid-sentence as she turns, her eyes landing on Orin standing in the doorway, his arm draped casually over my shoulders. The brief flash of shock that crosses her face doesn't go unnoticed by me—or Orin. She recovers quickly, her expression smoothing into something neutral, but it's too late. We've already seen it.

"Orin," she says evenly.

"Auntie, it's been far too long since I graced you with my presence," Orin says smoothly, stepping further into the kitchen and dragging me along with him like a prop. "I could smell your cooking all the way from the driveway. Thought I'd come see what you're spoiling my brother with these days."

Irina doesn't miss a beat, her smile polite but strained. "You must join me for dinner then. I'd love to hear all about what you've been up to," she says, turning her back to stir whatever is simmering on the stove. "Your brother should be along shortly. He had to run an errand."

An errand. Malachi isn't here, and I don't need him to be. Not for this. If Orin thinks he can get under my skin, he's in for a surprise.

I pull away from Orin's hold, stepping into the kitchen ahead of him. The warmth of the room and the scent of whatever Irina is cooking wrap around me, as I breath in through my nose. Irina busies herself at the stove, and though she masks it well, I catch the way her shoulders stiffen ever so slightly as Orin moves closer.

"Smells amazing, Irina. What are we having?" I ask, leaning casually against the counter. My demeanor is steady, calm—everything I know Orin isn't expecting. His little games don't intimidate me, and I want him to see that.

Irina glances back, her lips curving into a small smile as she sets a stack of bowls on the counter. "A stew. Something hearty for a cold day."

"Perfect," I say, grabbing the bowls and moving to set the table before Orin can make a show of offering to help. He watches me, his arms crossing as he leans against the wall, a smug grin forming.

"Always so helpful, aren't you, Katja?" he says, and I notice the seedy gleam in his eyes—like he's waiting for me to snap.

"It doesn't hurt to lend a hand," I reply, matching his grin with one of my own. "Something you might want to try sometime."

Irina hides a half-smile behind her hand as she pretends to adjust the flame on the stove. Orin's icy blue eyes narrow slightly, the first crack in his composed facade. Good.

I move to the chair closest to Irina, deliberately putting the table between Orin and me.

He grabs my arm, tugging me down into the chair next to him before yanking my jacket off and tossing it carelessly over the back of the chair. The bastard does it to get under my skin, to remind me he can invade my space whenever he pleases. I clench my jaw, refusing to give him the reaction he's looking for.

"Oh, Orin dear, won't Katja get cold?" Irina's voice is light, but I hear the edge beneath it. She knows exactly what he's doing, trying to defuse the situation without escalating it.

I give her a subtle shake of my head, hoping she'll let it go. I don't need her stepping in—not when I can handle him myself.

Orin chuckles, the sound as grating as nails on a chalkboard. "This tough little Avid? She likes the cold." His hand slides under the table, squeezing my knee hard enough to make a point.

The urge to fling the bowl of stew in his thick bearded face is strong, but I won't let him get to me. I pick up my spoon and take a bite, focusing on the warm, savory flavors. The stew is good—chunks of tender steak, potatoes, carrots, and peas swimming in a rich broth. I think this might even be real meat, and Irina must have a special greenhouse to grow vegetables that taste this fresh—or maybe they were cultivated in the Depths. My stomach growls, and I focus on eating, hoping he'll lose interest if I don't engage.

Of course, it's Orin, so that's wishful thinking.

"You're awfully quiet tonight, Kat," he says. His hand doesn't move from my knee, the pressure a constant reminder of his presence. "My aunt here has taken you into her home, treating you far better than you deserve and even letting you eat at her fucking dinner table. I don't think I've heard a thank you yet."

And there it is. His power play. I set my spoon down gently, forcing myself to keep my expression neutral. "Thank you, Irina," I say, turning to her with genuine warmth. "The stew is lovely, and I'm very grateful you're such a kind host."

Irina gives me a small smile, but her attention shifts to Orin, her features hardening. "You're very welcome, Katja," she says before fixing her stern gaze on her nephew. "Orin, you know I don't believe in mistreating Avids in this house. They're like us. I'm not my brothers."

I admire her for saying it so plainly. Irina might live out here in isolation, but she's not afraid to stand her ground, even with Orin looming over her.

He snorts, leaning back with an exaggerated sigh. "Mistreating them?" he echoes. "I don't think you believe in them at all, Auntie. That's the problem. You want to sit out here in the middle of nowhere, playing house, pretending the rest of the world doesn't exist."

I take another slow bite, keeping my eyes on the bowl, refusing to engage. Let him argue with Irina if he wants. I've got no interest in playing his games tonight.

"You don't have to believe in the world's darkness to know it exists, Orin," Irina says sharply. "But I also don't have to invite it into my home."

His laugh is cold, humorless. "And yet here I am. Since I'm here, maybe I can show you how entertaining an Avid can be. Consider it a token of my appreciation for this fine meal." His tone is sharp, laced with the threat of something sinister. My chest tightens, my spoon hovering over the bowl.

"That won't be necessary," Irina cuts in quickly.

Orin waves her off like she's said nothing of importance, the glint in his eyes sharpening. "Nonsense. If my father thought Kat should stay here, she might as well make herself useful." His gaze slides to me. "You know, I miss Uncle Jamie. Why don't we have Kat here translate a little chat for us?"

My stomach tightens as I glance toward Irina, catching the unease on her face. I didn't even know she had a husband—let alone that he'd died. The sadness that tugs at my chest is immediate, the urge to help her strong. But the look she gives me isn't one of someone asking for help. It's a warning.

"Thank you, but I'll pass for now," Irina says tightly, her polite veneer cracking enough to show the tension simmering beneath.

Orin grouses, "Come on, Auntie, don't be shy. Wouldn't it be nice to hear from Jamie again? Or maybe you're afraid of what he'd have to say." His smile widens as he leans forward, and the room feels colder, the air heavier.

"I said no, Orin," Irina yells, her voice like steel now. Her hand tightens slightly on her wine glass, and I can tell she's barely holding herself back.

I clench my hands under the table, willing myself to stay calm, though everything inside me screams to tell him off. The tension between them feels like a lit fuse, and I can't help but wonder how far Orin is willing to push tonight.

"Come on, Kat, give us a taste." Orin says, turning to face me fully now in his chair.

"You know I can't without knowing what he looks like," I say, hoping he can't procure anything.

Orin's chair scrapes loudly against the floor as he stands, his hand clamping into my hair before I have a chance to react. Pain radiates across my scalp as he pulls me up and forces me forward. I stumble, catching my balance, but his grip doesn't loosen.

"Goddamn it, Orin, not in my house!" Irina gets to her feet, her hands braced on the table, her expression thunderous. "I won't tolerate this behavior."

Orin doesn't even glance at her. His grip tightens as he drags me out of the room, the chill of the hallway air making me acutely aware of how exposed I feel. My boots scrape against the wooden floor, and my pulse pounds in my ears, but I don't fight back. Not yet. Not when I need to pick my moment.

He stops in front of a long table lined with framed photos, their glossy surfaces catching the faint overhead light. Without ceremony, he snatches one up and shoves it in my face, his fingers practically pressing the glass to my nose.

"Here. Take a good look."

I blink at the image of a younger Irina standing beside an older man, at least ten, maybe fifteen years her senior. His dark suit is tailored to perfection, his posture radiating control, his hand resting on her shoulder possessively. Irina's smile is faint, almost forced, her body tilted slightly away from him.

The man's face is sharp and cold, a charisma that borders on menace. He looks like the kind of man Marco or Viktor would consider an equal—an ally, perhaps.

"That's your memory now," Orin sneers, pressing a finger to my temple. "Seared into your pretty little head. Now, summon him."

He yanks me back toward the dining room, the photo clattering onto the table as we go. My pulse quickens as I glance back, catching a fleeting glimpse of Irina's face, her lips pressed into a thin line, her hands clenched at her sides. There's something there—something she isn't saying. But whatever it is, I don't have time to dwell on it. Orin drags me through the doorway and shoves me down into the same chair as before.

The room is silent except for the rustle of Orin's jacket as he leans over me, his fingers pressing into the back of my chair.

"Well?" he says, daring me.

I glance at Irina her eyes locked on Orin. She doesn't speak, doesn't move, and the silence presses heavier than Orin's grip. Whatever this is, it's not about me. A darker, bigger conflict than I can see has been brewing, and I want to know what the history is here.

"She clearly doesn't want this. I won't do it. I won't

summon him. You're not the boss of me, Orin. Marco is, and I don't see him here right now," I say.

Orin's eyes narrow, sharp as daggers, and if looks could kill, I'd already be dead. His hand tightens on my thigh, fingers digging in hard enough to bruise. "Summon him now, demon," he growls, his voice low and venomous. "Or I swear to god, you will not like what happens when I drag you back home."

The threat sends a cold shiver down my spine, the phantom burn of the brand on my back flaring to life as if it remembers. My fingers curl into the edge of the chair, knuckles white, but I refuse to give him the satisfaction of seeing me falter.

My gaze flicks to Irina, and her expression softens enough to tell me it's okay, though the tight set of her jaw tells me she hates this as much as I do. Her small nod feels like permission, like a lifeline, and I cling to it.

I close my eyes, inhaling slowly, trying to steady the storm raging inside me. The photo of Jamie is burned into my memory now, his sharp features etched in perfect clarity. I focus on them, on every line and shadow of his face, on the way he stood beside Irina with an air of control. I reach for the energy I know is there, lingering beyond the veil.

It starts as a faint chill, an ache in the air that slowly grows heavier, colder, until it wraps around me like a second skin. The room hums with something electric, the pressure thickening until my breath feels caught in my chest.

I open my eyes, and there he is.

Jamie stands before us, his presence commanding even in death. The air around him ripples like heat waves on asphalt, his sharp features as they were in the photo. His dark eyes sweep the room, and it feels like he's truly alive.

"He's here. What do you want to say?" My pulse pounds in my ears as I watch Jamie. His gaze lingers on Irina first, softening before sliding over to me. His head tilts slightly, an expression of curiosity crossing his face, like he's surprised I can see him at all. It's a reaction I've seen before, but it doesn't make it any less unsettling.

Orin shifts beside me, impatient. "Tell him to say something only I would know, so I know you're not making this up."

I glance at Orin then back at Jamie, who's now watching Orin with an almost amused expression. "He can hear you. I don't need to repeat it."

The ghostly man glares at us, piecing together what's happening in front of him. He doesn't like what he sees.

"Tell this little prick I should have taken more than the belt to him when I caught him stealing that nice bourbon out of my office as a young chap," Jamie says with dry amusement. I stare at him for a beat before turning to Orin, repeating the words verbatim.

Orin's grin widens, his hand lifting to rub his chin as if mulling over his next move. Irina shifts in her chair. Her gaze darts to where I'm staring, her expression torn between disbelief and dread, like she's teetering on the edge of speaking but can't quite bring herself to.

I don't blame her. The energy in the room is suffocating.

"Anything else you'd like to add?" Orin finally says, his voice smooth but sharp, like he's trying to bait Jamie—or me. "Or are we here to relive my rebellious youth? Why don't we talk about the day you died, Uncle?"

Jamie chuckles, his translucent form tilting his head toward me. "I've got plenty to say, girl, but only if you're smart enough to keep it to yourself."

I raise an eyebrow at him, my lips pressing into a tight line. Of course he'd drop some cryptic shit and expect me to pick up the pieces. Typical.

"I don't think your uncle's a fan of yours," I say, hoping to rattle Orin enough to end this charade.

Orin's grin falters, and his fingers twitch against the table before he forces the smirk back into place.

"Tell my wife I love her," Jamie says. I glance at Irina, repeating it, and watch as her eyes well with tears. She looks surprised, almost disbelieving. I wish I knew the story there—what kind of history lies tangled between these two. There's pain in her expression, yes, but there's something else I can't name.

Jamie steps closer. "Don't repeat what I'm about to say unless you're absolutely certain who you can trust. My wife—you can trust her. She has a good heart." His gaze locks with mine, and I nod ever so slightly.

"What's happening?" Orin snaps, leaning closer, his fingers tightening on my leg like a vice.

I don't dare look at him. "Nothing," I lie, keeping my gaze fixed on Jamie. "He keeps fading in and out. I think he's trying to hug his wife or something." It's the best excuse I can conjure under pressure.

Jamie's expression hardens, his translucent form flickering slightly. "You're looking for answers in all the wrong places. The truth you need to survive what's coming can be found where the wolves prowl." His voice lingers in my ears, even as he begins to dim. I blink at him, wanting to scream *What does that mean?* But Orin is right here, watching me like a hawk.

The sound of the front door opening echoes down the hallway, heavy footsteps approaching. Irina's shoulders visibly relax, though her hands tremble slightly as she adjusts the tablecloth.

Jamie flickers once more, his form beginning to dissolve. His gaze shifts toward Irina one last time. "When you're alone, tell her I'm sorry. I regret my actions, and all is well with us now...and forever."

I nod as his image fades entirely. Malachi's voice cuts

through the room as he turns the corner. "What the fuck is going on here?"

He strides into the dining room, his dark eyes immediately zeroing in on Orin's hand still resting on my leg. Tension radiates from him in waves, and Orin, of course, doesn't flinch. Instead, he leans back leisurely, as smarmy as ever.

"Family bonding," Orin drawls, giving my leg a condescending pat before finally removing his hand. "You know, making the most of this precious time together. I even reunited Aunt Irina with Uncle Jamie."

Malachi's jaw tightens, his glare shifting to me briefly, likely checking for any signs that something's wrong. I don't say a word, but the way his eyes flicker over me is enough to send a calming ripple through my nerves.

"Outside. We need to talk," Malachi orders as he stands rigid in the doorway. Orin lets out a low laugh, putting his hands up in mock surrender like this is all some kind of joke.

"I'll see you soon, demon," he whispers in my ear, his breath brushing against my skin, and I fight the urge to recoil. His words hang in the air like a threat, and I glare at him, refusing to let him see me flinch.

Orin rises from his chair, taking his time as if savoring the tension he's created. He adjusts his jacket and flashes that contemptuous smile as he saunters toward Malachi. "It was great seeing you, Auntie," he calls callously. Irina doesn't respond, her hand clenching the edge of the table as she watches him go.

The front door slams shut behind them, and I spring to my feet, eager to see what happens next.

Chapter Twenty-Four

RULE 24 OF THE NEW ORDER: EVERYTHING LOOKS LIKE CHAOS UNTIL THE RIGHT PIECE FALLS INTO PLACE—BUT NEVER MISTAKE DISORDER FOR DEFEAT.

"THE LIVING ROOM will give you the best view," Irina says as if reading my mind. I don't waste a second, rushing toward it and creeping up to the window. I stay low, careful not to be seen, and peek through the curtains.

Malachi is leaning against the doorframe with his arms crossed, his dark eyes fixed on Orin.

"You're starting to make a habit of this," Malachi says finally, his voice calm but laced with steel. "Poking around where you don't belong."

Orin shrugs, unbothered. "Looking out for family. Someone has to keep you in line, little brother."

Malachi laughs to himself. He pushes off the frame, closing the space between them until he's standing toe-to-toe with Orin.

"Family?" Malachi repeats. "You really want to talk about family? Because the way I see it, the only reason you're still breathing is because I haven't decided otherwise."

Orin tenses, his deranged grin faltering a bit. "Big talk for someone playing babysitter to Father's pet."

"Careful," Malachi murmurs. He leans in slightly, his gaze unwavering. "You don't want to test me. Not today."

Orin lets out a dry laugh, but there's a flicker of unease in his eyes. "What's your problem, Mal? She's an Avid. A tool. Don't tell me you're getting all worked up over her."

Malachi straightens, rolling his shoulders like he's shaking off the weight of the conversation. "My problem is you. Showing up uninvited. Grabbing what doesn't belong to you. Acting like you're untouchable when we both know that's not true."

Orin raises an eyebrow, his cocky façade slipping slightly. "Are you threatening me?"

Malachi steps closer, so close their faces are almost level. "I don't make threats, Orin. I make promises. You put your hands on her again, and I'll make sure the next hole you dig is for yourself."

Orin doesn't move, but his grin falters completely, replaced by something darker—something more cautious. "You've got a funny way of showing loyalty to Father," he mutters, stepping back. "Maybe I'll let him know where your priorities really lie."

"Do that," Malachi says, cold. "See how well that works out for you."

They stare at each other for a moment before Orin lets out a sharp laugh, holding up his hands. "Fine. You want her? She's all yours for now. Enjoy her while you can, but don't come crying to me when it all blows up in your face." He scratches at his beard thoughtfully then gestures toward the house. "Mark my words, there's something off about her. She's headed for a bad end and doesn't know how to stay out of trouble."

Malachi watches him get into his car, his fists clenched at his sides, his jaw tight. Only when Orin disappears down the road does he relax slightly, rolling his neck before turning back to the house.

I move to the front door, and as soon as Malachi steps inside, he closes the space between us, his arms pulling me into him. My forehead presses against his chest, the steady rhythm of his heartbeat calming me. The tension from earlier begins to unravel, his warmth like a shield against everything that happened tonight. My heart clenches, a warning I ignore. I've been so careful to keep my distance to protect my heart and keep my feelings in check, but I fear it's a battle I'm losing, and I lean into it now.

He slides his hand across my back, his touch firm and grounding. After a moment, his fingers find my shoulders. He leans back slightly, cupping my face, his thumbs gently moving over my cheeks as he studies me.

"Are you hurt? I should have known better than to leave you. Bash kept calling—he made a breakthrough with Avidian. I should have made him come here instead," he says as he shrugs off his coat. Draping it over my shoulders, he tucks the edges close around me like a blanket. The fabric is warm and smells faintly of him, a scent that makes me want to bury myself in it.

I shake my head. "No, I'm fine. Really. What did Bash have to show you?" I ask, pulling the coat tighter, letting the familiar weight of it settle me.

"He's been working on a way to control the inhalation better. He's created a mask with a button you can press to release just the right amount, so it lasts longer. It's still in the early stages, but I'll show it to you later. For now, let's get you inside before you freeze."

I nod. "We should check on Irina."

He searches my face then steps aside, one hand lingering on my arm as we head to the dining room. Irina sits at the table, the flickering candlelight casting shadows over her features. She clutches her wine glass, her fingers tightening and releasing as though trying to steady herself. Her eyes flick between us, softening slightly when they meet mine.

"I haven't seen Orin in a long time," she says, setting the glass down. Her hand hovers near the stem for a moment before she folds her fingers in her lap. "Dare I say he's gotten worse."

Malachi pulls out a chair, sitting down across from her. He runs a hand over the back of his neck, the tension in his posture betraying his frustration. "Orin's always been the same. You've been lucky to avoid him until now."

Irina lets out a sharp breath, leaning back in her chair. "Lucky," she mutters, shaking her head. She turns to me, her expression softening. "Are you sure you're alright, Katja? He can be..."

I sit straighter, adjusting Malachi's coat as if it could shield me from the memory of Orin's presence. "I'm fine. Thank you though. I'm sorry he showed up here. You didn't deserve that."

Irina waves, brushing the apology away, though her fingers tremble slightly as she picks up her glass again. "It's not your fault. Orin has a knack for making himself unwelcome."

Malachi leans forward, his elbows braced on the table. His jaw tightens, his knuckles brushing the wood as he speaks. "He won't be back anytime soon. I made that clear."

Irina tilts her head but doesn't press for details. Instead, she looks to the hallway as though expecting to see Orin's shadow creeping back through the door.

"Good," she says after a pause. Her hands curl around the glass, steady now. "The less I see of him, the better. You two should rest. You both look exhausted."

I think it's more of an excuse because she wants to be alone, and I respect that.

Malachi nods, and we both stand to leave, but something pulls me back. I glance over my shoulder at Irina, her face pale and drawn. "Jamie said he's sorry," I tell her. "He said he regrets his actions and that all is well, now and forever."

She inhales sharply, her hand trembling as it covers her mouth. Her eyes glisten, and she blinks rapidly, as if trying to keep herself from unraveling. Not wanting to intrude any further, I turn away, letting her have the moment to herself. Malachi doesn't say a word as he gently guides me toward the door.

The chill outside hits hard, and I shiver despite the thick coat draped around me. Malachi takes one look at my bare legs and shakes his head, muttering under his breath as he lifts me effortlessly into his arms.

Once inside, he sets me down gently and moves to the fireplace, kneeling to build a fire. I kick off my boots and shed the coat, watching him work as the familiar crackle of flames fills the space.

"How long was I out this time?" I ask, pacing near the fire, the heat warming my chilled skin.

He glances up at me, tossing another log into the flames before standing and dusting his hands off. "Almost three days."

"Fuck." I sink into the couch, running a hand through my hair. "Anything happen while I was out?"

Malachi leans against the mantel, arms crossed, his expression tight. "Apparently Orin showed up, which you already know. If I had any idea he would show up, I wouldn't have left you at all. Viktor's getting restless. And my father called— twice."

"Twice?" I arch a brow, already dreading whatever that means. "What did he want?"

Malachi shrugs, his discomfort showing. "Probably to remind us that the clock is ticking and to make sure you're not slacking. He was vague, as usual, but I don't think he liked the idea of you being out of commission for this long."

I sigh, resting my head back against the couch. "Great."

Malachi moves closer, sitting next to me on the couch. "Kat," he says softly. "We'll figure this out, but you need to take it easy. Whatever Bash did to amplify your power, I don't think we should try it again."

"We have other things to think about right now. First, tell me everything you know about your uncle and Irina," I say, shifting to rest against Malachi's chest. "What happened there? Because I know something bad went down."

He nods slowly, his arm tightening around me as he plays with a strand of my hair. "I don't know everything," he begins, "but I know Irina loved Jamie. He was quite a bit older than her, and she fell for him hard. It was only after she'd fallen that she started to see him for what he really was."

I don't say anything, waiting for him to continue, but my stomach starts to knot at the implication.

"He ran one of the largest underground trafficking rings to ever exist," Malachi finally says, his tone grim. "He was the one who got my father and uncle into it."

I jolt upright, disbelief washing over me. "What? Seriously?"

He nods, his fingers pausing in my hair. "Yeah. They were already into trading stolen goods and drugs, but I don't think they started acquiring Avids until Uncle Jamie came along and showed them the way."

The thought makes my blood freeze. The tangled web of evil runs deeper than I imagined.

"Irina loved him," Malachi continues, "but once she started to uncover the full picture of what he was doing...she killed him."

I sit up fully, turning to face him. Pieces start falling into place—the tension in Irina's demeanor, the forgiveness Jamie begged me to pass on. "What did Marco and Viktor do about it?" I ask.

Malachi shrugs. This is taxing on him, but I need to know more. "I was young, so I don't know all the details, but they love their little sister. I think they looked the other way. She played it off as an accident on the ranch, but I'm sure they knew better."

I swallow hard, imagining the guilt and isolation Irina must have endured. "Love makes you do crazy things, I guess," I murmur. "But even though he was clearly a terrible person, my heart hurts for her. She loved him, and she was still able to...do what she had to do."

I'm unable to fathom making that kind of choice. I've pictured killing Marco and Orin more times than I can count, but to kill someone I love? To live with that weight?

Malachi watches me, his hand sliding up to rest on my shoulder. "She doesn't talk about it, and I don't blame her," he says, "but she's stronger than people realize. She did what had to be done, and after that she started the Syndicate and now Solace. I think she's been trying to undo all of his bad deeds and the guilt that haunts her."

"Knowing all of this makes what Jamie's spirit told me even more peculiar," I say, shifting to face Malachi fully. His brow arches in curiosity, waiting for me to elaborate. "He said, 'The truth you need to survive what's coming can be found where the wolves prowl.' Does that mean anything to you?"

He leans back slightly, the firelight casting sharp shadows over his face. "No," he admits, "but there's a reason the Volkov family crest is a wolf. Volkov means 'wolf' in Russian. Marco and Viktor have been referred to as wolves for years—predators who always hunt in packs."

I blink. "That can't be a coincidence."

"It's not," Malachi says, the edge in his voice unmistakable.

He rubs his hand over his jaw, lost in thought. "If Jamie was trying to warn you, it might mean there's something tied to the family. A place, maybe. Somewhere Marco and Viktor conduct business or keep their secrets. Wherever 'where the wolves prowl' is, it's connected to them. And you said Jamie told Irina he was sorry and forgave her."

I lean closer, a chill creeping up my spine despite the heat of the fire. "Yes...but why would Jamie want to help me? He was the one who brought them into this in the first place."

Malachi's eyes narrow, his focus shifting to the flames. "Maybe he's trying to atone," he says distantly.

I start to wonder what would make a person change like that, when suddenly Malachi is off the couch, pulling his boots on with quick, deliberate movements.

"Get dressed. I'll be right back."

"What are you doing? Where are we going?" I ask, scrambling to my feet.

"I'm going to ask my aunt about what Jamie said. Get ready, and I'll bring the truck around. We need to go back to the Depths."

He's out the door, the cold air rushing in behind him.

I rush to the bedroom and grab a pair of black pants and a long-sleeve shirt, quickly pulling them on before reaching for my jacket. I see Carmen's journal on the bed and shove it into my jacket pocket, zipping it up.

My hands move quickly as I lace up my boots, my heart racing in anticipation. By the time I tug my ponytail tight and check my reflection in the small mirror by the door, I hear the low rumble of the truck pulling up outside.

That was fast.

Grabbing my gloves, I throw them on as I head out into the biting cold, the truck's headlights cutting through the night. Malachi is already in the driver's seat, his hand drumming impatiently on the wheel. He looks over as I climb into the cab, his expression unreadable.

"What did Irina say? Does she know what Jamie meant?" I ask as Malachi floors it down the driveway, the tires kicking up snow behind us.

"She does," he says tersely, "and you're not going to like the answer."

Chapter Twenty-Five

RULE 25 OF THE NEW ORDER: NEVER ASSUME THE
ENEMY ISN'T ALREADY TWO STEPS AHEAD—IT'S
WHEN YOU'RE COCKY THAT THEY STRIKE.

"WHEN WERE you going to fill me in on all of this?" I ask as I take in the room around me.

We've entered a part of the Depths I've never seen before, and it feels like I've stepped into another world all over again. The space is massive, easily the size of an aircraft hangar, segmented into nine distinct quadrants, each one seemingly designed for a specific purpose.

At least twenty people are spread throughout the lab, some working in small clusters, others practicing their gifts in isolation. The air hums with raw energy, a subtle charge that seems to sink into my skin and make my hair stand on end.

The first quadrant catches my attention immediately. Padded walls line the area, the kind you'd see in a gymnastics center but reinforced with something thicker, almost metallic. A young woman stands in the middle of the room, her hands glowing faintly as she conjures an orb of fire, spinning it rapidly before hurling it at a target on the far wall. The flames erupt on impact, but the walls absorb the blast like it's nothing. She smiles as an older man claps her on the back and points out adjustments to her form.

Aurora would love this.

The next section is enclosed in what looks like unbreakable glass, the kind that shimmers faintly under the fluorescent lights. Inside, two Avids are sparring—one wielding crackling bolts of electricity, the other forming shimmering shields of translucent energy to block the strikes. Their movements are fast, fluid, and terrifyingly precise, the clash of power echoing faintly through the glass barrier. These are all useful fucking powers.

These Avids are ready for battle, and I'm over here seeing ghosts.

Another area has rows of tables covered in vials of swirling, vibrant liquids—Avidian. Several people are seated, sipping from small doses of it while others monitor them, taking notes on tablets. Actually, I have no idea who is an Avid and who isn't, because everyone in here could be using Avidian.

A boy with silver streaks in his hair suddenly stands, his eyes wide as he looks down at his hand. He flexes his fingers, and a dense, golden mist forms around him, coiling and swirling like a living thing.

The quadrants are equipped for everything. One is filled with strange obstacles—walls to climb, spinning blades, and other death-trap-like mechanisms meant to hone reflexes and agility. Another features tanks of water where a woman submerges herself completely, holding her breath far longer than any human could as her skin seems to glisten like a fish's scales.

Near the back, a group gathers around what looks like a makeshift shooting range, only instead of weapons, they're using their gifts. A man with green eyes hurls jagged shards of ice at moving targets, each one hitting dead center.

"You're awake! How are you feeling? That was a trip the other day." Bash's voice pulls me from my trance. He's striding toward me, looking sheepish but animated.

"I'm good. Don't worry about me," I say, though my focus remains on the room. "Want to explain what's going on here since Malachi seems...distracted?" I gesture toward Malachi, who stands a few steps away, arms crossed, his gaze fixed on something in the distance like he's deep in thought.

Bash grins, though it doesn't quite reach his eyes. "Welcome to our little experimental playground. This is where we push boundaries, test limits, and make sure Avids have the tools to survive out there. Each quadrant is designed to train or experiment with different abilities. And we're fine-tuning the effects of Avidian. Both for them and us."

"Us?" I ask, narrowing my eyes.

"For Avids," Bash clarifies. "If a dose works, it grants temporary access to that specific gift. Avids can practice harnessing other abilities this way, and non-Avids—well, it levels the playing field when necessary." He gestures to the boy with the golden mist, who now seems to be summoning it into a shape—a weapon.

"Levels the playing field? Or creates a new kind of weapon?"

Bash hesitates, crinkling his nose and rubbing at his chin. "Depends on how you look at it, but what you're seeing here is controlled. Everyone in this room has agreed to be part of the experiments, and it's helping them. Look around—these Avids are getting stronger, more precise."

I take it all in, my skin prickling with unease and fascination. I glance back at Malachi, who continues to watch a group in one of the sparring quadrants.

"Bash, can you give us a minute?"

He looks at Malachi then back at me. "Of course." He

heads over to the nearest table and starts talking to someone holding a vial.

Malachi seems to barely notice when I approach him.

"Why are you being so weird and cryptic? You drag me down here and don't say anything. You said Irina knew what Jamie meant, but you still haven't filled me in. Care to share?" I shove Malachi's arm, hoping to snap him out of whatever is occupying his mind.

He blinks, as if remembering I'm still here, then grabs my wrist. "Yes, let's go to my office."

I barely have time to react as he walks over to one of the cabinets in the corner of the lab, shoving random items into a backpack. My curiosity is still fixed on the room behind me, on the Avids practicing their gifts and the buzz of power that makes the air feel electric. I want to stay, to watch, to see other abilities in this strange and fascinating place. But Malachi is already tugging me out and down the hall, leaving the lab behind.

We reach a door, and he pushes it open. The room inside is a stark contrast to the sterile, industrial feel of the lab. It's... cozy. The walls are lined with bookshelves filled with an eclectic mix of titles, their spines worn from use. A dark-mahogany desk sits in the center of the room, papers and note-books scattered across its surface. Two chairs face the desk, and off to the side there's a large leather couch next to a sleek black fridge. The space feels lived-in, personal, and completely unexpected.

I glance around, taking it all in, before my attention lands back on Malachi. He moves to his desk, drops the backpack onto it, and starts rifling through the contents with a single-minded intensity.

I cross my arms, planting myself in the middle of the room. "What the fuck is going on, Malachi?" My irritation rises, fueled by his silence and the way he keeps brushing me off. "You've been acting off since we got here, and I'm tired of being left in the dark."

"My aunt said 'where the wolves prowl' could be Jamie's old hunting cabin," Malachi explains, spreading a worn map across his desk. His fingers trace over faded lines, stopping at a remote spot. "He used to take trips there often, especially with Marco and Viktor. It's isolated, deep in one of the last forests left in the Western District, and only accessible with four-wheel drive. It's the perfect place to hide something."

My concern sharpens, the implications settling heavy in my gut. "How far away is this cabin?" I ask, leaning over the map.

"About an hour from here," he replies, pulling open a drawer and rummaging through its contents.

"I take it we're going?" I say, my voice dry.

"We're not going anywhere," he says without looking up. "You're staying here with Bash, where it's safe. I'll check it out and come back as soon as I can."

I startle, offended. "Excuse me?" I take a step closer to the desk. "You think I'm going to sit here and twiddle my thumbs while you head off into the unknown? With Marco's history, Jamie's cryptic warnings, and Orin's lovely visit fresh in my mind? No fucking way."

"Kat," he says, finally looking up, his tone even. "It could be dangerous."

I bark out a humorless laugh. "You think my life hasn't been a constant parade of danger? News flash, Malachi, I've been surviving worse situations than this for years. Dangerous is my normal. And I'm not staying behind."

He scowls bitterly. "I don't even have my team here," he says, gesturing at the map. "They're still at the safe house near Viktor's compound. I wasn't planning on taking action—only scoping the place out, gathering intel."

"Sounds like a low-risk operation, which means I'll be even safer tagging along. What could go wrong?"

He gives me a look, the corner of his mouth twitching as if fighting a smile. "You don't take no for an answer, do you?"

"Not when the alternative is being left behind with Bash, wondering if you're walking into a trap." I narrow my eyes at him. "You've got two choices: take me with you, or waste time arguing until I find a way to follow you anyway."

His smirk finally breaks through, but there's a flicker of something else in his expression—pride, maybe? "Fine," he relents, folding the map with a decisive snap. "But if we're doing this, you follow my lead. No going rogue. Got it?"

I grin. "I wouldn't dream of it."

He steps around the desk, his hands firm but gentle as they grab my waist and lift me effortlessly onto the map. My breath catches when he leans in, his fingers brushing a strand of hair behind my ear before his lips meet mine. The kiss is slow, deliberate, and intoxicating. When his tongue grazes mine, my mind betrays me, wandering to thoughts of him—his hands, his mouth, his body—everywhere at once, a flush of heat racing through me.

"Fuck, I wanted a night with you all to myself," he mutters, frustrated. His forehead rests against mine as I wrap my legs around him, pulling him closer.

"We can arrange that," I say, my hands slipping under his shirt, fingertips grazing the warmth of his skin. I press a kiss to his neck, savoring the way his breathing quickens under my touch.

His hands tighten on my hips as he pulls back enough to meet my eyes. "You're so fucking unexpected...in the best way possible," he says, his lips crashing back onto mine in a way that makes me forget everything for a moment. But then he steps back, a low groan escaping him as if it physically pains him to stop.

He says, "I need to grab a few more supplies and check in with Rain. Stay here and relax. I'll come get you soon, and we'll head out together."

I narrow my eyes, skeptical. "How do I know you're not going to leave without me?"

His expression softens as he reaches for my hands. "I would never lie to you like that," he says firmly. He reaches for his backpack, pulling it off his shoulder and handing it to me. "Here. It's packed with everything we'll need. If I was going to ditch you, I wouldn't leave this behind. There's some extra room in there—grab a few drinks or snacks from the fridge if you want. I won't be gone long, promise."

I take the backpack, but not without a small, suspicious squint. "Alright, hand it over."

He pulls me in for one last kiss, pressing his lips softly to the top of my head. "I'll be back soon," he says, his voice warm and certain. I watch as he strides down the hallway, disappearing around the corner.

As soon as Malachi is gone, I stretch out on the couch and remember the weight of Carmen's journal tucked inside my jacket. Carmen was young, in love, and meticulous enough to keep a journal—there's no way she didn't write about her boyfriend. And right now, he's my number one suspect.

I unzip the pocket and pull out the journal, flipping past the early pages filled with mundane daily entries. My fingers slow as I hit something promising—Carmen describing a man she met at a coffee shop.

"Dreamy eyes. Dark hair. He asked to see me again..."

Now we're getting somewhere.

A sudden knock at the door has me shoving the journal back into my pocket and zipping it closed. My heart jumps as I stand, halfway expecting Bash, but when I open the door, a girl around my age stands on the threshold. She's petite with black hair that spills over her shoulders, her nervous energy crackling in the way she tucks a strand behind her ear looking down.

"Hi, you're Katja, right? Bash told me a bit about you. I'm Isla," she says.

"Yeah," I reply, holding the door wider. "Do you want to come in?"

"Thank you. Um, I saw Malachi leave, and I thought maybe we could talk for a minute." She glances behind me, like she's not sure she should be doing this.

"Sure. What's on your mind?" I gesture toward the chairs in front of the desk. Isla perches on one, crossing her ankles and curling her hands in her lap. Her shoulders are tense, like she's bracing for something.

"I'm like you...an Avid, I mean," she squeaks.

I sit across from her, my interest piqued. "Go on."

"Solace saved me about a year ago, and I've been working with Bash ever since," she explains, her fingers fidgeting with the hem of her sweater.

"What's your gift?" I lean forward, eager to know more.

"That's why I'm here. I think maybe I can help you," Isla says, glancing at the door like she doesn't want to get caught in here. "Bash told me you can see the dead. He mentioned your projecting and that you're trying to solve a case—"

"Wow," I cut in, smirking, "Bash really does have a big mouth."

Her cheeks turn pink, and she shakes her head quickly. "He does, but only because he trusts me. We work together all the time, and I promise he's not running around sharing your business. I swear I won't say anything either."

I study her for a moment then nod. "It's fine. I'm not mad. How do you think you can help me?"

"When I touch someone, I can see things. Usually, it's memories they don't want me to see—trauma, secrets. It plays out in my mind, like a movie," she says, meeting my eyes.

That's...useful. Way more useful than my gift. "Amazing. And awful, depending on how you look at it," I say.

She laughs softly, covering her mouth like she's not used to laughing much. "It can be both. Anyway, Bash and I made this for you today. He was going to give it to you later, but we didn't want to upset Malachi since... Well, Bash said he was a little shaken after what happened."

She fishes a small vial out of her pocket and holds it out. I take it, turning the glass over in my hand. The liquid inside is mesmerizing, a swirling galaxy of shimmering stars. I've seen Avidian before, but I don't think it's something I'll be used to anytime soon.

"I saw Malachi leave and thought it was better to give this to you directly. You can decide whether to tell him or not. Either way, I won't say anything," she adds.

I want to hug her. "Thank you. Seriously, this means a lot. You really think it'll work on the dead?"

She nods, her expression firm. "If you can touch them, it should work. But make sure you use it at the right time. It kicks in fast—about a minute after inhaling—but it won't last long."

"Wait, Malachi told me Bash made a mask for this to work. Is that true?" I ask, and she shakes her head.

"He's been working on a mask, and it's almost done, but you don't need it for this. The Avidian will work right away if you inhale it. The mask helps release it gradually, so it lasts longer."

"Nice, sounds useful."

"Yes, very useful. The next step is figuring out how to combine different powers in the mask, so they're released all at once. Plus, the mask makes it easier for the team. Instead of digging around in their pockets for vials in the dark, they'll have vials clipped directly to the front of the mask, ready to release with the press of a button. There's even a dial to control the potency."

I grip the vial tightly, feeling a surge of hope I haven't felt in days.

"I can't wait to see it in action. But thank you for this. You have no idea how much this could help," I say, and she smiles, rising to her feet.

As much as I want to get away from Marco and be free, making progress on his brother Viktor's case will keep the heat off me.

"Good luck," Isla says, tucking her hands into her pockets and heading for the door. I watch her go, my mind already racing with possibilities.

I glance at the Avidian in my hand, the temptation to summon Carmen and Damian gnawing at me. I could do it now—use the vial and finally see the truth for myself. No more games, no more riddles. But Malachi will be back any minute, and the thought of adding this to his already full plate stops me. Tonight is already loaded with enough unknowns. I'll wait. Better to tell him about the journal and the Avidian when things settle down.

I tuck the vial safely in my pocket next to the journal, zipping it up tight, grateful for its sturdiness. I'd hate to crack it open accidentally. I cross to the fridge, pulling out a couple of water bottles and one of those pre-made cheese and cracker packs. I add a container of insect-based protein crackers for good measure, shoving everything into the backpack Malachi left behind. An energy drink catches my eye, and I grab that too. If I can't have coffee, at least I won't be dragging all night. Tossing it into the pack, I zip it up and slide it onto the desk.

I'm about to pull out Carmen's journal again to start

reading when the door swings open, and Malachi steps inside, a duffel bag slung over one shoulder.

"What's in there?" I ask, nodding at the bag.

"Binoculars, night vision, weapons—stuff," he says with a wink, setting it down briefly before slinging the backpack over one arm and the duffel over the other.

"Did you pack snacks?" he asks, and his grin widens as I point to the pack on his back.

"Snacks and drinks, all in there," I tell him.

He throws an arm over my shoulder, steering me toward the door. "Let's go see where the wolves prowl, shall we?"

Chapter Twenty-Six

RULE 26 OF THE NEW ORDER: THE TRUTH RARELY SHOUTS—IT WHISPERS, WAITING FOR THE RIGHT EARS TO HEAR.

"DO YOU LIKE TO HIKE?" Malachi asks, breaking the quiet from the driver's seat.

I chuckle softly. "Um, let me think...at night, in the snow, in the middle of a forest? Sure, why not."

We've been driving for nearly an hour, the last fifteen minutes requiring four-wheel drive as the trail grows rougher. The forest around us is dense, the towering evergreens stretching endlessly into the dark sky above. The moon tonight is a faint sliver, barely enough to light our way, and with thick clouds hanging low, the world outside the truck is cloaked in near-total darkness.

"Good," he says with a grin. "Because we can't drive all the way to the cabin. We're going to have to hike in if we want to go unnoticed."

I sigh. Of course. Not exactly how I envisioned spending the night, but I'd still rather be here with him than letting him do this alone. Malachi pulls off the trail, weaving the truck deeper into the trees until we're well-hidden. Finally, he kills the engine and reaches into the back seat for the backpack.

He flips the bag open, rummaging through it before pulling out a small case. The vials he grabbed from the lab earlier glint in the dim cabin light.

"Are those what I think they are?" I ask, watching him closely.

"Avidian," he confirms, holding out two small vials, one with a red cap and one with a green. "Put these in your pocket. I'm hoping we won't need them, but you never know."

I take the vials, turning them over in my hand for a moment before sliding them into the opposite pocket of the one where I already have something hidden. "I thought Solace wasn't using Avidian yet."

"We're not," he admits reluctantly. "These are still experimental. Only tested in the lab. I've never used either of them, but that doesn't mean they won't work."

I press my lips together to keep from blurting out something sarcastic, like how comforting that is. Instead, I ask, "What does the red one do?"

"It boosts strength. Not only physically but overall. You'll hit harder, throw better, run faster. Basically, you'll be a better fighter for a short window of time, maybe twenty to thirty minutes."

I nod, my stomach twisting slightly. "That could come in handy."

"And the green cap?" I ask.

"It enhances healing," he explains, slipping a green-capped vial into his pocket. "It's not miracle-level. A fatal wound will still kill you, but a deep cut? You'd recover without even a scar."

I let out a slow, steadying breath. "OK, great."

"Hey, it's better than nothing. Besides, I don't plan on letting you get hurt."

I roll my eyes. "Avoid getting mortally wounded. Got it."

He chuckles then slings the backpack over one shoulder

and reaches for the duffel bag of gear. I hop out of the truck, my boots sinking into the snow as I pull my jacket tighter around me. The air is sharp, biting against my cheeks, and the forest is eerily quiet, the only sound the soft wind weaving through the trees.

"Give me a minute," he says, opening the bags and moving a few things around. He puts a small blade in his boot and straps several knifes to his waist. Then he moves a few things from the duffle to the backpack, throwing the duffle in the backseat of the truck and putting the backpack on. Once ready, he turns to face me with a mask in his hand.

The mask isn't what I expected at all. I'm not sure what I thought it would look like, but definitely not this. It's a strange blend of something futuristic and an old gas mask straight out of my history book—like it was pulled from a scientist's twisted imagination.

It covers the bottom half of the face, its matte black surface catching the light with a faint, oily sheen. Two large, cylindrical filters sit on either side, vented with intricate patterns that resemble industrial fans. Their edges are lined with small, dotted ridges with embedded LED lights. The filters give it the unmistakable look of a traditional gas mask, but with a mechanical, almost sinister edge—as if it was built for survival in an unbreathable world.

But it's the vials that grab my attention as he loads it full of red-capped tubes that latch into the mask. Smaller than the potion-sized bottle of Avidian I saw in the lab, these are more like the vial Isla gave me. Several test tubes line the front of the mask now, each filled with mesmerizing Avidian. The contents shimmers faintly, almost alive, shifting with a slow, hypnotic rhythm. Beneath each vial is a tiny circular button, likely meant to release the contents at the press of a finger.

Malachi turns the mask in his hands, pointing out its

smaller details as he gives a quick explanation of how it works, clearly excited by what Bash has created. On one side, there's a small dial that he can twist and press to control the release of the Avidian.

I can tell Bash was far more concerned with control than comfort.

"So, you're not just experimenting with Avidian tonight, but you thought you'd try out this new mask too. It looks and sounds amazing, but what if it doesn't work?" I ask skeptically.

"Bash wouldn't let me take it if he thought it would fail," he says, making sure it's adjusted properly on his face. "Hopefully, I won't have to use it at all. But if I do, it's the perfect opportunity to see how it holds up in a real-world situation—not a lab."

I nod, uncertain whether it's a good idea or not, but there's no arguing with his reasoning.

Malachi moves around to my side, his eyes hardening into something more serious. "Stay close to me. We'll keep to the trail for as long as we can, but once we get closer to the cabin, we'll need to go off-road. I don't want to risk being seen."

I nod, swallowing the lump of nerves gathering in my throat. "Lead the way."

The hike starts off manageable, the packed snow on the trail making it easier to move without sinking too much. Malachi is silent, scanning the trees as we move, his sharp focus making it clear he's done this a hundred times before. Me? Each step feels heavier than the last as my legs fight the resistance of the snow.

"Remind me to work out more," I mutter under my breath, my boots catching on a root buried under the snow. Malachi glances over his shoulder, grinning despite the tension in his shoulders. "You're doing fine. Keep up."

"Thanks for the pep talk, coach. I can see why you're the Solace team leader."

After another twenty minutes, Malachi slows, his hand lifting to signal me to stop. I come up beside him, my breath fogging in the freezing air. "What is it?" I whisper.

He tilts his head, listening. "Thought I heard something," he murmurs, scanning the tree line ahead. "Probably an animal, but stay quiet."

Wild animals. As if this wasn't already creepy enough.

We press on, veering off the main trail. The snow here is untouched, the ground uneven and riddled with hidden obstacles. Malachi's movements are fluid, silent, while I feel like every step I take is a disaster waiting to happen.

Suddenly, he stops again, his hand reaching for mine to pull me behind him. "Do you see that?" he whispers.

I squint, following his line of sight. In the distance, past a break in the trees, a faint light flickers. It's not bright, but it's unmistakable—someone is out here.

"Could be the cabin," I say quietly.

Malachi shakes his head. "The cabin doesn't have electricity, and that's not a fire. That's a portable light, like a lantern or—"

"Or someone's here," I finish, the weight of the realization hitting me. My stomach knots as Malachi gestures for me to crouch. We stay low, moving through the trees with more caution now. My heart pounds louder with each step, every crunch of snow beneath my boots making me wince.

As we get closer, the light becomes clearer, and so do the voices. Two men, maybe three. They're speaking in low tones, their words muffled by the wind, but it's enough to confirm we're not alone.

Malachi motions for me to stay put as he edges forward, his movements deliberate, his hand resting on the hilt of a knife strapped to his thigh. I crouch lower, my breath coming in shallow bursts as I keep my eyes on him, waiting, watching.

He creeps closer to the light, disappearing behind a thick tree trunk, and for a moment all I can hear is the blood rushing in my ears.

A branch snaps behind me.

I whip around, my pulse leaping into my throat, but it's too late. A rough hand clamps over my mouth, and a strong arm wraps around my waist, dragging me back. I kick and thrash, panic surging through me, but the man's grip is iron. His hold is too strong. I hate being trapped.

Desperate, I bite down hard on the hand over my mouth, tasting sweat and dirt. He curses, his grip loosening enough for me to elbow him in the ribs. He stumbles back, and I turn, catching a glimpse of his face—a bearded, rough man with unfamiliar eyes.

Before he can recover, Malachi appears like a shadow out of nowhere, slamming into the man with enough force to send them both to the ground. The man doesn't stand a chance. Malachi's knife glints in the faint light as he presses it to the man's throat, his voice low and deadly. "How many of you are there?"

The man grits his teeth, glaring up at Malachi. "Enough to bury you," he spits.

Malachi's jaw tightens, and he presses the blade harder, drawing a thin line of blood. "Wrong answer."

Before he can push further, another figure emerges from the forest charging toward Malachi. I act on instinct, grabbing the nearest branch off the ground and swinging it with everything I have. It cracks against the man's head, and he drops like a stone.

"Kat!" Malachi barks, but there's no time to argue. More movement in the trees catches my eye, and I realize how outnumbered we are.

"They're surrounding us!" I shout, reaching for the red-capped vial in my pocket and deciding now is as good a time as any to try it.

My fingers tremble as I pop the top. A sparkling mist swirls out, and I inhale the vapor. The effect is immediate—a rush of heat, strength flooding my limbs, sharpening my senses. I've never felt anything quite like it, but I suddenly feel pure power coursing through me.

Malachi glances at me, his eyes narrowing, but there's no time for questions. More figures close in, and the fight begins.

"I take it you wouldn't listen if I told you to run?" Malachi asks, handing me a large knife, his eyes sharp and scanning the darkness around us as bodies move through the trees.

"Not a chance," I reply, gripping the handle tightly, trying to ignore the chill racing down my spine.

He presses one of the buttons on his mask, and a row of LED lights flickers briefly, casting a soft glow across his face. For a moment, his eyes widen, the Avidian taking full effect. It distracts me for a split second—long enough for something to go horribly wrong.

The faint crunch of snow behind me snaps me out of my daze, and I spin around.

"Touch her, and I promise your death won't be a slow one," Malachi growls, his voice cutting through the night like ice, a coldness in his tone that chills me to my core. And for some reason a part of me relishes it.

"I'm going to do more than touch her," the man sneers, stepping from the shadows, his hulking form blocking the moonlight.

Before I can react, Malachi moves in a blur, his body a flash of steel and fury. He shoves me back, my feet slipping in the snow as he crashes into the man. I barely have time to blink before the gleam of his knife flashes in the moonlight, and the sickening sound of steel slicing into flesh echoes through the still night.

The man grunts as the blade twists in his gut, the wet sound of impact following quickly. The stench of blood fills the air, and I scrunch my nose, trying to suppress the nausea crawling up my throat.

Malachi pulls the knife free with a swift, practiced motion, and kicks the man's body in the chest, sending him sprawling face-first into the snow. No need to finish the job—Malachi promised him a slow death.

I watch as the crimson liquid blooms into the white snow, staining it black in the cold light.

"Fuck," I breathe, stumbling back a step, my heart pounding in my ears.

Malachi doesn't look at me, his focus locked on the figure now slumped against the snow. His chest rises and falls quickly, his muscles taut, but there's no hesitation, no panic.

"Stay sharp," he says, barely sparing me a glance as he wipes the blood from his knife. "There's more of them."

I nod, clutching the blade he gave me, scanning the tree line for movement.

Something to the left catches my eye. Another figure steps out from behind a tree, their stance tense, weapon raised. I don't think, just throw. My knife slices through the air, grazing the side of their arm.

"Nice aim," Malachi says, impressed. But there's no time to celebrate.

The man snarls, throwing himself at me, but Malachi is there again, a blur of speed and strength. With one swift motion, he slams the hilt of his blade into the man's temple, dropping him instantly.

I glance around wildly, the forest suddenly alive with shadows. More figures are emerging, their footsteps crunching against the snow, and I know this isn't over.

"Mal, how many—"

"Doesn't matter," he interrupts, gripping my arm and tugging me closer. "Stick by me. Don't hesitate, and don't hold back."

I nod as he pulls another blade and presses it into my hand.

These men clearly aren't trained like Malachi. Watching him in action now, I understand why he's the Solace team leader. Part of me is terrified, but the other part is exhilarated. I don't know how much of this is his natural ability and how much is the Avidian, but he takes out several men without breaking a sweat, not a single scratch on him. All I manage to do is stab two guys in the arm, and even that feels like sheer luck from the Avidian.

Only one man remains, larger than the others, his broad shoulders cutting a menacing silhouette against the moonlight. He and Malachi circle each other like predators, the man wielding a knife in one hand and some kind of rod in the other.

Everything happens in a blur. A sharp hiss escapes Malachi's lips, followed by the sickening sound of flesh meeting steel. Red splatters the snow, staining it like spilled ink. Before I can think, my body takes over.

I sprint forward and leap onto the man's back, digging my nails into his face with one hand and slamming my blade into the side of his neck with the other. He thrashes violently, trying to throw me off, but he roars in agony, staggering, when I push the hilt of my blade in deeper.

That's when Malachi strikes, stabbing him twice in the chest, two quick blows. The man starts to stagger. A gurgled sound leaves his mouth as he coughs up blood. I rip my knife free from his neck and blood flows down the front of his chest as he collapses face-first into the snow.

Malachi yanks me off him, gripping my arms and hauls me to my feet.

"Don't ever do that again," he growls, his eyes blazing.

For some reason, I smile, my adrenaline still pumping. Maybe the Avidian doesn't only make you stronger—it makes you fearless too. Reckless. I'll have to ask Bash about that later.

We both scan the surrounding forest, but everything is silent now, eerily still. Malachi moves quickly, kneeling beside the bodies, checking their pockets and patting them down. His movements are efficient, methodical, and his focus is razor-sharp.

"These don't look like men my father would typically employ. What the fuck were they doing out here?"

"Maybe they were hunting?" I offer weakly.

"Then why attack us?" he counters, frustrated.

I press my lips together, thinking about it for a minute. "People are crazy, and men are cruel. I have no idea why they attacked us, but nothing would surprise me at this point."

He looks up at me, his eyes softening in a way that makes my chest tighten. There's something raw in his stare, a kind of empathy I don't know what to do with. Before I can dwell on it, my gaze drops to the gash across his arm.

"You're bleeding," I say, grabbing his arm to get a closer look.

"It's fine," he says, brushing me off.

"It's not fine. Take the healing vial," I insist.

"This isn't that bad," he replies, shaking his head. "I'd rather save it in case we need it later."

I scowl but don't argue. He tears a strip from his shirt and hands it to me. I wrap it around his arm as tightly as I can, tying the makeshift bandage with shaky fingers.

"Happy now?" he asks.

"Not even close," I mutter, stepping back and scanning the

darkness again. The cabin looms in the distance among the trees.

"Come on," he says. "Let's see what we can find before someone else shows up." He twists the knob on the side of his mask.

"Is there a limit on how much of that you should do at one time?" I ask, raising an eyebrow.

"Not that I know of." He shrugs, and I'm sure this is something Bash would have tested. I hope he's not lying to me so I don't worry.

THE CABIN MIGHT HAVE SEEMED CLOSE through the trees, but it's deceiving. We're forced to descend into a gully and then climb back up—twice—before it feels like we're making any real progress. My lungs are burning by the time we're halfway there, and Malachi keeps an arm wrapped around me, steadying me when my footing slips or I sink too deep in the snow.

"Did you feel anything from the Avidian?" I ask between gasps, trying to keep my focus on something other than the ache in my legs.

He glances at me. "Yeah. It was like everything I normally do was...amplified. My brain felt faster, my body stronger—more lethal."

I nod, sucking in air. "I felt it too. It's like I wasn't afraid to jump into the fight."

"You weren't," he says, chuckling softly. "You were downright feral. Remind me to stay on your good side."

I laugh weakly, the sound strained but genuine. "Noted."

He adjusts his grip on me as we crest another incline, his hand firm but careful on my arm. The trees around us grow denser, their branches stretching over us like skeletal fingers, blocking out what little moonlight we have. The shadows deepen, and the air feels colder.

"We're almost there. Let's stop here for a minute. I want to take a look around before we get any closer," Malachi murmurs. He sets his pack down and pulls out a pair of night vision goggles. He slips them on and scans the area.

I crouch beside him, watching as his gaze sweeps across the cabin and surrounding woods. His focus is intense, his body completely still as he assesses every detail. He lowers the goggles and looks at me.

"No movement. The cabin's dark, and I don't see anyone nearby. It's safe to approach—for now."

"Let's get this over with," I whisper, gripping the knife hidden in my pocket as Malachi stows the goggles.

We press on, the silence of the forest unnerving. The closer we get, the heavier the air feels, like the woods themselves are watching us.

As we crest another small rise, a howl rips through the silence. It's long, mournful, and impossibly loud, echoing through the trees like a warning. My heart lurches, and I whip my head toward the sound, my breath hitching.

Malachi freezes, his hand shooting out to steady me. "Stay close," he says.

Another howl joins the first, then another, and soon the forest is alive with the haunting sound. My stomach tightens as dark shapes moves through the forest ahead. My blood runs cold as the figures emerge into view, their eyes glowing faintly in the night.

"Wolves," I whisper, but as they come closer, I realize these aren't normal wolves.

They're massive, easily twice the size of any wolf I've seen before. Their fur is patchy and uneven, matted with what looks like dried blood. Their limbs are unnaturally long, their muscles bulging in ways that seem wrong, twisted. And their eyes are too bright, too intelligent, like there's something else behind them, something unnatural.

"Fuck," Malachi mutters, stepping in front of me, his knife drawn. "They look like they've been experimented on."

The closest wolf snarls, its lips peeling back to reveal jagged, oversized teeth. Saliva drips from its maw, steaming as it hits the snow.

I take a step back, my blade trembling in my grip, suddenly feeling too small. "What do we do?"

Malachi's eyes flick between the wolves, assessing. "We don't run. That'll trigger their instincts. Stay behind me and—"

Before he can finish, one of the wolves charges. Malachi moves faster than I can process, stepping into its path and slashing his knife across its shoulder. The creature howls in pain but doesn't stop, lunging for him again.

Another wolf leaps from the side, and I barely manage to dodge, slashing wildly with my knife. The blade connects, cutting deep into its side, but it doesn't slow the creature much.

Malachi kicks the first wolf back and pulls me closer to him. "Stay with me. Don't let them separate us."

The wolves close in, their movements unnervingly coordinated. They're not attacking randomly—they're hunting.

"Fuck this," Malachi growls, pressing one of the tiny buttons on the front of the mask again and turning the knob.

Another wolf leaps, and he meets it in midair, driving his knife into its throat. Blood sprays across the snow as the wolf collapses with a yelp, but the others don't hesitate.

One lunges at me, and I slash at its face, barely managing to keep it at bay. The sheer force of its weight knocks me back into the snow, and I lose my footing. The beast is on top of me in an instant, its heavy, wet maw dripping dangerously close to my face. My blood runs cold as its rancid breath washes over me.

Without thinking, I shove my blade upward, driving it directly into the beast. It lets out a low growl, jumping off me and circling back to the trees, drops of blood staining the snow as it moves.

I scramble to my feet, my heart pounding as I look for Malachi.

He's a whirlwind of motion, trying to fend off wolf after wolf, but there are too many.

"Malachi!" I shout as one of the wolves charges at him from behind.

He spins in time, his knife flashing as it finds its mark. The wolf collapses, but he's breathing heavily now, his movements slowing.

The remaining wolves pause, perhaps wary now that they've met stiff resistance, their glowing eyes fixed on us as they regroup. My chest heaves, my hand shaking as I grip my knife tighter.

"We can't stay here," Malachi says, his voice steady despite the utter chaos. "We need to get to the cabin."

I nod, swallowing hard. "Let's go."

Together, we start to back away, the wolves following at a distance, their eyes never leaving us.

The wolves' snarls grow louder with every step we take, their frothing maws snapping. One lunges at Malachi, and he fends it off with a brutal swing of his knife, but I barely have time to feel relief before another grabs me from behind. Its claws rake across my back as I'm knocked to the ground, and I scream as its teeth sink into my leg. The pain is sharp and unrelenting.

"Kat!" Malachi's voice roars, his eyes blazing with terror as he spins to face me. He doesn't hesitate. The blade in his hand arcs through the air, embedding itself deep into the wolf's shoulder. The beast releases me with a pained whimper and stumbles off, but the others aren't retreating. They're circling, their growls vibrating in the air like a sinister symphony.

My leg burns, the pain unbearable, but I force myself not to cry. I bite my lip so hard it tastes like copper. The last thing I want is to show weakness—not now, not here. And God, I hope that thing didn't have rabies.

Malachi reaches my side and shrugs off his backpack. "Put this on," he orders, shoving it into my arms. His voice is steady, but his eyes betray the panic he's barely keeping at bay.

I nod, clutching the bag as he helps me to my feet. I wobble but manage to slip the straps over my shoulders. Before I can protest, he kneels.

"Get on," he says, leaving no room for argument.

I climb onto his back, wrapping my arms around his shoulders and my legs around his waist as tightly as I can manage. He steadies me with one hand and grips his knife with the other, moving backward toward the cabin with deliberate steps.

I feel the wet warmth of blood seeping down my leg, the thick liquid sticking to my skin as we step back. One of the creatures approaches, its massive black form blending with the night. It lowers its snout to the snow, directly where my blood has stained the white ground. The animal sniffs deeply, its nose twitching, and then it tilts its head at me—its eyes glinting with a strange, unnerving intelligence.

A chill crawls up my spine as it stares me down, and then with an eerie, bone-chilling howl, it shatters the silence of the night. The sound is raw, primal—something that rattles my very bones.

I squeeze Malachi tighter, every instinct inside me screaming to run, to escape the sharp, hungry gaze of the creature. But I can't tear my eyes away.

God, I don't want to die like this. My mind races with intrusive thoughts of what it would feel like to be torn apart, the sheer horror of being devoured alive. And next to Malachi, of all people—the man I have feelings for, feelings I'm not ready to name but can't deny.

Another howl pierces the night, distant but sharp, and it cuts through my spiraling thoughts like a blade. Malachi freezes mid-step, his grip on me tightening. The wolves stop, their heads snapping toward the sound. They exchange looks, their postures shifting as if communicating something we can't understand.

Then, as suddenly as they appeared, they're gone. The pack bolts into the darkness, vanishing between the trees like shadows.

I barely have time to process what happened before Malachi is running. His strides are long and powerful, his breath ragged as he barrels toward the cabin. I cling to him, my fingers digging into his shoulders, and force myself to keep my eyes open, scanning the forest for any sign of movement.

The cabin looms ahead, dark and silent. It's so close. *Please, let it be unlocked.*

Malachi reaches the door and slams into it with his shoulder. By some miracle, it swings open. He rushes inside, setting me on a table before barricading the door with whatever he can find. Chairs, a heavy dresser, anything that will hold.

He moves to the windows next, shoving furniture against them until only slivers of moonlight sneak through. Finally, he finds a candle on the stove, lighting it and bringing it over to me. Its flickering glow casts long shadows on the wooden walls, but it's enough to push back the suffocating darkness.

My breath comes in shallow gasps, and I clutch the edges of the table, trying to ground myself. The air inside the cabin feels heavy but safe. For the first time since the wolves appeared, I feel like I can breathe.

Malachi steps closer, his eyes scanning me, lingering on my leg. "You're bleeding," he says.

I glance down at my torn pants, the blood staining my skin, and manage a weak smile. "It's a scratch."

He pulls his mask off and cringes at my leg. "That's not a scratch, Kat."

He's angry—not at me but at whatever twisted hand dealt us this night.

Chapter Twenty-Seven

RULE 27 OF THE NEW ORDER: WHERE THERE'S
SMOKE, THERE'S FIRE—AND SOMETIMES YOU MUST
EMBRACE THE BURN.

"TAKE THIS NOW," Malachi says, handing me the healing vial.
I quickly pull the one from my pocket and shove it toward him.

"Only if you take this one," I counter, holding firm. His
eyes narrow, the kind of look that says he's about to argue, but I
cross my arms and dig in.

"Your injury is far worse than mine," he insists. "I don't
want to waste it. What if those things come back?"

"Then you'll need to be at full strength," I retort. "Take it,
or I won't either."

His jaw tightens, and I know I've won when he pops the
top off the vial and inhales the shimmering contents in one
sharp breath. "You're impossible sometimes. Do you know
that?" he mutters, shaking his head.

"I pride myself on it," I say, smiling as I take my own dose.
The warmth spreads through me instantly, and the sharp pain
in my leg fades almost entirely.

Malachi lets out a short laugh, tossing the empty vial onto
the counter.

In an instant, he closes the distance between us, his mouth

crashing into mine with a force that sends me sliding back on the smooth surface of the table. My legs part instinctively as I grab at the front of his shirt, tugging him closer while he devours me with hungry kisses.

One of his arms wraps around my back, and the other shoves into my hair, holding me to him. All I want is to be closer to him. I can't get enough of him—his lips, his body, his scent. His teeth graze my lip, and I moan as he rocks his hips into me.

When he finally pulls back, his forehead rests against mine, and I realize I'm panting, struggling to catch my breath.

"Fuck," he mutters, his voice ragged. "There were a few moments out there where I thought I might never get to do that again."

I slide my hand down his chest, feeling the steady thrum of his heartbeat.

"Then don't stop."

His grin is both wicked and tender as his fingers grasp my chin, tilting my face up to his. "I need to see you. All of you." His hand releases my chin, trailing down my neck and then further in a slow, soothing motion before it reaches the hem of my shirt. "Let me."

I lift my arms without hesitation, and he pulls my top off over my head, tossing it aside. His eyes rake over me, and I don't shy away from his gaze. Instead, I reach back, unclasp my bra, and let it fall to the floor.

"I'm not sure what I want more right now—to worship you or ruin you."

I run my teeth over my bottom lip. "Why not both?"

That infuriatingly sexy smile spreads across his lips, and I clasp my hands around his neck, pulling him into me, capturing his mouth with mine. I can feel the hard press of him between my legs, his arousal straining against his pants, and it ignites a fire inside me. My hand slides down, pressing against the bulge, and his groan vibrates against my lips. His tongue explores my mouth with a desperation that feels like he's trying to memorize every part of me.

The tension that's been building between us is about to explode, and I'm ready for it. I want to burn for him, with him, until there's nothing left.

Malachi's kiss softens, becoming achingly tender as his hands slide up my thighs to settle on my hips, his grip firm as though he's afraid to let me go. The sensation sends sparks racing through me, and I arch into him, my heart pounding like a drum in my chest. His lips leave mine, trailing down my jaw and onto my neck and down to my breasts, where he nips and sucks in all the right places.

"You're more than I deserve, but I'm selfish enough to want you anyway." His breath is hot against my skin, and a shiver crawls down my spine.

"Then stop talking about what you deserve and let me show you what I want."

Before I finish speaking, my hands are already sliding under his shirt, desperate to feel the heat of his skin. He helps me, pulling it off in one swift motion and tossing it aside. I take a moment to look at him, to admire the lines of his chest and the way the candlelight dances across his skin.

He's so damn beautiful. I've known it since the moment I first saw him—his broad frame, that perfect smile, the effortless power in the way his muscles flex. His mouth twists into the charming smirk he wears so well. "See something you like?"

"Wouldn't you like to know."

I slide off the table and reach for him, my lips demanding to taste him again. I kiss him, frantic and messy, and he lets me explore his mouth, matching my intensity. My hands move to his belt, fumbling to undo it without breaking the kiss, but his hands stop me, a low laugh rumbling in his chest.

"What?" I pull back to look at him, and he grabs my hips, lifting me and placing me back onto the edge of the table.

"You shouldn't be standing on your ankle yet."

"I told you it's fine," I argue, reaching for his waist again, but he catches my hands in his, holding them firmly.

"I'll decide when it's fine." He lifts my hand to his lips, brushing a slow kiss across my knuckles. His eyes burn into mine, like smoldering embers glowing with flecks of gold.

Fuck.

I want him to take his time, but I also want him on me and inside me right now. My body is already burning with anticipation—I need more.

He releases my wrists, his fingers finding the waistband of my pants. He doesn't rush, sliding them down along with my panties in one fluid motion, his hands grazing my skin and leaving a trail of fire in their wake. One boot falls to the ground with a thud, then the other, the sound matching the frantic beat of my heart.

When I'm completely bare in front of him, he pushes my thighs open and wraps an arm around my lower back, tugging me to the very edge of the table.

The hard press of his cock against me makes my breath hitch, and I curse the fabric of his pants for being between us.

My hands move to his stomach, trailing over the coiled muscles there, and then slide up to wrap around his neck, coaxing him to kiss me again. His mouth claims mine, his tongue tracing my bottom lip before trailing to my ear. He nibbles at the sensitive skin, and as I'm about to beg for more, his hand cups my center.

One finger presses inside me, and my body reacts instantly,

tightening around him. A groan escapes my lips as my head falls back, exposing my neck to his kisses.

"You're so fucking perfect." His lips brush my throat. "So wet for me, Kat."

I place my hand over his, pressing it to me harder, and he glides another finger inside me. It's too much and not enough all at once. I need more of him—every piece of him—but the thought also terrifies me.

"So impatient," he teases, and I don't disagree.

His thumb grazes my clit, and my hips jerk in response, seeking more of the delicious pressure.

I go completely still when he lowers his mouth to my center, his lips replacing his thumb. His tongue parts my flesh with exquisite precision, my back arches, and I can't stop the raw, needy sound that tears from my throat. My fingers tangle in his hair, holding him to me as his tongue works magic, circling and stroking. One of his hands keeps a steady hold on my thigh, anchoring me in place, while the other continues its intoxicating rhythm inside me.

"Malachi," I breathe, and his responding hum sends vibrations through me that push me closer to the edge.

The world fades until there's nothing but him—his touch, his mouth, the way he's unraveling me so completely, like he's always known exactly how. This isn't just about desire. It's about trust. About stepping into something I've never allowed myself to imagine.

I've spent so long running, so long surviving, that I forgot what it feels like to simply be. To let someone in. And now, with Malachi, I feel like I can.

The way he touches me isn't just hungry—it's deliberate, like he's memorizing every inch of me, like he wants to erase every scar left behind by the life I've lived. His focus is all-consuming, and for the first time I feel like more than just my gift or my past.

I didn't think I'd ever want this. I didn't think I'd ever trust someone enough to have this. But here I am, wanting him, needing him in a way that scares me and excites me all at once.

For so long, I've believed that I was broken. That someone like me couldn't have a future, let alone happiness. But right now, with his hands on me, with the fire in his eyes pulling me in, I want to believe.

I want to believe I can have more.

That I can have him.

I can have Malachi.

And right now, I want him more than I've ever wanted anything.

I glance down at him, and air stalls in my lungs. His focus is entirely on me, like I'm the only thing that matters in the world. There's hunger in his gaze, yes, but there's something else too. Something softer, more consuming. It's devotion. Worship. The way his hands move over me, the way his mouth lingers, pulling shivers and gasps from me with every touch... I've never felt more wanted.

More seen.

Suddenly, he pulls back, his fingers slipping out of me as he stands. My body protests the loss of him, but the way his hands move to undo his pants ignites a new wave of suspense. My eyes are fixed on him, my breathing uneven as I watch his movements. He doesn't rush, his focus locked on mine with an intensity that makes my nerves alight.

"Tell me you've never done this before." His pants hit the floor, and he steps out of them with a confidence that's both captivating and overwhelming.

My breathing falters.

He's hard and thick, and I can't tear my eyes away. He's so fucking perfect, and the urge to taste him builds low in my stomach. But I don't move—my body frozen, caught in the intensity of the moment.

Heat floods my cheeks, and the air between us crackles, alive with tension. I've waited so long for this, and now that it's here, it feels like I might combust under the weight of it.

"Tell me I'm the only one." He takes a step toward me.

I meet his unrelenting stare. "There's only you," I whisper.

He takes a step closer and then another, until he's standing between my legs again. His large hands slide up my thighs, his lips brushing against mine in a kiss that's somehow softer than before but no less consuming. God, I want to cling to him, unshakable, like a shadow bound to its source.

I wrap my arms around his neck as he presses against me. I can feel him at my entrance, his warmth searing into my skin. He touches my breasts and teases my nipples, taking his time kissing my neck then my jaw and my mouth.

"No one else will ever touch you like this." His lips brush against mine, his hands tightening on my hips. "Because you're mine, Kat. Only mine."

The raw hunger in his claim sinks into me, and the way he says my name sends a sharp ache through my chest—one I know I should ignore but can't.

"Prove it," I whisper between kisses.

"I intend to. Over and over again." He starts to push inside me, taking his time, the pressure building as he stretches me in a way that steals the air from my lungs. My breath hitches, my nails digging into his shoulders as my legs wrap around his waist, anchoring myself to him.

"Easy," he says, his voice a low rasp, rough with restraint. His hand moves to cup my cheek, his thumb brushing softly against my skin. "Tell me if it's too much."

I shake my head, unable to speak, my chest heaving as he presses deeper. Every glorious inch of him fills me, a mix of pleasure and sharp, sudden pain making my body tremble. When I think he can't possibly go deeper, he does, and a soft whimper escapes me.

His forehead presses gently to mine, his eyes searching my face.

"Stay with me. Look at me."

I squeeze my eyes shut against the overwhelming sensation, but the gentle brush of his fingers through my hair draws me back. "I want to see your face when I make you fall apart."

I force my eyes open, locking onto his. The intensity in his stare anchors me, and he stays perfectly still, giving me a moment to adjust. His hands find my waist, his thumbs brushing soothing circles into my skin. Slowly, the pain starts to ebb, replaced by something deeper, something more consuming. When I nod, he takes the cue.

He pulls out slowly, the sensation leaving me wanting more, and then thrusts back in. My head falls back, a shaky breath turns into a moan as he fills me, stretching me in ways I've never experienced.

"Malachi," I exhale, gripping him tighter as he thrusts again, his movements gaining confidence and strength.

"Say my name again, and I might lose control."

Fuck, this is him in control. The way he moves, the way he looks at me—I'm already consumed, drowning in him. But God, I want to feel him lose it. "Malachi," I cry out again.

With a growl, he lifts me off the table, pressing me against the wall. The cool surface contrasts with the heat of his body, his arm firm around my waist as he holds me effortlessly. His other hand tangles in my hair, cradling the back of my head as he moves in and out of me with a rhythm that leaves me unraveling.

"You feel so damn good. You have no idea what you do to me, Kat."

I cling to him, my arms wrapped tight around his neck as waves of pleasure crash over me, leaving me speechless, building higher with every thrust. My cries fill the room, the sound of our bodies colliding almost drowned out by the pounding of my heartbeat in my ears.

"I'll never get enough of you—the way you tremble, the way you moan when I'm buried this deep inside you."

"If I'd known it would be this good, I wouldn't have waited so long," I manage to say between thrusts.

He chuckles before his lips find mine again, his kiss hungry, his tongue exploring my mouth as if he can't get enough. The connection is overwhelming, raw, and utterly consuming.

"Mine," he breathes against my lips, his voice a ragged growl. The possessiveness sends a shiver down my spine as he grips me harder, moving faster, deeper, until I'm crying out his name. The pleasure peaks, my entire body tightening around him as I shatter all at once.

With a few final, deep plunges, his body stills against me. I feel the swell and twitch of his cock deep inside me as his breathing slows. The intensity of the moment lingers, my body still trembling as I cling to him, utterly spent.

He stays inside me for a moment longer, his grip on me loosening as his lips brush my temple.

When he finally pulls out, he lowers me to my feet slowly, steadying me as my legs threaten to give out. I lean into him, burying my face in the crook of his neck, feeling his arms wrap protectively around me. The world feels distant. The only thing anchoring me is him.

WE DECIDE NOT to risk a fire, not with the possibility of drawing attention to the cabin. Luckily, there's a small closet stocked with heavy blankets and clean, albeit old, sheets. We layer the bed, bundling ourselves beneath the covers to keep warm, relying on body heat to do the rest. Malachi pulls me close, my back pressed firmly against his warm chest, and drapes an arm over my waist, his hand resting on my stomach. His warmth seeps into me, and I feel safe despite the craziness that's been surrounding us all night.

"At first light, we'll head back. I don't want to risk putting you in any more danger by going to the truck in the dark," he murmurs, his lips brushing the top of my head. The gesture is so gentle, so intimate, and I savor the feeling.

I don't respond right away. My mind is too preoccupied, replaying every moment we've shared tonight. The passion between us, the intensity—it lingers, intoxicating and all-consuming. It's impossible to ignore the yearning that still simmers under my skin. I dare to think I want more of him, and that thought alone thrills me.

"How are you feeling? Are you... Does it hurt?" he asks hesitantly, seemingly afraid of the answer.

I shake my head, my lips curving into a smile he can't see. "I feel amazing," I say, deciding to let the honesty slip out without second-guessing it. For once, I don't want to hold my cards too close to my chest. Not with him. He deserves to know how good he makes me feel.

His grip on me tightens slightly, and I feel the lazy drag of his fingertips as he traces patterns on my bare skin. "Do you want me to stop calling you demon?" he asks suddenly, catching me off guard.

The unexpectedness of the question makes me laugh louder than I mean to, and I quickly slap a hand over my mouth. "That's so random," I giggle, unable to stop myself.

"I know." He shifts behind me, getting comfortable. "I started calling you that to mess with you, but now I like it. Then after hearing my father call you that, I realized it might not be something you want to hear."

I tilt my head slightly, surprised by how much thought he's put into something so small. "I like it when you say it. Trust me, it doesn't sound the same coming from you. And when I'm with you, I'm not thinking about him at all," I say.

He exhales, his breath warm against the back of my neck, and I feel him relax behind me. "Good. I like calling you my clever demon," he murmurs.

"So possessive," I tease, though the flutter in my chest betrays how much I love it.

He pulls me closer until there's no space left between us.

"Why does my father call you a demon?" he asks, his hand trailing over my bare skin.

I shrug, nonchalant. "I think he's superstitious. He's always said seeing the dead is the work of the devil, so I must be one of his creatures. I don't mind, really. It actually makes some of the guards fear me, and I kind of like that."

He chuckles, but eventually a calm silence settles between us.

I ask, "What happens when this ends? When we get back and everything goes back to normal?"

The weight of reality is pressing against the edges of this fragile moment.

"This is my normal now, you're my normal now. The world will have to adjust," Malachi says without hesitation, his tone so steady it leaves no room for doubt.

I blink, caught off guard by the simplicity in his answer, the certainty in his voice. But the reality of Marco looms large in my mind, and I can't help but press further. "Care to clue me in on your plan when Marco shows up to claim me?"

His fingers, which had been tracing lazy patterns along my arm, still for a moment. "I'm still working on it," he admits, uneasy. "But trust me, Kat—no one is taking you away from me. If Orin or anyone else ever tries to hurt you again, I'll bury them so deep the wolves won't find their bones."

I shiver, but not from the cold. He's making a vow, one he intends to keep no matter the cost. His fingers move again, this time brushing against my bare skin with a tenderness that contrasts with the deadly promise he made.

"You make it sound like you own me now," I say, teasing him, though I'm curious too.

"I don't own you, Kat." He leans in so close that his breath warms my cheek and brushes his lips against my ear. "But I'll destroy anyone who tries to."

I can't tell whether I should feel comforted or terrified—or maybe a little of both. I turn over in his arms to face him, our heads resting on the worn pillows next to each other.

"I never would have imagined this." I stare into the flickering shadows cast by the single candle on the nightstand. My thoughts drift back to that night in the park when everything started—when I had no idea how much my life was about to change. How much he would change it.

Malachi tilts his head, watching me. "What do you mean?"

"I had given up," I admit. "On life, on the idea of ever finding someone I'd want to let in. I didn't think I'd ever feel like this about a man. And even if I did, it's not like I ever thought I'd get the freedom to act on it." I glance down at his chest, feeling too vulnerable to meet his eyes, swallowing hard. "But now...after everything I've been through, I wouldn't change a single moment—not if it meant it wouldn't lead me here. To this moment. To you."

The silence that follows is heavy but not uncomfortable. Malachi doesn't rush to fill it. Instead, his hand brushes against my cheek, the calluses on his fingers soft against my skin. He tucks a strand of hair behind my ear, touching my chin and coaxing me to look at him, his dark-brown eyes searching mine.

"You know," he says, shaking his head, "I knew you'd ruin me the moment I saw you. That night in the park. Those eyes, that smart-ass mouth of yours..." His lips curve in a grin, and I feel it in my chest. "And when you bit my ear instead of kissing me, called me out on my shit flirting—I was done for."

I laugh softly, the memory vivid in my mind. "You were such a cocky jerk. I didn't trust you for a second."

"You didn't have to," he says with a shrug. "But the more I got to know you—even when you made it painfully difficult—I knew you were going to destroy me. And I didn't even care."

"I think I knew I was falling for you," I say, my lips quirking into a smile, "the moment I saw you reading that spicy romance book. You looked so smug about it, until you got caught. Then you tried to hide it like a teenager with a dirty magazine."

He groans, dropping his forehead to my shoulder. "I was hoping you forgot about that."

"Never," I tease, giggling. "It was adorable."

He pulls back, mock glaring. "Hey, spicy romance books are top-tier literature. I've learned important lessons from them."

"Oh, I'm sure you have," I say, still laughing.

"Don't laugh at me. Those books taught me how to flirt with dangerous demons and live to tell the tale," he says, squeezing me tight enough to make me gasp.

"You're ridiculous," I say, breathless but smiling as he holds me closer.

His fingers trace lazy patterns along my back where they wrap around me. "You're not what I expected, Kat. But you're what I needed."

I rest my head against his chest, feeling his heartbeat under my cheek. "Same," I say quietly. "Exactly the same."

I WAKE WITH A START, momentarily disoriented, until the events of last night flood back—the cabin, the wolves, Malachi, and how he felt inside me, followed by the conversation that came after.

"Why are you smiling like that?" Malachi's voice draws my attention to the doorway. He's standing there, fully dressed, arms crossed, one eyebrow raised.

"Why are you watching me sleep like a creep?" I shoot back, grabbing a pillow and tossing it at him. He catches it with ease, laughing as he steps further into the room. "You're all dressed. Why didn't you wake me?"

I sit up and tug the blankets tighter. The cold bites at my skin, visible puffs of breath forming with every word.

"You looked too cute to disturb. Plus, I kept watch all night," he says casually, as if staying up in this freezing cabin after everything that happened was no big deal. "Didn't feel right to sleep here."

Guilt prickles in my chest. "You should've woken me. I would've taken shifts with you." I grab the other pillow and throw it at him. This time, he lets it hit him before closing the distance between us in two strides. His lips crash against mine, hard and unrestrained, like he's been dying to kiss me all night. When he pulls away, breathless and grinning, I can't help but giggle.

"What was that for?" I ask, my cheeks flushing despite the cold.

"Because you're adorable." His grin widens, and he grabs

the bundle of clothes from a nearby chair, handing them to me. "Now, get dressed. Stay put. I'll go get the truck and pick you up."

My eyes widen, and I'm about to protest when I realize I really don't want to make that hike back down. "I can come with you. My ankle feels fine—a little sore but mostly healed."

He shakes his head, firm. "No. Those wolves could still be out there, and it's safer if you stay here."

"I don't like this," I say, narrowing my eyes at him. "You better not go dying on me out there. I mean it—be careful."

He leans in, kissing me again, softer this time, and when he pulls back, there's a playful glint in his eye. "I'll be fine. Plus, no offense, but I'll move a lot faster without you."

I swat at his arm, but he dodges, chuckling. "Now, come barricade the door after me," he says, already heading for it.

I scramble out of bed, pulling on the clothes he brought me as quickly as I can. The cold hits me like a slap, but I ignore it, rushing to follow him. Once he's gone, I lock the door and push the table back in front of it, as he instructed.

The room feels eerily quiet without him, the silence amplifying my unease. I clutch the knife he gave me, double-checking the blade like it'll somehow make me feel safer.

"Don't get yourself killed, Malachi," I mutter under my breath. "I mean it."

Time drags. I remind myself it hasn't been more than fifteen minutes, maybe less, but it feels like hours. Malachi told me the hike would take longer, so I shouldn't worry. Still, I can't stop pacing. My nerves are getting the better of me, and I decide to distract myself by searching the cabin for anything useful.

Maybe there's something here that could make this place feel less ominous—or better yet, something to help if trouble comes back.

Everything is coated in dust and cobwebs, the air stale like no one's stepped inside for years. The cabin is a single story with four bedrooms. Two of them are identical to the one Malachi and I slept in, twin beds covered in worn sheets. Then there's the master bedroom, which has a massive bed taking up most of the space. For a moment, I'm thankful we didn't choose this room. The cramped bed we shared last night forced us to stay close, pressed together for warmth, and somehow that felt...perfect.

But this room has its charm. A huge, claw-foot tub sits in the corner, and my mind flashes to the idea of soaking in it with Malachi, steam rising around us, his hands on my skin. I shake the thought away and slide open the master closet door.

Empty.

The stark bar inside is bare, not a coat, jacket, or even a pair of old boots to hint that someone used to live here. What am I even looking for? A part of me expects a hunting cabin to have gear—weapons, tools, something—but there's nothing. Jamie's been dead a while, I think, and maybe this place has been vacant ever since.

I turn to leave when I notice another door on the far wall past the bed. Strange. A second closet in the same room? That feels...off. Maybe this one holds something useful. My heartbeat quickens as I approach, pulling the door open.

A rush of freezing air hits me like a slap to the face.

I flinch, blinking against the sudden brightness. White snow and sunlight pour through the open doorway, and it takes a second for my eyes to adjust.

A back door.

We had no idea there was another way out of this cabin. I glance down, and my stomach drops.

On the snow-covered ground, right outside the door, is a pile of cigarette butts. Fresh ones.

Not buried by snow, not covered in frost—fresh.

One of them is still smoking.

My breath catches as I take a slow step back, my pulse pounding in my ears. Someone's been here.

Someone's here.

Chapter Twenty-Eight

RULE 28 OF THE NEW ORDER: THE MOMENT YOU
LET YOUR GUARD DOWN IS THE MOMENT THE
KNIFE FINDS YOUR BACK.

I LUNGE FORWARD to slam the door shut, my hands shaking and my breath ragged. As the latch is about to catch, the force of a boot slams it open, and before I can react, he's on me.

Orin's arms clamp around me from behind like steel bands, his breath hot against my ear. "Bad move, menace."

Panicking, I fumble for the knife Malachi gave me, my fingers clumsy as they close around the handle. With a wild swing, I drive it into Orin's shoulder, the blade sinking into muscle with a sickening sound. He roars, reacting enough for me to break free. I bolt through the open door and plunge into the snow.

Each step is a struggle, the heavy snow swallowing my boots and slowing me down. I can't stop. It's too late now. I stabbed him. There's no turning back. Every instinct screams at me to keep moving, to put as much distance between us as possible.

My mind spirals with the consequences of what I've done. There's no way Orin will let this go. If he catches me now... I cannot let my mind go there.

The snow muffles my frantic footfalls, but I can still hear him behind me, his voice cutting through the cold. "You think you can run from me, demon? I'll tear you apart!"

I veer left, away from where I think Malachi might be, knowing I can't lead Orin to him. The cabin disappears behind me, swallowed by the dense forest. Branches snag my clothes, and the cold bites into my exposed skin, but I push forward, my focus narrowing to a single objective: run and hide.

The snow deepens, the drifts pulling at my legs like hands trying to drag me down. My lungs burn, my heart pounds, and still I run, weaving between trees, my body aching with every movement. My mind latches onto one thought, repeating like a mantra: *He can't catch me. He can't take me.*

I spot a fallen tree ahead, its massive trunk forming a hollow beneath it. Without thinking, I dive toward it, scrambling into the narrow space. Snow and dirt press against my body, but I don't care. I curl in on myself, barely breathing, my knife clutched tightly in my hand.

The forest falls silent except for the pounding of my heart. I strain to hear any sound over the blood rushing in my ears. Footsteps crunch closer, and I hold my breath.

"Come on, Katja. You can't hide forever. I'll find you, and when I do..." Orin's voice drifts through the trees, taunting, reveling.

I cover my mouth to stifle a sob, the icy air stinging my eyes. Every fiber of my being wants to bolt, to keep running, but I force myself to stay still. Be invisible. Be nothing.

The footsteps stop. Too close.

But I wasn't thinking there could be another. My focus was too fixed on Orin, on his voice slicing through the quiet, on the sheer desperation to stay hidden. I wasn't paying attention to my surroundings.

I peer out cautiously from beneath the fallen tree, my eyes

scanning the distance. I catch a glimpse of Orin moving between the trees, his figure a shadow against the pale snow.

Relief is short-lived. Arms wrap around me from behind, steel-strong and unyielding.

Frantic, I whirl around, the knife in my hand raised and ready to strike. My aim is true, the blade angled toward the chest of whoever grabbed me, but I falter the moment I see his face.

Banks.

His expression is torn, conflicted. I hesitate for a heartbeat, the blade trembling in my grip, and that's all the time Orin needs.

Before I can react, Orin is there, his shadow looming over me like a storm. The force of his blow lands against the side of my head, the crack ringing in my ears as pain blossoms, hot and immediate. My knees buckle, the knife slipping from my fingers into the snow.

The world tilts, my vision blurring at the edges. Somewhere through the haze, I think I see Banks's mouth move, his lips shaping words I can't quite hear. "I'm sorry." Maybe. Or maybe it's wishful thinking. I can't be sure of anything now as the darkness pulls me under.

"NICE OF YOU TO JOIN US," Orin says mockingly as I stir, the throbbing in my head pulling me from the fog. I force my eyes open and take in my surroundings. I'm on the couch in Marco's plane. The realization hits like a punch to the gut.

I sit up quickly, pressing my hand to the side of my head, which stings.

"Sorry about that," Orin continues, lounging in the seat

across from me with a smug smile. "But you didn't give me much of a choice now, did you?" He winks.

My fingers itch to wrap around his neck, to do anything that would wipe that grin off his face. But I know better. I'm not strong enough. Not here, not now.

"Where are we going?" I ask, my voice steady despite the storm inside me.

Orin's smile widens, sharp and full of malice. "You don't get to ask questions." He shakes his head like I'm a misbehaving child, and the urge to lunge at him becomes almost unbearable. Maybe I can rake my nails across his smug face or knee him where it counts. It wouldn't fix anything, but damn it would feel good.

"You and my brother had quite a night. Things got really hot in that cabin. Who knew what a woman you've become?"

He leers at my clothes, and bile rises in my throat. He saw us. He heard us. My skin crawls, humiliation and rage warring inside me. I clench my fists to keep from showing any sign of weakness.

"You were looking good under all this," he says, gesturing with a lazy smirk that makes me want to vomit.

For a split second, I imagine the sound of his nose breaking beneath my fist. It's almost enough to make me lose control. Almost. Instead, I grit my teeth and glare at him, letting my hatred do the talking for now.

"I've got to give it to my brother. He really has a way with women." Orin chuckles, his tone light, but every word feels like a dagger. I force myself to take a steadying breath.

Malachi.

God, I didn't even think to scream for him when I was running—not that he would've heard me. I hope he's okay. What if he was captured too?

No, he'd be here if that were the case.

But he went back to the cabin to get me... He must have been horrified to see the back door open, find me missing, and piece together the chaos I left behind.

"Did you read the journal? Did you at least solve the case while digging your demon claws into my little brother?"

I sneer at him, clenching my fists to keep from lashing out. Like I'm some kind of monster who tainted Malachi. Please.

"I haven't yet," I answer flatly, knowing better than to provoke him further.

He stares me down. "Do you have it with you?" he asks, his voice low, a barely-contained threat.

I open my jacket, slowly unzipping the inner pocket and pulling out Carmen's journal. My fingers brush against the Avidian vial tucked inside, and I quickly zip the pocket back up, keeping it hidden. They can't know about that. Not Orin, not Marco—no one.

"It's here," I say, holding up the journal.

"Good." His lips curl into a cruel grin. "You can read it now. Father will want answers when we get there, and I told him I'd make sure you have them ready."

The knot in my stomach tightens further. Marco. Of course. My mouth feels dry as I swallow.

"Can I read on the bed?" I ask. "I can't focus with you staring at me like that." My excuse feels weak, but it's all I can manage under his oppressive gaze. Really, I need to get away from him—need space to think, to act, to destroy the evidence of the Avidian before we land.

Orin narrows his eyes, studying me for a long, tense moment. With a wave of his hand, he says, "Go."

I don't wait for him to change his mind. I'm on my feet and heading toward the back of the plane before he can say another word. My heart pounds in my chest as I step into the small bedroom, close the door behind me, and finally exhale.

Get it together, Kat. Focus.

I decide to hold off on the Avidian for now. If I'm going to use it, I need all the pieces first. Whether we're heading to Viktor's or back to Marco's, I have time to figure this out. No need to rush.

I take a few steadying breaths, forcing my nerves to settle.

Everything is going to be okay.

Sliding onto the bed, I pull the journal open and start flipping through the pages, skimming for anything useful. Carmen's handwriting is small and neat, looping across the paper in a way that feels oddly personal. Mostly they are mundane entries about her life—a few mentions of some new guy she's seeing, scattered complaints about her job, and a running list of grievances about how awful everyone is.

The more I read, the more I feel a pang of sympathy for her. It sounds like her life at Viktor's estate was hell. Not that I'd expect anything else—it's Viktor, after all. But seeing it like this, in her own words, makes it all hit differently. She was trapped in a life she hated, surrounded by people who treated her like shit. I wonder if she ever felt as hopeless as I have.

I flip to the final entry, and the first couple of lines stop me cold.

Shit. I should have started here.

This isn't like the other entries.

BRIAN HAS *some kind of vendetta against Damien. I finally agreed to help him after he explained everything to me. He's been so mysterious, so closed off since I met him, I was starting to think "Brian" might not even be his real name.*

I think the mystery is partly what drew me to him—that and his charming smile, his built body, oh, and his huge cock that he knows how to use in ways I couldn't have dreamed of. Okay, I guess Brian has a lot of good things going for him, but now he's finally opened up to me. He let me in, told me his secret.

I feel so much better knowing he cares enough about me to trust me with all of this. And I have to help him. Solace is going to change the world, and if I can be even a small part of that, I'll do whatever it takes.

Starting with seducing Damien.

Tonight

I BOLT UPRIGHT, my heart pounding as if it's trying to break free from my chest. My hand flies to my mouth, muffling a gasp that threatens to turn into a scream. The room feels too small, the air too thick, and I start shaking my head, desperate to rid myself of the intrusive thoughts swirling like a storm in my mind.

This can't be true.

It can't.

Carmen's boyfriend was in Solace—the organization Malachi leads. My Malachi. No, not mine. My head throbs as I try to process the journal, each line replaying in my mind like a sick mantra.

"Brian." She said Brian might not even be his real name.

God, what if Malachi is Brian? He's charming, strong. And he's good at seducing women. My stomach churns violently, and I press my hand harder against my mouth, as if I can physically hold back the bile rising in my throat. Tears spill down my cheeks, hot and unwelcome, as the weight of doubt crushes me.

I clutch the journal tighter, my fingers digging into its worn cover. Carmen never described him, not in detail. No hair color, no eye color, nothing. She left me nothing to confirm or deny what I'm thinking. My head spins, and the room tilts, my breathing growing shallow and erratic.

"Malachi," I whisper, the name a plea and a curse all at once. I want to believe it's not him. I need to believe it's not him. But a sliver of doubt worms into my heart, planting seeds of suspicion I can't uproot.

I close my eyes, pressing my forehead against my knees, trying to steady myself, to think rationally. Malachi would have told me. He's had so many chances to tell me. Unless this is the part of him he didn't want me to see. Unless there is something larger at play here that I'm not seeing for what it is.

I swipe at the tears on my cheeks, my hands trembling as I force myself to breathe. One, two, three deep breaths—each more deliberate than the last. The air burns in my lungs, but it's enough to clear some of the fog in my mind. I've been here before, teetering on the edge of chaos, but I won't let myself fall.

Get a grip, Kat.

I close the journal and press it against my chest, as if doing so could somehow silence the storm of emotions threatening to tear me apart. Malachi isn't here. I don't have answers, and jumping to conclusions now won't get me anywhere. I need to keep my head. I need to be the Kat Sinclair who's survived far worse than this, the one who perfected her stoic facade in the face of unimaginable horrors.

I can't let my emotions cloud my judgment. Not now. Not when everything feels like it's hanging by a thread.

I take another breath, this one steadier, and push the intrusive thoughts aside, at least for now. They'll creep back—I know they will—but I'll deal with them when I have more to go on. When I see Malachi again, if I see him again. That thought cuts deep, sharper than I'm prepared for, and it takes everything in me not to crumble under the weight of it.

I shake my head, dismissing the ache in my chest. *Focus.* I need to be calm, calculated, and practical. Treat this like any other case. Set emotions aside. Piece the clues together.

I toss the journal onto the bed and run my hands down my thighs, getting a grip. I can't lose myself in paranoia. Not yet. If I want answers, I'll have to face this head-on, step by step. No assumptions. No hysteria.

I can figure this out.

I sit frozen, the journal still resting on the bed beside me, my mind racing as I piece together the scattered fragments of this nightmare. Carmen's betrayal, her anger, her desperation—it all started to make sense when I saw those first images she shared. She was furious at her boyfriend for something so terrible for watching and letting things go too far with Damien that night. She said she loved him. And Damien...warned me. Over and over again, he warned me.

"He's closer than you realize."

I thought it was Damien's sick game, his need to taunt me, to keep me spinning in circles. But now? It feels like he was giving me the answers the entire time, wrapped in riddles and cruelty. The way he wouldn't help me, the way he seemed almost gleeful every time I stumbled—it wasn't about me. He was fucking with Malachi too. If he knew Malachi was the killer, then all of his taunts were calculated, every jab aimed at cutting deeper.

The memories rush back like an unforgiving tide. Malachi in the park that night. It was late, really late, and he was upset—so visibly shaken that I couldn't get a read on him. I chalked it up to a bad day, an off moment, but now I wonder if it was something else. Something darker. What if things went wrong? What if he'd killed Carmen and Damien and I ran into him in the aftermath? He has access to a plane, to resources that most people couldn't dream of. It would've been a stretch but doable.

And then there's Solace. The organization isn't large, and

Malachi is its leader. Could something like this—two murders, calculated and personal—really have happened without him knowing? Without his involvement? The answer is there, glaring at me, and it's one I can't bring myself to say out loud.

No, it couldn't.

I struggle to breathe. The very real possibility that none of this was Malachi doesn't absolve him. Even if he didn't pull the trigger—or, in this case, thrust the knife—someone in Solace did. And if he didn't know, then he's blind. If he did...

I clench my fists, nails digging into my palms as I force the intrusive thoughts to settle. I don't want to believe any of it, but the pieces fit too perfectly to ignore.

And yet...Malachi saved me. He's been the one standing between me and the worst of this world. He's been my anchor, the only person who's made me feel alive in years. How do I reconcile that with this possibility? How do I face him when everything inside me is screaming that he might be the very monster I've been trying to find? Killing Damien is one thing, but Carmen too and then playing me the entire time...being intimate with me and all the things we've shared all while he was keeping this from me.

The tears threaten to fall again again, but I swallow them down, locking them away. There's no time for emotions. No time for doubt. Not now. If I'm going to survive this, if I'm going to get the answers I need, I have to stay sharp.

The truth will come out, and I know how to find it once and for all. I get up, quietly lock the door, and reach into my pocket, pulling out the small vile.

Avidian.

Chapter Twenty-Nine

RULE 29 OF THE NEW ORDER: THE TRUTH IS A
DOUBLE-EDGED SWORD—BE READY TO BLEED
WHEN YOU FIND IT.

I TURN the vial of Avidian over in my hands, my thumb running along the smooth glass as though the motion could steady my nerves. Inside, the liquid swirls like a living galaxy, dark and mesmerizing, pulling at me with equal parts temptation and dread...I fear what it will show me, but I have to be ready to accept the truth.

I exhale sharply, trying to quiet the doubts rattling around my head. There's no turning back now. My fingers tremble as I pop the cap off. The vapor rises immediately, shimmering like stardust before it disappears into the air. I hesitate for a fraction of a second before I inhale deeply. The vapor burns as it hits my lungs, sharp and bitter, but the effect is instantaneous. My vision blurs and sharpens again, clearer than ever before, the edges of the room suddenly more vivid.

Carmen.

Her name is a chant in my mind, a beacon I focus all my energy on. I picture her face, her presence, calling her back from whatever liminal space Damien has forced her into. "Carmen," I whisper aloud.

The room grows colder, a biting chill that raises the hairs on my arms, and then she's there—flickering into existence like a weak signal trying to hold steady.

She's sitting on the bed beside me, fragile and translucent, her face a mixture of relief and sorrow.

"I know it's been hard for you to reach me," I say softly, for fear of her disappearing on me again. "I know Damien's been keeping you from me, and I know... I know you've been through something horrible." I pause, searching her face for any sign of hesitation, but she watches me, her eyes flickering with the faintest spark of hope. "Give me your hand, Carmen. Let me see what happened. You deserve justice. You deserve peace."

She hesitates, her form flickering in and out like a candle fighting against the wind. Her gaze shifts to her lap, and for a second I think she's going to disappear again. But then she nods, her movements jerky, uncertain. Slowly, she extends her hand, resting it lightly on her leg, her fingers trembling like she's afraid of what I'll find.

I don't have time for hesitation. My heart pounds as I reach out, my fingers hovering above hers before making contact. The moment our skin connects, the world around me implodes. Cold crashes over me like a tidal wave, pulling me under. I gasp sharply and realize I'm no longer in the bedroom on the plane—I'm somewhere else entirely.

Somewhere darker.

And I see everything.

Damien's voice filters through the door, muffled but clear enough to cause my skin to prickle. "In case I fall asleep, come get me before dawn."

Carmen freezes mid-pace, her eyes flicking to the mirror. She smooths her hair, adjusts the strap of her top, and takes a steadying breath. Her hand trembles as it brushes the fabric of her skirt, smoothing imaginary wrinkles. She looks anxious, even scared.

There's a knock at the door, and she rushes to open it, her steps hesitant despite the forced smile on her face. Damien steps inside, his movements cocky as he kicks the door shut behind him without taking his eyes off her.

"I've been thinking about you all day," he says, his voice low, laced with hunger. "I want another taste."

The air between them feels heavy, charged. Carmen's lips quirk upward in a nervous smile. She doesn't back away as he closes the distance, his hands immediately finding her waist, tugging up her skirt.

The scene blurs for a moment, fragments flashing in and out like a film reel skipping frames. Suddenly, they're on the bed, Damien's body pressing into hers, moving with a rhythm that feels aggressive, but she moans like she's into it. Carmen's face is turned away, her gaze fixed on the door over his shoulder.

The door. It's closed—or is it?

I whip around and see it's ajar, a sliver of dim hallway light creeping into the room. My stomach knots as I catch the faintest movement—a shadow, someone watching. Carmen said he watched. This has to be him. This must be "Brian."

The figure in the hallway doesn't enter, doesn't move closer. He stands there, a dark silhouette framed by the door. Carmen keeps glancing at him, her tension palpable even from where I'm standing. She's not nervous—she's terrified.

The door swings open abruptly, flooding the room with light. Damien turns, shielding his eyes with his arm. "Fuck, it's early," he mutters, clearly mistaking the figure for whomever was meant to wake him.

The man doesn't answer. His head tilts slightly, and even though his face is hidden in shadow, the weight of his presence fills the room. Carmen sits up, clutching the sheet to her chest. Her wide eyes dart between Damien and the figure in the doorway.

Damien sneers, turning back to Carmen. "You came for a show? Fine. I'll give you a show." He thrusts into her harder, and she cries out—whether in pleasure or pain, I can't tell, but she goes along with it, not pushing him away at all.

The man in the doorway steps forward, and my heart clenches. He's calm, eerily so, as if none of this fazes him. The light catches the edge of a blade in his hand. He moves with precision, calculated and deliberate, as he blows out the candle on the desk.

The room plunges into darkness, and the sounds come next —a shuffle of feet, a gasp, the wet, sickening slice of a blade meeting flesh. Carmen screams, and when the lights flash back on, the scene is chaos.

Blood.

So much blood.

Damien's body sprawls on the bed, his throat slit, crimson pooling beneath him. The man in the hoodie looms over him, his back to me as he pulls another blade from his waistband.

Carmen, still clutching the sheet, stumbles to the corner of the room, her hand clamped over her mouth as though she's fighting to keep from vomiting. Her eyes are wide, glassy with shock, as she watches the man plunge the blade into Damien's chest again and again, methodical and unflinching.

The room reeks of death, and I can't look away from the grotesque scene. Carmen takes a step forward, her bare feet sticking to the blood-slick floor.

"Brian, what the fuck are you doing?" she whispers, her voice cracking.

The man doesn't answer. He slices into Damien's flesh

with a precision that's more clinical than angry, as though he's dissecting, not killing.

"This wasn't the plan," Carmen chokes out, her voice rising. "You said you would stop him before it went that far. You watched him... How could you?"

The man finally straightens, turning his head enough to glance at her. His hood obscures most of his face, but the faintest hint of a jawline is visible. His voice is low, cold. "Plans change."

I can't tell if it's Malachi. I need to see more.

"You used me!" Carmen yells, the sheet slipping slightly as she steps closer to him. "You—"

"Stop." His tone is sharp, final, and it silences her instantly.

"I know you said we had to cut him up, had to make it look like someone else—" Carmen raves. "I can't do this. I can't... Brian, this is wrong. It's all wrong." Her hands tremble as she paces.

The scene flickers, blurs like a warped film reel again, before snapping back into focus. Time has shifted—I don't know how much—but now Carmen stands in the corner of the room, her body rigid, her hands clenched into fists. Brian looms in front of her, hood pulled low over his face, his movements tense, coiled like a predator waiting to strike.

"I'm going to expose you," Carmen spits, her voice trembling but steady enough to cut through the silence. "I'm going to expose Solace. You think you're doing good? You think this makes you better than them? Well, it doesn't. Call it whatever you want, but murder is still murder."

Brian freezes, his hands rising to his hood, gripping his head as if trying to physically hold back whatever he's feeling. For a moment, I think he's going to argue, but the scene flickers again, the air shimmering as time skips forward. When it clears, Carmen is on the ground, her legs kicking weakly as Brian's hands close around her throat. Her nails dig into his skin, clawing, but he doesn't relent. Her struggles grow weaker, slower, until her body stills.

I gasp, clutching my chest, the Avidian still coursing through my veins like fire. When I blink, the plane's dim interior comes into focus, and I realize Carmen is gone. She's not lingering like Damien, not staying to share more or explain herself. She's...gone.

What I saw—what she showed me—it's too much, and yet it's not enough. Not enough to piece everything together but more than enough to know the truth is worse than I imagined.

I can't tell if it was Malachi or not. God, I thought I'd know for sure. The voice was familiar—too familiar—but not quite his. Maybe I've been too rash, jumping to conclusions without enough proof. Maybe I need to give him the benefit of the doubt.

Carmen's nails were clawing into Brian's wrists, and I don't remember seeing any marks on Malachi in the park. But then again, I wasn't looking for something like that, and his suit could've easily hidden the evidence.

One thing's clear now. The man Carmen was seeing killed her and Damien, and he did it for Solace. It wasn't random. Carmen's murder didn't seem planned though. It felt messy, like he was trying to sway her to his side, but when she reacted the way she did—threatening to expose him and Solace—he panicked. He killed her without thinking, without a plan. Does that make it better? No. If anything, it makes it worse.

My gut is screaming that it wasn't Malachi. It couldn't have been. But even if he's innocent, this throws everything I thought I knew about Solace and the Syndicate out the window. Are things really what they seem? Or have I been a pawn in some bigger, more sinister game?

"We're about to land. Get out here," Orin barks, banging on

the door so hard the walls rattle. I practically leap off the bed, his interruption jolting me out of my spiraling thoughts.

I stomp on the empty Avidian vial, feeling a small sense of satisfaction as it crumbles into shards beneath my boot. Carefully, I wrap the pieces in a tissue, ensuring no trace of the shimmering residue remains, and toss it into the small trash bin. The action feels symbolic, like I'm burying what I've seen, though the truth is far from gone—it's seared into my mind.

I move back to the seat across from Orin, settling in as if I hadn't glimpsed the ugliest parts of someone's soul. My calm facade slides into place, practiced and steady, masking the chaos inside me. But no amount of composure can quiet the knot in my stomach, the way my pulse thunders in my ears.

I force myself to hold Orin's gaze, or rather his smug, infuriating face. I don't flinch. I don't fidget. I can't let him see even a flicker of fear, even though inside I'm terrified of what's coming next.

Chapter Thirty

RULE 30 OF THE NEW ORDER: DARKNESS NEVER
DIES—IT ONLY CHANGES HANDS.

A BARK FOLLOWED by a warm sensation in my lap wakes me. I open my eyes to see Mischka jumping in my lap. My head feels like it's been stuffed with cotton and dipped in acid. Every breath is shallow, tinged with the metallic tang of damp air. When I try to move, my limbs feel sluggish, like they're weighed down by invisible chains.

Where the fuck am I?

The floor beneath me is cold, hard concrete. I blink against the dim light filtering through a single bare bulb swinging overhead. It casts long, erratic shadows across the room, distorting the shape of the basement I suddenly realize I'm in.

A basement. Marco's basement.

I sit up too quickly, and a sharp pain shoots through my skull. I press my palm to my forehead, trying to ground myself. How did I get here?

I glance down, noticing the dirty scrapes on my arms and legs. My jacket is gone, my boots too, leaving me in my socks and the same clothes I wore at the cabin. The faint memory of

Orin's sneer flashes in my mind. Did he drug me? How long have I been here?

The walls of the basement are stone, old and damp, with rivulets of water trailing down like veins. A staircase stands to my left, leading up to a heavy wooden door with no visible handle. Across the room, a single metal chair and table sit under the flickering light, like something out of an interrogation scene.

I give Mish a pet, and she jumps down before disappearing as I push myself to my feet, legs trembling. I stagger toward the door, testing its weight. Locked, of course.

A sound—soft, almost imperceptible—sends a jolt of adrenaline through me. It's coming from the shadows in the far corner of the basement. I spin around, heart pounding, trying to make sense of what I'm hearing.

"Hello?" My voice comes out hoarse.

Silence.

I take a cautious step forward, peering into the darkness. Something shifts, a faint rustling, and a shape emerges—a figure slumped against the wall. My stomach drops.

It's a person.

"Who's there?" I demand and edge closer.

The figure doesn't move, and as I step into the faint light, I see why. It's a man tied to a chair, his head lolling forward. Blood mats his hair, streaks down his face and neck. For a second, I think he's dead, but then his chest rises, barely, and I realize he's breathing.

Holy shit.

I crouch down, reaching out to lift his chin. His skin is clammy, his lips cracked and pale.

Banks.

"What the hell did they do to you?" I murmur, shaking him

gently. His eyelids flutter, and he lets out a low groan, but he doesn't wake.

"Don't touch that sympathizer." Orin's voice cuts through the silence. The echo of his polished shoes on the concrete stairs fills the dimly lit space as he descends. My stomach churns at the word—sympathizer? What happened while I was out? I press my fingers to my temple, trying to sift through the fragments of memory, but my mind is blank.

Did Banks...

No, there's no way.

"You look like shit, and Marco wants to see you," Orin continues, his tone cold as he tosses a wet, soapy rag at me, followed by a pile of clothes that land at my feet with a dull thud. My fingers instinctively flinch away from the damp cloth.

"Get cleaned up," he orders, plopping down on the bottom stair, his eyes raking over me with that unsettling expression he always wears, the one that makes my body tense up.

"You're going to sit there and watch?" I glare at him, holding the rag like it's toxic.

His smirk deepens, the dim light casting harsh shadows across his sharp features. "Of course. I wouldn't miss the show."

I clench my jaw, the anger bubbling beneath the surface, but I swallow it down, knowing better than to rise to his bait right now. I grab the clothes and move to the farthest corner of the room, turning my back to him. The damp chill of the basement seeps into my skin, but I force myself to keep my movements steady, defiant even in this small act.

"Don't take too long," he calls out suggestively. "Marco doesn't like to be kept waiting."

I inhale deeply, the metallic tang of the air mixing with the faint soap scent from the rag.

Stay calm, Kat. For now.

Once I'm dressed in the black dress and tights Orin tossed

at me—hardly ideal for an escape but precisely what Marco would expect—I try to steady my breathing. It's not a practical choice, but Orin knows Marco likes his "pets" presentable. My skin still feels grimy despite wiping it down, but there's no time to linger. I quickly braid my hair to the side, tying it off with a frayed ribbon from the pile of clothes. A poor attempt to look polished when I still feel like a caged animal.

"You clean up nice, parasite," Orin says. He motions for me to go ahead of him, always so happy when he gets to order me around.

I fight the urge to spit some retort back at him, opting to stay silent. My pulse hammers in my ears as I move toward the stairs. Each step feels heavier than the last.

Orin's presence behind me feels like a weight pressing down on my spine, his eyes burning into the back of my head. I want to run. I want to bolt, fight, scream, make him bleed for everything he's done. But not yet.

Not yet.

As we climb the stairs, my thoughts race. I've tasted freedom now—felt what it's like to be beyond their reach. I can't stay here, not after I've known what it's like to be more than a pet here.

When we reach the top of the stairs, Orin opens the door, reaching past me and gesturing mockingly like he's some sort of gentleman. "After you," he drawls, his grin widening when I brush past him.

"Can we stop at my bathroom, please? I really need to go. And look—" I gesture at myself, throwing in a touch of exasperation for good measure. "I don't even have shoes. Marco won't approve of this sloppy look."

Orin narrows his icy blue eyes, as if deciding whether to indulge me or not. Then, to my surprise, he nods once, motioning for me to lead the way.

"Fine. Make it quick," he says, following me into my bedroom. He sits on the edge of my bed, his sharp gaze tracking my every move as I step into the adjoining bathroom.

I close the door with a soft click, exhaling a shaky breath. At least he didn't follow me in here to watch. Small mercies, I suppose.

The bathroom feels impossibly small under the weight of my nerves. I glance at myself in the mirror. I don't look as bad as I feel, but the cut on my forehead tells a different story. My eyes are tired, the kind of tired that doesn't fade with sleep, and my cheeks are still smudged with traces of grime.

I quickly use the toilet then grab my toothbrush. I know hygiene should be the least of my worries right now, but I can't shake the need to brush my teeth. I feel disgusting, like layers of this place are clinging to me.

As I brush, my mind starts to churn. I don't have much time. I rinse, pat my face dry, and open the door, moving to my closet in a hurry. Orin watches me with a lazy smirk, his amusement barely hidden.

I grab a pair of black loafers—polished enough to meet Marco's standards but far more practical than heels. They'll pass inspection, and more importantly they'll be easier to run in if it comes to that.

I slip them on quickly, avoiding Orin's stare as I straighten. "Ready," I say, my voice steady despite the anxiety building in my chest.

"Good. Let's not keep my father waiting."

We walk through the halls toward Marco's wing of the house, and everything looks as it always does. Security guards stand at key points, their postures rigid and alert, while the usual servants move about, heads down, carrying trays or tending to the decor. It's unsettling how normal it all seems— like I've stepped back in time to a life I no longer fit into.

Calling this place home feels wrong now.

When we reach the large double doors to Marco's private rooms, Orin knocks. The sound echoes in the marble hall. A moment later, the door opens, and to my surprise I'm met by a tall man with deep-blue eyes and slicked back hair, it's Gary—the more level-headed of Marco's sons.

He spares me a glance, the expression on his clean-shaven face tight, before stepping past us without a word. He doesn't even acknowledge Orin. His shoulders are rigid, and the irritation radiating off him is evident as he storms down the hall.

"There she is." Marco's voice draws my attention. "It's been too long, my little demon."

I step into the room, every nerve on edge. Marco's suite is as grand as ever, ostentatious like the rest of the estate. The white marble floors gleam under the warm glow of the chandelier, and the walls are equally pristine. A massive bed dominates one side of the room, draped in gold and cream silks, while a sitting area flanks a gold-trimmed fireplace. It's immaculate, controlled, and deeply unsettling.

I take a few hesitant steps forward, my footsteps swallowed by the soft rug beneath me. The heavy doors close behind me, the sound final, and Orin lingers long enough to earn a pointed wave from Marco.

"Leave us," Marco says, not even sparing him a glance.

Orin doesn't argue, his retreating footsteps fading quickly down the hall.

I'm alone with Marco.

"Come, sit." Marco motions toward one of the large leather chairs in front of the fire, his tone smooth, almost too casual.

I hesitate but force my feet to move, crossing the room to the chair. He watches me with the calculated gaze of a predator as I lower myself into the seat, sinking slightly into the expensive cushion.

"I know you must feel neglected," he says, swirling the whiskey in the glass he poured from the drink cart. "But know it hasn't been by choice."

His voice drips with false warmth, each word polished and practiced. It's too proper, too nice—Marco always hides his most despicable intentions behind a veil of politeness, and it sets my teeth on edge.

"Can I get you a drink?" he offers, holding his own glass aloft as if it's an extension of his charm.

I shake my head, a polite refusal. The thought of drinking anything he offers twists my stomach.

Marco chuckles softly, a sound that feels more sinister than amused. "Suit yourself." He takes a slow sip, his eyes never leaving me, and settles into the chair across from me, his posture impossibly relaxed, like he's completely in control. Because, of course, he thinks he is.

"Carmen's boyfriend, Brian, killed her and Damien," I say, keeping my voice steady, almost detached. The sooner I say it, the less time Marco has to probe. "He caught her with Damien and went on a jealous rampage."

I meet Marco's gaze head-on, refusing to flinch under his scrutiny. Whatever Orin has told him, I can't let it shake me. Solace doesn't need to be dragged into this, and I'll do whatever it takes to keep that part of the truth buried.

Marco doesn't respond right away, his sharp eyes assessing me as he swirls his whiskey. The silence stretches, heavy and deliberate.

"Brian," he repeats, testing the name like he's rolling it over in his mind, trying to fit it into the larger puzzle.

I nod once.

"Viktor will be pleased," he says finally, leaning back in his chair. "You did the job you were supposed to do."

I keep my expression neutral, offering no response. It's

what he expects—subdued compliance. Inside, I'm screaming. *Please, Marco, let this drop. Let me go back to my room so I can figure out how the hell to escape this place once and for all.*

"The girl's journal," he says, breaking the silence. "Was it helpful?"

"Yes," I answer, keeping my tone measured. "Without it, I would have come to the same conclusion, but it did speed up the process."

I shift in the chair, the unease building with every second he watches me.

"I haven't been able to reach my son to confirm yet," Marco says before taking another slow drink of whiskey, and I know he must be talking about Malachi. "But Orin told me some alarming things."

My stomach tightens, and I bite the inside of my cheek to keep from reacting.

"Oh." I glance at the fire, trying to stay the perfect picture of nonchalant.

"Malachi has always been my sharpest son, but he inherited too much of his mother's heart," Marco says.

He hasn't asked me a direct question yet, and I won't give him more than I have to.

"He trusts too easily," Marco continues, swirling the whiskey in his glass before downing the last of it. He sets the glass on the side table with a soft clink, his eyes fixed on me. "I'm no fool, Katja. I know he's been moving behind my back for some time now."

A chill ripples down my spine, but I sit still, focusing on keeping my breathing steady.

Marco leans forward slightly, his voice dropping lower. "That's why I took you to that warehouse, to see Boris and his Avids. A reminder of what your life could look like should I decide you are no longer useful. Should I decide I can no longer trust you."

My stomach twists into a violent knot. I fight the urge to leap out of this chair, to grab something sharp, anything, and tear him apart with my bare hands. The image of burning this whole place to the ground flashes through my mind—Marco, Orin, the entire rotten operation—all of it reduced to ash. My chest heaves as the fury threatens to spill over, but I force my hands to steady and my voice to come out even.

"I have given you no reason to doubt me," I say.

Marco studies me, the silence between us heavy and dangerous. He smiles faintly. "That is...debatable," he replies. "You are keeping things from me, even now."

He pauses, his hand moving to his chest, rubbing it absent-mindedly. His features twitch slightly, and then it happens. He falters, his words slurring. "I know... I... I..."

Marco slumps back in his chair, his body suddenly limp, and the glass topples from the table, shattering against the floor.

I freeze, my heart hammering in my chest as I watch him sink further into the chair, his eyes fluttering shut.

Then it hits—the deep rumble of an explosion shakes the walls, followed by shouting.

For a second, everything stills. Then chaos takes over.

MARCO IS STILL BREATHING, and I frantically search for a weapon. Now is my chance to end him. I hear footsteps coming down the hall and quickly run to hide next to the bed.

Malachi's voice in the hall sends a wave of adrenaline coursing through me. "Keep clearing the property. Come to me when you find her."

I press myself flat against the side of the bed, my heart

pounding as the door swings open. His tall frame fills the doorway, but his sharp eyes zero in on Marco slumped in the chair. His jaw tightens, the flicker of rage barely contained beneath his calm exterior. Then his gaze shifts to me, crouched by the bed, and everything in him changes.

"Kat."

He strides across the room in several quick steps, pulling me to my feet and into his arms. His hold is crushing, fierce, like he's been fighting the entire world to get here. Before I can say anything, his mouth is on mine, desperate and consuming. All the tension, the fear, the anger—it all melts away in the heat of him. My hands clutch his shoulders, and I kiss him back like I've been starving for this.

Malachi pulls back enough to meet my eyes. "You're okay?" His voice is rough, strained.

"I'm okay," I whisper, but my voice trembles with everything I need to say. Relief, anger, the questions. He looks at me like I'm the only thing that matters.

He moves quickly, lifting me and setting me on the edge of the bed. His hands roam over my body, pulling me closer, fingers tangling in my hair as his lips crash against mine. The kiss is so fierce, so consuming, that I forget to breathe. My chest tightens, desperate for air.

"Malachi," I gasp when he pulls back, my lungs burning but my heart racing for more.

"When I got back to the cabin and you weren't there..." He pulls me against him, wrapping his arms tightly around me, and his lips press to the top of my head. "You don't know the hell I went through, the things that went through my head."

I melt into his embrace, taking in the sight of him—fully dressed in black tactical gear from head to toe, his chest rising and falling with the weight of his breaths. He looks like a soldier, a man ready to face war. The image sends a pang of something sharp and unfamiliar through me.

"I know," I whisper, my voice barely audible. "I'm sorry—"

"Don't." He cuts me off, his grip tightening. "You don't have to apologize. Not for this."

"I know," I say, nodding as my eyes scan over him. I'm torn, debating whether this is the right time. "I saw what happened to Carmen. I saw who killed them, and I read Carmen's journal. Her boyfriend was in Solace. Why did you keep all of that from me? Why did you want Damien dead?"

I immediately realize that wasn't the most tactful way to ask, but the questions are burning in me.

His eyes soften, and I can see the conflict in him. He's wishing we could talk about this another time, but I can't hold back anymore. I need to know. At least the short version.

"You're right," he says, running a hand over his face. "I haven't told you everything, and that's because, in the beginning, I didn't know if I could trust you. And once I could... Well, there are things we haven't talked about yet. Things we need to talk about, but not like this."

His hands gently cup my face, and I force myself to swallow the lump in my throat.

Sighing, he continues, "I thought I could trust Damien. He hated his father, wanted to make a difference. I thought I could recruit him into Solace, make him a double agent, get intel on Viktor. He was being shady. I had to send one of my men in undercover. He saw a girl who worked there and used that as an in."

"Carmen," I say.

He nods, his face drawn. "Yeah, he posed as her boyfriend. Used her to get close to Damien, to find out if we could trust him. And it turns out...we couldn't. Damien was playing both sides, planning to sell us out to Viktor. I had to make it look like an accident, and I—"

The truth hits me like a freight train. "So you didn't do it. You sent one of your men, Brian, to kill them that night, and all this time Damien's been toying with me because he knew the truth and hates all of you."

"Brian—no."

A faint rustling pulls our attention to Marco. He stirs, his head rolling to one side before his eyes flutter open. Malachi moves instantly, striding over to him with purpose, pulling thick rope from his bag.

"Come on, we'll finish this conversation later," he says, motioning for me to follow as he starts binding Marco to the chair.

"How is he like this?" I ask, still reeling from the breakneck turn of events.

"We drugged his whiskey. Then we watched and waited." His voice is clipped, leaving no room for further explanation. There's more to this—so much more—but now isn't the moment for follow-up questions.

Marco's eyes slowly regain focus, roaming the room until they land on us. His expression hardens, his gaze settling on Malachi with a disarming calm.

"Son," Marco wheezes, "you didn't have to go through all this effort to get my attention. If you wanted my pet so badly, you could have asked."

I don't bother hiding my disgust. I let him see exactly how I feel about him. His gaze lingers on me, assessing, calculating, before his lips curl into a slow, sinister smile.

"Isn't this a pretty picture? My demon falling for my son. And you," he adds, addressing Malachi, "what do you think you are? Her savior? Do you even know what you're doing?"

"I'm sorry, Father," Malachi says, stepping back, his jaw

tight with barely restrained fury. "But I'll be taking more than your pet tonight. Let's start with your life."

I snap my head toward him, my heart lurching. Is he serious? Is he really going to do it?

Marco chuckles, the sound hollow and biting, as though he can't fathom the possibility. "You're not going to kill me," he says with smug certainty. "You don't have what it takes. I was telling Katja how you have too much heart. You always have."

He leans back in the chair, not even trying to break free of the restraints, dark amusement dancing in his eyes, like he's toying with us even now. But there's something Marco isn't seeing—something he's underestimating. Because the look on Malachi's face isn't hesitation. It's cold, calculated rage.

I wonder if Marco's wrong. Maybe Malachi does have what it takes. Maybe he's had it all along.

"What does 'where the wolves prowl' mean?" Malachi demands.

I add, "And what the hell were those creatures near Jamie's hunting cabin? Those weren't wolves—those were monsters. What did you do to them?"

Marco looks casually at the fire, his expression infuriatingly calm, as if we're discussing the weather. "You two have been busy. Dare I say, you might even make a good team. A pity you're so determined to choose the wrong side."

I roll my eyes. More games. More riddles. I want answers, not another fucking monologue.

Malachi doesn't give Marco a chance to play coy. In one fluid motion, he pulls out a knife and drives it into Marco's thigh. The blade sinks in deep, the sickening squish of metal against flesh making my stomach twist. Marco grunts, his fingers curling around the arms of his chair. Shock flashes across his face for a moment before something twisted takes its place—a laugh. Dark and low, it spills out of him like poison.

"Do you really think I don't know what my sister's been up to?" Marco's voice is a rasp of mock amusement, his teeth bared in a twisted grin. "You think I don't have someone on the inside? That I haven't been watching you and your Solace pet project? Why do you think I let it go on so long?" He leans forward slightly, despite the knife still lodged in his leg, like he's sharing some grand secret. "I allowed it because it benefits me. The Syndicate might be changing science, but don't think for a second I'm not ahead of the curve. I have my own creations—ones you haven't even begun to comprehend."

Malachi's jaw visibly tightens, and I cross my arms, stepping closer. "From where I'm standing, it looks like you're two steps behind."

Marco chuckles again, the sound more unhinged this time—like he's teetering on the edge of sanity. "You think you've won? You haven't even seen the board yet, girl. You haven't seen the bigger picture." He tips his head back, that guttural laugh sending goosebumps across my flesh.

It's unnerving. I've never seen Marco this animated, this alive. Maybe it's the drugs still running through his veins—or maybe it's because he knows something we don't. But beneath that deranged amusement, I see a man who knows his time is running out.

And I don't plan on letting him die before he tells us everything.

"Why didn't we find anything at the cabin?" Malachi asks, his gaze fixed on Marco.

Marco doesn't flinch. "Son, you should've looked harder. I got the idea from you and the Depths, after all," he says, shrugging what he can of his shoulders in his restraints.

I shake my head, disbelief creeping in. How did we miss it? The underground operation, hidden beneath our noses? We would've figured it out eventually, but time wasn't on our side, and fucking Orin had to show up. I push the frustration aside, focus returning to the present.

Malachi opens his mouth to speak, but before he can, a knock echoes through the room. The door swings open, and in steps a woman with long black hair, clad in the same tactical gear as Malachi. My heart stutters, and I can't help but wonder. Is this the same woman who helped us save Aurora that night in the snow?

"Boss, the property's secure. Everyone's loaded up and waiting on your orders," she says.

Malachi nods in acknowledgment, but his mind is elsewhere. "What about my brothers?"

She shakes her head, her expression cold. "No sign of them. They bailed the second they sensed trouble."

I want to laugh. Fucking cowards, both of them.

"We should probably leave soon, before reinforcements show up," she adds, the obvious truth hanging between us. Malachi nods in agreement, turning to walk back toward me as she exits.

Marco's voice cuts through the tension. "You're running out of time, son. And I don't think you've got what it takes to do it. My leg may be one thing, but can you really put that knife through my heart?"

Malachi looks at me, his gaze intense. "I don't have to have what it takes. Because she does."

For a moment, time stills. I blink, my pulse quickening as the weight of what he's saying sinks in. Malachi reaches out, his hand gently cupping my face. He faces me fully, ignoring Marco completely.

"Do you want this?" he asks, his voice low, the question hanging in the air between us. "After everything he's done to you, say the word, and it's yours. If not, I'll handle it for both of us."

A heavy beat thrums in my chest, and the answer bursts forth from me like I've been holding it back for far too long. "I want it," I say, my voice steady, the conviction clear.

I've never been more certain in my life.

Marco needs to die.

The thought of whatever horrors he's concocted in his underground lab makes my stomach twist. For so long, I believed he was the lesser evil—the good twin. But now I see him for what he truly is. I have questions for Malachi, but right now none of that matters. We need to find Marco's lab, save the Avids, the animals...whatever souls are trapped down there, suffering through unspeakable things.

Malachi's touch pulls me back to the moment. His fingers trail over my face again, grounding me. Then he leans down, pressing a soft kiss to the top of my head before pulling away.

"I'll give you privacy," he says, handing me a large knife he pulled from his waistband. "You heard her—the property's secure. I'll be waiting for you out front when you're ready."

He walks to the door, not sparing a single glance at his father when Marco calls his name. "And don't take too long, Kat," Malachi adds. The door clicks shut behind him.

The room feels colder now, the crackle of the fire the only sound in the silence. I turn to face Marco, my body tense, my thoughts swirling. It's the two of us now.

"Katja, I've been like a father to you. I saved you from that place—the life you would've had without me," Marco says, his voice thick with conviction. He believes it. And that's the fucked-up part.

For as long as I can remember, I've lived in the shadow of death. I've seen more of it than anyone should, and through it all, I've wondered what it would be like to end a life. To be the one who pulls the trigger, who takes the life from someone else.

What it must feel like to do the unthinkable. I've imagined killing Marco more times than I care to admit.

And now, standing here, I finally know I have what it takes.

I move around him, circling until I'm behind him. My hand wraps around the hilt of the knife, and I press it lightly against his throat, enough to make his skin tremble. He shudders, his breath catching. I lean in, my voice a whisper in the stillness.

"This is the devil's work. And I'll do it gladly."

You wanted a demon, Marco? I'll show you one.

I feel the weight of the blade in my hand, the steady pressure as I prepare to end him. But then something shifts. Out of the corner of my eye, I catch a flicker of movement. I freeze. My heart skips, my mind reeling.

No, not now. Why now?

I close my eyes, willing the image to go away, but when I open them again, he's closer—Cade...my Cade. His presence is like a heavy weight, pulling at my chest. His green eyes burn into me, bright and unyielding. His black hair falls over his forehead, like it always did. He's here. But he's not saying anything.

I can't do this. Why now?

My pulse pounds in my ears. I've never tried to communicate with his spirit before. I've kept my distance, unwilling to let him haunt me. But now, here he is, standing right in front of me—silent, staring. He looks different but not, and I can't breathe. My heart aches, and my vision blurs. Why is he here?

Is this a sign? Am I about to make a mistake?

Did I somehow summon him? Did my subconscious call him to me because I'm about to kill Marco?

"Brian," Marco says, his voice cutting through the tension like a blade of its own.

The sound of the knife hitting the marble floor rings in my ears. I don't even register dropping it. My hand trembles as I step back too far, the cool stone of the wall pressing against my back. My breath comes in shallow bursts, unsure whether to clutch my chest or cover my mouth. My whole body shakes.

"Cade."

When I say it, something inside me unravels. I can barely comprehend what's happening.

He's here.

He's alive.

His nod is all the answer I need. "You're alive... You're Brian." I can't believe it. My mind spins, trying to make sense of the impossible.

I start shaking, my body betraying me, trembling with the weight of this revelation.

"Don't cry, Kitty Kat," he says.

I lose it. His voice, the same familiar sound I never thought I'd hear again, brings everything crashing down. The tears flood down my face, my stomach twisting as I try to catch my breath. This can't be happening.

"But if—"

"If you're here, if you're alive and you're Brian, then—what have you done, Cade?" My voice cracks, tears slipping freely down my face as my hands tremble. But I don't move. I can't.

My body feels like it's shutting down, as if this moment—this impossible moment—has stolen the strength from my limbs.

I let him wrap his arms around me. I let him pull me close, my head pressing against his chest, feeling the steady beat of a heart I thought was gone.

I tell myself it's a hallucination, that none of this is real. But Marco saw him too.

How is this possible?

I don't know how much time passes, but Cade says a few things—words I can't process, not when the accident keeps replaying in my mind, when I saw him die, when I watched him die.

He was dead. And now he's here.

Suddenly, a noise snaps me back to reality, distant but urgent. Before I can register it, Cade jerks me, his grip tightening as his eyes search mine. His face is taut, emotion flickering there.

And then I look past him.

Marco's gone.

No!

I run to the chair, my pulse roaring in my ears as I stop short, staring at the sagging ropes where his body had been. Panic claws at my throat, and I kneel down, my hands shaking as I reach for a single glass vial that lies on the floor, almost hidden in the shadows. I pick it up, turning it over in my hand, feeling the weight of it—one single drop of dark, viscous liquid inside.

It's not Avidian.

But what is it?

I look up at Cade, my stomach flips, my heart hammering, as his eyes study me, piercing through me like he knows every secret I've kept. Finally, my voice comes—broken but steady. "You're supposed to be dead."

"What have you done, Cade?"

He shakes his head slowly and reaches for me, but I take an involuntary step back, half in shock and half afraid of what truth he's about to reveal.

"You don't know how many nights I've spent searching for you," he murmurs. "How many times this moment has played out in my head. Over and over."

He takes a step closer, and I don't think I'm breathing. "You were always meant to be mine, and now... Now I can finally bring you home."

Ashley R. O'Donovan is an author of fantasy romance born and raised in Monterey, California, Ashley loves spending time with her friends and family, and when she's not writing, you can almost always find her cuddled up with one of her dogs reading a book, or catching the latest horror movie with her husband.

If you enjoyed this book, please consider leaving a review on Amazon and keeping in touch with Ashley on social media. She loves hearing from readers and is exciting to share more of her stories with the world.

**

For more books and updates:
www.AuthorARO.com